EX LIBRIS

VINTAGE CLASSICS

MARY LAVIN

Mary Lavin was an award-winning writer best known for her short stories. Born in East Walpole, Massachusetts, to Irish parents, she returned to live in Ireland as a child and spent most of her life in County Meath, where many of her stories are set. She was a writer under contract to the *New Yorker* magazine and received many honours, including the James Tait Black Memorial Prize, a number of Guggenheim fellowships and an honorary doctorate from the National University of Ireland. She received the title of Saoi from Aosdána and is the first female writer to have a public space named after her in Dublin.

ALSO BY MARY LAVIN

Tales from Bective Bridge
The House in Clewe Street: A Novel
The Becker Wives, & Other Stories
Mary O'Grady: A Novel
A Likely Story
The Stories of Mary Lavin: Vol. 1
Happiness and Other Stories
A Memory and Other Stories
The Second-Best Children in the World
The Stories of Mary Lavin: Vol. 2
The Shrine and Other Stories
A Family Likeness and Other Stories
The Stories of Mary Lavin: Vol. 3
In a Café

MARY LAVIN

AN ARROW IN FLIGHT

Selected Stories

SELECTED AND INTRODUCED BY
Colm Tóibín

VINTAGE CLASSICS

1 3 5 7 9 10 8 6 4 2

Vintage Classics is part of the Penguin Random House group of companies

Vintage, Penguin Random House UK, One Embassy Gardens,
8 Viaduct Gardens, London SW11 7BW

penguin.co.uk/vintage-classics
global.penguinrandomhouse.com

First published in Great Britain by Vintage Classics in 2026
First published in the United States of America by Scribner in 2026

Copyright © The Estate of Mary Lavin 2026
Introduction copyright © Colm Tóibín 2026

The moral right of the author has been asserted

Penguin Random House values and supports copyright. Copyright fuels creativity, encourages diverse voices, promotes freedom of expression and supports a vibrant culture. Thank you for purchasing an authorised edition of this book and for respecting intellectual property laws by not reproducing, scanning or distributing any part of it by any means without permission. You are supporting authors and enabling Penguin Random House to continue to publish books for everyone. No part of this book may be used or reproduced in any manner for the purpose of training artificial intelligence technologies or systems. In accordance with Article 4(3) of the DSM Directive 2019/790, Penguin Random House expressly reserves this work from the text and data mining exception.

Printed and bound in Great Britain by Clays Ltd, Elcograf S.p.A.

The authorised representative in the EEA is Penguin Random House Ireland,
Morrison Chambers, 32 Nassau Street, Dublin D02 YH68

A CIP catalogue record for this book is available from the British Library

ISBN 9781529956481

Penguin Random House is committed to a sustainable future
for our business, our readers and our planet. This book is made
from Forest Stewardship Council® certified paper.

Contents

Introduction by Colm Tóibín	ix
TRASTEVERE	1
IN THE MIDDLE OF THE FIELDS	23
A MEMORY	43
A CUP OF TEA	95
A STORY WITH A PATTERN	115
THE GREAT WAVE	143
IN A CAFÉ	169
ASIGH	191
HAPPINESS	219
THE YELLOW BERET	239
CHAMOIS GLOVES	261
THE LONG AGO	281
AT SALLYGAP	301
SARAH	327
THE HAYMAKING	341
THE CUCKOO SPIT	369

Introduction

Like Myra in her story 'A Memory', Mary Lavin lived in a mews house behind Fitzwilliam Square in Dublin. She also had a house on a bend of the River Boyne in County Meath, north of Dublin, a place inhabited by some other characters in her fiction. When I came to Dublin as a student in 1972, Mary Lavin was a familiar presence in the city. I watched her as she moved with a sort of stateliness in the Reading Room of the National Library, or as she sat in a small café known as the Country Shop, or as she drank coffee in Bewley's in Grafton Street. She was usually alone. She wore black. Her hair was parted in the middle and pulled untidily into a bun at the back. Her gaze was kind and sad and oddly distracted, but it had a funny strength as well. She had spent her life describing others and finding strategies to create versions of herself on the page; it was not easy to categorise her.

Although Lavin's stories were mostly set in Dublin or in County Meath, they did not deal in predictable local colour. And although they were mainly set in the 1940s and 1950s, they have not dated. But neither are they timeless. They belong fiercely to their own moment and emerge from a vision that is exact and precise, deceptively gentle, and then sharp and direct.

I have no clear memory of how I knew that Mary Lavin was a widow with children at a young age, but I might have read it in the *Irish Times*. I was interested in the word 'widow' and I would have paid real attention to a writer, or anyone at all indeed, who was a widow, since my mother was one. Or it may have been when we studied a story by Mary Lavin in secondary school called 'The Widow's Son'.

I had read a good deal of Lavin's work by the time I first saw her in the city. Some of her stories dealt directly with how grief becomes sorrow, how much silence there was around grief in Irish culture – how, in particular, a woman who lost her husband might feel the loss as a palpable absence and then set about concealing her feelings. One of these stories is 'In the Middle of the Fields'. Its first sentence makes clear that her heroine is alone in an isolated rural place. The next sentence reads: 'And yet she was less lonely for him here in Meath than elsewhere.'

The loss Lavin is portraying here is complex, or it comes in a complex guise. People think the protagonist wants to talk about her dead husband, or be reminded of what she has lost. 'They thought she hugged tight every memory she had of him. What did they know about memory?' She rather hopes for a time when she had 'forgotten him for a minute'. It is clear that her grief does not have to be named as 'grief', or brought out for inspection. It is private and untrustworthy and not stable.

In Lavin's stories a newly widowed woman has to remake the rules for herself, including the most ordinary rules of behaviour. Her characters' behaviour could become irrational and hard to explain; they often did the very opposite of what they intended. Being unmoored by loss affects their every thought – even when they are not thinking about loss – and their every action.

In 1981, when an edition of her *Selected Stories* came out in paperback, I went to her house in County Meath and interviewed Mary Lavin for a magazine. The house was modern and beautiful. The long living room was, I remember, on two levels and the walls were filled with paintings. Her conversation was rambling and fascinating. She had a way of starting something and then letting it lead her elsewhere, but part of her mind never left the point to which she would eventually return. 'What was I saying?' she would ask. But she would know what she was saying. She told me that she often wrote a story in bed and then worked on many, many drafts. And, when I asked her how would she decide to write one story if she had several in her mind, she told me that she had a contract with the *New Yorker* magazine, but they only paid for the stories they used, and thus each time she began a new story, she chose to write the one they were least likely to take. And sometimes, she said, she was right and sometimes she was wrong. But she would not have written merely to please them, or for the money.

Re-reading the stories now, it is clear that they include a great sense of mystery and wisdom and a use of voice and tone which seems effortless. Part of their power comes from what has been left out. Mary Lavin was more interested in a character she had invented in all its strangeness and individuality than she was in wider society; she was more interested in families than politics; she was more interested in the drama around the solitary figure than large questions of identity. It is the clarity of these interests and her refusal as an artist to be diverted from them that make her work seem now undated, make her stories have the still and severe presence of a painting by Morandi or William Scott. Her stories chart the aura around small hidden dramas and provincial lives. She, from her own reading of Russian and French literature, knew that such limits had created a great tradition, the stories of Tolstoy or Turgenev, for example, or the best work of Flaubert.

Mary Lavin removes the props by which we might read her women easily; she refuses to allow us to come to know them by an obvious set of signals or tensions. They live in a twilight time. Their desires are numerous and ambiguous and require a great deal of detail to describe. And because Mary Lavin is working with the short story rather than the novel, what happens in her fiction must have the noise of delicacy and then a fierce or piercing after-effect. She is not prepared to be simple about this, but she is capable of distracting the reader from this by a set of strategies which suggest simplicity of approach.

Lavin's women protagonists who are not widows are often placed under pressure so that they appear different from those around them – more sensitive, more guarded, more intelligent, more concerned with strangeness or interested in excitement. Gloria in 'Trastevere' and Mag in 'The Yellow Beret' offer the stories a drama around fragility. In 'A Story with a Pattern', Ursula's intellectual curiosity is seen not only as unusual, but an impediment to happiness, a disruptive force. In 'The Haymaking', Fanny's lack of knowledge of the countryside makes her seem an eccentric and nervous figure against the solidity and unthinking masculinity of Christopher, her farmer husband.

In the story 'In a Café', the dead husband is given the same name as the husband in 'In the Middle of the Fields' – Richard. Once more he does not appear, but he hovers over everything, or his loss does. Mary, the protagonist, arrives early at a café off Grafton Street in Dublin. She is to meet another widow, a younger woman, Maudie. As Mary waits, what she has lost does not come to her simply: 'It happened so often. In her mind she would see a part of him, his hand, his arm, his foot perhaps, in the finely worked leather shoes he always wore, and from it, frantically, she would try and build up the whole man.'

There are paintings on the wall of the café, and they have been done by an artist who comes and sits at a nearby table. She notices his hands first. Then there are a number of awkward connections and disconnections between Mary and Maudie and the artist, who is foreign. Lavin makes this awkwardness stand for a great deal, for the idea that in a time of grief nothing is free from tension, least of all the most ordinary encounter, the most casual moment. In any case, Mary Lavin has a particular skill in making the casual moment or the random detail pull in energy towards itself, remain true and modest but manage to send out signals.

The signals here, as in 'In the Middle of the Fields' and 'The Cuckoo Spit', are sexual and they are, by necessity, deeply confused. The artist gives Mary the address of his studio, which is very close, and when Maudie departs, Mary has an urge to visit him. It is clear that when she was married she would never have done such a thing. Once more then, Lavin explores a moment of pure instability in the poetics of solitude. This moment will come in many guises. It will be impulsive and surprising. It will offer a hint of what love is, but also will come like a parody of a love lost. And this time it will bring in its wake something that was not available before – an image of the lost husband which is complete. In Mary's mind now, the mind that could not see Richard in full before, he comes 'towards her tall, handsome, and with his curious air of apartness from those around him. He had his hat in his hand, down by his side, as on a summer's day he might trail a hand in water from the side of a boat.'

That last image is visually satisfying; it suggests a position for the hand which is casual, languid, relaxed, but it also does other work: the boat is moving, the hand is in water, thus the image is also, by suggestion, the image of someone quietly moving, in this case moving away further into death, further away from her, as he seems to be moving closer.

I remember asking Mary Lavin about her story 'Happiness' in that house near the Boyne in the summer of 1981. I was aware of course that, like the mother in the story, she had three daughters, since I knew Caroline Walsh, her youngest. And I must have recognised Father Hugh in the story, since someone very like him was coming in and out of the actual room, hoping that the interview would soon end. He – Michael Scott – too had been a priest and he was now her husband.

I must have asked her about 'using' autobiographical material in fiction. And she turned her wise and calm gaze about me and smiled. And I remember what she said clearly. She said: 'And I predicted my own death in that story. I used my own death.'

In 'Happiness' Lavin found a voice which was close to her actual voice, and it was close too to her daughter Caroline's. The daughter in the story recounts her mother's vagaries and whims, the way she spoke, the way her daughters and her friend the priest had watched over her as a young widow. The story sets out to lull the reader into trusting that the voice speaks of matters which are odd and gentle, almost eccentric.

And then the voice takes on an undertow which is unforgettable in its precision. It moves from the domestic to a set of images which are disturbing, sharp, and ruthlessly set out.

I remember Mary Lavin that day more than forty years ago, gaze unflinching as the style in the story, voice deep and strong, an aura around her of what it means to have faced things, to have fearlessly created an image close to the image of the woman's head as she sank into death. The mother's head in the story 'Happiness' could equally have been Mary Lavin's words which 'sank so deep into the pillow it seemed that it would have been dented had it been a pillow of stone'.

Colm Tóibín, 2025

AN ARROW
IN FLIGHT

TRASTEVERE

THE LIGHTS WERE CHANGING AT THE CORNER OF MADISON AND SIXTY-ninth. To get across in time, Mrs Traske walked fast. Then, just as she reached the other side, she heard her name called. How nice to be hailed in the street like that on her first day back in New York! She turned expectantly. But the young man who called out had missed the light, and a river of cars now flowed between them. From the far bank he was waving frantically, and although she could not quite place him, Mrs Traske stood and waited, smiling reassurance.

Who was he? His face was certainly familiar, so she kept smiling. He was pleasant, eager and intelligent-looking. When the lights changed again, he bounded across.

'Mrs Traske! You remember me? Paul Martin. We met in Rome.'

Given an instant more, she'd have placed him. He was one of the young poets she'd met this summer. Rome was full of them, but this one was much the nicest.

'Of course!' she said. 'You took me to Trastevere – myself and my daughter.'

She'd been particularly grateful that he'd included Gloria; pretty young daughters were sometimes harder to entertain than people were aware. On the other hand, it must have been easier for him to be nice to Gloria than to a middle-aged novelist! Most of the poets in Rome were a bit contemptuous of Mrs Traske, especially when they heard she was staying on the Via Veneto. Fortunately, she had reached an age at which she was able to absolve herself for putting comfort before atmosphere. Their stay in Rome had been nearing an end when they met Paul. Hearing that they had never been across the river to Trastevere, he promptly offered to escort them. He planned an interesting afternoon, and – what they appreciated most – suggested they end the day with a visit to friends of his who had an apartment in a magnificent old medieval palazzo in the quarter.

'I thought you were still in Rome, Mr Martin,' she said, and, assuming that they were both going the same way, she started to walk on. But he did not move and did not let go of her hand. In fact, he gripped it tighter, and she realised that he was upset. The odd thing was that he seemed to connect her in some way with his distress.

'Oh, Mrs Traske, you don't know how good it was to look up and see you. I was in a telephone booth across the street. You of all people, I thought. I didn't know you were in New York. I just *had* to call out to you. You remember those friends of mine in Trastevere, the ones we had dinner with that evening – Simon Carr and Della?'

He was really very disturbed. He kept wiping his forehead.

'To look up like that and see you!' he cried. 'Someone who knew them! I'd only just heard, you see – just a minute before. I don't know any details yet, but oh God, Mrs Traske, she killed herself – Della did – last night!'

'Oh, no!' Now she gripped *his* hand. 'How terrible. I can't tell you how sorry I am.' Sorry for him, she meant; he was so upset – the young woman she'd only met on that one occasion. Naturally, she was sorry for her, too, and for her poor husband. Yet her immediate sympathy went out to the young man in front of her. He was so *very* young in his grief. 'What happened?' she asked. 'Was there another woman?'

Paul was shocked. He threw up his hands in protest. 'He was hers, body and soul!' he cried.

'What was it, then?'

'That's what's so awful!' the young man cried. 'I don't know. I only heard she was dead. I was just going to put in a call to Rome – over there,' he said, nodding back, 'when I saw you. Oh, God, isn't it hard to believe? They were insanely in love. You must have seen that for yourself the evening in Trastevere.' With both hands now, he held on to her. 'What frightens me is that Simon may kill himself. He won't be able to live without her.' A wild look came into his eyes. 'And Della won't rest in the grave without him. She'll – '

But at this point Mrs Traske disengaged her hands. 'Now, don't talk rubbish,' she said. She was suddenly impatient with him. 'Let's walk on,' she said. 'Better still, come along to my hotel and have some lunch. It's quite near. You'll feel different when you've eaten something. We can talk.'

But Paul sprang away. 'I can't,' he cried. 'I've got to put in that call to Rome. I may have to go back there at once.' For another instant, he stood in front of her. 'Thank you again just for being here!' he cried. Then he was gone.

Shaken, Mrs Traske walked on alone. The poor girl, she thought – young woman, rather, for surely Della was a little older than her husband. Or was she? It may only have been his dependence on her that gave that impression. No matter, it was all very sad. As to Mr Martin's fears of a double suicide, however, she would not, quite frankly, give a fig for them. Widowed young herself, and having enough good sense not to make public by marriage a second, late but deeply satisfying relationship, she had her own concept of love.

What *had* happened, though? All she could recall of Della was that she was beautiful, with fine eyes and shining black hair. The evening Gloria and she had spent with the three young people ought to have been entirely enjoyable, but somehow it was not. Once or twice, it had seemed that Della was too dominating, but since the young men didn't seem to mind – quite the contrary – Mrs Traske had seen no reason to let it worry *her*.

Walking along Madison Avenue, she began to wonder. No more than Paul did she feel like lunch. She had an impulse to ring Mack, but she resisted it. He'd barely be back in his office, having met her at the boat and stayed to settle her in at the hotel. Anyway, she'd be seeing him for dinner. She stopped. She must be near Central Park. Ah, yes, she could see the tops of the trees. Perhaps she'd walk for a while in the sun there. According to her New York friends, Central Park was dangerous, but surely not in broad daylight? If one was to believe Mr Martin, not as dangerous as love! For although she'd snubbed him, Paul had made her think, with his fanciful notions of love. Crossing the avenue, Mrs Traske went in the direction of the park. She'd miss out lunch altogether. After forty, it did no harm to skip a meal. She'd never been able to do that in Rome. There, she was hungry all the time. It made her ravenous just to walk down some of those narrow streets dedicated entirely to food – whole shops given over to one commodity: cheese, pasta, salami; stalls of fruit and vegetables arranged with as much regard to colour, shape, and size as the mosaics in the Vatican workshop. Passing them, her fingers used to itch to press a fleshy fig or a fat peach to see if it was as prime as it looked. But she was scared she'd set off an avalanche that would bury her up to the neck in apples and pears, figs, tomatoes, pomegranates, melons, aubergines.

The day in Trastevere, they had eaten an excellent luncheon at her hotel, and yet they had no sooner crossed the Ponte Palatino than she was famished again, tantalised by the smells that came streaming out of apartment windows – the smell of hot cooking oil, garlic, oregano. All the walking they did made her twice as hungry. Paul had shown them everything – basilicas, crypts, palaces, fountains, piazzas. He was tireless. What they loved best were the narrow streets, like the Via dell'Atleta, that plunged them into the atmosphere of Trastevere, with orange peel underfoot and gaily coloured washing strung across overhead like bunting.

Thinking of what happened to her in one of those little streets, Mrs Traske had to smile. It was intensely hot and they were all perspiring, and so, although she was wearing only a light silk dress, she was relieved, really, when out of the sky a few drops of rain fell on her bare arm. She turned her face upward to receive them, 'As if,' Gloria said afterwards, laughing, 'as if you were a flower, Mother!' Only it wasn't rain! Overhead, high above, when she looked up she saw the bare bottom of a man-child, held out by his mother in her strong brown arms.

How they laughed. Then Paul tactfully suggested that perhaps they ought to be getting on, as Della would be expecting them. She liked to eat early, because she had a job, he explained; she was always ready to eat the minute she got home from the office.

'Oh, we mustn't keep her waiting,' Mrs Traske said, for from the first she had assumed they were going to eat in the apartment. That seemed the whole point of the visit. They had seen the outside of enough old palazzos.

'Wait till you see their apartment!' Paul cried. 'I told you, didn't I, it's in one of the oldest palazzos in Rome, with balconied windows and studded doors – and they have a terrace garden on the roof. There it is!' he announced as they entered a *piazzale* off which ran a street as narrow as a gully.

Impressed, they stood and stared at the massive ornamented façade that projected over the thoroughfare.

'There are disadvantages, of course, as you can see,' Paul said when they got nearer and an acrid odour assailed them from the brimming garbage bins that had not yet been emptied. Like cornucopias, the bins spilled out a largesse of lobster claws, fish heads, eggshells, decayed flowers, and the pulp of rotted fruit. And from the lavish heap, as they went past, a swarm of flies rose into the air with an iridescent glitter, hissing like geese.

'Sorry for that,' Paul said easily. 'It's the price for living in the quarter. But look at that carving!' He pointed up at the magnificent portico.

They were having trouble, however, getting past the garbage bins, and in the hallway itself they had to push their way through a horde of small children playing on the marble floor and the lower steps of the great marble staircase. The hallway was infested with children. They were very sweet, very appealing, but she had to hold her skirts clear of their grubby little fingers. When they reached the stairs she had to laugh out loud at one small fat infant who was trying to get up the great marble step. His diaper, heavy with urine, hung down under him like an udder, and left a wet track after him wherever it touched the steps.

'Like a snail!' said Gloria, and she lifted him to one side so they could pass, although in fact the wide staircase was so broad they could easily have got past him. All three of them could have gone up it abreast. A magnificent staircase. And on the walls, set in plaster, there were wonderful ceramic medallions, although elsewhere on the plaster, up as high as they could reach, the children had been busy with chalk and crayon.

'I don't advise looking too closely,' Paul cautioned uneasily. And, indeed Mrs Traske had just seen a very crude drawing. It wasn't all the work of children, not by any means. Not wishing to embarrass the young man, she launched into a generality. 'Graffiti fascinate me,' she said. 'I read a most interesting article on the subject recently.'

The words were hardly out of her mouth when a door opened overhead and a voice called down. 'What kept you? We're starving.'

Such familiarity was warming, and the Traskes hurried up, but when Mrs Traske got to the landing she couldn't help stopping again and exclaiming at the rich Venetian red of the walls that was so well set off by the pure white of the door and the pedimented architrave. 'What glorious colour!' she cried to the young man standing on the landing – Simon?

He smiled. 'It was extravagant of us to decorate the landing, because it doesn't belong to us legally. It's supposed to be communal, but as we're at the top we took a chance and did the landing, too, when we were doing up the rest.'

Gloria and Paul had joined them.

'I always say,' said Paul, 'that this landing sounds a trumpet for what is to come!' Stepping past Simon, he threw the door of the apartment fully open.

At the sight of the room within, Mrs Traske gasped and gave another rapturous exclamation.

'You sound surprised, Mother,' Gloria said sharply. 'Mr Martin did try to prepare us.'

Mrs Traske smiled at her daughter, grateful to her for helping her transform her surprise into more tactful terms of appreciation.

'But how could anyone be prepared for such dramatic colours?' Mrs Traske said quickly. 'That glowing ruby, and now this green. It's as green as the campanile,' she added when, stepping into the room, she saw the dome of Santa Maria in Cappella through one of the great windows at the far end. She turned back to her host. 'Is your wife an artist?' she asked.

For no reason that she could see, Simon and Paul both laughed – quite loudly, too.

'Well, then, it is the room of a poet,' she murmured. The room demanded a fitting tribute.

At this point, the door of a kitchenette opened and a young woman came out. Della? Like her husband, she dispensed with greetings and joined at once in the conversation. Again, the familiarity had the effect of putting the Traskes at ease. 'The room of a poet?' the young woman repeated, questioningly, and she looked around it like a stranger. 'You should have seen the room where he lived before we were married,' she said, but she took her husband's arm and squeezed it affectionately. She nodded at the prints on the wall. 'The prints were Simon's, of course,' she said. 'I only reframed them. And the old desk was his – I just had it stripped and waxed. And the books are his.' But she frowned slightly, because some of the books looked a bit ragged. She hugged his arm tighter. 'I think the colour was your idea, too, wasn't it? Or was it Paul's?' She reached out and drew Paul to her. 'I only paid for things!' She turned to Mrs Traske. 'Perhaps you're right,' she said. 'Perhaps it is the room of a poet, but with the tone raised an octave or two – by money.'

The mention of money in this way would have made Mrs Traske uncomfortable if it were not that the young men – both of them – were so obviously delighted with Della.

'I must tell you,' Paul said. 'Della has one of the best jobs in Rome.' He laughed. 'That's why they came here – and me, too.'

Did he live with them? Mrs Traske wondered. This room was so spacious there could not be very much sleeping accommodation beyond it.

Paul seemed to read her mind. 'I don't live *with* them,' he said. 'I only live *off* them.'

At this, again all three laughed, and Mrs Traske laughed with them. She could see, though, that Gloria found Della rather overpowering. What a strong personality. Standing there in the middle of her beautiful room, with the two young men linked to her, she suddenly presented an extravagant image to the mind of Mrs Traske – an image of a Maypole, festooned with ribbons, which, as they gyrated, bound the young men closer and closer to her.

'Simon, aren't you going to offer them a drink?' Unlinking herself, Della picked up an empty glass that had evidently been her own, then put it down again. 'I won't have any more,' she said, and it was hard not to feel this was a reprimand to them for being late. All the same, Mrs Traske and Gloria took the drinks that, without choice, were offered to them, and Mrs Traske began at once to sip hers as an example to Gloria, who loathed Campari and found it as hard to swallow as cough syrup.

'It was good of you to come,' Della said then, unexpectedly. 'We've heard a lot about you from Paul.'

Mrs Traske had started to give the self-deprecatory smile with which she usually acknowledged over-facile praise of her work when Della continued. 'About your generosity to young people, I mean,' she said.

How glad Mrs Traske was then for those frank admissions concerning Della's salary, because if money had been in short supply she would have thought the young woman was leading up to a request for a loan. As things were, it did cross her mind that they might be expecting something other than money from her. She turned to Simon. 'I regret to say I haven't read any of your poetry,' she murmured.

Della took her empty glass. 'How could you?' she said. 'It's never been published,' and before Mrs Traske could say anything more she put up her hand as if in warning. 'Don't suggest reading it in manuscript,' she cried, 'unless you are an Egyptologist or a hieroglyphist,' and, reaching out, she joined the two young men to her again. 'They call themselves writers, and no one can read their writing.' She laughed. 'And they can't spell.' She laughed again. 'They don't even know the meaning of words. Do you know what this fellow here thought?' She hugged Paul tighter to her. 'He thought "temerity" meant timidity! And this fellow here' – she hugged her husband's arm – 'this fellow thought a hysterectomy was a lobotomy! Not that one can blame him too much for that; the medieval philosophers all thought the womb was the centre of the emotions.' She let them go. 'Oh, they are hopeless cases. I don't know what they'd do if they didn't have me to look after them.'

And, indeed, to Mrs Traske it was beginning to seem as if she did give them strength. In the large room where she and Gloria stood apart as separate people, the three young people seemed to stand as closely grouped together as when they were linked.

'Take the girl's glass,' Della said to Simon. 'And if we're ready, let's go and eat.'

But it was over to the door through which they had come in she walked, and, opening it, she led them out on to the landing.

'Are we not going to eat here?' said Mrs Traske. Too late she knew she'd let slip that she was disappointed. She hadn't seen the room properly, hadn't looked at the prints or the books, and, above all, she hadn't had time to look out of the window at the wonderful view of Trastevere. She glanced regretfully around.

'Do you mind?' Della said, almost offensively, and she held the door open. Mrs Traske couldn't help feeling she'd been put under a compliment.

'We'd be happy to take pot luck, you know,' she said nervously. 'Gloria wouldn't mind giving a hand. She's quite a good cook. She makes a delicious omelette.' The truth was that after months of living in hotels and eating out, she herself would have enjoyed helping with a meal. She thought again of the vegetable stalls, and she could almost feel the snap of young beans under her fingers, and the swish of spinach.

Della however had turned away. 'We never eat in the apartment,' she said. 'There's a trattoria in the cellar of the palazzo – you must have seen the sign in the hallway when you were coming up here. We eat there every night – in fact we only eat up here on very rare occasions.'

'Sad occasions, not joyful,' Paul explained quickly. 'If one of them is sick, or something like that.'

'The smell of cooking hanging around the apartment all evening would disgust me,' Della said.

Still Mrs Traske was not happy. 'We shouldn't have come for a meal at all,' she murmured.

'But why should you think that?' Simon said. 'It's not that Della is tired or anything; it's just that we can afford to eat out – because of her job.'

'That's right,' Della said more graciously. 'If it weren't for my job, we probably wouldn't be able to eat at all!' She saw Gloria look surprised, and she gave a little laugh. 'Don't worry,' she said, and she nodded at her husband. 'He pays in other ways.' She paused. 'He washes the nappies.' When both Mrs Traske and Gloria failed to conceal their surprise at this, she shrieked with laughter. 'Figuratively speaking!' she cried. 'We haven't any little nappies.'

Mrs Traske looked nervously at Simon. As both he and Paul laughed, however, she tried to laugh, too. Gloria only stared.

'Don't worry,' Paul whispered reassuringly as they went down the stairs. 'Della knows what she's doing. Other people's extravagances are her economies.'

But it was no longer her social obligations that concerned Mrs Traske. 'Are they long married?' she asked.

'About three months,' Paul said. He leaned closer. 'They were living together for some time in London, but when Della got this great job in Rome they decided to get married.' He lowered his voice still more. 'I don't think Simon liked the idea of marriage at first – that's what Della meant about the little nappies – but he knew he couldn't live without her.' He grinned. 'I can hardly live without her myself. I'm over here on a grant, and I'm staying in a good enough pensione, but – well, I spend all my time here in their apartment. I'm afraid I lean on her too. She's that kind of person. I'd heard of people like her before, but I never met one – people whose strength is a kind of magnet for people like Simon and me, who are pretty helpless when it comes to living. It's true!' he said when Mrs Traske looked quizzically at him.

They were at the bottom of the great stairs, and now she could see that there was a greasy sign on the wall and a steeper, darker stair leading down to the trattoria in the cellar.

The trattoria was small but packed with people. When Della appeared, however, the little fat patron, his face glistening with sweat, ran forward at once to meet them, as if he'd been rolled at them like a ball, and began to bow them towards the only empty table in the room, way at the back near the service doors.

'*Signore! Signora!*' He beamed until suddenly he saw Mrs Traske and Gloria. Thinking them a separate party, he was thrown into confusion, and more sweat broke from his face – it might have been rubbed all over with oil. For a moment, it was as if he were some lower form of life that would divide in two, both halves able to go forward and bestow welcomes alike on the two parties at the same time. But this being impossible, he clapped his hands and, summoning a waiter in a long lank apron down to his boots, ordered him to attend on the strangers. '*La carta per gli Inglesi!*' he cried. Then, as he realised that they were together, one single party, a beatific smile of relief broke over his face. '*Momento!*' he cried to the waiter. '*Carta per tutti.*' Without waiting to be obeyed, he dashed over to a service table and rushed back with a fistful of menus so greasy and wine-stained they were positively succulent, and dealt them out.

'*Prego.*' He gave one to Della. '*Prego.*' One to Mrs Traske. '*Prego, prego, prego,*' he cried, dealing one to each person. But the next instant he gathered them up again and discarded them. Like a conductor disdaining the score, he began to extol from memory the delights of his kitchen. '*Pollo al diavolo? Saltimbocca? Abbacchio alla cacciatora?* Tonight it is tender' – he bowed to Gloria – 'like the eyes of the *Signorina.*' Then, conspiratorially, he lowered his voice. '*Osso buco,*' he whispered. 'Tonight it is – ' He stopped, and, placing a kiss on his fat fingers, he blew it heavenward. As there was still no response, he was silent for a moment. Then he raised his voice again. 'Steak!' he cried. Just the one word. But now he was no longer a restaurateur; he was a generalissimo. He held up his hand for their attention. '*Momento!*' he cried, and he stumped off through the service doors. When he emerged again, it was triumphantly, with a piece of raw steak on the palm of his hand; blood from it oozed through his fingers. 'Never a steak like this,' he said solemnly. 'Never!'

All except Mrs Traske and Gloria gave the steak a close scrutiny, Della even lifting it up and turning it over. But Simon winked at Gloria, and put on a face of mock dismay. 'What good is that when there are five of us,' he said.

'*Scusi?*' Angelo did not immediately catch that a joke was meant. Then, offended, he frowned. 'I speak of the little Florentine heifer from which we take the steak!' he said with dignity. '*Molto* steak, *molto!*' he corrected. And, assuming that an order had been given, he handed the meat to the waiter. His hands free, he clapped them commandingly. 'Steak *per tutti!*' he cried.

Mrs Traske would have preferred an omelette, and Gloria loathed steak. To make matters worse, Della had called 'Underdone!' after the little patron.

'*Capisco!*' Angelo cried, and was about to scuttle off.

'But I – ' said Gloria.

Angelo stopped.

It was Simon, though, who had arrested him. 'Wait a minute, Angelo,' Simon said. 'Tonight I think I'll try the *osso buco*.'

'Simon!' Della was astonished. 'You know you hate sloppy dishes.'

'*Osso buco*,' Simon repeated.

'Simon!' Della caught him by the arm. 'It will take ages – twenty minutes, at least – you know that? You don't want to wait that long.'

But Angelo was all eagerness to comply. 'For the *Signore* – no!' he cried. Prudently measuring the distance between him and the other tables, he lowered his voice. 'For the one who comes in off the street, yes, maybe, but *per il cliente – il Signore* – no, no. I fix it myself, at once.' He held up five fat fingers. '*Cinque minuti*.'

Della sat back. 'Well, bring ours when it's ready, Angelo – without waiting,' she said. She still looked puzzled. She turned to Mrs Traske. 'I don't believe I've ever known him to eat *osso buco*,' she said. Then, as Angelo was hurrying away, she called again, 'Underdone!'

Mrs Traske looked at her. No matter what the two men said, it seemed to Mrs Traske that Della did look tired. It could, of course, have been that she was hungry, because she had picked up a roll and begun to pluck out the soft inner dough.

'It's all very well for Simon and Paul,' she said. 'They lunch here, too – that is to say, if they get up for lunch at all.' Suddenly she looked strangely at Mrs Traske. 'What time do you begin your day?'

Surprised, Mrs Traske hesitated. 'Do you mean when I'm at home, or do you mean here in Rome? This morning, we didn't get up very early, because Paul warned us that we'd have a tiring day trudging around and seeing the sights.'

As Paul nodded, Della gave him an affectionate smile. 'Did you really show them everything?' she asked him. 'For you the day must have been exceptionally exacting.'

Paul laughed. 'Della doesn't think writing poetry is work at all,' he said.

'But she married a poet!' Mrs Traske said, feeling she had to defend the young woman.

It was a shock to find that instead she had annoyed her. 'I married a man – a man like any other man, I hope,' Della said sharply. 'I don't see why allowances should be made for him on account of his work. I'd be insulted if anyone made allowances for *me* on account of *mine*.'

'Oh, but – ' Mrs Traske began, when Gloria spoke up.

'Mother never expects allowances to be made for her, either,' she said hotly. 'But it's not the same as if she was just a lawyer or a paediatrician! When she's working she can't sleep and she can't eat and she gets upset over nothing. Writers are sometimes working when we think they're only standing looking out of the window! Didn't you know that?' she demanded crossly, and so like a small child her mother had to smile.

Fortunately, Della was not offended. On the contrary, she was amused. 'Do you mean that Simon here may be working when he's fast asleep at three o'clock in the afternoon?'

Gloria was not to be put off so easily. 'That's not fair,' she said. 'It *is* true his mind could be working – unconsciously – and that takes a lot out of a person. The artist has always been regarded as a sacrificial figure and – '

'Gloria!' Mrs Traske just couldn't let her go on. 'She has been reading *The Wound and the Bow*,' she said to Della by way of apology.

Della brushed the apology away, however, and actually encouraged the girl. 'Go on,' she said. 'I'm interested. I take it that you feel my husband here is some special kind of being.'

Uncertain suddenly, Gloria looked for help from her mother, but the ice was thin; it would never bear the weight of two.

'Well,' said Gloria slowly, to gain time as she searched around in her mind. 'Writers and artists, and people like that – they do have special insights, don't you think?'

Della looked at her with a grave expression. Then, equally gravely, she looked at Simon. 'You think' – she paused – 'you think he may be some kind of a nut?'

Here Paul exploded with laughter, and Mrs Traske would have laughed if she weren't a bit anxious about Gloria, who could easily have burst into tears.

The girl felt too strongly for that, though. 'Put it that way if you like!' she cried. 'I suppose some people *do* think poets are nuts. Just because they don't measure success by money!' Her cheeks were flaming.

And Della was apparently touched. She laid a hand on the girl's arm. 'How nice it must be to have you for a daughter,' she said with real sweetness, but then she turned sharply to Mrs Traske. 'Of course, it's true you writers *are* above money, isn't that so?' she said, and to Mrs Traske's amazement her eyes travelled – really quite insolently – over her dress, and came to rest on her opal-and-diamond brooch.

Compelled now to speak up herself, Mrs Traske looked Della in the eye. 'My husband was a stockbroker,' she said.

At that moment, luckily, the steaks arrived.

'Let's begin, shall we?' Della said when, except for Simon, they were all served. 'Poor Simon,' she said. 'I told you it would take twenty minutes. Now aren't you sorry you're not one of the common herd?'

'*Momento. Momento,*' Angelo clucked.

'Go easy, Gloria. You'll get indigestion,' Mrs Traske said trying to slow her down, although she sympathised with her motives for gulping it off – the steaks were positively blue.

Slow as they all went – and even Della ate slowly – they were finished before Angelo came back proudly bearing, breast-high, the platter of *osso buco*.

'It looks good,' Gloria said as she handed her empty plate to a waiter.

'It smells delicious, Simon,' Della said, and as Angelo took her plate she reached out and snatched her fork. Leaning across the table, she stuck the fork into the *osso buco*. To the astonishment of all of them, Simon, who had just picked up his own fork, threw it down on the plate with a clatter.

'Why, Simon, what's the matter?' Della cried. 'I only wanted . . .'

Simon didn't look at her. He pushed his plate across the table. 'If you wanted it, why didn't you order it? There. You can have it.'

'But Simon!' Della was so taken aback she held her fork in the air, halfway to her mouth. Unnoticed, the meat fell from the prongs. Then, quietly and carefully, she picked it up and put it on her side plate and laid the fork back on the table, straightening it as if she were laying a place setting. 'I only wanted to see if it tasted good,' she said, in a voice that for her was low and indistinct.

'I don't want it,' Simon said.

Stupefied, they all stared.

'Will you have a steak, then?' Della asked.

'No. I'm not hungry,' Simon said. 'You eat it if you want it.'

Della looked down at the full plate in front of her. 'But I don't want it,' she said. 'I had what I ordered – I only . . .' Then she didn't attempt any more apology. 'Don't be absurd, Simon. We'll wait for our dessert until you've eaten. Eat it up,' she said, pushing back the plate. She turned in exasperation to Paul. 'What's the matter with him?' she cried. 'Tell him not to be childish.' She turned to her husband. 'Eat it up, Simon.'

Simon, however, had leaned back and was calling Angelo. 'Take this away,' he said, pointing to the plate.

Angelo stared at him.

'Don't worry, Angelo,' Della said quickly. 'It's just that he's not hungry.' As the patron took up the plate but stood uncertainly with it held low, like a collection plate, she jumped up from her chair and whispered something into his ear. 'Go along, Angelo,' she said then, out loud, 'and bring our dessert.' She turned back to those at the table. 'What will you have? Fruit? Cheese?' To Gloria she spoke kindly, as if she were a child. 'How about a *cassata* for you?'

Embarrassed, they all nodded acceptance of what apparently was decreed for them.

It hardly seemed possible that the awkwardness would pass. Thinking of it now, Mrs Traske, walking in the sunlight, felt that there, in that incident – if anywhere – was a hint of why the young woman had killed herself. But no. As she recalled it, after that things had gone well. Nothing more was said about the *osso buco*. Simon was suddenly in better form. Indeed, the next quarter of an hour was the most pleasant of the whole evening. They were all soon at ease, and for the first time Simon showed a real interest in the Traskes and their travels. 'How long are you going to be in Rome?' he'd asked.

'I'm not sure yet,' she'd replied without much thought, eager only to keep the conversation on a safe topic. 'We intended going to Milan the day after tomorrow, but somehow or other, on the way here from Florence, we missed out on Viterbo, and I'm told – '

'Oh yes, yes. You can't leave without seeing Viterbo.' He laughed. 'Though, mind you, I was only there once, years ago, and I didn't see much of it. I was drunk. Very drunk.' He turned to Paul. 'You remember that day?' He turned back to Mrs Traske. 'We'd hired an old car and we were supposed to turn it in in Rome, but we didn't really expect it would last out the trip. We were driving along when we saw the sign for Viterbo, and felt we ought to see it, so we turned off the main road. We thought we might eat there. But after we'd driven down some of the old streets – Viterbo is *all* old streets, and they're *all* crooked, *all* dark, *all* damp, even on the hottest day – well, we didn't think much of it, and we certainly didn't feel like eating there, and so we were trying to find the way out again when the old car gave a jolt. Blump it went. And then blump again. Blump, blump, blump. Paul, you remember?'

Paul was convulsed with laughter. 'Go on!' he cried.

Simon went on. 'Can you imagine a flat tyre in a place like that? We looked at each other in despair, threw up our hands, and decided to drive on. Blump we went, blump, blump, blump, blump, blump. We began to think we'd punctured all four tyres. And then to make things more hectic, although when we first drove into the place it was like a city of the dead, not a living soul in sight, *now* from all sides people appeared. Men, women, children – especially children. The children started running after us, shouting and yelling. I stepped on the gas. In a backward place like that, a pack of children is as bad as a pack of wolves. We tried to put a bit of distance between us and them, and I thought we were getting up speed when all of a sudden the kids dropped back. They stopped dead, in fact, and huddled together. The last I saw of them they were staring with their mouths wide open. Then I was jerked back as all of a sudden the ground went from under the car. Next thing there was a loud smack and a great almighty splash. We hadn't a puncture at all. We'd driven down a flight of steps into the river. That was all!'

'Oh, Simon, you never told me that story,' Della said. 'I want to go there. I want to see those steps.'

She was laughing so happily Mrs Traske thought that perhaps after all no harm had been done by the incident of the *osso buco*.

'How did you get the car out of the river, Mr Carr?' Gloria asked.

Dear girl. How they laughed at her.

'You must never look beyond the end of a good story, Gloria,' Paul said. 'Your mother could have told you that.'

They were all happy again.

'We certainly won't miss Viterbo after this,' Mrs Traske said, and she began to draw on her gloves. 'Which means we will be staying another day in Rome, so why don't you all have lunch with me tomorrow at my hotel?'

'But Della doesn't eat lunch,' Simon said in dismay.

'I have a snack at the canteen,' Della explained.

'Oh, what a pity,' Gloria said, and Mrs Traske turned to Paul, whom Angelo had released from his chair by pulling the table out from the wall. 'Perhaps you and Simon . . .' she began.

Uncertainly, both men looked at Della.

'Why not?' Della said. 'It would be a change for Simon.' She paused. 'A change from lying in bed, I mean.'

Once again for a moment, Mrs Traske's heart sank at what sounded to her like an unnecessary gibe, but again the young men seemed to see it in some other light, because they both laughed. It seemed settled that the young men would come to lunch.

Meanwhile, they were moving towards the stairs, and Paul had run up the steps to call a taxi.

'What time?' Simon said.

'How about noon?' she said, and she was just about to compliment Angelo on the meal as he bowed them out, his face now in the heated room glistening as if he was sweating glycerin.

Della, who had been looking at the little patron, suddenly turned to her husband. 'Simon! I forgot. You can't go. You've got to lunch *here* tomorrow. Isn't that right, Angelo?' she asked, smiling at him.

'*Si, si, Signora.*' Angelo bobbed his head up and down.

Della reached out and patted him. 'You are a dear, Angelo,' she said, before she took Simon's arm and began to move towards the door. 'Angelo is keeping your *osso buco* for your lunch tomorrow,' she said. 'Those sloppy dishes improve by keeping – the flavour comes out with standing overnight.' Then she turned to Mrs Traske and put out her hand. 'You'll be in Rome again,' she said indifferently.

Simon said nothing, and somehow Mrs Traske didn't look at him as she shook hands. He had pulled away from Della, Mrs Traske saw out of the corner of her eye. She started to go up the dark stairs, and when she reached the street Paul was there with the taxi. She thought it best to let the others explain about the lunch to him. She and Gloria got into the car.

As it drove away, she looked back at the three of them standing on the kerb. Simon seemed taller than she'd realised, and Della was really quite small. That Maypole image had been absurd, she thought, and even Paul's description of her as a tower of strength didn't seem right any more. Mrs Traske stopped. Was it possible that Della wasn't strong at all – that she had all the time been taking strength, not giving it as the young men thought?

Mrs Traske was surprised to find that her eyes had filled with tears. She wiped them away and looked around for a seat. She'd exhausted herself with her efforts to probe human motive, and now she felt curiously lonely. She sighed, and looked at her watch. She never liked to ring Mack during office hours, but perhaps just this once she might do so. He might slip out for a cup of coffee with her. It would be nice to meet him at this banal time of day and not wait for the more circumspect hours of evening.

She sighed again. Life was so short. And she remembered something Mack had once said, to which she had not attached importance at the time. She had said that she did not see much point in getting married at their age, when they had not much left to give each other, and he had shaken his head in disagreement.

'At least we do not diminish each other,' he said.

Were they making a mistake, she wondered, she and Mack? In spite of how often they thrashed things out and discarded the idea of marrying – laughed at the mere notion – perhaps after all . . .

She had come to a gate leading back into the street, and there would be a phone booth close by. She'd call Mack anyway. Even on the phone he was able to cheer her up – make her happy, make her laugh. She walked faster. For a woman of her years, her step at that moment was light.

IN THE MIDDLE
OF THE FIELDS

LIKE A ROCK IN THE SEA, SHE WAS ISLANDED BY FIELDS, THE HEAVY grass washing about the house, and the cattle wading in it as in water. Even their gentle stirrings were a loss when they moved away at evening to the shelter of the woods. A rainy day might strike a wet flash from a hay barn on the far side of the river. Not even a habitation! And yet she was less lonely for him here in Meath than elsewhere. Anxieties by day, and cares, and at night vague, nameless fears, these were the stones across the mouth of the tomb. But who understood that? They thought she hugged tight every memory she had of him. What did they know about memory? What was it but another name for dry love and barren longing? They even tried to unload upon her their own small purposeless memories. 'I imagine I see him every time I look out there,' they would say as they glanced nervously over the darkening fields when they were leaving. 'I think I ought to see him coming through the trees.' Oh, for God's sake! she'd think. She'd forgotten him for a minute.

It wasn't him she saw when she looked out at the fields. It was the ugly tufts of tow and scutch that whitened the tops of the grass and gave it the look of a sea in storm, spattered with broken foam. That grass would have to be topped. And how much would it cost?

At least Ned, the old herd, knew the man to do it for her. 'Bartley Crossen is your man, ma'am. Your husband knew him well.'

Vera couldn't place him at first. Then she remembered. 'Oh yes, that's his hay barn we see, isn't it? Why, of course, I know him well, by sight.' And so she did, splashing past on the road in his big muddy car, the wheels always caked with clay, and the wife in the front seat beside him.

'I'll get him to call around and have a word with you, ma'am,' said the herd.

'Before dark,' she cautioned.

But there was no need to tell Ned. The old man knew how she

always tried to be upstairs before it got dark, locking herself into her bedroom, which opened off the room where the children slept, praying devoutly that she wouldn't have to come down again for anything, above all, not to answer the door. That was what in particular she dreaded: a knock after dark.

'Ah, sure, who'd come near you, ma'am, knowing you're a woman alone with small children that might be wakened and set crying? And, for that matter, where could you be safer than in the middle of the fields, with the innocent beasts asleep around you?' If he himself had come to the house late at night for any reason, to get hot water to stoup the foot of a beast, or to call the vet, he took care to shout out long before he got to the gable. 'It's me, ma'am!' he'd shout.

'Coming! Coming!' she'd cry, gratefully, as quick on his words as their echo. Unlocking her door, she'd run down and throw open the hall door. No matter what the hour! No matter how black the night!

'Go back to your bed now, you ma'am,' he'd say from the darkness, where she could see the swinging yard lamp coming nearer and nearer like the light of a little boat drawing near to a jetty. 'I'll put out the lights and let myself out.' Relaxed by the thought that there was someone in the house, she would indeed scuttle back into bed, and, what was more, she'd be nearly asleep when she'd hear the door slam. It used to sound like the slam of a door a million miles away. There was no need to worry. He'd see that Crossen came early.

It was well before dark when Crossen did drive up to the door. The wife was with him, as usual, sitting up in the front seat the way people sat up in the well of little tub traps long ago, their knees pressed together, allowing no slump. Ned had come over with them, but only he and Crossen got out.

'Won't your wife come inside and wait, Mr Crossen?' she asked.

'Oh, not at all, ma'am. She likes sitting in the car. Now, where's the grass that's to be cut? Are there any stones lying about that would blunt the blade?' Going around the gable of the house, he looked out over the land.

'There's not a stone or a stump in it,' Ned said. 'You'd run your blade over the whole of it while you'd be whetting it twenty times in another place.'

'I can see that,' said Bartley Crossen, but absently, Vera thought. He had walked across the lawn to the rickety wooden gate that led into the pasture, and leaned on it. He didn't seem to be looking at the fields at all though, but at the small string of stunted thorns that grew along the riverbank, their branches leaning so heavily out over the water that their roots were almost dragged clear of the clay. When he turned around he gave a sigh. 'Ah, sure, I didn't need to look. I know it well,' he said. As she showed surprise, he gave a little laugh, like a young man. 'I courted a girl down there when I was a lad,' he said. 'That's a queer length of time ago now, I can tell you.' He turned to the old man. 'You might remember.' Then he looked back at her. 'I don't suppose you were born then, ma'am,' he said, and there was something kindly in his look and his words. 'You'd like the mowing done soon, I suppose? How about first thing in the morning?'

Her face lit up. But there was the price to settle. 'It won't be as dear as cutting meadow, will it?'

'Ah, I won't be too hard on you, ma'am,' he said. 'I can promise you that.'

'That's very kind of you,' she said, but a little doubtfully.

Behind Crossen's back, Ned nodded his head in approval. 'Let it go at that, ma'am,' he whispered as they walked back towards the car. 'He's a man you can trust.'

When Crossen and the wife had driven away, Ned reassured her again. 'A decent man,' he said. Then he gave a laugh, and it was a young kind of laugh for a man of his age. 'Did you hear what he said about the girl he courted down there? Do you know who that was? It was his first wife. You know he was twice married? Ah, well, it's so long ago I wouldn't wonder if you never heard it. Look at the way he spoke about her himself, as if she was some girl he'd all but forgotten. The thorn trees brought her to his mind. That's where they used to meet, being only youngsters, when they first took up with each other.

'Poor Bridie Logan! She was as wild as a hare. And she was mad with love, young as she was. They were company-keeping while they were still going to school. Only nobody took it seriously, him least of all, maybe, till the winter he went away to the agricultural college in Clonakilty. They started writing to each other then. I used to see her running up to the postbox at the crossroads every other evening, and sure, the whole village knew where the letter was going. His people were fit to be tied when he came home in the summer and said he wasn't going back, but was going to marry Bridie. All the same, his father set them up in a cottage on his own land. It's the cottage he uses now for stall-feds, it's back of his new house. Oh, but you can't judge it now for what it was then. Giddy and all as she was, as lightheaded as a thistle, you should have seen the way Bridie kept that cottage. She'd have had it scrubbed away if she didn't start having a baby. He wouldn't let her take the scrubbing brush into her hands after that.'

'But she wasn't delicate, was she?'

'Bridie? She was as strong as a kid goat, that one. But I told you she was mad about him, didn't I? Well, after she was married to him she was no better. Worse, I'd say: She couldn't do enough for him. It was like as if she was driven on by some kind of fever. You'd only to look in her eyes to see it. Do you know! From that day to this, I don't believe I ever saw a woman so full of going as that one. Did you ever happen to see little birds flying about in the air like they were flying for the divilment of it and nothing else? And did you ever see the way they give a sort of a little leap in the air, like they were forcing themselves to go a bit higher still, higher than they ought? Well, it struck me that was the way Bridie was acting, as she rushed about that cottage doing this and doing that to make him prouder and prouder of her. As if he could be any prouder than he was already with her condition getting noticeable.'

'She didn't die in childbed?'

'No. Not in a manner of speaking, anyway. She had the child, nice and easy, and in their own cottage too, only costing him a few shilling for one of those women that went in for that kind of job long ago. And all went well. It was no time till she was let up on her feet again. I was there the first morning she had the place to herself. She was up and dressed when I got there, just as he was going out to milk.

' "Oh, it's great to be able to go out again," she said, taking a great breath of the morning air as she stood at the door looking after him. "Wait, why don't I come with you to milk?" she called out after him. Then she threw a glance back at the baby to make sure it was asleep in its crib by the window.

' "It's too far for you, Bridie," he said. The cows were down in a little field alongside the road, at the foot of the hill below the village. And knowing she'd start coaxing him, Bartley made off as quick as he could out of the gate with the cans. "Good man!" I said to myself. But the next thing I knew, Bridie had darted across the yard.

' "I can go on the bike if it's too far to walk," she said. And up she got on her old bike, and out she pedalled through the gate.

' "Bridie, are you out of your mind?" Bartley shouted as she whizzed past him.

' "Arrah, what harm can it do me?" she shouted back.

'I went stiff with fright looking after her. And I thought it was the same with him, when he threw down the cans and started down the hill after her. But looking back on it, I think it was the same fever as always was raging in her that was raging in him, too. Mad with love, that's what they were, both of them, she only wanting to draw him on, and he only too willing.

' "Wait for me!" he shouted, but before she'd even got to the bottom she started to brake the bike, putting down her foot like you'd see a youngster do, and raising up such a cloud of dust we could hardly see her.'

'She braked too hard?'

'Not her! In the twinkle of an eye she'd stopped the bike, jumped off, turned it round, and was pedalling madly up the hill again to meet him, with her head down on the handlebars like a racing cyclist. But that was the finish of her.'

'Oh no! What *happened*?'

'She stopped pedalling all of a sudden, and the bike half stopped, and then it started to slide back down the hill, as if it had skidded on the loose gravel at the side of the road. That's what we both thought happened, because we both began to run down the hill too. She didn't get time to fall before we got to her. We got her in the bed, and the neighbours came running, but she was gone before night.'

'Oh, what a dreadful thing to happen! And the baby?'

'Well, it was a strong child. And it grew into a fine lad. That's the fellow that drives the tractor for him now, the oldest son. Barty they called him not to confuse him with Bartley.'

'Well, I suppose his second marriage had more to it, when all was said and done.'

'That's it. And she's a good woman, the second one. Look at the way she brought up that child of Bridie's, and filled the cradle, year after year, with sons of her own. Ah sure, things always work out for the best in the end, no matter what!' the old man said, and he started to walk away.

'Wait a minute, Ned,' Vera called after him urgently. 'Do you really think he forgot about her, until today?'

'I'd swear it,' said the old man. Then he looked hard at her. 'It will be the same with you, too,' he added kindly. 'Take my word for it. Everything passes in time and is forgotten.'

As she shook her head doubtfully, he shook his empathetically.

'When the tree falls, how can the shadow stand?' he said. And he walked away.

I wonder! she thought as she walked back to the house, and she envied the practical country people who made good the defaults of nature as readily as the broken sod knits back into the sward.

Again that night, when she went up to her room, Vera looked down towards the river and she thought of Crossen. Had he really forgotten? It was hard for her to believe, and with a sigh she picked up her hairbrush and pulled it through her hair. Like everything else about her lately, her hair was sluggish and hung heavily down, but after a few minutes under the quickening strokes of the brush, it lightened and lifted, and soon it flew about her face like the spray over a weir. It had always been the same, even when she was a child. She had only to suffer the first painful drag of the bristles when her mother would cry out, 'Look! Look! That's electricity!' And a blue spark would shine for an instant like a star in the grey depths of the mirror. That was all they knew of electricity in those dim-lit days when valleys of shadow lay deep between one piece of furniture and another. Was it because rooms were so badly lit then that they saw it so often, that little blue star? Suddenly, she was overcome by longing to see it again, and, standing up impetuously, she switched off the light. It was just then that, down below, the iron fist of the knocker was lifted and, with a strong, confident hand, brought down on the door. It was not a furtive knock. She recognised that even as she sat stark with fright in the darkness. And then a voice that was vaguely familiar called out from below.

'It's me, ma'am. I hope I'm not disturbing you?'

'Oh, Mr Crossen!' she cried out with relief, and unlocking her door, she ran across the landing and threw up a window on that side of the house. 'I'll be right down!' she called.

'There's no need to come down, ma'am,' he shouted. 'I only want one word with you.'

'Of course I'll come down.' She went back and got her dressing gown and was about to pin up her hair, but as she did she heard him stomping his feet on the gravel. It had been a mild day, but with night a chill had come in the air, and for all that it was late spring, there was a cutting east wind coming across the river. 'I'll run down and let you in from the cold,' she called, and, twisting up her hair, she held it against her head with her hand without waiting to pin it, and she ran down the stairs in her bare feet and opened the hall door.

'Oh? You were going to bed, ma'am?' he said apologetically when she opened the door. And where he had been so impatient a minute beforehand, he stood stock-still in the open doorway. 'I saw the lights were out downstairs when I was coming up the drive,' he said contritely. 'But I didn't think you'd gone up for the night.'

'Not at all,' she lied, to put him at his ease. 'I was just upstairs brushing my hair. You must excuse me,' she added, because a breeze from the door was blowing her dressing gown from her knees, and to pull it across she had to take her hand from her hair, so the hair fell down about her shoulders. 'Would you mind closing the door for me?' she said, with some embarrassment, and she began to back up the stairs. 'Please go inside to the sitting room off the hall. Put on the light. I'll be down in a minute.'

Although he had obediently stepped inside the door, and closed it, he stood stoutly in the middle of the hall. 'I shouldn't have come in,' he said. 'You were going to bed,' he cried, this time in an accusing voice as if he dared her to deny it. He was looking at her hair. 'Excuse my saying so, ma'am, but I never saw such a fine head of hair. God bless it!' he added quickly, as if afraid he had been too familiar. 'Doesn't a small thing make a big differ,' he said impulsively. 'You look like a young girl.'

In spite of herself, she smiled with pleasure. She wanted no more of this kind of talk, all the same. 'Well, I don't feel like one,' she said sharply.

What was meant for a quite opposite effect, however, seemed to delight him and put him wonderfully at ease. 'Ah sure, you're a sensible woman, I can see that,' he said, and, coming to the foot of the stairs, he leaned comfortably across the newel post. 'Let you stay the way you are, ma'am,' he said. 'I've only one word to say to you. Let me say here and now and be off about my business. The wife will be waiting up for me, and I don't want that.'

She hesitated. Was the reference to his wife meant to put *her* at ease? 'I think I ought to get my slippers,' she said cautiously. Her feet were cold.

'Oh, yes, you should put on your slippers,' he said, only then seeing that she was in her bare feet. 'But as to the rest, I'm long beyond taking any account of what a woman has on her. I'm gone beyond taking notice of women at all.'

But she had seen something to put on her feet. Under the table in the hall there was a pair of old boots belonging to Richard, with fleece lining in them. She hadn't been able to make up her mind to give them away with the rest of his clothes, and although they were big and clumsy on her, she often stuck her feet into them when she came in from the fields with mud on her shoes. 'Well, come in where it's warm, so,' she said. She came back down the few steps and stuck her feet into the boots, and then she opened the door of the sitting room. She was glad she'd come down. He'd never have been able to put on the light. 'There's something wrong with the centre light,' she said as she groped along the skirting board to find the plug of the reading lamp. It was in an awkward place, behind the desk. She had to go down on her knees.

'What's wrong with it?' he asked, as, with a countryman's interest in practicalities, he clicked the switch up and down to no effect.

'Oh, nothing much, I'm sure,' she said absently. 'There!' She had found the plug, and the room was lit up with a bright white glow.

'Why don't you leave the plug in the socket?' he asked critically.

'I don't know,' she said. 'I think someone told me it's safer, with reading lamps, to pull the plugs out at night. There might be a short circuit, or mice might nibble at the cord, or something. I forget what I was told. I got into the habit of doing it, and now I keep on.' She felt a bit silly.

But he was concerned about it. 'I don't think any harm could be done,' he said gravely. Then he turned away from the problem. 'About tomorrow, ma'am,' he said, somewhat off handedly, she thought. 'I was determined I'd see you tonight, because I'm not a man to break my word, above all, to a woman.'

What was he getting at?

'Let me put it this way,' he said quickly. 'You'll understand, ma'am, that as far as I am concerned, topping land is the same as cutting hay. The same time. The same labour. The same cost. And the same wear and tear on the blade. You understand that?'

On her guard, she nodded.

'Well now, ma'am, I'd be the first to admit that it's not quite the same for you. For you, topping doesn't give the immediate return you'd get from hay.'

'There's *no* return from topping,' she exclaimed crossly.

'Oh, come now, ma'am! Good grassland pays as well as anything. You know you won't get nice sweet pickings for your beasts from neglected land, but only dirty old tow grass knotting under their feet. It's just that it's not a quick return, and so, as you know, I told you I'd be making a special price for you.'

'I do know,' she said impatiently. 'But I thought that part of it was settled and done.'

'Oh, I'm not going back on it, if that's what you think,' he said affably. 'I'm glad to do what I can for you, ma'am, the more so seeing you have no man to attend to these things for you, but only yourself alone.'

'Oh, I'm well able to look after myself,' she said, raising her voice. Once again her words had an opposite effect to what she intended. He laughed good-humouredly. 'That's what all women like to think,' he said. 'Well, now,' he went on in a different tone of voice, and it annoyed her to see he deemed to think something had been settled between them, 'it would suit me, and I'm sure it's all the same to you, if we could leave your little job till later in the week, say till nearer to the time of the haymaking generally. Because by then I'd have the cutting bar in good order, sharpened and ready for use. Whereas now, while there's still a bit of ploughing to be done here and there, I'll have to be chopping and changing, between the ploughs and the mower, putting one on one minute and the other the next.'

'As if anyone is still ploughing this time of the year! Who are you putting before me?' she demanded.

'Now, take it easy, ma'am. I'm not putting anyone before you, leastways, not without getting leave first from you.'

'Without telling me you're not coming, you mean.'

'Oh, now, ma'am, don't get cross. I'm only trying to make matters easy for everyone.'

She was very angry now. 'It's always the same story. I thought you'd treat me differently. I'm to wait till after this one, and after that one, and in the end my fields will go wild.'

He looked a bit shamefaced. 'Ah now, ma'am, that's not going to be the case at all. Although, mind you, some people don't hold with topping, you know.'

'I hold with it.'

'Oh, I suppose there's something in it,' he said reluctantly. 'But the way I look at it, cutting the weeds in July is a kind of topping.'

'Grass cut before it goes to seed gets so thick at the roots no weeds can come up,' she cried, so angry she didn't realise how authoritative she sounded.

'Faith, I never knew you were so well up, ma'am,' he said, looking at her admiringly, but she saw he wasn't going to be put down by her. 'All the same now, ma'am, you can't say a few days here or there could make any difference?'

'A few days could make all the difference. This farm has a gravelly bottom to it, for all it's too lush. A few days of drought could burn it to the butt. And how could I mow it then? And what cover would there be for the "nice sweet pickings" you were talking about a minute ago?' Angrily, she mimicked his own accent without thinking.

He threw up his hands. 'Ah well, I suppose a man may as well admit when he's bested,' he said. 'Even by a woman. And you can't say I broke my promise.'

'I can't say but you tried hard enough,' she said grudgingly, although she was mollified that she was getting her way. 'Can I offer you anything?' she said then, anxious to convey an air of finality to their discussion.

'Not at all, ma'am. Nothing, thank you. I'll have to be getting home.'

'I hope you won't think I was trying to take advantage of you,' he said as they went towards the door. 'It's just that we must all make out as best we can for ourselves, isn't that so? Not but you are well able to look after yourself, I must say. No one ever thought you'd stay on here after your husband died. I suppose it's for the children you did it?' He looked up the well of the stairs. 'Are they asleep?'

'Oh, long ago,' she said indifferently. She opened the hall door.

The night air swept in. But this time, from far away, it brought with it the fragrance of new-mown hay. 'There's hay cut somewhere already,' she exclaimed in surprise. And she lifted her face to the sweetness of it.

For a minute, Crossen looked past her out into the darkness, then he looked back at her. 'Aren't you never lonely here at night?' he asked suddenly.

'You mean frightened?' she corrected quickly and coldly.

'Yes! Yes, that's what I meant,' he said, taken aback. 'Ah, but why would you be frightened? What safer place could you be under the sky than right here with your own fields all about you.'

What he said was so true, and he himself as he stood there, with his hat in his hand, so normal and natural it was indeed absurd to think that he would no sooner have gone out the door than she would be scurrying up the stairs like a child. 'You may not believe it,' she said, 'but I am scared to death sometimes. I nearly died when I heard your knock on the door tonight. It's because I was scared that I was upstairs,' she said, in a further burst of confidence. 'I always go up the minute it gets dark. I don't feel so frightened upstairs.'

'Isn't that strange now?' he said, and she could see he found it an incomprehensibly womanly thing to do. He was sympathetic all the same. 'You shouldn't be alone. That's the truth of the matter,' he said. 'It's a shame.'

'Oh, it can't be helped,' she said. There was something she wanted to shrug off in his sympathy, while at the same time she appreciated the kindliness. 'Would you like to do something for me?' she asked impulsively. 'Would you wait and put out the lights down here and let me get back upstairs before you go? Ned often does that for me if he's working here late.' After she had spoken she felt foolish, but she saw at once that, if anything, he thought it only too little to do for her. He was genuinely troubled about her. And it wasn't only the present moment that concerned him; he seemed to be considering the whole problem of her isolation and loneliness.

'Is there nobody could stay here with you, at night even? It would have to be another woman, of course,' he added quickly, and her heart was warmed by the way, without a word from her, he rejected that solution out of hand. 'You don't want another woman about the place,' he said flatly.

'Oh, I'm all right, really. I'll get used to it,' she said.

'It's a shame, all the same,' he said. He said it helplessly, though, and he motioned her towards the stairs. 'You'll be all right for tonight, anyway. Go on up the stairs now, and I'll put out the lights.' He had already turned around to go back into the sitting room.

Yet it wasn't quite as she intended for some reason, and it was somewhat reluctantly that she started up the stairs.

'Wait a minute! How do I put out this one?' he called out from the room before she was halfway up.

'Oh, I'd better put out that one myself,' she said, thinking of the awkward position of the plug. She ran down again, and, going past him into the little room, she knelt and pulled at the cord. Instantly the room was deluged in darkness. And instantly she felt that she had done something stupid. It was not like turning out a light by a switch at the door and being able to step back into the lighted hall. She got to her feet as quickly as she could, but as she did, she saw that Crossen was standing in the doorway. His bulk was blocked out against the hall light behind him. 'I'll leave the rest to you,' she said to break the peculiar silence that had come down on the house. But he didn't move. He stood there, the full of the doorway, and she was reluctant to brush past him.

Why didn't he move? Instead he caught her by the arm, and, putting out his other hand, he pressed his palm against the door jamb, barring her way.

'Tell me,' he whispered, his words falling over each other, 'are you never lonely at all?'

'What did you say?' she said in a clear voice, because the thickness of his voice sickened her. She had barely heard what he said. Her one thought was to get past him.

He leaned forward. 'What about a little kiss?' he whispered, and to get a better hold on her he let go the hand he had pressed against the wall, but before he caught at her with both hands she had wrenched her all free of him, and, ignominiously ducking under his armpit, she was out next minute in the lighted hall.

Out there, because light was all the protection she needed from him, the old fool, she began to laugh. She had only to wait for him to come sheepishly out. But here was something she hadn't counted on;

she hadn't counted on there being anything pathetic in his sheepishness, something really pitiful in the way he shambled into the light, not raising his eyes. And she was so surprisingly touched that before he had time to utter a word she put out her hand. 'Don't feel too bad,' she said. 'I didn't take offence.'

Still he didn't look at her. He just took her hand and pressed it gratefully, his face turned away. And to her dismay she saw that his nose was running water. Like a small boy, he wiped it with the back of his fist, streaking his face. 'I don't know what came over me,' he said slowly. 'I'm getting on to be an old man. I thought I was beyond all that.' He wiped his face again. 'Beyond letting myself go, anyway,' he amended miserably.

'Oh, it was nothing,' she said.

He shook his head. 'It wasn't as if I had cause for what I did.'

'But you did nothing,' she protested.

'It wasn't nothing to me,' he said dejectedly.

For a minute, they stood there silent. The hall door was still ajar, but she didn't dare to close it. What am I going to do with him now, she thought, I'll have him here all night if I'm not careful. What time was it, anyway? All scale and proportion seemed to have gone from the night. 'Well, I'll see you in the morning, Mr Crossen,' she said, as matter-of-factly as possible.

He nodded, but made no move to go on. 'You know I meant no disrespect to you, ma'am, don't you?' he said, looking imploringly at her. 'I always had a great regard for you. And for your husband, too. I was thinking of him this very night when I was coming up to the house. And I thought of him again when you came to the door looking like a young girl. I thought what a pity it was him to be taken from you, and you both so young. Oh, what came over me at all? And what would Mona say if she knew?'

'But surely you wouldn't tell her? I should certainly hope not,' Vera cried, appalled. What sort of a figure would she cut if he told the wife about her coming down in her bare feet with her hair down her back. 'Take care would you tell her!' she warned.

'I don't suppose I ought,' he said, but he said it uncertainly and morosely, and he leaned back against the wall. 'She's been a good woman, Mona. I wouldn't want anyone to think different. My sons could tell you. She's been a good mother to them all these years. She never made a bit of difference between them. Some say she was better to Barty than to any of them. She reared him from a week old. She was living next door to us, you see, at the time I was left with him,' he said. 'She came in that first night and took him home to her own bed, and, mind you, that wasn't a small thing for a woman who knew nothing about children, not being what you'd call a young girl, in spite of the big family she gave me afterwards. She took him home and looked after him, although it isn't every woman who would care to be responsible for a newborn baby. That's a thing a man doesn't forget easy. There's many I know would say that if she hadn't taken him someone else would, but no one only her would have done it the way she did. She used to keep him all day in her own cottage, feeding him and the rest of it. But at night, when I'd be back from the fields, she'd bring him home and leave him down in his little crib by the fire alongside of me. She used to let on she had things to do in her own place, and she'd slip away and leave us alone, but that wasn't her real reason for leaving him. She knew the way I'd be sitting looking into the fire, wondering how I'd face the long years ahead, and she left the child there with me to distract me from my sorrow. And she was right. I never got long to brood. The child would give a cry, or a whinge, and I'd have to run out and fetch her to him. Or else she'd hear him herself maybe, and run in without me having to call her at all. I used often think she must have kept every window and door in her place open, for fear she'd lose a sound from either of us. And so, bit by bit, I was knit back into a living man. I often wondered what would have become of me if it wasn't for her. There are men and when the bright way closes to them there's no knowing but they'll take a dark way. And

I was that class of man. I told you she used to take the little fellow away in the day and bring him back at night? Well, of course, she used to take him away again coming on to the real dark of night. She used to keep him in her own bed. But as the months went on and he got bigger, I could see she hated taking him away from me at all. He was beginning to smile and play with his fists and be real company. "I wonder ought I leave him with you tonight," she'd say then, night after night. And sometimes she'd run in and dump him down in the middle of the big double bed in the room off the kitchen, but the next minute she'd snatch him up again. "I'd be afraid you'd overlie him. You might only smother him, God between us and all harm!"

' "You'd better take him," I'd say, I used to hate to see him go myself by this time. All the same, I was afraid he'd start crying in the night, and what would I do then? If I had to go out for her in the middle of the night, it could cause a lot of talk, there was talk enough as things were, I can tell you, although there was no grounds for it. I had no more notion of her than if she wasn't a woman at all. Would you believe that? But one night when she took him up and put him down, and put him down and took him up, and went on and went on about leaving him or taking him, I had to laugh. "It's a pity you can't stay along with him, and that would settle all," I said. I was only joking her, but she got as red as fire, and the next thing she burst out crying. But not before she'd caught up the child and wrapped her coat around him. Then, after giving me a terrible look, she ran out the door with him. Well, that was the beginning of it. I'd no idea she had any feelings for me. I thought it was only for the child. But men are fools, as women well know, and she knew before me what was right and proper for us both. And for the child too. Some women have great insight into these things. That night God opened my own eyes to the woman I had in her, and I saw it was better I took her than wasted away after the one that was gone. And wasn't I right?'

'Of course you were right,' she said quickly.

But he had slumped back against the wall, and the abject look came back into his eyes. 'And to think I shamed her as well as myself.'

I'll never get rid of him, Vera thought desperately. 'Ah, what ails you?' she cried impatiently. 'Forget it, can't you?'

'I can't,' he said simply.

'Ah, for heaven's sake. It's got nothing to do with her at all.'

Surprised, he looked up at her. 'You're not blaming yourself, surely?' he asked.

She'd have laughed at that if she hadn't seen she was making headway. Another stroke and she'd be rid of him. 'Why are you blaming any of us?' she cried. 'It's got nothing to do with any of us, with you, or me, or the woman at home waiting for you. It was the other one you should blame, the girl, your first wife, Bridie! Blame her!' The words had broken uncontrollably from her. For a moment, she thought she was hysterical and that she could not stop. 'You thought you could forget her,' she cried, 'but see what she did to you when she got the chance.'

He stood for a moment at the open door. 'God rest her soul,' he said, without looking back, and he stepped into the night.

A MEMORY

JAMES DID ALL RIGHT FOR A MAN ON HIS OWN. AN OLD WOMAN FROM the village came in for a few hours a day and gave him a hot meal before she went home. She also got ready an evening meal needing only to be heated up. As well, she put his breakfast egg in a saucepan of water beside the paraffin stove, with a box of matches beside it in case he mislaid his own. She took care of all but one of the menial jobs of living. The one she couldn't do for him was one James hated most – cleaning out ashes from the grate in his study and lighting up the new fire for the day.

James was an early riser and firmly believed in giving the best of his brain to his work. So, the minute he was dressed he went out to the kitchen and lit the stove under the coffee pot. Then he got the ash bucket and went at the grate. When the ashes were out the rest wasn't too bad. There was kindling in the hot press and the old woman left a few split logs for getting up a quick blaze. He had the room well warmed by the time he had eaten his breakfast. His main objection to doing the grate was that he got his suit covered with ashes. He knew he ought to wear tweeds now that he was living full-time at the cottage, but he stuck obstinately to his dark suit and white collar, feeling as committed to this attire as to his single state. Both were part and parcel of his academic dedication. His work filled his life as it filled his day. He seldom had occasion to go up to the University. When he went up it was to see Myra, and then only on impulse if for some reason work went against him. This did happen periodically in spite of his devotion to it. Without warning a day would come when he'd wake up in a queer, unsettled mood that would send him prowling around the cottage, lighting up cigarette after cigarette and looking out of the window until he'd have to face the fact that he was not going to do a stroke. Inevitably the afternoon would see him with his hat and coat on, going down the road to catch the bus for Dublin – and an evening with Myra.

This morning he was in fine fettle though, when he dug the shovel into the mound of grey ash. But he was annoyed to see a volley of sparks go up the black chimney. The hearth would be hot, and the paper would catch fire before he'd have time to build his little pyre. There was more kindling in the kitchen press, but he'd have felt guilty using more than the allotted amount, thinking of the poor old creature wielding that heavy axe. He really ought to split those logs himself.

When he first got the cottage he used to enjoy that kind of thing. But after he'd been made a research professor and able to live down there all year around he came to have less and less zest for manual work. He sort of lost the knack of it. Ah well, his energies were totally expended in mental work. It would not be surprising if muscularly he got a bit soft.

James got up off his knees and brushed himself down. The fire was taking hold. The nimble flames played in and out through the dead twigs as sunlight must once have done when the sap was green. Standing watching them, James flexed his fingers. He wouldn't like to think he was no longer fit. Could his increasing aversion to physical labour be a sign of decreasing vigour? He frowned. He would not consider himself a vain man, it was simply that he'd got used to the look of himself; was accustomed to his slight, spare figure. But surely by mental activity he burned up as much fuel as any navvy or stevedore? Lunatics never had to worry about exercise either! Who ever saw a corpulent madman? He smiled. He must remember to tell that to Myra. Her laugh was always so quick and responsive although even if a second or two later she might seize on some inherently serious point in what had at first amused her. It was Myra who had first drawn his attention to this curious transference – this drawing off of energies – from the body to the brain. She herself had lost a lot of the skill in her fingers. When she was younger – or so she claimed – she'd been quite a good cook, and could sew, and that kind of thing, although frankly James couldn't imagine her being much good about the house. But when she gave up teaching and went into freelance translation her work began to make heavy demands on her, and she too, like him, lost all inclination for physical chores. Now – or so she said – she could not bake a cake to save her life. As for sewing – well here again frankly – to him the sight of a needle in her hand would be ludicrous. In fact he knew – they both knew – that when they first met, it was her lack of domesticity that had been the essence of her appeal for him. For a woman, it was quite remarkable how strong was the intellectual climate of thought in which she lived. She had concocted a sort of cocoon of thought and wrapped herself up in it. One became aware of it immediately one stepped inside her little flat. There was another thing! The way she used the word 'flat' to designate what was really a charming little mews house. It was behind one of the Georgian squares, and it had a beautiful little garden at the back and courtyard in front. He hadn't been calling there for very long until he understood why she referred to it as her flat. It was a word that did not have unpleasant connotations of domesticity.

Her little place had a marvellously masculine air, and yet, miraculously, Myra herself remained very feminine. She was, of course, a pretty woman, although she hated him to say this – and she didn't smoke, or drink more than a dutiful pre-dinner sherry with him, which she often forgot to finish. And there was a nice scent from her clothes, a scent at times quite disturbing. It often bothered him, and was occasionally the cause of giving her the victory in one of the really brilliant arguments that erupted so spontaneously the moment he stepped inside the door.

Yes, it was hard to believe Myra could ever have been a homebody. But if she said it was so, then it *was* so. Truth could have been her second name. With regard to her domestic failure, she had recently told him a most amusing story. He couldn't recall the actual incident, but it had certainly corroborated her theory of the transference of skill. It was – she said – as if part of her had become palsied, although at the time her choice of that word had made him wince, it was so altogether unsuitable for a woman like her, obviously now in her real prime. He'd pulled her up on that. Verbal exactitude was something they both knew to be of the utmost importance, although admittedly rarer to find in a woman than a man.

'It is a quality I'd never have looked to find in a woman, Myra,' he'd said to her on one of his first visits to the flat – perhaps his very first.

He never forgot her answer.

'It's not something I'd ever expect a man to look for in a woman,' she said. 'Thank you, James, for not jumping to the conclusion that I could not possibly possess it.'

Yes – that must have been on his first visit, because he'd been startled by such quick-fire volley in reply to what had been only a casual compliment. No wonder their friendship got off to a flying start!

Thinking of the solid phalanx of years that had been built up since that evening, James felt a glow of satisfaction, and for a moment he didn't realise that the fire he was supposed to be tending had got off to a good start, and part at least of his sense of well-being was coming from its warmth stealing over him.

The flames were going up the chimney with soft nervous rushes and the edges of the logs were deckled with small sharp flames, like the teeth of a saw. He could safely leave it now and have breakfast. But just then he did remember what it was Myra had been good at when she was young. Embroidery! She had once made herself an evening dress with the bodice embroidered all over in beads. And she'd worn it! So it must have been well made. Even his sister Kay, who disliked Myra, had to concede she dressed well. Yes, she must indeed have been fairly good at sewing in her young days. Yet one day recently when she ripped her skirt in the National Library she hadn't been able to mend it.

'It wasn't funny, James,' she chided when he laughed. 'The whole front pleat was ripped. I had to borrow a needle and thread from the lavatory attendant. Fortunately I had plenty of time – so when I'd taken it off and sewed it up I decided to give it a professional touch – a finish – with a tailor's arrow. It took time but it was well done and the lavatory attendant was very impressed when I held the skirt up! But next minute when I tried to step into it I found I'd sewn the back to the front. I'd formed a sort of gusset. Can you picture it. I'd turned it into trousers!'

Poor Myra! He laughed still more.

'I tell you, it's not funny, James. And it's the same with cooking. I used at least to be able to boil an egg, whereas now – ' She shrugged her shoulders. 'You know how useless I am in the kitchen.'

She had certainly never attempted to cook a meal for him. They always went out to eat. There was a small café near the flat and they ate there. Or at least they did at the start. But when one evening they decided they didn't really want to go out – perhaps he'd had a headache, or perhaps it was a really wet night, but anyway whatever it was, Myra made no effort to – as she put it – slop up some unappetising smather. Instead she lifted the phone, and got on to the proprietor of their little café and – as she put it – administered such a dose of coaxyorum – she really had very amusing ways of expressing herself – that he sent around two trays of food. Two trays, mind you. That was so like her – so quick, so clever. And tactful, too. That night marked a new stage in their relationship.

They'd been seeing a lot of each other by then. He'd been calling to the flat pretty frequently and when they went out for a meal, although the little café was always nearly empty, he had naturally paid the bill each time.

'We couldn't go on like that though, James!' she'd said firmly when he'd tried to pay for the trays of food that night. And she did finally succeed in making him see that if he were to come to the flat as often as she hoped he would – and as he himself certainly hoped – it would put her under too great an obligation to have him pay for the food every time.

'Another woman would be able to run up some tasty little dish that wouldn't cost tuppence,' she said, 'but – ' she made a face ' – that's out.

All the same I can't let you put me under too great a compliment to you. Not every time.'

In the end they'd settled on a good compromise. They each paid for a tray.

He had had misgivings, but she rid him of them.

'What would you eat if I wasn't here, Myra?' he'd asked.

'I wouldn't have *cooked* anything, that's certain,' she said, and he didn't pursue the topic, permitting himself just one other brief enquiry.

'What do other people do, I wonder?'

This Myra dismissed with a deprecating laugh.

'I'm afraid I don't know,' she said. 'Or care! Do you?'

'Oh Myra!' In that moment he felt she elevated them both to such pure heights of integrity. 'You know I don't,' he said, and he'd laid his hand over hers as she sat beside him on the sofa.

'That makes two of us!' she said, and she drew a deep breath of contentment.

It was a rich moment. It was probably at that moment he first realised the uniquely undemanding quality of her feeling for him.

But now James saw that the fire was blazing madly. He had to put on another log or it would burn out too fast. He threw on a log and was about to leave the study when, as he passed his desk, a nervous impulse made him look to see that his papers were not disarranged, although there was no one to disturb them.

The papers, of course, were as he had left them. But then the same diabolical nervousness made him go over and pick up the manuscript. Why? He couldn't explain, except that he'd worked late the previous night and, when he did that, he was always idiotically nervous next day, as if he half expected to find the words had been mysteriously erased during the night. That had happened once! He'd got up one morning as usual, full of eagerness to take up where he thought he'd left off only to find he'd stopped in the middle of a sentence – had gone to bed defeated, leaving a most involved and complicated sentence unfinished.

He'd only dreamed that he'd finished it off.

This morning, thank heavens, it was no dream. He'd finished the sentence – the whole chapter. It was the last chapter too. A little rephrasing, perhaps some rewording, and the whole thing would be ready for the typist.

Standing in the warm study with the pages of his manuscript in his hand James was further warmed by a self-congratulatory glow. This was the most ambitious thing he'd attempted so far – it was no less than an effort to trace the creative process itself back, as it were, to its source-bed. How glad he was that he'd stuck at it last night. He'd paid heavily for it by tossing around in the sheets until nearly morning. But it was worth it. His intuitions had never yielded up their meanings so fast or so easily. But suddenly his nervousness returned. He hoped to God his writing wasn't illegible? No. It was readable. And although his eye did not immediately pick up any of the particularly lucid – even felicitous – phrases that he vaguely remembered having hit upon, he'd come on them later when he was re-reading more carefully.

Pleased, James was putting down the manuscript, but on an impulse he took up the last section again. He'd bring it out to the kitchen and begin his re-reading of it while he was having his breakfast, something he never did, having a horror of food stains on paper. It might, as it were, recharge his batteries, because in spite of his satisfaction with the way the work was going, he had to admit to a certain amount of physical lethargy, due to having gone to bed so late.

It was probably wiser in the long run to do like Myra and confine oneself to a fixed amount of work per day. Nothing would induce Myra to go beyond her predetermined limit of two thousand words a day. Even when things were going well! It was when they were going well that paradoxically she often stopped work. Really her method of working amazed him. When she encountered difficulty she went doggedly on, worrying at a word like a dog with a bone – as she put it – in order, she explained, to avoid carrying over her frustration with it to the next day. On the other hand, when things were going well and her mind was leaping forward like a flat stone skimming the surface of a lake (her image again, not his, but good, good) *then* sometimes she stopped.

'Because then, James, I have a residue of enthusiasm to start me off next day! I'm not really a dedicated scholar like you – I need stimulus.'

She had a point. But her method wouldn't work for him. It would be mental suicide for him to tear himself away when he was excited. It was only when things got sticky he stopped. When an idea sort of seized up in his mind and he couldn't go on.

There was nothing sticky about last night though. Last night his brain buzzed with ideas. Yet now, sitting down to his egg, the page in his hand seemed oddly dull – a great hunk of abstraction. He took the top off the egg before reading on. But after a few paragraphs he looked at the numbering of the pages. Had the pages got mixed up? Here was a sentence that seemed to be in the wrong place. The whole passage made no impact. And what was this? He'd come on a line that was meaningless, absolutely meaningless – gibberish. With a sickening feeling James put down the manuscript and took a gulp of coffee. Then, by concentrating hard he could perceive – could at least form a vague idea of – what he'd been trying to get at in this clumsy passage. At one point indeed he had more or less got it, but the chapter as a whole – ? He sat there stunned.

What had happened? Could it be that what he'd taken for creative intensity had been only nervous exhaustion? Was that it? Was Myra right? Should he have stopped earlier? Out of the question. In the excited state he'd been in, he wouldn't have slept a wink at all – even in the early hours. And what else could he have done but go to bed? A walk, perhaps? At that time of night? On a country road in the pitch dark? It was all very well for Myra – the city streets were full of people at all hours, brightly lit, and safe underfoot.

Anyway Myra probably did most of her work in the morning. He didn't really know for sure of course, except that whenever he turned up at the flat there was never any sign of papers about the place. The thought of that neat and orderly flat made him look around the cottage and suddenly he felt depressed. The old woman did her best, but she wasn't up to very much. The place could do with a rub of paint, the woodwork at least, but he certainly wasn't going to do it. He wouldn't be able. James frowned again. Why was his mind harping on this theme of fitness? He straightened up as if in protest at some accusation, but almost at once he slumped down, not caring.

He got exercise enough on the days he went to Dublin. First the walk to the bus. Then the walk at the other end, because no matter what the weather, he always walked from the bus to the flat. It was a good distance too, but it prolonged his anticipation of the evening ahead.

Ah well! He wouldn't be going today. That was certain. He gathered up his pages. He'd have to slog at this thing till he got it right. He swallowed down the last of his coffee. Back to work.

The fire at any rate was going well. It was roaring up the chimney. The sun too was pouring into the room. Away across the river in a far field cattle were lying down: a sign of good weather, it was said.

Hastily, James stepped back from the window and sat down at his desk. It augured badly for his work when he was aware of the weather. Normally he couldn't have told if the day was wet or fine.

That was the odd thing about Dublin. There, the weather did matter. There he was aware of every fickle change in the sky, especially on a day like today that began with rain and later gave way to sunshine. The changes came so quick in the city. They took one by surprise, although one was alerted by a thousand small signs, whereas the sodden fields were slow to recover after the smallest shower. In Dublin the instant there was a break in the clouds, the pavements gave back an answering glint. And after that came a strange white light mingling water and sun, a light that could be perceived in the reflections underfoot without raising one's eyes to the sky at all. And how fast then the paving stones dried out into pale patches. Like stepping stones, these patches acted strangely on him, putting a skip into his otherwise sober step!

Talk of the poetry of spring. The earth's rebirth! Where was it more intoxicating than in the city, the cheeky city birds filling the air with song, and green buds breaking out on branches so black with grime it was as if iron bars had sprouted. Thinking of the city streets, his feet ached to be pacing them. James glanced out again at the fields with hatred.

Damn, damn, damn. The damage was done. He'd let himself get unsettled. It would be Dublin for him today. He looked at the clock. He might even go on the early bus. Only what would he do up there all day? His interest in Dublin had dwindled to its core, and the core was Myra.

All the same, he decided to go on the early bus. 'Come on, James! Be a gay dog for once. Get the early bus. You'll find plenty to do. The bookshops! The National Library! Maybe a film? Come on. You're going whether you like it or not, old fellow.'

Catching up the poker, James turned the blazing logs over to smother their flames. A pity he'd lit the fire, or rather it was a pity it couldn't be kept in till he got back. It would be nice to return to a warm house. But old Mrs Nully had a mortal dread of the cottage taking fire in his absence. James smiled thinking how she had recently asked why he didn't install central heating. In a three-roomed cottage! Now, where on earth had she got that notion, he wondered, as he closed the door and put the key under the mat for her. Then, as he strode off down to the road, he remembered that a son of hers had been taken on as houseman in Asigh House, and the son's wife gave a hand there at weekends. The old woman had probably been shown over the house by them before the Balfes moved into it.

The Balfes! James was nearly at the road, and involuntarily he glanced back across the river to where a fringe of fir trees in the distance marked out the small estate of Asigh. Strange to think – laughable really – that Emmy, who once had filled every cranny of his mind, should only come to mind now in a train of thought that had its starting point in a plumbing appliance!

Here James called himself to order. It was a gross exaggeration to have said – even to himself – that Emmy had ever entirely filled his mind. He'd only known her for a year, and that was the year he finished his Ph.D. He submitted the thesis at the end of the year, and his marks, plus the winning of the travelling scholarship, surely spoke for a certain detachment of mind even when he was most obsessed by her?

He glanced back again at the far trees. Emmy only stood out in his life because of the violence of his feeling for her. It was something he had never permitted himself before; and never would again. When the affair ended, it ended as completely as if she had been a little skiff upon a swiftly flowing river, which, when he'd cut the painter, was carried instantly away. For a time he'd had no way of knowing whether it had capsized or foundered. As it happened, Emmy had righted herself and come to no harm.

Again, James had to call himself to order. How cruel he made himself seem by that metaphor. Yet for years that was how he'd felt obliged to put it to himself. That was how he'd put it to Myra when he first told her about Emmy. But Myra was quick to defend him, quick to see, and quick to show him how he had acted in self-defence. His career would have been wrecked, because of course with a girl like Emmy marriage would have become inescapable. And, of course, then as now, marriage for him was out. It was never really in the picture.

Later, after Myra appeared on the scene, he came to believe that a man and woman could enter into a marriage of minds.

'But when one is young, James,' Myra said, 'one can't be expected to be both wise and foolish at the same time.'

A good saying. He'd noticed, and appreciated, the little sigh with which she accompanied her words, as if she didn't just feel *for* him but *with* him. Then she asked the question that a man might have asked.

'She married eventually I take it, this Emmy?'

'Oh good lord, yes.' How happy he was to be able to answer in the affirmative. If Emmy had not married it would have worried him all his life. But she did. And, all things considered, surprisingly soon.

'Young enough to have a family?' Myra probed, but kindly, kindly. He nodded. 'I take it,' she said then more easily, 'I take it she married that student who – '

James interrupted, 'The one she was knocking around with when I first noticed her?'

'Yes, the one that was wrestling with that window when you had to step down from the rostrum and yank it open yourself?'

Really Myra was unique. Her grasp of the smallest details of that incident, even then so far back in time, was very gratifying.

He had been conducting a tutorial and the lecture room got so stuffy he'd asked if someone would open a window? But when a big burly fellow – the footballer type – tried with no success, James strode down the classroom himself, irritably, because he half thought the fellow might be having him on to create a diversion. And when he had to lean in across a student whose chair was right under the window, he was hardly aware it was a girl, as he exerted all his strength to bring down the heavy sash. Only when the sash came down and the fresh air rushed in overhead did he find he was looking straight into the eyes of a girl – Emmy.

That was all. But during the rest of the class their eyes kept meeting. And the next day it was the same. Then he began to notice her everywhere, in the corridors, in the Main Hall, and once across the Aula Maxima at an inaugural ceremony. And she'd seen him too. He knew it. But for a long time, several weeks, there was nothing between them except this game of catch-catch with their eyes. And always, no matter how far apart they were, it was as if they had touched.

James soon found himself trembling all over when her eyes touched him. Then one day in the library she passed by his desk and he saw that a paper in her hand was shaking as if there was a breeze in the air. But there was no breeze. Still, deliberately, he delayed the moment of speaking to her because there was a kind of joy in waiting. And funnily enough when they did finally speak neither of them could afterwards remember what their first spoken words had been. They had already said so much with their eyes.

Myra's comment on this, though, was very shrewd. 'You had probably said all there was to say, James.' Again she gave that small sigh of hers that seemed to put things in proportion: to place him, and Emmy too, on the map of disenchantment where all mankind, it seems, must sojourn for a time. And indeed it was sad to think that out of the hundreds of hours that he and Emmy had spent together, wandering along the damp paths of Stephen's Green, sitting in little cafés, and standing under the lamps of Leeson Street where he was in lodgings, he could recall nothing of what was said. 'You probably spent most evenings trying out ideas for your thesis on her, poor girl.' Myra had a dry humour at times, but he had to acknowledge it was likely enough, although if so, Emmy used to listen as if she were drinking in every word.

When he'd got down at last to the actual writing of the thesis they did not meet so often. In fact he could never quite remember their last meeting either. Not even what they had said to each other at parting. Of course long before that they must have faced up to his situation. He'd been pretty sure of getting the travelling scholarship, so it must have been an understood thing that he'd be going away for at least two years. And in the end, he left a month sooner than he'd intended. They never actually did say goodbye. He'd gone without seeing her – just left a note at her digs. And for a while he wasn't even sure if she'd got it. She'd got it all right. She wrote and thanked him. How that smarted! *Thanked* him for breaking it off with her. Years later, telling Myra, he still felt the sting of that.

Myra was marvellous though.

'Hurt pride, my dear James. Nothing more, don't let it spoil what is probably the sweetest thing in life – for all of us, men or women – our first shy, timid love.' There was a tenderness in her voice. Was she remembering some girlish experience of her own? The pang of jealousy that went through him showed how little Emmy had come to mean to him.

Myra put him at ease.

'We all go through it, James, it's only puppy love.'

'Puppy love! I was twenty-six, Myra!'

'Dear, dear James.' She smiled. 'Don't get huffy. I know quite well what age you were. You were completing your Ph.D., and you were old enough to conduct tutorials. You were not at the top of the tree, but you had begun the ascent!'

It was so exactly how he'd seen himself in those days, that he laughed. And with that laugh the pain went out of the past.

'Dear James,' she said again, 'anyone who knows you – and loves you,' she added quickly, because they tried never to skirt away from that word 'love', although they gave it a connotation all their own, 'anyone who loves you, James, would know that even then, where women were concerned, you'd be nothing but a lanky, bashful boy. Wait a minute!' She sprang up from the sofa. 'I'll show you what I mean.' She took down the studio photograph she'd made him get taken the day of his honorary doctorate. 'Here!' She shoved the silver frame into his hands, and going into the room where she slept, she came back with another photograph. 'You didn't know I had this one?' He saw with some chagrin that it was a blow-up from a group photograph taken on the steps of his old school at the end of his last year. 'See!' she said. 'It's the same face in both, the same ascetical features, the same look of dedication.' Then she pressed the frame end face inward, against her breast. 'Oh James, I bet Emmy was the first girl you ever looked at! My dear, it was not so much the girl as the experience itself that bowled you over.'

Emmy was not the first girl he'd looked at. In those days he was always looking at girls, but looking at them from an unbridgeable distance. When he looked at Emmy the space between them seemed to be instantly obliterated. Emmy had felt the same. That day in class her mind had been a million miles away. She was trying to make up her mind about getting engaged to the big burly fellow, the one who couldn't open the window; James could not remember his name, but he was a type that could be attractive to women. The fellow was pestering her to marry him, and the attentions of a fellow like that could have been very flattering to a girl like Emmy. She was so young. Yet, after she met *him* it was as if a fiery circle had been blazed around them, allowing no way out for either until he, James, in the end had to close his eyes and break through, not caring about the pain as long as he got outside again.

Because Myra was right. Marriage would have put an end to his academic career. For a man like him it would have been suffocating.

'Even now!' Myra said, and there was a humorous expression on her face, because of course, in their own way, he and Myra *were* married. Then, in a businesslike way, as if she were filling up a form for filing away, she asked him another question. 'What family did they have?'

'She had five or six children, I think, although she must have been about thirty by the time she married.' James couldn't help throwing his eyes up to heaven at the thought of such a household. Myra, too, raised her eyebrows.

'You're joking?' she said. 'Good old Balfe!' But James was staring at her, hardly able to credit she had picked up Emmy's married name. He himself had hardly registered it, the first time *he'd* heard it, so that when last summer Asigh House had been bought by people named Balfe, it simply hadn't occurred to him that it could have been Emmy and her husband until one day on the road a car passed him and the woman beside the driver reminded him oddly of her. The woman in the car was softer and plumper and her hair was looser and more untidy — well, fluffier anyway — than Emmy's used to be, or so he thought, until suddenly he realised it *was* her. Emmy! She didn't recognise him though. But then she wasn't looking his way. She was looking out over the countryside through which she was passing. It was only when the car turned left at the crossroad the thought hit him, that she had married a man named Balfe, and that Balfe was the name of the people who'd bought Asigh. It was a shock. Not only because of past associations, but more because he had never expected any invasion of his privacy down here. It was his retreat, from everything and everyone. Myra — even Myra — had never been down there. She was too sensible to suggest such a thing. And he wouldn't want her to come either.

Once when he'd fallen ill he'd lost his head and sent her a telegram, but even then she'd exercised extreme discrimination. She despatched a nurse to take care of him, arranging with the woman to phone her each evening from the village. Without once coming down, she had overseen his illness — which fortunately was not of long duration. She had of course ascertained to her satisfaction that his condition was not serious. The main thing was that she set a firm precedent for them both. It was different when he was convalescing. Then she insisted that he come up to town and stay in a small hotel near the flat, taking his evening meal with her, as on ordinary visits except — James smiled — except that she sent a taxi to fetch him, and carry him back, although the distance involved was negligible, only a block or two.

Remembering her concern for him on that occasion, James told himself that he could never thank her enough. He resolved to let her see he did not take her goodness for granted. Few women could be as self-effacing.

Yet, in all fairness to Emmy, she had certainly effaced herself fast. One might say drastically. After that one note of thanks — it jarred again that she had put it like that — he had never once heard or seen her until that day she passed him here on the road in her car. So much for his fears for his privacy. Unfounded! For days he'd half expected a courtesy call from them, but after a time he began to wonder if they were aware at all that he lived in the neighbourhood? After all, their property was three or four miles away, and the river ran between. It was just possible Emmy knew nothing of his existence. Yet somehow, he doubted it. As the crow flies he was less than two miles away. He could see their wood. And was it likely the local people would have made no mention of him? No, it was hard to escape the conclusion that Emmy might be avoiding him. Although Myra – who was never afraid of the truth – had not hesitated to say that Emmy might have forgotten him altogether!

'Somehow I find that hard to believe, Myra,' he'd said, although after he'd made the break, there had been nothing. Nothing, nothing, nothing.

But Myra was relentless.

'You may not like to believe it, James, but it could be true all the same,' she said. Then she tried to take the hurt out of her words by confessing that she herself found it dispiriting to think a relationship that had gone so deep, could be erased completely. 'I myself can't bear to think she did not recognise you that day she passed you on the road. *She* may have changed – you said she'd got stouter – ' That wasn't the word he'd used, but he'd let it pass ' – whereas you, James, can hardly have changed at all, in essentials, I mean. Your figure must be the same as when you were a young man. I can't bear to think she didn't even *know* you.'

'She wasn't looking straight at me, Myra.'

'No matter! You'd think there'd have been some telepathy between you; some force that would *make* her turn. Oh, I can't bear it!'

She was so earnest he had to laugh.

'It is a good job she didn't see me,' he said. Emmy being nothing to him then, it was just as well there should be no threat to his peace and quiet.

Such peace; such quiet. James looked around at the sleepy countryside. The bus was very late though! What was keeping it?

Ah, here it came. Signalling to the driver, James stepped up quickly on to the running-board so the man had hardly to do more than go down into first gear before starting off again. In spite of how few passengers there were, the windows were fogged up and James had to clear a space on the glass with his hand to see out. It was always a pleasant run through the rich Meath fields, but soon the unruly countryside gave way to neatly squared-off fields with pens and wooden palings, where cattle were put in for the night before being driven to the slaughterhouse.

James shuddered. He was no countryman. Not by nature anyway. He valued the country solely for the protection it gave him from people. When he lived in Dublin he used to work in the National Library, but as he got older he began to feel that in the eyes of the students and the desk-messengers, he could have appeared eccentric. Not objectionably so, just rustling his papers too much, and clearing his throat too loudly; that kind of thing. He'd have been the first to find that annoying in others when he was young. The cottage was much better. It also served to put that little bit of distance between him and Myra which they both agreed was essential.

'If I lived in Dublin I'd be here at the flat every night of the week,' he'd once said to her. 'I'm better off down there – I suppose – stuck in the mud!'

That was an inaccurate – an unfair – description of his little retreat, but the words had come involuntarily to his lips, which showed how he felt about the country in general. The city streets of Dublin were so full of life, and the people were so dapper and alert compared with the slow-moving country people. Every time he went up there he felt like an old fogy – that was, until he got to Myra's – because Myra immediately gave him back a sense of being alive. Mentally at least Myra made him feel more alive than twenty men.

The bus had now reached O'Connell Bridge, where James usually descended, so he got out. He ought to have got out sooner and walked along the Quays. One could kill a whole morning looking over the book barrows. Now he would have to walk back to them.

Perhaps he ought not to have come on the early bus? It might not be so easy to pass the time. And after browsing to his heart's content and leaning for a while looking over the parapet on to the Liffey, it was still only a little after 1 o'clock when he strolled back to the centre of the city. He'd have to eat something and that would use up another hour or more. He'd buy a paper and sit on over his coffee.

James hadn't bargained on the lunchtime crowds though. All the popular places were crowded, and in a few of the better places, one look inside was enough to send him off! These places too were invaded by the lunchtime hordes, and the menu would cater for these barbarians. If there should by chance happen to be a continental dish on the menu – a goulash or a pasta – it would nauseate him to see the little clerks attacking it with knife and fork as if it was a mutton chop.

At this late hour how about missing out on lunch altogether? It never hurt to skip a meal, although, mind you, he was peckish. How about a film? He hadn't been in a cinema for years. And just then, as if to settle the matter – James saw he was passing a cinema. It was exceptionally small for a city cinema, but without another thought he bolted inside.

Once inside, he regretted that he hadn't checked the time of the showings. He didn't fancy sitting through a newsreel, to say nothing of a cartoon. He had come in just in the middle of a particularly silly cartoon. He sat in the dark fuming. To think he'd let himself in for this stuff. It was at least a quarter of an hour before he realised with rage that he must have strayed into one of the newfangled newsreel cinemas about which Myra had told him. For another minute he sat staring at the screen, trying to credit the mentality of people who voluntarily subjected themselves to this kind of stuff. He was about to leave and make for the street, when without warning his eyes closed. He didn't know for how long he had dozed off, but on waking he was really ravenous. But wouldn't it be crazy to eat at this hour and spoil his appetite for the meal with Myra? He could, he supposed, go around to the flat earlier – now – immediately? Why wait any longer? But he didn't know at what hour Myra herself got there. All he knew was that she was always there after seven, the time he normally arrived.

But wasn't it remarkable now he came to think of it, that she *was* always there when he called. Very occasionally at the start she had let drop dates on which she had to go to some meeting or other, and he'd made a mental note of them, but as time went on she gave up these time-wasting occupations. There had been one or two occasions she had been going out, but had cancelled her arrangements immediately he came on the scene. He had protested of course, but lamely, because quite frankly it would have been frightfully disappointing to have come so far and found she really had to go out.

Good God – supposing that were to happen now? James was so scared at the possibility of such a catastrophe he determined to lose no more time but get around there quick. Just in case. He stepped out briskly.

The lane at the back of Fitzwilliam Square, where Myra had her mews, was by day a hive of small enterprises. A smell of cellulosing and sounds of welding filled the air. In one courtyard there was a little fellow who dealt in scrap iron and he made a great din. But by early evening, the big gates closed on these businesses, the high walls made the lane a very private place, and the mews-dwellers were disturbed by no sound harsher than the late song of the birds nesting in the trees of the doctors' gardens.

Walking down the lane and listening to those sleepy bird-notes gave James greater pleasure than walking on any country road. His feet echoed so loudly in the stillness that sometimes before he rapped on her gate at all, Myra would come running out across the courtyard to admit him. A good thing that! Because otherwise he'd have had to rap with his bare knuckles; Myra had no knocker.

'You know I don't encourage callers, James,' she'd said once, smiling. 'Few people ferret me out here – except you; and, of course, the tradesmen. And I know their step too! It's nearly as quiet here as in your cottage.'

'Quiet?' He'd raised his eyebrows. 'Listen to those birds; I never heard such a din!'

Liking a compliment to be oblique, she'd squeezed his arm as she drew him inside.

This evening however James was less than halfway down the lane when at the other end he saw Myra appear at the wicket gate. If she hadn't been bare-headed he'd have thought she was going out!

'Myra?' he called in some dismay.

She laughed as she came to meet him. 'I heard your footsteps,' she said. 'I told you! I always do.'

'From this distance?'

She took his arm and smiled up at him. 'That's nothing! It's a wonder I don't hear you walking down the country road to get the bus.' She matched her step with his. Normally he hated to be linked, but with Myra it seemed to denote equality, not dependence. Suddenly she unlinked her arm. 'Well, I may as well confess something,' she said more seriously. 'This evening I was listening for you. I was expecting you.'

They had reached the big wooden gate of the mews and James, glancing in through the open wicket across the courtyard, was startled to see, through the enormous window by which she had replaced the doors of the coach house, that the little table at which they ate was indeed set up, and with places laid for two! She wasn't joking, then? An unpleasant thought crossed his mind – was she expecting someone else? But reading his mind, Myra shook her head.

'Only you, James.'

'I don't understand – '

'Neither do I!' she said quickly. 'I *was* expecting you though. And I ordered our trays!' Here she wrinkled her nose in a funny way she had. 'I made the order a bit more conservative than usual. No prawns!' He understood at once. He loved prawns. 'So you see,' she continued, 'if my oracle failed, and you didn't come, the food would do for sandwiches tomorrow. As you know, I'm no use at hotting up leftovers. It smacks too much of – '

He knew. He knew.

'Too wifey.' He smiled. And she smiled. This was the word they'd ear-marked to describe a certain type of woman they both abhorred.

'You could always have fed the prawns to the cat next door,' James said. 'Whenever I'm coming he's sitting on the wall smacking his lips.'

'But James,' she said, and suddenly she stopped smiling, 'he doesn't know when you're coming – any more than me!'

'Touché,' James admitted to being caught out there. He wasn't really good at smart remarks. 'Ah well, it's a lucky cat who knows there's an even chance of a few prawns once or twice a month. That's more than most cats can count on.' Bending his head he followed her in through the wicket. 'Some cats have to put up with a steady diet of shepherd's pie and meat loaf.'

They were inside now, and he sank down on the sofa. Myra, who was still standing, shuddered.

'What would I do if you were the kind of man who *did* like shepherd's pie?' she said. 'I'm sure there are such men.' But she couldn't keep up the silly chaff. 'I think maybe I'd love you enough to try and make it – ' she laughed ' – if I could. I don't honestly think I'd be able. The main thing is that you are *not* that type. Let's stop fooling. Here, allow me to give you a kiss of gratitude – for being you.'

Lightly she laid her cheek against his, while he for his part took her hand and stroked it.

It was one of the more exquisite pleasures she gave him, the touch of her cool skin. His own hands had a tendency to get hot although he constantly wiped them with his handkerchief. He had always preferred being too cold to being too hot. Once or twice when he had a headache – which was not often – Myra had only to place her hand on his forehead for an instant and the throbbing ceased. This evening he didn't have a headache but all the same he liked the feel of her hand on his face.

'Do that again,' he said.

'How about fixing the drinks first?' she said.

That was his job. But he did not want to release her hand, and he made no attempt to stand up. Unfortunately just then there was a rap on the gate.

'Oh bother,' he said.

'It's only the catering service,' Myra said, and for a minute he didn't get the joke. She laughed then and he noticed she meant the grubby little pot-boy who brought the trays around from the café.

'Let me get them,' he said, but she had jumped up and in a minute she was back with them.

'I must tell you,' she said. 'You know the man who owns the café? Well, he gave me such a dressing-down this morning when I was ordering these.' James raised his eyebrows as he held open the door of the kitchenette to let her through. 'Just bring me the warming plate, will you please, James,' she said interrupting herself. 'I'll pop the food on it for a second while we have our little drink.' She glanced at her watch. 'Oh, it's quite early still.' She looked back at him. 'But you were a little later than usual, I think, weren't you?'

'I don't think so,' he said vaguely, as he fitted the plug of the food warmer into the socket. 'If anything, I think I was a bit earlier. But I could be wrong. When one has time to kill it's odd how often one ends up being late in the end!'

'Time to kill?'

She looked puzzled. Then she seemed to understand. 'Oh, James.

You make me tired. You're so punctilious. Haven't I told you a thousand times that you don't have to be polite with me? If your bus got in early you should have come straight to the flat! Killing time indeed! Standing on ceremony, eh?'

He handed her her drink.

'You were telling me something about the proprietor of the café – that he was unpleasant about something? You weren't serious?'

'Oh, that! Of course not.'

Yet for some reason he was uneasy. 'Tell me,' he said authoritatively.

Naturally, she complied. 'He was really very nice,' she said. 'He intended phoning me. He just wanted to say there was no need to wash the plates before sending them back. I'm to hand them to the messenger in the morning just as they are – and not *attempt* to wash them.' Knowing how fastidious she was, James was about to pooh-pooh the suggestion, but she forestalled him. 'I can wrap them up in the napkins, and then I won't be affronted by the sight. And I need feel under no compliment to the café – it's in their own interests as much as in mine. They have a big washing machine – I've seen it – with a special compartment like a dentist's sterilisation cabinet, and of course they couldn't be sure that a customer would wash them properly. You can imagine the cat's lick some women would give them!'

James could well imagine it. He shuddered. Myra might hate housework, but anything she undertook she did to perfection. Unexpectedly she held out her glass.

'Let's have another drink,' she said. They seldom took more than one. 'Sit down,' she commanded. 'Let's be devils for once.' This time though she sat on the sofa and swung her feet up on it so he had to sit in the chair opposite. 'There's nothing that makes the ankles ache like thinking too hard,' she said.

James didn't really understand what she meant but he laughed happily.

'Seriously!' she said. 'I am feeling tired this evening. I'm so glad you came. I think maybe I worked extra hard this morning because I was looking forward to seeing you later. Oh, I'm so glad you came, James. I would have been bitterly disappointed if you hadn't showed up.'

James felt a return of his earlier uneasiness.

'I'm afraid that premonition of yours is more than I can understand,' he said, but he spoke patiently, because she was not a woman who had to be humoured. 'As a matter of fact I never had less intention of coming to town. I'd already lit the fire in my study when I suddenly took the notion. I had to put the fire out!'

At that, Myra left down her glass and swung her feet back on to the floor.

'What time did you leave?' she asked, and an unusually crisp note in her voice took him unawares.

'I thought I told you,' he said apologetically, although there was nothing for which to apologise. 'I came on the morning bus.'

'Oh!' It was only one word, but it fell oddly on his ears. She reached for her drink again then, and swallowed it down. Somehow that too bothered him. 'Is that what you meant by having to kill time?' she asked.

'Well – ' he began, not quite knowing what to say. He took up his own drink and let it down fairly fast for him.

'Oh, don't bother to explain,' she said. 'I think you will agree though it would have been a nice gesture to have lifted a phone and let me know you were in town and coming here tonight.'

'But – '

'No buts about it. You knew I'd be here waiting whether you came or not. Isn't that it?'

'Myra!'

He hardly recognised her in this new mood. Fortunately the next moment she was her old self again.

'Oh James, forgive me. It's just that you've *no* idea – simply *no* idea – how much it meant to me tonight to know in advance – ' She stopped and carefully corrected herself ' – to have had that curious feeling – call it instinct if you like – that you were coming. It made such a difference to my whole day. But now – ' her face clouded over ' – to think that instead of just having had a hunch about it, I could have known for certain. Oh, if only you'd been more thoughtful, James.' Sitting up straighter, she looked him squarely in the eye. 'Or were you going somewhere else and changed your mind?'

What a foolish question.

'As if I ever go anywhere else!'

Her face brightened a bit at that, but not much.

'You'll hardly believe it,' she said after a minute, 'but I could have forgiven you more easily if you had been going somewhere else, and coming here *was* an afterthought. It would have excused you more.'

Excused? What was all this about? He must have looked absolutely bewildered, because she pulled herself up.

'Oh, James, please don't mind me.' She leant forward and laid a hand on his knee. 'Your visits give me such joy – I don't need to tell you that – I ought to be content with what I have. Not knowing in advance is one of the little deprivations that I just have to put up with, I suppose.'

But now James was beginning to object strongly to the way she was putting everything. He stood up. As if his doing so unnerved her, she stood up too.

'It may seem a small thing to ask from you, James, but I repeat what I said – you could have phoned me.' Then, as if that wasn't bad enough, she put it into the future tense. 'If you would only try, once in a while, to give me a ring, even from the bus depot, so I could – '

' – could what?' James couldn't help the coldness in his voice, although considering the food that was ready on the food warmer, his question, he knew, was ungenerous. On the other hand he felt it was absolutely necessary to keep himself detached, if the evening was not to be spoiled. He forced himself to speak sternly. 'Much as I enjoy our little meals together, it's not for the food I come here, Myra. You must know that.' He very, very nearly added that in any case he paid for his own tray, but when he looked at her he saw she had read these unsaid words from his eyes. He reddened. There was an awkward silence. Yet when she spoke she ignored everything he had said and harked back to what she herself had said.

'Wouldn't it be a very small sacrifice to make, James, when one thinks of all the sacrifices I've made for you? And over so many years?' Her words, which to him were exasperating beyond belief, seemed to drown her in a torrent of self-pity. 'So many, many years,' she whispered.

It was only ten.

'You'd think it was a lifetime,' he said irritably. Her face flushed.

'What is a lifetime, James?' she asked, and when he made no reply she helped him out. 'Remember it is not the same for a woman as for a man. *You* may think of yourself as a young blade, but I . . .'

She faltered again, as well she might, and bit her lip. She wasn't going to cry, was she? James was appalled. Nothing had ever before happened that could conceivably have given rise to tears, but it was an unspoken law with them that a woman should never shed tears in public. Not just unspoken either. On one occasion years ago she herself had been quite explicit about it.

'We do cry sometimes, we women, poor weaklings that we are. But I hope I would never be foolish enough to cry in the presence of a man. And to do it to you of all people, James, would be despicable.' At the time he'd wondered why she singled him out. Did she think him more sensitive than most? He'd been about to ask when she'd given one of her witty twists to things. 'If I did, I'd have you snivelling too in no time,' she said.

Yet here she was now, for no reason at all, on the brink of tears, and apparently making no effort to fight them back.

Myra was making no effort to stem her tears because she did not know she was crying. She really did despise tears. But now it seemed to her that perhaps she'd been wrong in always hiding her feelings. Other women had the courage to cry. Even in public too. She'd seen them at parties. And recently she'd seen a woman walking along the street in broad daylight with tears running down her cheeks, not bothering to wipe them away. Thinking of such women, she wondered if she perhaps had sort of – she paused to find the right word – sort of denatured herself for James?

'Denatured': it was an excellent word. She'd have liked to use it then and there but she had just enough sense left to keep it to herself for the moment. Some other time when they were talking about someone else, she would bring it out and impress him. She must not forget the word.

When Myra's thoughts returned to James she felt calmer about him. He was not unkind. He was not cruel – the opposite in fact. What had gone wrong this evening was more her fault than his. When they'd first met she had sensed deep down in him a capacity for the normal feelings of friendship and love. Yet throughout the years she had consistently deflected his feelings away from herself and consistently encouraged him to seal them off. Tonight it seemed that his emotional capacity was completely dried up. Despair overcame her. She'd never change him now. He was fixed in his faults, cemented into his barren way of life. Tears gushed into her eyes again but this time she leant her head back quickly to try and prevent them rolling down, but they brimmed over and splashed down on her hands.

'Oh, James, I'm sorry,' she whispered, but she saw her apology was useless; the damage was done. Then her heart hardened. What harm? She wasn't really sorry. Not for him anyway. Oh, not for him. It was for herself she was sorry.

Grasping at a straw, then, she tried to tell herself, nothing was ever too late. Perhaps tonight some lucky star had stood still in the sky over her head and forced her to be true to herself for once. James would see the real woman for a change. Oh, surely he would? And surely he would come over and put his arm around her. He would: he would. She waited.

When he did not move, and did not utter a single word, she had to look up.

'Oh no!' she cried. For what she saw in his eyes was ice. 'Oh James, have you no heart? What you have done to me is unspeakable! Yet you can't even pity me!'

James spoke at last. 'And what, Myra, what may I ask, have I done to you?'

'You have – ' She stopped, and for one second she thought she'd have control enough to bite back the word, but she hadn't. 'You have denatured me,' she said.

Oh God, what had she done *now*? Clapping her hands over her mouth too late, she wondered if she could pretend to some other meaning in the words. Instead, other words gushed out, words worse and more hideous. Hearing them she herself could not understand where they came from. It was as if out of the corners of the room she was being prompted by the voices of all the women in the world who'd ever been let down, or fancied themselves badly treated. The room vibrated with their whispers. Go on, they prompted. Tell him what you think of him. Don't let him get away with it. He has got off long enough. To stop the voices she stuck her fingers into her ears, but the voices only got louder. She had to shout them down. She saw James's lips were moving, trying to say something, but she could not hear him with all the shouting. When she finally caught a word or two of what he said she herself stopped trying to penetrate the noise. Silence fell. She saw James go limp with relief.

'What did you say? I – I didn't hear you,' she gulped.

'I said that if that's the way you feel, Myra, there's nothing for me to do but to leave.'

She stared at him. He was going over to the clothes' rack and was taking down his coat. What had got into them? How had they become involved in this vulgar scene? She had to stop him. If he went away like this would he ever come back? A man of his disposition? Could she take him back? Neither of them was of a kind to gloss over things and leave them unexplained knowing that unexplained they could erupt again – and again. Something had been brought to light that could never be forced back underground. Better all the same to let their happiness dry up if it must, than be blasted out of existence like this in one evening. Throwing out her arms she ran blindly towards him.

'James, I implore you. James! James! Don't let this happen to us.' She tried to enclose him with her arms, but somehow he evaded her and reached to take his gloves from the lid of the gramophone. Next thing she knew he'd be at the door.

'Do you realise what you're doing?' She pushed past him and ran to the door pressing her back against it, and throwing out her arms to either side. It was an outrageous gesture of crucifixion, and she knew she was acting out of character. She was making another and more frightful mistake. 'If you walk out this door, you'll never come through it again, James.'

All he did was try to push her to one side, not roughly, but not gently.

'James! Look at me!'

But what he said then was so humiliating she wanted to die.

'I am looking, Myra,' he said.

There seemed nothing left to do but hit him. She thumped at his chest with her closed fists. That made him stand back all right. She had achieved that at least! If she was not going to get a chance to undo the harm she'd done, then she'd go the whole hog and let him think the worst of her. She was ashamed to think she had been about to renege on herself. She flung out her arms again, not hysterically this time, but with passion, real, real passion. Let him see what he was up against. But whatever he thought, James said nothing. And he'd have to be the one to speak first. Myra couldn't trust herself any more.

In the end, she did have to speak. 'Say something, James,' she pleaded.

'All right,' he said then. 'Be so kind, Myra, as to tell me what you think you're gaining by this performance?' He nodded at her outstretched arms. 'This nailing of yourself to the door like a stoat!'

The look in his eyes was ugly. She let her arms fall at once and running back to the sofa flung herself face down upon it screaming and kicking her feet.

She didn't even hear the door bang after him, or the gate slam.

Outside in the air James regretted that he had not shut the door more gently, but after the coarse and brutal words he had just used it was inconsistent to worry about the small niceties of the miserable business. His ugly words echoed in his mind, and he felt defiled by them. He had an impulse to go back and apologise, if only for his language. Nothing justified that kind of thing from a man. He actually raised his hand to rap on the gate, but he let it fall, overcome by a stronger impulse – to make good his escape. But as he hurried up the lane his unuttered words too seemed base and unworthy – a mean-minded figure of speech – that could only be condoned by the fact that he had been so grievously provoked, and by the overwhelming desire that had been engendered in him to get out in the air. If Myra had not stood aside and let him pass, he'd have used brute force. All the same nothing justified the inference that he was imprisoned. Never, never had she done anything to hold him. Never had he been made captive except perhaps by the pull of her mind upon his mind. He'd always been free to come or go as he chose. If in the flat they had become somewhat closed in of late it was from expediency – from not wanting to run into stupid people. If they had gone out to restaurants or cafés nowadays some fool would be sure to blunder over and join them, reducing their evening to the series of banalities that passed for conversation with most people. No, no, the flat was never a prison. Never. It was their nest. And now he'd fallen out of the nest. Or worse still been pushed out. All of a sudden James felt frightened. Was it possible she had meant what she said? Could it be that he would never again be able to go back there? Nonsense. She was hysterical.

He stood for a minute considering again whether he should not perhaps go back? Not that he'd relish it. But perhaps he ought to do so – in the interests of the future. No, he decided. Better give her time to calm down. Another evening would be preferable. If necessary he'd be prepared to come up again tomorrow evening. Or later this same evening? That would be more sensible. He looked back. She must be in a bad state when she hadn't run out after him. Normally she'd come to the gate and stay standing in the lane until he was out of sight. Even in the rain.

James shook his head. What a pity. If she'd come to the gate he could have raised his hands or something, given some sign – the merest indication would be enough – of his forgiveness. He could have let her see he bore no rancour. But the gesture would not want to be ambiguous. Not a wave; that would be overcordial, and he didn't want her stumbling up the lane after him. No more fireworks, thank you! But it would not want to appear final either. A raised hand would have been the best he could do at that time. He was going to walk on again when it occurred to him that if he'd gone back he need not have gone inside. Just a few words at the gate, but on the whole it was probably better to wait till she'd calmed down. Then he could safely take some of the blame, and help her to save face. Fortunately he did not have the vanity that, in another man, might make such a course impossible. It was good for the soul sometimes to assume blame – even wrongly. James immediately felt better, less bottled up. He walked on. But he could not rid his thoughts of the ugly business. He ought to have known that no woman on earth but was capable, at some time or another, of a lapse like Myra's. And Myra, of course, was a woman. How lacking he'd been in foresight. He'd have to go more carefully with her in future. Next time they met, although he would not try to exonerate himself from the part he'd played in the regrettable scene, at the same time it would not be right to rob her of the therapeutic effects of taking her share of the blame. He felt sure that, being fair-minded people, both of them, they would properly apportion the blame.

Anyway he resolved to put the whole thing out of his mind until after he'd eaten. To think he'd eaten nothing since morning! After he'd had some food he'd be better able to handle the situation.

James had reached the other end of the lane now and gone out under the arch into Baggot Street again. Where would he eat? He'd better head towards the centre of the city. It ought not to be as difficult as it had been at midday, although an evening meal in town could be quite expensive. He didn't want a gala-type dinner, but not some awful slop either that would sicken him. He was feeling bad. The tension had upset his stomach and he was not sure whether he was experiencing hunger pangs or physical pain. Damn Myra. If she'd been spoiling for a fight, why the devil hadn't she waited till after their meal? She'd say this was more of his male selfishness, but if they had eaten they'd have been better balanced and might not have had a row at all. What a distasteful word – the word 'row'! Yet, that's what it was – a common row. James came to a stand again. He wouldn't think twice of marching back and banging on the gate and telling her to stop her nonsense and put the food on the table. She was probably heartbroken. But if that was the case she'd have come to the door with her face flushed and her hair in disorder. Sobered by such a distasteful picture he walked on. He could not possibly subject her to humiliation like that. It would be his duty to protect her from exposing herself further. Perhaps he'd write her a note and post it in the late-fee box at the G.P.O. before he got the bus for home. She'd have it first thing in the morning, and after a good night's sleep she might be better able to take what he had to say. He began to compose the letter.

'*Dear Myra –* ' But he'd skip the beginning: that might be sticky. He'd have to give that careful thought. The rest was easy. Bits and pieces of sentences came readily to his mind – '*We must see to it that, like the accord that has always existed between us, discord too, if it should arise, must be –* '

That was the note to sound. He was beginning to feel his old self again. He probably ought to make reference to their next meeting? Not too soon – this to strike a cautionary note – but it might not be wise to let too much time pass either –

'*because, Myra, the most precious element of our friendship –* '

No, that didn't sound right. After tonight's scene, 'friendship' didn't appear quite the right word. A new colouring had been given to their relationship by their tiff. But here James cursed under his breath. 'Tiff.' Such a word! What next? Where were these trite words coming from? She'd rattled him all right. Damn it. Oh damn it.

James abandoned the letter for a moment when he realised he had been plunging along without regard to where he was headed. Where would he eat? There used to be a nice quiet little place in Molesworth Street, nearly opposite the National Library. It was always very crowded but with quite acceptable sorts from the library or the Art College. He made off down Kildare Street.

When James reached the café in Molesworth Street however and saw the padlock on the area railings, he belatedly remembered it was just a coffee shop, run by voluntary aid for some charitable organisation, and only open mornings. He stood, stupidly staring at the padlock. Where would he go now? He didn't feel like traipsing all over the city. Hadn't there been talk some time ago about starting a canteen in the National Library! Had that got under way? He looked across the street. An old gentleman was waddling in the library gate with his briefcase under his arm. James strode after him.

But just as he'd got to the entrance, the blasted porter slammed the big iron gate – almost in his face. He might have had his nose broken.

'Sorry, sir. The library is closed. Summer holidays, sir.'

'But you just let in someone! I saw that man – '

James glared after the old man who was now ambling up the steps to the reading room.

'The gentleman had a pass, sir,' the porter said. 'There's a skeleton staff on duty in the stacks and the director always gives out a few permits to people doing important research.' The fellow was more civil now. 'It's only fair, sir. It wouldn't do, sir, would it, to refuse people whose work is – ' But here he looked closer at James and, recognising him, his civility changed into servility. 'I beg your pardon, Professor,' he said. 'I didn't recognise you, sir. I would have thought you'd have applied for a permit. Oh dear, oh dear!' The man actually wrung his hands. 'If it was even yesterday, I could have got hold of the director on the phone, but he's gone away – out of the country too, I understand.'

'Oh, that's all right,' James said, somewhat mollified by being recognised and remembered. He was sorry that he, in turn, could not recall the porter's name. 'That's all right,' he repeated. 'I wasn't going to use the library anyway. I thought they might have opened that canteen they were talking about some time back – ?'

'Canteen, sir? When was that?' The fellow had clearly never heard of the project. He was looking at James as if he was Lazarus come out of the tomb.

'No matter. Good evening!' James said curtly, and he walked away. Then, although he had never before in his life succumbed to the temptation of talking to himself, now, because it was so important, he put himself a question out loud.

'Have I lost touch with Dublin?' he asked. And he had to answer simply and honestly. 'I have.' He should have known the library was always closed this month. If only there was a friend on whom he could call. But he'd lost touch with his friends too.

He looked around. There used to be a few eating places in this vicinity, or rather he could have sworn there were. It hardly seemed possible they were *all* closed down. Where on earth did people eat in Dublin nowadays? They surely didn't go to the hotels? In his day the small hotels were always given over at night to political rallies or football clubs. And the big hotels were out of the question. Not that he'd look into the cost at this stage. He stopped. If it was anywhere near time for his bus he wouldn't think twice of going straight back without eating at all.

It was all very well for Myra. She ate hardly anything anyway. He often felt that as far as food went, their meal together meant nothing to her. Setting up that damned unsteady card table, and laying out those silly plates of hers shaped like vine leaves and too small to hold enough for a bird. They reminded him of when his sisters used to make him play babby-house.

Passing Trinity College, James saw there was still two hours to go before his bus, but it was just on the hour. There might be a bus going to Cavan? The Cavan bus passed through Garlow Cross, only a few miles from the cottage. How about taking that? He'd taken it once years ago, and although he was younger and fitter in those days, he was tempted to do it. His stomach was so empty it was almost caving in, but he doubted if he could eat anything now. He felt sickish. He might feel better after sitting in the bus. And better anything than hanging about the city.

At that moment on Aston Quay James saw the Cavan bus. It was filling up with passengers, and the conductor and driver, leaning on the parapet of the Liffey, were taking a last smoke. James was about to dash across the street, but first he dashed into a sweetshop to buy a bar of chocolate, or an apple. The sensation in his insides was like something gnawing at his guts. He got an apple and a bar of chocolate as well, but he nearly missed the bus. Very nearly. The driver was at the wheel and the engine was running. James had to put on a sprint to get across the street, and even then the driver was pulling on the big steering wheel and swivelling the huge wheels outward into the traffic before putting the bus in motion. James jumped on the step.

'Dangerous that, sir,' said the young conductor.

'You hadn't begun to move!' James replied testily, while he stood on the platform getting his breath back.

'Could have jerked forward, sir. Just as you were stepping up!'

'You think a toss would finish me off, eh?' James said. He meant the words to be ironical, but his voice hadn't been lighthearted enough to carry off the joke.

The conductor didn't smile. 'Never does any of us any good, sir, at any age.'

James looked at him with hatred. The fellow was thin and spectacled. Probably the overconscientious sort. Feeling no inclination to make small talk, he lurched into the body of the bus, and sat down on the nearest seat. He was certainly glad to be off his feet. He hadn't noticed until now how they ached. Such a day. Little did he think setting off that it would be a case of About Turn and Quick March.

James slumped down in his seat, but when he felt the bulge of the apple in his pocket he brightened up, and was about to take it out when he was overcome by a curious awkwardness with regard to the conductor. Instead, keeping his hand buried in his pocket he broke off a piece of the chocolate and surreptitiously put it into his mouth. He would nearly have been too tired to chew the apple. He settled back on the seat and tried to doze. But now Myra's words kept coming back. They were repeating on him, like indigestion.

To think she should taunt him with how long they'd known each other? Wasn't it a good thing they'd been able to put up with each other for so long? What else but time had cemented their relationship? As she herself had once put it, very aptly, they'd invested a lot in each other. Well, as far as he was concerned she could have counted on *her* investment to the end. Wasn't it their credo that it didn't take marriage lines to bind together people of their integrity. He had not told her, not in so many words – from delicacy – but he had made provision for her in his will. He'd been rather proud of the way he'd worded the bequest too, putting in a few lines of appreciation that were, he thought, gracefully, but more important, tactfully expressed.

Oh, why had she doubted him? Few wives could be as sure of their husbands as she of him – but he had to amend this – as she *ought* to be, because clearly she had set no value on his loyalty. What was that she'd said about the deprivations she'd suffered? *'One of the many deprivations!'* Those might not have been her exact words, but that was more or less what she'd implied. What had come over her? He shook his head. Had they not agreed that theirs was the perfect solution for facing into the drearier years of ageing and decay? That dreary time was not imminent, of course, but alas it would inevitably come. The process of ageing was not attractive, and they both agreed that if they were continually together – well, really married, for instance – the afflictions of age would be doubled for them. On the other hand, with the system they'd worked out, neither saw anything but what was best, and best preserved, in the other. As the grosser aspects of age became discernible, if they could not conceal them from themselves, at least they could conceal them from each other. To put it flatly, if they had been married a dozen times over, that would still be the way he'd want things to be at the end. It was disillusioning now to find she had not seen eye to eye with him on this. Worse still, she'd gone along with him and paid lip service to his ideals while underneath she must all the time have dissented.

Suddenly James sat bolt upright. That word she used: 'deprivation.' She couldn't have meant that he'd done her out of children? What a thought! Surely it was unlikely that she could have had a child even when they first met? What age was she then? Well, perhaps not too old but surely to God she was at an age when she couldn't have fancied putting herself in *that* condition? And what about all the cautions that were given now on the danger of late conception? How would *she* like to be saddled with a retarded child? Why, it was her who first told him about recent medical findings! And – wait a minute – that was early in their acquaintance too, if he remembered rightly. He could recall certain particulars of the conversation. They had been discussing her work, and the demands it made on her. She was, of course, aware from the first that *he* never wanted children, that he abhorred the thought of a houseful of brats, crawling everywhere, and dribbling and spitting out food. They overran a place. As for the smell of wet diapers about a house, it nauseated him. She'd pulled him up on that though.

'Not soiled diapers, James. The most slovenly woman in the world has more self-respect than to leave dirty diapers lying about. But I grant you there often is a certain odour – I've found it myself at times in the homes of my friends, and it has surprised me, I must say – but it comes from *clean* diapers hanging about to air. At worst it's the smell of steam. They have to be boiled you know.' She made a face. 'I agree with you, though. It's not my favourite brand of perfume.'

Those were her very words. If he were to be put in the dock at this moment he could swear to it. Did that sound like a woman who wanted a family? Yet tonight she had insinuated – James was so furious he clenched his hands and dug his feet into the floorboards as if the bus were about to hurtle over the edge of an abyss and he could put a brake on it.

Then he thought of something else: something his sister, Kay, had said.

It was the time Myra had had to go into hospital for a few weeks. Nothing serious, she'd said. Nothing to worry about, or so she'd told him. Just a routine tidying-up job that most people – presumably she meant women – thought advisable. Naturally he'd encouraged her to get it over and done with: not to put it on the long finger. The shocking thing was how badly it had shaken her. He was appalled at how frightful she'd looked for months afterwards. Finally the doctors ordered her to take a good holiday, although it hadn't been long since her summer holidays. She hadn't gone away that summer, except for one long weekend in London, but she'd packed up her work and he'd gone up more often.

But the doctor was insistent that this time she was to go away. Oddly enough, her going away had hit him harder than her going into hospital. If they could have gone away together it would have been different. That, of course, was impossible. There was no longer a spot on the globe where one mightn't run the risk of bumping into some busybody from Dublin.

'What will I do while you're away?' he'd asked.

'Why don't you come up here as usual,' she suggested, 'except you need order only one tray.'

But she overestimated the charm of the flat for its own sake. And he told her so.

'Nonsense,' she said. 'Men are like cats and dogs; it's their habitat they value, not the occupants.'

'I'll tell you what I'll do,' he said finally. 'I'll come up the day you're coming back and I'll have a fire lit – how about that?'

'Oh, James, you are a dear. It would make me so glad to be coming back.'

'I should hope you'd be glad to be coming back anyway?'

'Oh yes, but you must admit it would be extra special to be coming back to find you here – in our little nest.'

There! James slapped his knee. *That* was where he'd got the word 'nest'. He had to hand it to her; she was very ingenious in avoiding the word 'home'. She was at her best when it came to these small subtleties other people overlooked. And the day she was due back he had fully intended to be in the flat before her, were it not for a chance encounter with his sister Kay, and a remark of hers that upset him.

Kay knew all about Myra. Whether she approved of her or not James did not know: Kay and himself were too much alike to embarrass each other by confidences. That was why he found what she said that day so extraordinary.

'Very sensible of her to go away,' Kay had said, 'otherwise it takes a long time, I believe, to recover from that beastly business.' Beastly business? What did she mean? Unlike herself, Kay had gone on and on. 'Much messier than childbirth, I understand. Also, I've heard, James, that it's worse for an unmarried woman – ' she paused '– I mean a childless woman.' Then feeling – as well she might – that she'd overstepped herself, she looked at her watch. 'I'll have to fly,' she said. And perhaps to try and excuse her indiscretion she resorted to something else that was rare for Kay – banality. 'It's sort of the end of the road for them, I suppose,' she said, before she hurried away leaving him confused and dismayed.

He had never bothered to ask Myra what her operation had been. He didn't see that it concerned him. At any age there were certain danger zones for a woman that had to be kept under observation. But what if it had been a hysterectomy! Was that any business of his? Medically speaking, it wasn't all that different from any other ectomy – tonsillectomy, appendectomy. What was so beastly about it? If it came to that, the most frightful mess of all was getting one's antrums cleaned out. He knew all about *that*. Anyway the whole business was outside his province. Or at least he had thought so then.

Then, then, then. But now, now it was as if he'd been asked to stand up and testify to something. It was most unfair. Myra herself had never arraigned him. Neither before nor after. Admittedly he had not given her much encouragement. But he could have sworn that she herself hadn't given a damn at the time. Ah, but – and this was the rub, the whole business could have bred resentment, could have rankled within her and gone foetid. Considered in this new light the taunts she had flung at him tonight could no longer be put down to hysteria and written off – something long festering had suppurated. He put his hand to his head. Dear God, to think she had allowed him to bask all those years in a fool's paradise!

He closed his eyes. Thank heavens he hadn't demeaned himself by going back to try and patch things up. He'd left the way open should he decide to sever the bond completely. Perhaps he ought to sever it, if only on the principle that if a person once tells you a lie, that puts an end to truth between you forever. A lie always made him feel positively sick. And God knows he felt sick enough as it was. There was a definite burning sensation now in his chest as well as his stomach. He looked around the steamy bus. Could it be the fumes of the engine that were affecting him? He'd have liked to go and stand on the platform to get some fresh air, but he hated to make himself noticeable, although the bus was now nearly empty. He stole a look at the other passengers to see if anyone was watching him. He might have been muttering to himself, or making peculiar faces. Just to see if anyone would notice he stealthily, but deliberately, made a face into the window, on which the steam acted like a backing of mercury. And sure enough the damn conductor was looking straight at him. James felt he had to give the fellow a propitiating grin, which the impudent fellow took advantage of immediately.

'Not yet, sir,' he said. 'I'll tell you when you're there!'

Officious again. Well, smart as he was, he didn't know his countryside. Clearing a space on the foggy glass, James looked out. It was getting dark outside now but the shape of the trees could still be seen against the last light in the west. The conductor was wrong! They *were* there! He jumped to his feet.

'Not yet, sir,' the blasted fellow called out again, and loudly this time for all to hear.

Ignoring him, James staggered down the bus to the boarding platform, where, without waiting for the conductor to do it, he defiantly hit the bell to bring the bus to a stop. The fellow merely shrugged his shoulders. James threw an angry glance at him, and then, although the bus had not quite stopped, deliberately and only taking care to face the way the bus was travelling so that if he did fall it would be less dangerous, he jumped off.

Luckily he did not fall. He felt a bit shaken, as he regained his balance precariously on the dark road, he was glad to think he had spiked that conductor. He could tell he had by the smart way the fellow hit the bell again and set the bus once more in motion, that for all his solicitude on the Quays, he'd hardly have noticed if one had fallen on one's face on the road: or cared.

And Myra? If Myra were to read a report of the accident in the newspaper tomorrow, how would *she* feel? More interesting still – what would she tell her friends? Secretive as their relationship was supposed to be, James couldn't help wondering if she might not have let the truth leak out to some people. Indeed, this suspicion had lurked in his mind for some time, but he only fully faced it now.

What about those phone calls she sometimes got? Those times when she felt it necessary to plug out the phone and carry it into her bedroom? Or else talk in a lowered voice, very different from the normal way in which she'd call out 'wrong number' and bang down the receiver? Now that he thought about it, the worst giveaway was when she'd let the phone ring and ring without answering it at all. It nearly drove him mad listening to that ringing.

'What will they think, Myra?' he'd cry. When she used to say the caller would think she was out, he nearly went demented altogether at her lack of logic.

'They wouldn't keep on ringing if they didn't suspect you were here,' he exploded once.

Ah! The insidiousness of her answer hadn't fully registered at the time. *Now* it did though.

'Oh, they'll understand.' That was what she'd said.

Understand what? He could only suppose she had given her friends some garbled explanation of things.

'Oh damn her! Damn her!' he said out loud again. There was no reason now why he shouldn't talk out loud or shout if he liked here on the lonely country road. 'Damn, damn,' he shouted. 'Damn, damn, damn!'

Immediately James felt uncomfortable. What if there was someone listening? A few yards ahead, to the left, there was a lighted window.

But suddenly he was alerted to something odd. There should not be a light on the left. The shop at the crossroads should be on the other side. He looked around. Could that rotten little conductor have been right? Had he got off too soon? Perhaps that was why the fellow had hit that bell so smartly? To give him no time to discover his mistake?

For clearly he *had* made a mistake, and a bloody great one. He peered into the darkness. But the night was too black, he could see nothing. He had no choice but to walk on.

By the time James had passed the cottage with the lighted window, his eyes were getting more used to the dark. All the same when a rick of hay reared up to one side of the road it might have been a mountain! Where was he at all? And a few seconds later when unexpectedly the moon slipped out from behind the clouds and glinted on the tin roof of a shed in the distance it might have been the sheen of a lake for all he recognised of his whereabouts. Just then, however, he caught sight of the red tail light of the bus again. It had only disappeared because the bus had dipped into a valley. It was now climbing out of the dip again, and going up a steep hill. Ah! he knew that hill. He wasn't as far off his track as he thought. Only a quarter of a mile or so, but he shook his head. In his present state that was about enough to finish him. Still, things could have been worse.

Meanwhile a wisp of vapoury cloud had come between the moon and the earth and in a few minutes it was followed by a great black bank of cloud. Only for a thin green streak in the west it would have been pitch dark again. This streak shed no light on his way but it acted on James like a sign, an omen.

He passed the hayrick. He passed the tin shed. But now another mass of blackness rose up to the left and came between him and the sky. It even hid the green streak this time though he was able to tell by a sudden resinous scent in the air and a curious warmth that the road was passing through a small wood. His spirits rose at once. These were the trees he could see from his cottage. Immediately, his mistake less disastrous, the distance lessened. If only that conductor could know how quickly he had got his bearings! The impudent fellow probably thought he'd left him properly stranded. And perhaps as much to spite the impudent fellow as anything else, when at that instant a daring thought entered his mind and he gave it heed. What if he were to cut diagonally across this wood? It could save him half a mile. It would actually be putting his mistake to work for him.

'What about it, James? Come on. Be a sport,' he jovially exhorted himself.

And seeing that his green banner was again faintly discernible through the dark trees, he called on it to be his lodestar, and scrambled up on the grass bank that separated the road from the wood.

James was in the wood before it came home to him that of course this must be Asigh wood – it must belong to the Balfes! No matter. Why should he let that bother him? The wood was nowhere near their house as far as he remembered its position by daylight. It was composed mostly of neglected, self-seeded trees, more scrub than timber – almost waste ground – ground that had probably deteriorated into commonage.

As he advanced into the little copse – wood was too grand a designation for it – James saw it was not as dense as it seemed from the road, or else at this point there was a pathway through it. Probably it was a shortcut well known to the locals, because even in the dark, he thought he saw sodden cigarette packets on the ground, and there were toffee wrappers and orange peels lodged in the bushes. Good signs.

Further in, however, his path was unexpectedly blocked by a fallen tree. It must have been a long time lying on the ground because when he put his hand on it to climb over, it was wet and slimy. He quickly withdrew his hand in disgust. He'd have to make his way round it.

The path was not very well defined on the other side of the log. It looked as if people did not after all penetrate this far. The litter at the edge of the wood had probably been left by children. Or by lovers who only wanted to get out of sight of the road? Deeper in, the scrub was thicker, and in one place he mistook a strand of briar for barbed wire it was so tough and hard to cut through. You'd need wire clippers!

James stopped. Was it foolhardy to go on? He'd already ripped the sleeve of his suit. However the pain in his stomach gave him his answer. Nothing that would get him home quicker was foolish.

'Onward, James,' he said wearily.

And then, damn it, he came to another fallen tree. Again he had to work his way around it. Mind you, he hadn't counted on this kind of thing. The upper branches of this tree spread out over an incredibly wide area. From having to look down, instead of up, he found that – momentarily of course – he'd lost his sense of direction. Fortunately, through the trees, he could take direction from his green banner. Fixing on it, he forged ahead.

But now there were new hazards. At least twice, tree stumps nearly tripped him, and there were now dried ruts that must have been made by timber lorries at some distant date. Lucky he didn't sprain his ankle. He took out his handkerchief and wiped his forehead. At this rate he wouldn't make very quick progress. He was beginning to ache in every limb, and when he drew a breath, a sharp pain ran through him. The pains in his stomach were indistinguishable now from all the other pains in his body. It was like the way a toothache could turn the whole of one's face into one great ache. The thought of turning back plagued him too at every step. Stubbornly, though, he resisted the thought of turning. To go on could hardly be much worse than to go back through those briars?

A second later James got a fall, a nasty fall. Without warning, a crater opened up in front of him and he went head-first into it. Another fallen tree, blown over in a storm evidently, because the great root that had been ripped out of the ground had taken clay and all with it, leaving this gaping black hole. Oh God! He picked himself up and mopped his forehead with his sleeves.

This time he had to make a wide detour. Luckily after that the wood seemed to be thinning out. He was able to walk a bit faster, and so it seemed reasonable to deduce that he might be getting near to the road at the other end. His relief was so great that perhaps that was why he did not pause to take his bearings again, and when he did look up he was shocked to see the green streak in the sky was gone. Or was it? He swung around. No, it was there, but it seemed to have veered around and was now behind him. Did that mean he was going in the wrong direction? Appalled, he leant back against a tree. His legs were giving way under him. He would not be able to go another step without a rest. And now a new pain had struck him between the shoulders. He felt around with his foot in the darkness looking for somewhere to sit, but all he could feel were wads of soggy leaves from summers dead and gone.

Perhaps it was just as well – if he sat down he might not be able to get up again. Then the matter was taken out of his hands. He was attacked by a fit of dizziness, and his head began to reel. To save himself from falling he dropped down on one knee and braced himself with the palms of his hands against the ground. Bad as he was, the irony of his posture struck him – the sprinter, tensed for the starter's pistol! Afraid of cramp he cautiously got to his feet. And he thought of the times when, as a youngster playing hide-and-seek, a rag would be tied over his eyes and he would be spun around like a top, so that when the blindfold was removed, he wouldn't know which way to run.

Ah, there was the green light! But how it had narrowed! It was only a thin line now. Still, James lurched towards it. The bushes had got dense again and he was throwing himself against them, as against a crashing wave, while they for their part seemed to thrust him back. Coming to a really thick clump he gathered up enough strength to hurl himself against it, only to find that he went through it as if it was a bank of fog, and sprawled out into another clearing.

Was it the road at last? No. It would have been lighter overhead. Instead a solid mass of blackness towered over him, high as the sky. Were it not for his lifeline of light he would have despaired. As if it too might quench he feverishly fastened his eyes on it. It was not a single line any more. There were three or four lines. Oh God, no? It was a window, a window with a green blind drawn down, that let out only the outline of its light. A house? Oh God, not Balfe's? In absolute panic James turned and with the vigour of frenzy crashed back through the undergrowth in the way he had come. This time the bushes gave way freely before him, but the silence that had pressed so dank upon him was shattered at every step and he was betrayed by the snapping and breaking of twigs. When a briar caught on his sleeve it gave out a deafening rasp. Pricks from a gorse bush bit into his flesh like sparks of fire, but worse still was the prickly heat of shame that ran over his whole body.

'Damn, damn, damn,' he cried, not caring suddenly what noise he made. Why had he run like that? – Like a madman? – Using up his last store of strength? What did he care about anyone or anything if only he could get out of this place? What if it was Balfe's? It was hardly the house? Probably an outbuilding? Or the quarters of a hired hand? Why hadn't he called out?

Sweat was breaking out all over him now and he had to exert a superhuman strength not to let himself fall spent, on the ground, because if he did he'd stay there. He wouldn't be able to get up. To rest for a minute he dropped on one knee again. The pose of the athlete again! Oh, it was a pity Myra couldn't see him, he thought bitterly, but then for a moment he had a crazy feeling that the pose was for real. He found himself tensing the muscles of his face, as if at any minute a real shot would blast off and he would spring up and dash madly down a grassy sprint track.

It was then that a new, a terrible, an utterly unendurable pain exploded in his chest.

'God, God!' he cried. His hands under him were riveted to the ground. Had he been standing he would have been thrown. 'What is the matter with me?' he cried. And the question rang out over all the wood. Then, as another spasm went through him other questions were torn from him. Was it a heart attack? A stroke? – In abject terror, not daring to stir, he stayed crouched. 'Ah, Ah, Ahh . . .' The pain again. The pain, the pain, the pain.

'Am I dying?' he gasped, but this time it was the pain that answered, and answered so strangely James didn't understand, because it did what he did not think possible: it catapulted him to his feet, and filled him with a strength that never, never in his life had he possessed. It ran through him like a bar of iron – a stanchion that held his ribs together. He was turned into a man of iron! If he raised his arms now and thrashed about, whole trees would give way before him, and their branches, brittle as glass, would clatter to the ground. 'See Myra! See!' he cried out. So he had lost his vigour? He'd show her! But he had taken his eyes off the light. Where was it? Had it gone out? 'I told you not to go out,' he yelled at it, and lifting his iron feet he went crashing towards where he had seen it last.

But the next minute he knew there was something wrong. Against his face he felt something wet and cold, and he was almost overpowered by the smell of rank earth and rotting leaves. If he'd fallen he hadn't felt the fall. Was he numbed? He raised his head. He'd have to get help. But when he tried to cry out no sound came.

The light? Where was it. 'Oh, don't go out,' he pleaded to it, as if it was the light of life itself, and to propitiate it, he gave it a name. 'Don't go out, Emmy,' he prayed. Then came the last and most anguished question of all. Was he raving? No, no. It was only a window. But in his head there seemed to be a dialogue of two voices, his own and another that answered derisively 'What window?' James tried to explain that it was the window in the classroom. Hadn't he opened it when the big footballer wasn't able to pull down the sash? He, James, had leant across the desk and brought it down with one strong pull. But where was the rush of sweet summer air? There was only a deathly chill. And where was Emmy?

With a last desperate effort James tried to stop his mind from stumbling and tried to fasten it on Myra. Where was *she*? She wouldn't have failed him. But she *had* failed him. Both of them had failed him. Under a weight of bitterness too great to be borne his face was pressed into the wet leaves, and when he gulped for breath, the rotted leaves were sucked into his mouth.

A CUP OF TEA

'SHE'LL TAKE A CUP OF TEA, NO MATTER HOW LATE IT IS WHEN SHE gets here. You can leave the kettle at the back of the stove where it will keep the heat without spilling over and putting out the fire.'

'All right, ma'am,' said the servant girl, and she threw a baleful glance at a picture of Sophy, for whom all this trouble was being taken, and who had been expected since early morning, and would, as likely as not, arrive in the middle of the night, and get them all up out of their beds. The young servant's back was nearly broken from all the work that had been done in the last few days. They had scrubbed every floor in the house, cleaned all the windows, and they had gone as far as waxing Sophy's room twice in the one day because Sophy's mother had marked it so much with tracks of her feet going in and out with clean curtains and extra pillows, bunches of flowers and hot jars.

'She needs a holiday after all the hard work she has done,' said her mother as she pushed the kettle further back on the stove, and then changed her mind and left it where it had been.

'I hope she'll pass her examination,' said the servant, raising up from the floor in the hope of gaining a moment's rest by introducing a topic upon which her mistress always showed weakness and garrulity.

'Her examination!'

It was almost as if Sophy's mother had forgotten that Sophy had done any examination at all, so absorbed was she in the thought that her only daughter was coming home again after a three months' absence.

'Oh, her examination!' she repeated, carelessly as her eyes ran over the tray that was already set for Sophy's breakfast in bed next morning. 'Why, of course she'll pass. I expect she'll do very well, and get very good marks.'

'She's very clever, isn't she?' said the young girl, in a tone of voice in which she was careful to mingle mixed ingredients of envy and flattery, as a good farmer mingles his grasses with cocksfoot and ratstail and clover when he lays down a field.

'Oh, she has a good brain, I suppose,' said Sophy's mother, in an offhand manner that so far from deceiving the servant emboldened her to sit back on her hunkers and rest her limbs more freely.

'Why wouldn't she have brains!' said the young girl, 'I suppose she takes after her father!' And jerking her finger and thumb she was about to point upward in dumb show at the ceiling, for over their head was the study in which Sophy's father was buried in books and lost in the fumes of tobacco smoke. He was an amateur entomologist.

But Sophy's mother turned around sharply.

'What time do you expect to get that floor scoured? Do you expect to be at it all night, or why are you sitting back and taking your ease like that?'

The girl grabbed the scouring brush again and began to rub it hastily on the big bar of soap that she had held indifferently in her hand while she had taken her ease.

Except for the noise of the rough brush going over the flagged floor there was no sound then for a few minutes, but it was clear from the expression upon her face that Sophy's mother was still brooding on what the servant had said.

'There's a great deal of difference between a hobby and a degree from a university!' she said at last, 'and Sophy has done one of the hardest degrees in the university. There were only two girls in the Political Economy class, and only one in the class for the Study of International Relations.' She smiled. 'Her father spends a lot of his time up there in his study with his books and his collection cases, but I hardly think that he'd make much out of Sophy's books! Did you ever see them? I never saw such books. So heavy! And figures and diagrams on every second page.'

During this speech the mother's face relaxed somewhat and assumed an expression of satisfaction such as it had worn after Sophy's floor had been waxed the second time. 'Of course, my husband is a great authority on insects,' she said, grudgingly, as one who having very little respect for the position of another is nevertheless aware that upon the respect in which it is held by others his own importance depends. She was going to say something else, but just then the young servant ran to the window and began to pull off her apron and struggle to get it over her head.

'She's here! She's here!' cried the girl excitedly. And then, before the mother was into the living room and only halfway across the floor to the hallway, Sophy was running across the room to meet her, throwing her bag and scarf to either side of her, and putting out her arms to hug her mother with such a rattle of bracelets and metal buttons that although the cheeks that pressed against hers were soft and firm as plums and peaches her mother was reminded for a moment of Sophy's father and the way his watch chain used to rattle against the buttons on his waistcoat long ago when he gave her a salutation. That was before he took to wearing smoking jackets with buttons of braid or velvet, and gave up bothering to carry around a watch of any kind. But the impression only lasted a moment.

'Stand back from me,' she cried. 'Let me look at you! You look thin. I hope you're not trying to slim yourself. How did the car drive up without my hearing it? Did you have a tiresome journey? What time did you leave? I hope you stopped on the road for a rest!'

The mother's eyes flew from Sophy's face to her waist, from her waist to her hair, and from her hair to her hands with that confused, distracted, and haphazard curiosity that is so different from the steady gaze of a stranger which travels systematically from top to toe.

'How did you get on at your examination?' she asked, and then, before Sophy had time to answer even the last of the questions, her mother threw up her hands. 'Hold up your head! Don't stir!' she said, and she moved back as one moves back from a canvas at a picture gallery, the better to see it. 'You're too thin,' she said. 'It doesn't suit you. It throws up your likeness to your father. I often heard people drawing attention to it, but I could never see it myself. But I see it now! I'd swear I was looking at him, except for his moustaches. How odd I never saw it before. Sometimes, I thought there was a slight resemblance in the way you turned your head, but only at certain times, if you were upset or annoyed about something. I can't say it was ever anything definite. It was nothing at all like the way you resemble my own sisters in your walk and the way you hold yourself. But I suppose it's natural that you should resemble him in something. It's a good thing you didn't inherit his disposition!'

As she made the last remark she felt Sophy draw away her hand, which she had still kept clasped in hers while leaning back to scrutinise her. Instantly she regretted having let her tongue run away with her, but Sophy's face gave no sign of annoyance. She had released her hands, certainly, but she had smiled as she moved away and began to gather up her scarf, her bag, and her gloves. Still, her mother regretted the remark.

'How is he?' said the girl, and then suddenly she sank down into an armchair in case her mother might think for a moment that she was impatient to go up to him.

'You'll have to go up and see him. He mustn't have heard the car!' said her mother grudgingly, and then before she could stop herself she had given in to her spite again. 'I don't know why he didn't hear the car! His study is to the side of the house, and I was in the kitchen, away at the back!' But almost at once, she made an effort to undo the harm she had done. 'You had better run up and see him before you take off your hat and coat,' she said, and then she urged herself to be even more pressing. 'Please, dear!' she said, briskly. 'Don't sit down until you have gone up to him, if only for a minute. You need only say a few words; just to please him. There's no need to stay. Just a few words! Don't sit down till you do it. If you sit down you won't feel like getting up.' She walked over and taking her daughter's arm urged her to stand up by pressing her arm. 'I'll have your cases brought up to your room while you're gone, and when you come down we'll have a nice chat. I want to hear all you have to tell me. But not until you come down again!'

Sophy began to get up from the armchair slowly. She pouted and put on an air of unwillingness, feeling compelled by an impulse of pity and compassion to play up to the pretence of her own reluctance with which her mother was deluding herself.

'Hurry, dear! You'll be glad you went. Just tell him you got here safely. He'd feel so hurt if you didn't go up.'

'Why didn't he come down?' said Sophy, with a good appearance of resentment.

'He's coming to the final chapters of his work on those disgusting beetles he has all over the house,' said her mother, and she shuddered. 'He comes down for his meals because I insist, but he doesn't come down at all in the evenings. I see his light burning till all hours in the night. I say the book will want to bring in queer profits before it pays for all the lamp oil he's burned in the last five years! Although who's going to buy it is more than I can make out unless there are more than I think of dried-up unnatural people like himself, that see more value in a bee's foot than they see in the company of the human beings around them!' Again she recollected herself quickly and rushed on without drawing a breath. 'But go up,' she cried. 'Go to the door for a minute, anyway. There's no need to stay.'

But as Sophy went out of the room dragging her feet, the mother knew in her heart that the girl would not come down again until she had to be called, and perhaps called more than once. Even as she listened she heard the footsteps getting faster. They stopped dragging and soon broke into a run, taking the stairs two at a time. Suddenly she thought of the lassitude and disinclination that Sophy had shown about going upstairs, although she had been as fresh as a daisy when she first came in, and seemed to freshen up quickly enough when she got to the stairs. Had she too been pretending? And why? Her mother regretted her own polite pretence, and almost ran out into the hallway to shout up the stairs.

'Go on! Don't let me keep you. Go on. Run up to your father. Tell him all your news. Don't think of me. Don't tell me anything at all.'

But she shut her mouth tightly and went out to tell the maid that she could go to bed, there was nothing more to be done.

The maid was worn out. She sat on a chair in front of the range with her legs apart and her head bent as she tried to take a splinter out of her thumb by sucking it.

'What is the matter? Is your finger sore? Put a poultice of bread and water on it and leave it on till morning.' She looked around the kitchen. 'You can go to bed now,' she said, and then she remembered the bags. 'You can carry up the baggage to her room before you go,' she said, and then she went over to the pantry door. 'Did you leave out a jug of milk,' she asked, 'and a bowl of sugar? I forgot to ask her if she'd have a cup of tea, but I'm sure she'll want one.'

The girl rose up unsteadily to her feet and went into the pantry. She came out with a large jug of milk, but her face had a dubious expression, and when she came into the light of the kitchen she put the jug to her nose and smelled it, making a grimace as she did so.

'Don't do that,' shouted her mistress, nearly causing the girl to drop the jug. 'Where did you pick up that disgusting habit?'

'I only wanted to see if the milk was sour. How could I find out without smelling it?' said the girl, not fully aware of the error of what she had done, but painfully aware of the error of having been seen doing it.

'The milk couldn't be sour. It's the afternoon's milk. Give it to me!'

'All the same,' said the girl, and she handed over the jug, looking with interest to see in what superior way its condition would be tested by her mistress.

Sophy's mother took the jug and for a minute she seemed to hesitate, then she began to move it deliberately round and round in circles a long way from her nose, but presumably within the orbit of her olefactory organs, for as she did so she sniffed two or three times. But the presumption was wrong.

'There is no need to stick your nose right into the jug,' she said, then, feeling a need to modify her former remarks on the subject, as she raised the jug and brought it slightly nearer to her nose, before she circled it round once more. This time her nostrils dilated slightly. The young girl tossed her head and took out a hair-slide rather unnecessarily since she fastened it in her hair again a minute later in the exact same place where it had been before. 'Don't put your hands to your hair in the kitchen,' said her lady absentmindedly, but she was looking around the kitchen. 'Where is the small saucepan?' she said. 'Oh, there it is. Rinse it out with clean water for me. And then you can go to bed. This milk is perfectly fresh, but it will do it no harm to give it a boil. That will make sure of it for the morning. It will be cool before Sophy comes downstairs, I'm sure.'

The milk was well cooled when Sophy came down. Her mother had been up and down to her own room two or three times and had at last undressed and put on her slippers and dressing gown. She walked heavily each time she passed her husband's study, but the talk and laughing inside may have prevented her footsteps from being heard. When she passed the box room under the stairs she heard the young servant snoring and groaning in her sleep.

'Oh, Mother! I kept you up,' cried Sophy when at last she came down and saw the slippers and dressing gown. 'Why did you wait up? Why didn't you call me?' And then, as if answering both of her own questions, she summed up the situation. 'You should have gone to bed,' she said.

'I thought you might like some tea,' said her mother. 'I kept the fire in. It was nearly out, but I was just in time to throw on a few logs.'

'Oh, good!' said Sophy.

Her mother's spirits that had sunk in the last hour began to rise again.

'I have the tray set,' she said, 'and I'll have a cup with you. I never take tea at this hour because it keeps me awake but I'll be awake tonight, anyway, with excitement!'

Her spirits rose higher. She forgot her hurt at the hour Sophy had spent upstairs.

'I want to hear everything that happened since you went away. Begin at the beginning. Were you wet when you reached the station going back last time? I worried all night thinking of the long journey you had sitting in that cold railway carriage. They should have proper heating apparatus. It's disgraceful. Did you meet anyone going up in the train? Were you back on the right day? Were there any new people in your class?'

'I'm sure I told you all that in a letter,' said Sophy, taken aback at her mother's accurate memory of a day she had difficulty in recalling.

'I could hear it a dozen times,' said her mother. 'Tell me everything!'

'Oh, there's nothing unusual to tell,' said Sophy, taking up a biscuit and beginning to chew it.

'You found plenty to tell your father, it seems, judging by the length of time you stayed up with him,' said her mother irritably.

Sophy looked up. 'Oh, we were only talking,' she said vaguely, for she could not, in fact, remember much of the lazy banter that she and her father exchanged when they met. 'There's nothing much to tell. The exams were not too bad. The results will be in the paper.' She paused and tried to remember something else to tell. 'The second paper on the first day was a bit hard, but I think I'll pull through all right.'

'I can hardly believe it's your final examination,' said her mother. 'How time flies! I lie awake nights wondering if we did right in sending you to the university. It puts such a strain on a girl. I hope you'll stay home for a while, even after the results come out. Indeed, if you like I'll speak to your father about letting you stay home entirely. It's very nice to have a degree and feel independent, but there's no need to carry things too far and wear yourself out working when your father himself makes no attempts to add to his income, although he could earn more than any man in the town if he wasn't so odd!'

'You have the wrong idea, Mother. I had a definite idea in taking out my degree.'

The mother looked at her, at her glossy silk knees and her nice straight hair.

'Have you some plans?' she asked excitedly. 'I'm so happy to have you home. Tell me your plans. I want to hear them. I want to help.'

She remembered the way she went into her own mother's room years ago to sit in an armchair and brush her hair when she came back from a visit to a relation, telling her mother all about the dances to which she had gone, the partners with whom she had danced, about the underlinen her cousins had worn, the needlework they were doing, and even arranging her hair in the manner in which they had worn theirs so that nothing would be unknown to those at home of the way her time had been spent during her absence from them.

'One thing is certain,' she said suddenly, speaking out of a dream. 'You have my mother's hands. I never saw anything so remarkable. She would have been so pleased to know it, but I never thought of telling her.' She sighed and her faint sigh seemed to fill the air with ghostly memories and regrets, and Sophy moved in her chair, and stared down at her hands self-consciously, but seeing a loosened piece of cuticle on the forefinger of her left hand she became absorbed at once in trying to tear it off with the finger and thumb of her right hand, which she crooked to form a pincers. She gave two or three sharp tugs to the loose piece of skin but failed to tear it off each time. 'Don't do that,' said her mother. 'It will be sore all night. It will keep you awake.'

'I can't leave it alone,' said Sophy, tugging at it again.

'You can. Forget about it. Stop looking at it. Tell me more about your examination. Tell me about your friends and you'll forget all about it, and it will knit back into the skin.'

But Sophy could not forget the dead cuticle. It irritated her, and she kept at it. The mother spoke again in a dreamy voice.

'Poor mother's hands were all blackened and hardened from work, but she wouldn't have grudged you your easy life. She would have been the first to congratulate you on your independence in going to the university. How it would have amused her to see your hands so much like her own. I wish I had thought of telling her. It's only when people are gone from us that we remember all the little things we could have done to please them!'

'Ah!' said Sophy. She had torn off the cuticle and she put her finger up to her mouth to ease the sting of the pain. Then she looked around at the tray. 'How about the tea?' she said.

'The kettle is at the back of the stove,' said her mother. 'It will be almost boiling. I'll go out and get it. If we poke up the fire here it will bring the water to the boil in a minute.'

'Is there any use bringing up tea to father?' said Sophy when her mother came back into the room with the kettle.

'You can if you like,' said the woman, bending down to settle the kettle on the crackling logs in the grate. 'I know the reception I'd get if I interrupted him at his work! Anyone would imagine it was for my own good I went up to him, to hear the way he turned on me upon the few occasions I was unwise enough to enquire if he'd like anything before I went to bed!'

'Oh, I'm so hungry! I'm so thirsty!' said Sophy, breaking in upon her mother urgently. 'All the way down in the train I was thinking of those dear old cups with the impossible birds on them.' She held up one of the frail cups and stared at its hand-painted rim. But her mother understood the interruption and flushed.

'If that's the case it's a wonder you stayed upstairs so long,' she said bitterly, and once again, incongruously, she remembered the confidences that used to be exchanged between her own mother and herself long ago. It would have been such a relief, just once, to tell Sophy of some of the unpleasant things she had had to put up with while she was away. But Sophy was talking about the stupid old cups as if she wanted to stave off any chance of confidences. She was holding the cup in front of her with both hands and staring at it with burning cheeks and bright eyes. How could she be so excited about an old cup that she had seen in the china closet ever since she was able to toddle!

'Is it meant to be a real bird?' Sophy cried. 'Is it a peacock? Is it a nightingale? Whoever saw such feathers! Whoever saw such colours!' Her voice was feverish and she asked question after question, laughing nervously at the same time. But in her heart she was trying to form some sort of a prayer. 'Dear God, keep her from complaining about Father! I want to comfort her. I want to be understanding. I want to make her happy on my first night home. But I can't see things from her point of view.'

'Give me the cup,' said her mother. 'The tea is ready.' She caught the small cup almost roughly. She disliked it with a sudden passion and could have thrown it on the floor only it was belonging to a set. Instead, she began to talk as normally as she could. 'I'm looking forward to a cup of tea myself,' she said. 'Indeed, I'd take a cup every night if I had someone to take one with me. I used to love a cup at this hour. I don't know why I gave it up. You give up a great many things, one after another, when you are alone. Of course, I don't want company. I have my reading! I have my knitting! I have a big basket of socks to darn. It never seems to be empty!'

Poor mother. Sophy looked at her mother's face as it was bent over the fire and for a moment she envied the fine structure of bone that made the face so clear and attractive in spite of age, and she looked at the grey hair that was still so full of life that it sprang into curling tendrils whenever it escaped from the combs that held it. She thought of her own large pale face and straight hair that gave her a resemblance to her father. In spite of her mother's difficulty in seeing it, she herself knew a likeness was evident.

'The kettle is beginning to sing,' said her mother, just then. 'It's a good thing someone in the house has the heart to sing, as I often say to the maid, when your father has been particularly trying.'

Sophy looked around quickly for something with which she could attract her mother's attention away from the abyss over which she trembled again. Her eyes fell on the album that her mother had taken from her old home when she had left to get married. It was covered in faded blue velvet, with a large silver clasp.

'Did you paste in the picture of my class that I sent you at midterm?' she asked, and she leaned forward and took the album on her knee. It fell open at the page upon which she had gazed so frequently as a child, and which she had probably strained from the binding by the many times she leaned her elbows on the book to gaze better at the familiar picture. It was a photograph of her grandmother sitting in a wicker chair against a photographer's scenic screen of palms and clouds and trellis balustrades, and around her, grouped in formal postures, were her daughters, Sophy's mother, and Sophy's mother's sisters. And they all wore long white dresses with long white sleeves and high necks and wide white hats that tilted under the weight of floppy silk roses. They all wore gold brooches, and gold bracelets, and they all had great masses of nut-brown hair. And they sat with their arms entwined around each other's waists, while those of them nearest to the chair upon which their mother sat leaned back against her or looked up into her face. Sophy always paused a moment before she picked out her own mother from the group of charming girls. She remembered that her mother often told her that it took the photographer twenty minutes to try and pose them, spreading out his hands, and exclaiming in Italian, and entreating them to stop laughing just for one minute. And all at once she remembered the other stories her mother used to tell her too, when she was a little girl and easily pleased, the stories of beaux and bouquets, and the stories of larks and pranks that were played upon everyone; the singing, and laughing, and the playing upon the piano that had gone on all day long. And she tried to feel sorry for her mother, all alone now, sitting here in the evenings filled with the bitterness of those unfulfilled and foolish dreams.

But instead of a feeling of pity, Sophy felt an impatience and irritability – why did she marry the wrong man? But then another question formed itself in her mind as an answer to the first. Is it possible to be certain before it is too late that the man you are going to marry is the right man or not? But she was tired, and tiredness confused her mind, and she put both questions aside unanswered. Times have changed, she told herself easily. Women know more about men now than they did long ago. Marriages may break asunder nowadays, but they don't rot slowly.

'I hope you haven't given up sugar?' her mother asked. 'It's so foolish of girls to try and be thinner than Nature intended them to be.'

'Oh, I take sugar all right,' said Sophy – and then she could not resist a slight protest. 'I'm glad I take it because if I didn't I should hate to have you try and force me to do so, Mother!'

'Am I a scold?' said her mother, smiling and seeming to enjoy the idea as a joke. She passed the jug of milk. 'Put in the milk yourself. You say I always give you too much.'

But Sophy was staring into the jug.

'What is the matter with the milk?' she said, and she held it up to her nose.

'There's nothing the matter with it,' said her mother, anxiously looking at her.

'Ugh!' said Sophy. 'There's a scum on it! Ugh, it's disgusting! What is it?'

'Oh!' said her mother, relaxing in relief. 'I forgot to take off the scum. But it's nothing. It's quite all right. I just gave the milk a boil while you were upstairs. It wasn't sour, but it seemed on the point of turning. Boiling saves it, but it doesn't make any difference to the milk. You wouldn't notice any taste when it's in the tea. But I shouldn't have left the scum on it. That was stupid of me!' And she dragged off the scum with the back of a spoon. It crumpled up on the side of the jug like a piece of white silk. 'There's nothing disgusting about it at all!' she said again, as she saw her daughter's grimace.

'Boiled milk does give a taste to the tea,' said Sophy.

'Not at all,' said her mother, pouring out a cup. 'I often give it a boil at night.'

'Is there any milk in the kitchen that has not been boiled?' said Sophy, drawing her empty cup away as her mother went to pour the tea into it. She stood up with the cup in her hand.

'I'm afraid not,' said her mother, 'but I assure you this is quite all right. You won't notice the difference when it's in the tea! I promise you. I wouldn't have done it otherwise. I'm too particular about things!'

Sophy sat down and held out the cup. When it was filled she raised it to her lips and sipped at it.

'I taste it distinctly!' she said, lowering the cup again.

'You couldn't, dear.' Her mother sipped hers. 'I don't taste it.'

'Well, I do,' said Sophy, 'and what's more, I can't drink the tea.'

'But that's absurd,' cried her mother. 'It's just your imagination.'

'It's not imagination. I think you might have left a little milk without being boiled, when you know a cup of tea means so much to me after a long journey.'

'I tell you it makes absolutely no difference.'

'Oh, Mother! Let's not argue about it. I can't drink the tea; that's all! Oh, why did you boil it?'

The mother sat looking at her own tea, for which she, too, had suddenly a great distaste. Why did she boil the milk? She tried to remember. It wasn't sour. And even if it was beginning to turn it would have kept until Sophy had come down; a matter of thirty or forty minutes. Suddenly she remembered the way she had walked from room to room during those minutes, moving the kettle, stirring the fire, and filling in the time with aimless actions.

'Perhaps if you hadn't stayed so long upstairs I might not have had time to boil it!' she said, flinging out the excuse without caring what effect it had. The evening was spoiled, anyway. The whole week of work and preparation was spoiled too. Everything was spoiled.

Sophy got up from her chair. And now she looked very tired indeed. There was no mistaking the heavy black lines under her eyes and the way her mouth dropped at the sides.

'Don't harp on it, Mother,' she said, and she thought to herself that this was the way her father and mother acted when she was out of earshot.

'That's right!' said her mother. 'Lose your temper now! Go upstairs and bang your door! After all the trouble I took preparing for you this is all the thanks I get. It's good that I'm used to this kind of thing from your father!'

'Leave Father out of it!' cried Sophy.

'Two of a feather!' cried her mother.

Sophy threw out her hands in an appeal.

'I wish you wouldn't take it this way, Mother!'

'What other way can I take it?'

'You could admit that you made a mistake in boiling the milk without finding out whether I minded or not.'

'I can't see now or then why you did mind it,' said her mother. 'It makes no difference whatever to the taste of the tea. At home we always gave the milk a boil after supper to keep it from getting sour overnight.'

'I never heard of it being done anywhere else,' said Sophy. 'You did a lot of things at home that sound queer to me, if it comes to that!'

Her mother drew in a quick breath.

'I suppose you heard your father say that! He's always having a slap at my sisters!'

'He never even mentions them, if you want to know!'

'Oh, that doesn't deceive me. There are more ways of sneering than by word of mouth. And indeed, now that we're mentioning such things, let me tell you that your own attitude isn't what it might be at times. When the old cock crows, the young cock cackles.'

'Well, I can't help it, can I, if I'm like him?' said Sophy.

'There's no need to copy his ignorant traits,' said her mother.

Sophy stuck her fingers into her ears.

'I won't listen to talk like that,' she cried. 'It's unjust. I never knew him to say or do anything that wasn't just as it should be!'

'Maybe if you were at home a little more you might not have the same thing to say for very long.'

Sophy sprang to the door. 'I must say I'm glad I don't come home very often if this is the kind of reception I get! Good night!' And she banged the door.

Sophy went up to the bedroom where the floor had been waxed twice over, and where the stiff muslin curtains floated back and forth as the winds urged them.

As she undressed she thought of the girls in the white dresses who vexed the photographer by laughing so much he could not pose them properly and she thought of the photograph of her father that hung in the hall, showing a stiff and straight young man with a broad face and serious eyes with a stern look in them. And suddenly she ran to her case and opened it, tossing up her blouses and handkerchiefs as she ran her hand to the bottom and took out a small photograph in a small frame. It was a photograph of another young man, also straight and also stiff, with serious eyes and a stern look, because these are the attributes which young men usually wish to appear to possess when they have their photographs taken. Sophy stared at the photograph, and then she ran over to the mirror and stared at her own face. But she had not learned anything from looking at either face, for she sighed and got into bed.

Two or three times she leaned up on her elbow to hear if her mother had gone up to her own room, but she heard no sound, and several times she wanted to go down again and ask to be forgiven, but she knew that instead of coming to terms they would begin to argue again, so she lay still, and began instead to plan the things that she would do for her mother when she had money of her own to spend as she liked. But even this was difficult to do because her mother and herself so rarely liked the same things. The tears came into her eyes.

And then it suddenly seemed to Sophy that she had discovered a secret, a wonderful secret, that wise men had been unable to discover, and yet it was so simple and so clear that anyone could understand it. She would go through the world teaching her message. And when it was understood there would be an end to all the misery and unhappiness, all the misunderstanding and argument with which she had been familiar all her life. Everything would be changed. Everything would be different.

The footsteps that had stopped outside her door moved on, and then were silent. A door closed far away. The dream began to form again. People would all have to become alike. They would have to look alike and speak alike and feel and talk and think alike.

What a wonderful place the world would become. People would all look like the girls in the photograph, with white dresses and linked arms. But they would all think like herself and her father. It was so simple. It was so clear! She was surprised that no one had thought of it before. She saw the girls untwine their arms, and lift up the hems of their long dresses and step aside to admit her as she passed into their company.

A STORY WITH A PATTERN

THE TABLE WAS GETTING BLISTERED WITH WET BLUE RINGS AS GLASSES were laid down carelessly. The ashtrays were overflowing with fine white ash that blew softly over the slippery mahogany every time a breath of air came in through the wide-open windows, which, as a matter of fact, was not very often, for the afternoon was still, and the room was hot and crowded.

The first noise of the party had died down, and here and there groups of people with common interests had sorted themselves out from the crowd, and stood together, talking in low tones.

Coming towards me across the room was my hostess, and the middle-aged man that she guided by the elbow was staring at me boldly.

'Here is someone who is anxious to meet you!' said my hostess, and then being called from the other end of the room, she pressed my arm, and made an excuse, and hurried away without any attempt to make me acquainted with the man who evidently had some slight acquaintance with me already.

I could only look at him, and wait for him to speak.

'How do you do!' he said, and he put out his hand, and shook mine heartily. 'I'm glad to meet you! I've read a number of your stories, and I want to tell you what I think of them. You've got talent! Did you know that? You ought to take up writing. Take it up seriously, I mean! Give your time to it!' He paused. 'There's a lot of money to be made out of writing. Did you know that?' Then he lowered his voice. 'It's not everyone that can write, you know. It's not everyone has the time! It's not everyone has the education!'

And there and then, my new acquaintance gave me his opinions on books and writers in general. He had a high opinion of both, but although he had read a great many of the former he had never until this moment met one of the latter.

And while he talked I tried to sum him up. He was evidently one of those men in whom an eagerness for knowledge had developed only when it was too late for schooling to supply it; when he had entered upon some occupation or trade which had cut him off irrevocably from all chance of remedying his deficiencies. At times, however, he had a surprisingly adequate vocabulary, employed correctly and aptly, but this was probably acquired second-hand by listening to others.

Before the man had uttered three words I had seen that he was poorly educated, but before he had uttered a dozen I saw that it was a great loss to himself – and indeed to others – that this had been so, because his mind was eager and quick, and curious in the best sense of the word. The affair was irremediable now, however. He had all the faults one would expect. He was dogmatic where he should have been humble, forthright where he should have been delicate, and above all he confidently gave as original opinions that were unfortunately original only to himself, having been evolved by him in slow processes of thought, but which were commonplaces to people who knew how to avail themselves of the world's depository of knowledge. Men such as he waste great quantities of mental energy working out simple problems that have long ago been solved by others, and they waste precious time as well, so that middle age often finds them, after years of inquiry and application, in a state of mental immaturity at which a clever school-boy might be able to laugh with justice. But there is this to be said for them also: old age, when it comes, finds them still eager, still vehement, still consuming their own energy, and death they regard as but another problem to be tackled, and to that problem they can also bring an open mind, unhampered by the stale opinions, the false findings, and the unsuccessful probings of others.

His opinion might be worth hearing after all.

'Which of the stories did you like best?' I asked.

He looked at me. 'I beg your pardon,' he said, 'did I say I liked them? I thought they were written with a good style, and I thought you brought the people in them to life, but I don't think that I remember saying that I liked them.'

Now this, you will admit, was disconcerting.

'Yes,' said my friend. 'Your stories have a great many good qualities, but I wouldn't exactly say that I liked any of them.' As he repeated this he looked at me with his head a little to one side as if he would be better able to judge my reaction to his words by holding himself that way. And then, evidently discerning that I had been somewhat taken back, he put out his hands, one to either side of me, and pressed me together as you'd press a concertina. 'Don't be offended,' he said. 'Remember that I know nothing at all about the subject. You might be right; for all I know. All I can do is give you my opinion; that is to say, tell you what I think. And what I think, if I might venture to put it bluntly, is that your stories in their present form, good as they are, will never appeal to a man. They may appeal to women. But they'll never appeal to men. A man would only read a page or two of your work, and then he'd throw it aside. Because,' he paused, 'because a man wants something with a bit of substance to it, if you know what I mean? A man wants something a bit more thick, if you understand.'

And carefully pinching off a piece of the smoke-laden air around us, he held it between his forefinger and thumb to show me just how thick men liked their reading matter.

'Now your stories,' he said, 'are very thin. They have hardly any plot at all.'

'But don't you think . . . ?' I said, beginning to explain a point, but he brushed my unfinished sentence away, together with a bothersome bluebottle that had come our way at that moment.

'And the endings,' he said. 'Your endings are very bad. They're not endings at all. Your stories just break off in the middle! Why is that, might I ask?'

I'm afraid that I smiled superciliously.

'Life itself has very little plot,' I said. 'Life itself has a habit of breaking off in the middle.' I knew I was not being very explicit, but after all, his criticism had been casual enough! Perhaps I had become annoyed.

He, however, remained very affable, and he took up my argument blandly.

'But don't you see?' he exclaimed. 'It is just because life seems vague and disorderly, because it seems purposeless and chaotic, that people turn for distraction to books! We turn to books because in them we hope to find that the author, with a keener eye than ours, has been able to make a selection from the multiplicity of incidents that crowd upon us, and present them in a manner that will show that there is after all some relation between cause and effect.' He drew a deep breath. 'Only for books I would, long ago, have fallen into despair myself! But instead of that I read for a solid hour every night, before I put out the light. And so,' here he slackened the grip which he had retained upon my arms, and spread his hands out wide to either side of me, like great flat, protective wings, 'and so although I may not know much about writing, I can give you a plain man's opinion about your work. And mind you I may be able to give you some useful information!' He stopped for a moment. 'By the way,' he said quickly, 'would you mind telling me – I'm not asking out of curiosity, mind you, and there's no impertinence meant – but I'd like to know if you make much money out of your stories?'

'Well,' I began slowly, in order to gain time and find a suitable answer for the question. 'Well, you see . . .' I began.

But he cut me short again. 'I see nothing,' he said, abruptly. 'Don't tell me that you're not interested in whether your work sells or not, because that's only nonsense, if you'll excuse my saying so! Only a fool would say a thing like that. If you said that to a jackass he'd kick you, if you'll pardon the expression. Why do you write stories if you don't care whether they're read or not? And how can people read them if they don't buy them? Be reasonable about the matter! Admit that you'd like your stories to sell. And, as I said before, if you take my advice, they might!'

'What is your advice?' I said at last, testily enough it must be admitted.

'My advice is to give your stories more shape, to give them more plot; to give them more pattern, as it were!'

'That would be distorting the truth!' I said, and I was about to explain further.

'Why do you say that?' he cried, interrupting me. 'There may be times when life seems formless, and when our actions seem to be totally unrelated to each other, but for that again there are thousands of times when incidents in life not only show a pattern, but a pattern as clear and well-marked as the pattern on this carpet!'

He glanced down and my eyes followed his, to stare at the brilliant and constantly recurring medallions of the soft pile under our feet.

'I don't believe you could tell me one incident out of all the thousands!' I said.

'Will you put me to the test?' said he.

'If there is time,' I said, looking around, but no one appeared to have any sign of going.

'There's plenty of time. Let me see now . . .' And he paused.

'You can't think of one!' I cried.

'Can't I?' said he. 'If I'm having any trouble at all it's trying to choose one out of all the incidents that are crowding my mind into a state of confusion.' Still he paused for another space, and I was going to laugh at him when he looked up and cleared his throat.

'I'll tell you what I'll do,' said he. 'I'll tell you one of my father's stories, to save me having to make a choice among my own.'

'Your father read it in some old book, I suppose?'

'Oh, no, he didn't. I'm not going to cheat. This is a real, true story, and I often heard my father tell it. It's about a man that lived in the same town as him, long ago. They went to the same school, and they played together too, on wet days and the like, not indeed that Murty Lockhart was able to play very much. But that's all part of the story. Will I go on with it?'

I said that I wanted very much to hear the story, but I think my main reason for encouraging him to go on was that I wanted to hear how he would tell it. For, since the time he first came over to me with such a sophisticated manner, a change had taken place in both his manner and his voice, and even in his very vocabulary. With his first words about Murty Lockhart the emphasis he had been laying on every second word disappeared altogether and he became, instead, unsure, halting, and inclined to look at me questioningly in between every sentence. And when he was speaking a short time, I noticed with interest that it was not his voice at all I was listening to, but the voice of his father, who had told the story to him. His memory had stored not only the incidents of that story but the very words in which it had been told, and the very voice of the man who first strung them together. It was the voice of an aged and credulous man telling an incredible story with a kind of fright at its seeming purport. And as he told the story the very name of Murty Lockhart seemed to fill him with awe for he always uttered it in a lower voice than the rest of the sentence.

'When Murty Lockhart used to come to the parlour window of his house and look up and down the street from it, the people of the town who happened to be passing by at the time would say to each other, "Will you look at that devil up there thinking out some new badness," or "Hell isn't bad enough for that fellow – look at him piercing out at us with his eyes!"

'What they really meant, of course, was that three shillings was more than enough rent for his ugly, jerry-built houses, much less the ten or eleven shillings they'd be paying him. Murty owned pretty near all the town. I suppose, too, that he often heard what was said about himself and his houses, because you know, don't you, the way voices in the street float in through the windows in a country town, not like in a city where they are beaten down by the noises of the trams and buses. Oh, yes, he heard all that was said about him, never fear, but he took no offence, or, if he did, he never let on to it. He probably knew as well as everybody else that what is said out loud is better than what is said in a whisper, and that all that is said is seldom meant in any case! Let that be as it may, anyhow, but I may as well tell you that he himself was the very one that seldom or never said what he meant. It was either the bitter word covering up the soft thought or the soft word covering up the bitter thought. No one ever knew how to take him, or where they were with him, after he grew up. But my father used to say that as a child you couldn't find a sweeter disposition than Murty's in the length and breadth of the country, not if you were looking for a month of Sundays. But when he grew up he got sort of soured and even those that played with him oftenest in his own back garden were turned against him by his manner; all but my father, that is to say. But there again, my father never pitied him like the rest did, not even when he was a little nipper sitting by the window watching the other children racing up and down outside. My father didn't pity him. It would be more correct to say he was kind of scared of him. Well, maybe not scared, but a bit in awe of him, if you like. And what's more, he never lost that feeling he had about him through all the years afterwards, even when Murty got so well off that the pity of the town was turned into envy. Yes, indeed, the pity of the town turned into envy all right as time went on, because, as the people got older, they put less store on flashing limbs and red faces and began to think that when Murty owned half the town he wasn't in need of much pity, no matter what way his legs were!

'By the way, I forgot – did I? – to tell you that poor Murty had club feet?

'Yes, I forgot to tell you that. Wasn't that stupid of me, now? That's the most important part of the whole story; or pretty near!

'Yes, indeed, poor Murty had club feet from birth. That was why, you see, he couldn't knock around like the other young hooligans in the town. That was the reason why they had to come into his back garden if they wanted to play with him. Even then they had to take good care it was something quiet and easy they played, like catchers or conkers. They couldn't even give high catchers. If they did, or if there was the least sign of roughness, Murty's mother would pull aside the lace curtains and tap on the glass. It wasn't much fun playing with him, as you can imagine, specially for kids that were just after hearing news of the Boer War that was on at the time, and were leaping inside their boots to be off playing Zulus or having skirmishes in the lanes. But kids are good at heart, as you've noticed, no doubt, for all their contrariness at times, and they often and often gave up their games to come and play with little Murty. And dare any new kid say anything about his feet; or about anybody's feet, for that matter – you know how touchy kids are? – or there would be another kid ready to shut him up, double quick, or clip him under the jaw if need be! They were always ready to champion the poor kid. That was another reason afterwards why they found it difficult to understand how Murty could be so hard on them when they were all grown up – he and them, just because he had the upper hand on account of a bit of money. You see, his father left him a bit when he died; a bit more than Murty or anyone else expected. I suppose he felt the poor fellow needed more than most, on account of his feet. Anyway, Murty got the money and he didn't waste time in putting it to use. And he put it to such good use it wasn't long till he put himself above everyone in the whole town. I often thought when my father would be telling me about him that maybe he never liked having the kids championing him the way they used. Maybe he resented it. Maybe he didn't, though. I don't know. Nobody knows.'

At this point the storyteller stopped suddenly and looked at me.

'I suppose,' he said, 'that's where you'd end the story if you were telling it; with Murty not knowing why he was bitter against the town and the town not knowing either! But that's not where my story ends. That's not even the middle of it. Wait till you hear!'

He leaned back against the wall and continued.

'I always think it was curious, don't you, the way my father never felt any pity for him? He used to say that Murty's sort of yellow-coloured eyes used to fascinate him. He used to say, too, that he didn't think his feet were so terrible either, if it came to that. What was there to be gained after all, he used to say, by running the streets like lunatics the way the other kids and himself used to do? My father would have preferred reading to running any day. He always had his nose stuck in a book, or a Fourpenny Illustrated. It used to get on his own father's nerves to see him at it. His father and mother were always shooshing him out like a hen out of the house. So you can see, can't you, that my father would look on Murty as a privileged person in many many ways since he could sit all day reading a book and nobody would say, aye, yes or no to him.

'Murty used to sit at the window, sometimes reading, sometimes scribbling, and sometimes only sitting, and my father used to be a bit envious of him when he'd sweat past with a piece of rope between his teeth pretending he was a prairie horse, in some game or other he couldn't get out of, that the other kids were after planning. Later on when they were all a bit older it was more or less the same thing in a different way. Murty would be sitting at the window and my father would be rushing off to the ball-alley, that the parish priest had built for the young men, outside the town, and he used to look up and wave at Murty as much as to say "Well for you." If he had a second at all he used to run to the door to say hello to him and look over Murty's shoulder at the book in his hand while he was promising to come in for a while on the way back if he got a chance. And then, as he ran down the street, and out on to the road, his mind would be filled with the pictures he had glimpsed in Murty's book; pictures of stars and planets, and comets, and flaming meteors.

'My father always had a great curiosity about the sky and the stars and such-like things. In his day there wasn't as much known as there is now about astronomy, and what was known was not to be found out, either, I may tell you, by buying a Sixpenny Paper Cover. No, indeed, if you wanted to find out anything about anything at all in those days you had to read through a queer lot of print, in a queer lot of books; books that cost a nice penny, too, and were hard enough to come by even at that. Nowadays you can find out almost anything from a few pages in the middle of the Sunday paper. But not so then. I often wish he had lived long enough to see how easy it is to know everything there is to be known, because he was a man with a great respect for knowledge. Do you know, I think that he prized it higher than any other one thing. So you can see – can't you? – how he sort of envied Murty, club feet and all, and had a sort of awe of him as they both got older.

'Do you know? I've just thought of something I never hit on before in all the times I turned over this thing in my mind. I bet you anything you like, my father thought that Murty would discover something or other about the Other World! Could that ever have been the idea at the back of his mind, do you suppose? Because, now that I come to think of it, I often heard him saying that if a man thought for long enough, without his ever opening a book at all, he ought to be able to tell at the end of a long time whether there was a God or not! Maybe he thought Murty might get some strange knowledge by all his brooding and thinking. And maybe he thought that, if he did, he would let him share the secret. Do you suppose he could have had that in his head? Whether he had or not anyway he wasn't as horrified as the rest of the town when he heard what happened to Murty, because he always felt that Murty was creeping up closer and closer on the mysteries of the world, every hour he sat by the window, with his curious yellow eyes fixed on the rim of the sky, or what there was to be seen of it between the church opposite and the corner of the schoolhouse roof. But, of course, he didn't expect for an instant the thing would have the terrible turn it had, nor that anyone else would be dragged into it but Murty himself. He certainly would not have thought the one to be dragged into it would be Ursula Merrick, such a quiet, serious girl with smooth yellow hair and deep blue eyes. If it had even been a dark-haired girl; but there was nothing dark about Ursula at all. She looked brighter than most people, and happier, too, although, true enough, her happiness seemed deeper and slower-moving than other people's. Poor girl! May the Lord have mercy on her soul! She died a year after she married Murty.'

He stopped. 'Am I telling this very badly?' he said, looking at me uncertainly. 'Wasn't I a bloody fool to try telling a story to a professional storyteller?'

'Remember my bad endings,' I said.

'Oh, not bad,' he said, 'just weak. Anyhow, it isn't the way it's told that matters in this story: it's the story itself. All you have to know is what happened, and it doesn't matter much how you hear it. I only want to show you that things are not always as vague and pointless in life as you would have us believe in your stories. Will I go on?'

'Do, of course.'

'I was telling you about the way Ursula Merrick got drawn into the thing, wasn't I? Well, I should have told you first that Murty grew up to be so clever that when his father died and left him a few hundred pounds he wasn't a half-year older before he had doubled the sum by buying an old ramshackle hovel across the street, and building it up into a fine new shop and letting it out to a butcher, or maybe it was a baker, I forget which, that came to the town from Kinnegad. It was put up cheap, but it had a fine showy front to it, and the stand couldn't be bettered, on the main Dublin road, and the fellow that rented it was ready and willing to give Murty whatever money he asked for it. Murty – I need hardly tell you – asked enough for it! He asked enough to justify him in buying another tumbledown place further down the same street and tearing it down too and putting up another fine-fronted shop. He let the second one to a chemist.

'He did all this speculating, I may tell you, without as much as going outside the door of his own house. He figured it all out on paper and set a few men on the job. By the time the second shop was built people were beginning to look with less pity at him when he sat at the window-pane inside. And by the time he owned a block of houses, three more shops and, as well as that, a farm outside the town, as he did in a short number of years, there was hardly one remembered he had club feet at all. Murty himself, indeed, seemed to have pretty near forgotten it too, judging by the way he began to go out and about, to this place and that, leaning on his stick as lightly as if he carried it for swank. He was looked up to by everyone everywhere he went, although this was as much from fear as from respect, because by this time he had a finger in everyone's business and, if he didn't own the house a man lived in, he owned the ground under it, or had some hold on the place. You can see, therefore, that although they were a bit surprised they weren't altogether astonished when they saw he was paying attentions to Ursula Merrick. In fact, you know how it is in those country towns? – they had got so used to him by this time and, considering his money and the way he was looked up to and that, most people thought that the girl was doing well for herself. And the night they heard she was going to marry him they never gave a thought to his feet at all and went around telling each other what a stroke of luck it was for the girl. Maybe an odd young person here and there gave a kind of shudder, but that was all, and, getting used to the idea, they thought she had feathered her nest well, and that she would have the laugh at the other girls, who had married young shop-boys and mechanics without a penny to their name, when she'd be driving round in her motor car and giving meat teas to everyone that came to visit.

'But when Ursula and Murty were married a few months and there were no signs of the motor car, and no signs of the meat teas, and no signs in any other direction either of the fact that she was any better off than before, the talk began. First one old woman and then another began to say he was mean to her like he was to everyone else, and that she was looking back on her bargain, and that she had no right to marry a man like him, anyway. Any bit of scandal that came into their heads was out on their tongues a minute after. The rumours flew round to such an extent there was a regular swarm of them flying after her every time she put her foot outside the door. And would you believe it, the town turned against her in no time and people began to say she got her deserts for marrying a poor cripple just to get the use of his bit of money! They never thought for a moment she married him for any other reason, and I don't suppose it would have mattered what they thought, the poisonous old rips, if Murty himself didn't begin to wonder at his luck in getting her, when he came home every night and looked across the table at her: at her lovely face and her lovely yellow hair lit up with the candlelight. She must have been very good-looking, by all accounts, and the finest and fittest and best set-up man in the county might have wondered at his luck in winning her, much less a poor creature like himself with blunted feet and his shoes having to be made specially for him over in London!

'Murty began to think there must have been a string to his bargain somewhere and he no sooner thought this than he was dead set on finding it, and cutting it if he could. It was funny the way he first got suspicious; funny, I mean, the way a little thing can drag down such a lot on top of us if we don't leave it alone. Murty began to get suspicious when Ursula wouldn't order a fur coat for herself and wouldn't hear tell of getting a motor car. He noticed, too, that she put very little store on the trinkets and fancies he brought home to her if he had occasion to go to another town for a few hours. Even the servants in the house used to remark on the way she left them lying about, as if she put no more value on them than if they were junk. When he gave them to her she used to smile, they said, and thank him very much, but as likely as not she'd walk out of the room a minute or two after, and leave them lying about where anyone that had a mind to it could pocket them and walk off! She gave the impression, if you know what I mean, of not caring whether they were stolen or not; good things too, you know, brooches and little fur capes and bits of china. Murty used only laugh at first and tell the servants to put them away in a safe place till she missed them some day. But seldom or ever Ursula thought of them again. And after a while Murty got uneasy.

'You see, Murty, like everybody else, thought that Ursula had married him for his money, and that the more of it he let her see, the happier she'd be, and the less she'd be likely to feel bad when he couldn't go careering round with her to dances and evening parties, the way he imagined other young married couples did. The first day ever he saw her he set his heart on having her, and by that time, being accustomed to buying anything he fancied, he thought that he could buy her too. He was pretty badly in love with her, and although as he was getting to know her, I imagine, he must have had an odd doubt whether he'd get her as easy as he thought, nevertheless when she did agree to marry him it never crossed his mind it was for any other reason but because of his money.

'Now the strange part of the thing is that Murty would have seen nothing at all objectionable in her marrying him for his money. He was as proud as the devil with everyone, but he was as humble as could be with Ursula. He thought he could never buy her enough to keep her from regretting her decision. But when he saw she would rather go off walking in the rain than ride in a car, and that she'd rather wear a bit of velvet ribbon round her neck than a string of beads, he began to worry. So you see it was when he began to doubt that it was with his money he had got her, that the real trouble started, the very opposite of what the old back-biters in the town were thinking, as is often the way. Murty began to ponder over the whole thing and he tried hard to find another reason why she should have married him, and apart from money or love there aren't many reasons, you'll agree. She hadn't married him for his money, she made that plain enough, and he never, at any time, let himself think that the girl could have had any love for him. It was too bad he hadn't the least trace of conceit in him. If he had, things might have taken a different turn. If he had he might have found out in time what he learned too late, that Ursula Merrick, strangely enough, was in love with him before she married him, and not only that but that she became what you might call pitiably in love with him after her marriage. I say pitiably because she was one of those people whose feelings are deep and troublesome to them and they dare not show them to others. And I'd say pitiably in any case in the light of what happened in the end.

'Only for what happened, I suppose, I wouldn't be telling you the story at all, because I never yet heard a happy love story that was worth the breath used in telling it. It's only when all else around is dark and bitter that a glorious blaze of love like hers is shown up against the darkness. Yet I often thought when my father would be telling me about them, that it was a terrible pity Murty hadn't held a candle up to the big mirror over the fireplace, and taken a good look at his face one night without minding to see the rest of him. If he did he might have seen that years of studying and thinking had given his face a strong and stern kind of a look that made him as near to being handsome as he could well go without being so by nature. If he did he might have been able to put himself in Ursula's place for a minute and see some reason why she chose to spend her life face-to-face with him, if I might put it that way. Indeed, without going to that length at all he might have found time to remember that a girl like Ursula would have noble reasons, whatever they might be, for everything she did. But he didn't think. He just accepted other people's opinions about his marriage, which just goes to show that even a man that has spent his whole life in the pursuit of wisdom can fall as far from it as any fool, if he fails for a minute to think for himself and lets lesser people do his thinking for him. And if he had to have the opinion of others, and the best of us can't resist it at times, it was more than a pity he didn't look for it from my father, because I believe my father would have seen quicker than any man alive, and told him quicker, too, that Ursula Merrick was in love with her husband just as I told you she was, and that she wouldn't have married him if she wasn't.

'I told you before, didn't I, that my father was always kind of fascinated by Murty? Well, I suppose you might say my father was half in love with him himself, let alone Ursula, because love is a strange thing, although you can't talk as broadly about it now as you could once, because people think they are so well up now that they feel they must snigger and sneer and put two meanings on every word you say. But I think I'd be right in putting it like that, talking to you, and say without fear of being taken up wrong, that my father was a sort of in love with Murty all his life. He would have been the very person then, I think, to have made Murty see how fond his wife was of him, and how happy she was ever and always to be in his company without any greater entertainment in the way of drives or visitors.

'She used to sit, my father often remarked, as quiet as a mouse whenever there was company, outside the arc of the firelight with her head bent over a piece of sewing and only her white hands showing clearly in the smaller arc of the lamp on the table beside her. Murty often had my father and a few others in to talk and argue, and sometimes one of them would read out a passage aloud from some special book or other he had got hold of in the city. Ursula would be silent all evening, and my father thought for a long time that she was weaving her own thoughts with a needle as silent as the steel one in her hand, unheedful of what they were saying, but one night he noticed that she left the door ajar when she went into the dining room to set decanters on a tray and spread some biscuits out in a fan on a plate, as a small refreshment for the men. And once or twice he saw her come to the jamb of the door and stand there for a minute, and he knew then that she was listening all the time and probably grudging the space of floor she had to cross on her way for the refreshments, because it took her away from the conversation and left her likely to lose the continuity of what was being said.

'Now, it's a hard thing for us in this age to realise how strange a thing it must have been for women in my father's time, if they happened to be exceptionally intelligent and did not succeed in smothering their intellectual curiosity in the worries of domestic affairs. An odd one of them here and there, I know, cut through their obstacles and wrote books and poems, and travelled impudently round like men, but they were the rare ones, and if the truth were told they may have been more men than women in any case. But the quiet ones, the ones that were like Ursula, the ones with minds more receptive than creative, they were really and truly to be pitied. They probably went through life with a hunger for knowledge that even the richest harvest of personal experience was not enough to satisfy. When you think out in a wide stretch like that to either side of the story of Ursula and Murty you see at once, what nobody saw at the time, that it was a wonderful thing for her to meet a man like Murty, and to marry him, and live always within the radius of his wisdom and knowledge and within the magic circle of his talk, day and night. For Ursula was one of those women with rich accumulating sort of minds that stored up strange things they heard from time to time and wove them into her own life slowly, and after a long time had passed. Do you know that kind of woman? Perhaps if herself and Murty had been given another few years and she had gained confidence and courage to talk freely to him, he might have realised the bonds that bound her to him. But although she was one of those intelligent women who are almost a trouble to themselves they're so intelligent, she had no education beyond a general one such as is got in a country convent school, and even that benefited her little, because she probably found her own thoughts more interesting than anything that was chalked up on the blackboard. She looked into her own mind for the answers to all her questioning, and relied on her sensitive nerves more than she relied on the words of the rosy-faced nuns. But, since the greatest thinkers of all time have oftentimes had access to no deeper source of knowledge than hers, it is very possible that she could have talked better to Murty about life and death and the mysteries of man than any of the friends he invited in for that purpose; the parish priest, the doctor and, an odd time, my father, although my father, like Ursula, was only an amateur of philosophy, and one that listened more than he spoke.

'My father listened more than he spoke for the same reason that Ursula listened and never spoke; neither of them could have put their thoughts into ordered sentences and both could have been put on the dunce's stool by a single technical term. But they sometimes talked to each other, you see, and my father got to know how deep she was, deeper even than Murty he sometimes felt, as he listened to her untidy talk and saw the depth of her eyes. He used to watch her, too, in the church. He used to watch her stealthily from a dark end of the pew and he knew by her face she was not praying but forcing her mind to travel deeper and deeper into places of mystery and ignorance. Her eyes would be open wide like eyes that were dead.

'Now! you know now the kind of girl she was, you can see, can't you, how wonderful it was for her to sit and listen to Murty and his friends talking about things she'd never hear other women talk about – and all the time she sat silent under the lamp, sewing a piece of cloth, and not saying a word. You can imagine how she must have felt at night lying beside him in the dark and knowing that his mind was not banging aimless as a bat against the windows and walls of their house and the things of every day, but that it was flying out with her own over dark unislanded seas of thought. Anyone with an eye in his head, my father used to say afterwards, would have known by looking at her that she wouldn't be happy with the most robust and handsomest man in the country unless his mind was as edgy as Murty's, and that, by the same way of looking at things, she would always and ever have been as happy with Murty as she was for a short while, even if he was paralysed as well as crippled! But it wasn't till after it was too late that this was realised, and then the only kindness that could be done to her was not to mention her name, for fear Murty would hear it and fly into a fury of grief at the sound of it.

'It was a wonder he didn't do himself harm in one of those fits of grief. People were always nervous when they saw him going around alone, and the servants were almost too scared to sleep in the house with him. But my father said that when he didn't kill himself the night the child was born though, it wasn't likely he'd do it after. My father knew he'd never kill himself. My father, you must remember, looked on all that happened as the strange working of mysterious powers, and he felt that Murty Lockhart only began to live on that terrible night, even though his new life was dearly bought. My father felt that on that night Murty passed into the knowledge of the mysterious workings of God that he was all his youth seeking, and that Ursula, too, poor girl, was timidly trying to probe. Of course my father was a staunch believer, and that accounts for the turn he gave to the whole thing when he was telling it. You might put a different interpretation on it, and call it a strange coincidence, but in either case you'll have to admit there was a pattern in the events, and that the beginning worked around to the end in as perfect a circle as ever anyone saw.

'No matter what way you look on the thing, however,' said my companion, taking out a blue silk handkerchief and wiping his face with it, 'it's a good story. But I wish you could have heard my father tell it. I've told it badly enough up to now, but I'm afraid I'll make a proper mess of the end of it, although that's the most extraordinary part of it entirely. Well, anyway, to go on with it —

'Once Murty got suspicious he lost all balance and let his mind narrow in on itself until he had only one thought, and that was the thought that Ursula had married him for some reason he didn't yet know; and of course in a certain manner of speaking that was true too, but it was not from any deception or crookedness that that reason was kept from him, but from a mixture of dignity and modesty. It was from some such reasons of modesty, too, that she was so slow about telling him that they were going to have a child. She didn't tell him until she was carrying it for several months. Perhaps she wanted to shorten the time of waiting for him by keeping it a secret as long as ever she could. Who knows! Anyway, the tragedy was to be, it seems, and she didn't tell him in time. While she was laying up her secret joy for him he was hoarding and storing distrust of her in his heart. Then one day some old rip in the town made herself busy enough and good enough to offer Murty a bit of friendly advice on how he should treat his wife while she was in that condition. Those were the very words the old devil used, and Murty didn't know what she was talking about, not being a man given over much to talking with women. You can imagine him asking her "what condition?" and then pulling himself up short and remembering that there was only one significance put on most long words by women of that old one's type. You can imagine him realising what was meant by her talk and realising too the laughing stock he'd be all over the town when she went off and told the news that he didn't know his own wife was going to have a child. At this part of the story you'd pity him all right, but by the time he got home he was in a terrible rage. It was more than queer she didn't tell him, he thought. So it was – we all are agreed on that – but she wasn't an ordinary girl and you can't have it both ways. He went straight into the house and took one look at her and went out again. She must have thought it odd, but she was too preoccupied with her plans and thoughts to think long of anything those days. The servants thought nothing at all of it at the time, but afterwards it was the first thing that leaped to their minds. The day it happened they were too busy to think, because they were getting the attic ready. The attic was never used, but it had fine wide rooms with far views out from it, and neither noise nor dust seemed able to climb as high as it. She was going to open it up as a room for the child. They were getting it ready on the quiet, because they were in the know and it was to be nearly as big a surprise to Murty as the news of who was to use it! The day she decided to tell him was the day they were putting the finishing touches to the rooms. She just decided that a suitable time had arrived and she left down a duster she had in her hand and went downstairs and told him at about ten o'clock in the morning before he went out on his day's work inspecting his properties. She was so excited she probably didn't notice how quietly he took the news and how quickly he went out afterwards. In fact, she didn't have time to tell him about the attic, he went out so abruptly, but she thought nothing of it, he was always a bit abrupt, and so she decided she'd tell him later in the day and she went upstairs again and she went on with the directing of where to put this, and where to put that, and she was as happy as a thrush. Indeed, the servants were remarking on how happy she looked a minute before Murty's step was heard outside the front door and the way her face lit up when she said: "Here's my husband, back again. Now we'll tell him about the way we're fixing up the attic." The two servant women were as happy as herself, because it was expected that Murty would take his hand out of his pocket for more than to bless himself when the great day came. Certainly there wasn't one of them had the least suspicion of the dreadful tortured thought that had found its way into his mind. It was so vicious, so tortured, so misbegotten a thought, and most of all so unwarranted, that it would make you think after all that there might be something in the old people's saying that there's a twisted mind in a twisted body. The thought Murty had in his mind was so wrongful that I don't believe even you, listening to me here, could have any idea of what it was, and you'll be just as surprised as the servants and Ursula herself, poor girl, when he came out with it, standing at the foot of the banisters, looking up at the three women where they stood halfway up the stairs, their arms filled with blankets and pillows. Ursula was clutching the banisters they say, and staring at him as if a devil had looked out at her through his eyes. It was all so sudden. They were going up to the top of the house to put the last touches to the rooms, and the older of the two maids, who was in the family long before Ursula came into it, was eyeing her like a mother as if she doubted the wisdom of her climbing up three flights of stairs. Just as they were on the third step they heard Murty coming up to the hall door outside and turning the key in the lock. Ursula stopped and waited till he came in and then she called down to him gaily and asked him to come upstairs, she had something to show him. He made some excuse and gave her a dark look. She started to tease him very prettily and to coax him to change his mind, but he went on down the hall and didn't even turn round to answer her. The colour that hadn't been in her cheeks for several months came back with a violent flutter.

'"You don't have to come," she called down to him, "if you're not interested in the rooms that are being got ready for your own child!"

'She probably expected him to be softened out of whatever caprice of anger he was in. Who knows what she expected, but everyone knows a pure girl like her didn't expect what she got, anyway. He turned around with a snarl that held all the months' bitterness.

'"How do I know it's my child?" he shouted.

'They were all deafened and blinded and stupefied at his words. He stared at them and they staring back at him like ghostly people from the valleys of death. Then he shouted out all his suspicions in a storm of words, as if by their stinging spate he could bring back the fluttering blood to their faces again. And it wasn't until Ursula fell down on the step of the stairs where she stood that he stopped the mad words that were pouring out of his mouth.

'They got her to bed and the doctor came and no one as much as thought of Murty during the next forty-eight hours when her untimely labour was on her. He went over to my father, who lived across the road, and told him the whole story; told him how he loved Ursula so much it got to be a torture to him to think how unworthy he was of her. It wasn't until after he was married to her, he said, that the real torture of loving her came on him. Before they were married he only wanted her for her body but afterwards he wanted her thoughts and – his voice sank – her love. He told my father he knew she was in love with someone, because she used to keep saying over little words of gentleness in her sleep such as no one heard from her during the day. Then, when he heard she was going to have a child and when she didn't run to tell him, he began to think that he had found the reason why a healthy girl like her had married a cripple-foot like him. Even to my father Murty was ashamed to put his meaning any plainer, but my father knew what he meant. He watched her, Murty said, and he knew by the passionate look on her face that she was carrying the child of the lover she talked with in her sleep.

'And then, as Murty spoke it all came clearly to my father, as things sometimes do, that Ursula was in love with Murty and Murty didn't know it even yet. All that night they sat downstairs in my father's house watching up at the lights that were burning high in Murty's house. There were dim red rays in some rooms from the colza oil lamps that were lit before statues. There were bright pink lights from paraffin lamps whose wicks were turned up to their highest. And sometimes a light was seen to travel from window to window as a lamp was hurriedly caught up and carried from one place to another. Sometimes a lamp was snatched up hastily and carried downstairs so quickly that the shadows it struck from banister to banister fell on the windowpanes like bitter blows of a stick. And the hurrying lights told a tale of worry and dread to the watchers across the street.

'All that night my father tried to make Murty see that his wife had married him because she loved him, and that she probably loved him even more after she was married, but his words had to pierce through too much doubt and misery, and so when morning paled the window-panes across the street and left only a hard gilt core of lamplight where there had been a glaze of gold, Murty was still saying over and over again that he wanted to believe all my father said, but that he would have to have proof. It was the same old obstinacy he used to show in the arguments they had had many a night in the past.

'"This is another thing, Murty," said my father, "where there can be no proof. You must have faith."

'"Faith is a poor substitute for proof," said Murty with a glitter of despair in his eyes.

'My father went out and left him sitting by the grey powdered grate while he went out to find out how Ursula was, and he thought as he went, of how queer Murty was, even as a child, sitting between his mother's lace curtains, his eyes boring the distance, eyes that had seemed to him, even then, as if they would pierce the mysteries of darkness. But when he came back across the street a few minutes later he did not want to see those eyes, as he told Murty that Ursula was dead!'

The storyteller stopped and as I was overcome with such a feeling of horror at the turn the story had taken, I did not realise that it was not finished until his voice went on once more, lower and more uncertain.

'You see,' he said, 'my father was scared to look him in the face in case Murty'd see he was keeping something back from him; the news that was spreading poisonously over the whole town, that Ursula Lockhart had died giving birth to a stillborn child – whose feet were clubbed.'

We were both silent then, he from the strain of the story, I from the chill that had swept across me from the ending words of it. Then he spoke.

'Write out that story sometime,' he said self-consciously. 'That's the kind of story to write!'

'But I can't write that! How can I?' I said. 'That's your story.'

'A story on the tongue is nobody's story,' he said.

'Write it down yourself, then!' I said.

'I'm not a writer,' he said, and I must admit he said it indignantly.

'Well, you ought to be,' I said, being in my turn somewhat indignant.

'If I was, I'd miss hearing half of what goes on in the world, like you do,' said he. 'If you're wise you'll do as I say and write that out and get it printed. If you do, people will begin to think something of your work instead of throwing it into the wastebasket.'

'But afterwards? I'll have to go back again to my old methods.'

'Why?'

'Because I won't always be able to find stories like this to tell. This was only one incident. Life in general isn't rounded off like that at the edges; out into neat shapes. Life is chaotic; its events are unrelated; its . . .'

'There you go again!'

'But surely even now, you will admit . . .' I said, beginning to enter the discussion again, but this time my friend the storyteller glanced at me in a most peculiar way; you might almost say with dislike.

'Please don't start that nonsense again,' he said, and he casually walked away.

THE GREAT WAVE

THE BISHOP WAS SITTING IN THE STERN OF THE BOAT. HE WAS IN HIS robes, with his black overcoat thrown across his shoulders for warmth, and over his arm he carried his vestments, turned inside out to protect them from the salt spray. The reason he was already robed was because the distance across to the island was only a few miles, and the island priest was spared the embarrassment of a long delay in his small damp sacristy.

The islanders had a visit from their bishop only every four years at most, when he crossed over, as now, for the Confirmation ceremony, and so to have His Grace arrive thus in his robes was only their due share: a proper prolongation of episcopal pomp. In his albe and amice he would easily be picked out by the small knot of islanders who would gather on the pier the moment the boat was sighted on the tops of the waves. Yes: it was right and proper for all that the bishop be thus attired. His Grace approved. The bishop had a reason of his own too, as it happened, but it was a small reason, and he was hardly aware of it anywhere but in his heart.

Now, as he sat in the boat, he wrapped his white skirts tighter around him, and he looked to see that the cope and chasuble were well doubled over, so that the coloured silks would not be exposed when they got away from the lee of the land and the waves broke on the sides of the currach. The cope above all must not be tarnished. That was why he stubbornly carried it across his arm: the beautiful cope that came all the way from Stansstad, in Switzerland, and was so overworked with gilt thread that it shone like cloth of gold. The orphreys, depicting the birth and childhood of Christ, displayed the most elaborate work that His Grace had ever seen come from the Paramentenwerkstätte, and yet he was far from unfamiliar with the work of the sisters there, in St Klara. Ever since he attained the bishopric he had commissioned many beautiful vestments and altar cloths for use throughout the diocese. He had once, at their instigation, broken a journey to Rome to visit them. And when he was there, he asked those brilliant women to explain to him the marvel, not of their skill, but of his discernment of it, telling them of his birth and early life as a simple boy, on this island towards which he was now faced.

'Mind out!' he said sharply, as one of the men from the mainland who was pushing them out with the end of an oar threw the oar into the boat, scattering the air with drops of water from its glossy blade.

'Could nothing be done about this?' he asked, seeing water under the bottom boards of the boat. It was only a small sup, but it rippled up and down with a little tide of its own, in time with the tide outside that was already carrying them swiftly out into the bay.

'Tch, tch, tch,' said the bishop, for some of this water had saturated the hem of the albe, and he set about tucking it under him upon the seat. And then, to make doubly sure of it, he opened the knot of his cincture and retied it as tight about his middle as if it were long ago and he was tying up a sack of spuds at the neck. 'Tch, tch,' he repeated, but no one was unduly bothered by his ejaculation because of his soft and mild eyes, and didn't they know him? They knew that in his complicated, episcopal life he had to contend with a lot, and it was known that he hated to give his old housekeeper undue thumping with her flat iron. But there was a thing would need to be kept dry – the crozier!

'You'd want to keep that yoke there from getting wet through, Your Grace,' said one of the men, indicating the crozier that had fallen on the boards. For all that they mightn't heed his little-old-womanish ways, they had a proper sense of what was fitting for an episcopal appearance.

'I could hold the crozier perhaps,' said Father Kane, the bishop's secretary, who was further up the boat. 'I still think it would be more suitable for the children to be brought over to you on the mainland, than for you to be traipsing over here like this, and in those foreign vestments at that!'

He is thinking of the price that was paid for them, thought the bishop, and not of their beauty or their workmanship. And yet, he reflected, Father Kane was supposed to be a highly educated man, who would have gone on for a profession if he hadn't gone for the priesthood, and who would not have had to depend on the seminary to put the only bit of gloss on him he'd ever get – Like me, he thought! And he looked down at his beautiful vestments again. A marvel, no less, he thought, savouring again the miracle of his power to appreciate such things.

'It isn't as if *they'll* appreciate them over there,' said Father Kane, with sudden venom, looking towards the island, a thin line of green on the horizon.

'Ah, you can never say that for certain,' said the bishop mildly, even indifferently. 'Take me, how did I come to appreciate such things?'

But he saw the answer in the secretary's hard eyes. He thinks it was parish funds that paid for my knowledge, and diocesan funds for putting it into practice! And maybe he's right! The bishop smiled to himself. Who knows anything at all about how we're shaped, or where we're led, or how in the end we are ever brought to our rightful haven?

'How long more till we get there?' he asked, because the island was no longer a vague green mass. Its familiar shapes were coming into focus; the great high promontory throwing its purple shade over the shallow fields by the shore, the sparse white cottages, the cheap cement pier, constantly in need of repairs. And, higher up, on a ledge of the promontory itself there was the plain cement church, its spire only standing out against the sky, bleak as a crane's neck and head.

To think the full height of the promontory was four times the height of the steeple!

The bishop gave a great shudder. One of the rowers was talking to him.

'Sure, Your Grace ought to know all about this bay. Ah, but I suppose you forget them days altogether now!'

'Not quite, not quite,' said the bishop, quickly. He slipped his hand inside his robes and rubbed his stomach that had begun already to roll after only a few minutes of the swell.

When he was a little lad, over there on the island, he used to think he'd run away, some day, and join the crew of one of the French fishing trawlers that were always moving backwards and forwards on the rim of the sky. He used to go to a quiet place in the shade of the Point, and settling into a crevice in the rocks, out of reach of the wind, he'd spend the day long staring at the horizon; now in the direction of Liverpool, now in the direction of the Norwegian fjords.

Yet, although he knew the trawlers went from one great port to another, and up even as far as Iceland, he did not really associate them with the sea. He never thought of them as at the mercy of it in the way the little currachs were that had made his mother a widow, and that were jottled by every wave. The trawlers used to seem out of reach of the waves, away out on the black rim of the horizon.

He had in those days a penny jotter in which he put down the day and hour a trawler passed, waiting precisely to mark it down until it passed level with the pier. He put down also other facts about it which he deduced from the small vague outline discernible at that distance. And he smiled to remember the sense of satisfaction and achievement he used to get from that old jotter, which his childish imagination allowed him to believe was a full and exhaustive report. He never thought of the long nights and the early dawns, the hours when he was in the schoolroom, or the many times he was kept in the cottage by his mother, who didn't hold with his hobby.

'Ah, son, aren't you all I've got! Why wouldn't I fret about you?' she'd say to him, when he chafed under the yoke of her care.

That was the worst of being an only child, and the child of a sea widow into the bargain. God be good to her! He used to have to sneak off to his cranny in the rocks when he got her gone to the shop of a morning, or up to the chapel of an afternoon to say her beads. She was in sore dread of his even looking out to sea, it seemed! And as for going out in a currach! Hadn't she every currach crew on the island warned against taking him out?

'Your mammy would be against me, son,' they'd say, when he'd plead with them, one after another on the shore, and they getting ready to shove their boats down the shingle and float them out on the tide.

'How will I ever get out to the trawlers if I'm not let out in the currachs?' he used to think. That was when he was a little fellow, of course, because when he got a bit older he stopped pestering them, and didn't go down near the shore at all when they were pulling out. They'd got sharp with him by then.

'We can't take any babbies out with us – a storm might come up. What would a babby like you do then?' And he couldn't blame them for their attitude because by this time he knew they could often have found a use for him out in the boats when there was a heavy catch.

'You'll never make a man of him hiding him in your petticoats,' they'd say to his mother, when they'd see him with her in the shop. And there was a special edge on the remark, because men were scarce, as could be seen anywhere on the island by the way the black frieze jackets of the men made only small patches in the big knots of women, with their flaming red petticoats.

His mother had a ready answer for them.

'And why are they scarce?' she'd cry.

'And, don't be bitter, Mary.'

'Well, leave me alone, then. Won't he be time enough taking his life in his hands when there's more to be got for a netful of ling than there is this year!'

For the shop was always full of dried ling. When you thought to lean on the counter, it was on a long board of ling you leant. When you went to sit down on a box or a barrel it was on top of a bit of dried ling you'd be sitting. And right by the door, a greyhound bitch had dragged down a bit of ling from a hook on the wall and was chewing at it, not furtively, but to the unconcern of all, growling when it found it tough to chew, and attacking it with her back teeth and her head to one side, as she'd chew an old rind of hoof parings in the forge. The juice of it, and her own saliva mixed, was trickling out of her mouth onto the floor.

'There'll be a good price for the first mackerel,' said poor Maurya Keely, their near neighbour, whose husband was ailing, and whose son, Seoineen, was away in a seminary on the mainland studying to be a priest. 'The seed herring will be coming in any day now.'

'You'll have to let Jimeen out on that day if it looks to be a good catch,' she said, turning to his mother. 'We're having our currach tarred, so's to be all ready against the day.'

Everyone had sympathy with Maurya, knowing her man was nearly done, and that she was in great dread that he wouldn't be fit to go out and get their share of the new season's catch, and she counting on the money to pay for Seoineen's last year in the seminary. Seoineen wasn't only her pride, but the pride of the whole island as well, for, with the scarcity of menfolk, the island hadn't given a priest to the diocese in a decade.

'And how is Seoineen? When is he coming home at all?' another woman asked, as they crowded around Maurya. 'He'll soon be facing into the straight,' they said, meaning his ordination, and thinking, as they used the expression, of the way, when Seoineen was a young fellow, he used to be the wildest lad on the island, always winning the ass-race on the shore, the first to be seen flashing into sight around the Point, and he coming up the straight, keeping the lead easily to finish at the pier-head.

'He'll be home for a last leave before the end,' said his mother, and everyone understood the apprehension she tried to keep out of her voice, but which steals into the heart of every priest's mother thinking of the staying power a man needs to reach that end. 'I'm expecting him the week after next,' she said, then suddenly her joy in the thought of having him in the house again took over everything else.

'Ah, let's hope the mackerel will be in before then!' said several of the women at the one time, meaning there would be a jingle in everyone's pocket then, for Seoineen would have to call to every single cottage on the island, and every single cottage would want to have plenty of lemonade and shop-biscuits too, to put down before him.

Jimeen listened to this with interest and pleased anticipation. Seoineen always took him around with him, and he got a share in all that was set down for the seminarian.

But that very evening Seoineen stepped on to the pier. There was an epidemic in the college and the seminarists that were in their last year, like him, were let home a whole week before their time.

'Sure, it's not for what I get to eat that I come home, Mother!' he cried, when Maurya began bewailing having no feasting for him. 'If there's anything astray with the life I've chosen it's not shortage of grub! And anyway, we won't have long to wait?' He went to the door and glanced up at the sky. 'The seed will be swimming inward tomorrow on the first tide!'

'Oh, God forbid!' said Maurya. 'We don't want it that soon either, son, for our currach was only tarred this day!' And her face was torn with two worries now instead of one.

Jimeen had seen the twinkle in Seoineen's eye, and he thought he was only letting on to know about such things, for how would he have any such knowledge at all, and he away at schools and colleges the best part of his life.

The seed was in on the first tide, though, the next day.

'Oh, they have curious ways of knowing things that you'd never expect them to know,' said Jimeen's own mother. It was taken all over the island to be a kind of prophesy.

'Ah, he was only letting on, Mother,' said Jimeen, but he got a knock of her elbow over the ear.

'It's time you had more respect for him, son,' she said, as he ran out of the door for the shore.

Already most of the island boats were pulling hard out into the bay. And the others were being pushed out as fast as they could be dragged down the shingle.

But the Keely boat was still upscutted in the dune grass under the promontory, and the tar wetly gleaming on it. The other women were clustered around Maurya, giving her consolation.

'Ah sure, maybe it's God's will,' she said. 'Wasn't himself doubled up with pain in the early hours, and it's in a heavy sleep he is this minute – I wouldn't wake him up whether or no! He didn't get much sleep last night. It was late when he got to his bed. Him and Seoineen stayed up talking by the fire. Seoineen was explaining to him all about the ordination, about the fasting they have to do beforehand, and the holy oils and the chrism and the laying-on of hands. It beat all to hear him! The creatureen, he didn't get much sleep either, but he's young and able, thank God. But I'll have to be going back now to call him for Mass.'

'You'll find you won't need to call Seoineen,' said one of the women. 'Hasn't him, and the like of him, got God's voice in their hearts all day and they ever and always listening to it. He'll wake of himself, you'll see. He'll need no calling!'

And sure enough, as they were speaking, who came running down the shingle but Seoineen.

'My father's not gone out without me, is he?' he cried, not seeing their own boat, or any sign of it on the shore, a cloud coming over his face that was all smiles and laughter when he was running down to them. He began to scan the bay that was blackened with boats by this time.

'He's not, then,' said Maurya. 'He's above in his bed still, but leave him be, Seoineen – leave him be – ' She nodded her head back towards the shade of the promontory. 'He tarred the boat yesterday, not knowing the seed 'ud be in so soon, and it would scald the heart out of him to be here and not able to take it out. But as I was saying to these good people, it's maybe God's will the way it's happened, because he's not fit to go out this day!'

'That's true for you, Mother,' said Seoineen, quietly. 'The poor man is nearly beat, I'm fearing.' But the next minute he threw back his head and looked around the shore. 'Maybe I'd get an oar in one of the other boats. There's surely a scarcity of men these days?'

'Is it you?' cried his mother, because it mortally offended her notion of the dignity due to him that he'd be seen with his coat off maybe – in his shirtsleeves maybe – red in the face maybe along with that and – God forbid – sweat maybe breaking out of him!

'To hear you, Mother, anyone would think I was a priest already. I wish you could get a look into the seminary and you'd see there's a big difference made there between the two sides of the fence!' It was clear from the light in his eyes as they swept the sea at that moment that it would take more than a suit of black clothes to stop him from having a bit of fun with an oar. He gave a sudden big laugh, but it fell away as sudden when he saw that all the boats had pulled out from the shore and he was alone with the women on the sand.

Then his face hardened.

'Tell me, Mother,' he cried. 'Is it the boat or my father that's the unfittest? For if it's only the boat then I'll make it fit! It would be going against God's plenitude to stay idle with the sea teeming like that – look at it!'

For even from where they stood when the waves wheeled inward they could see the silver herring seed glistening in the curving wheels of water, and when those slow wheels broke on the shore they left behind them a spate of seed sticking to everything, even to people's shoes.

'And for that matter, wasn't Christ Himself a fisherman? Come, Mother – tell me truth! Is the tar still wet or is it not?'

Maurya looked at him for a minute. She was no match for arguing with him in matters of theology, but she knew all about tarring a currach. 'Wasn't it only done yesterday, son,' she said. 'How could it be dry today?'

'We'll soon know that,' said Seoineen, and he ran over to the currach. Looking after him they saw him lay the palm of his hand flat on the upturned bottom of the boat, and then they heard him give a shout of exultation.

'It's not dry surely?' someone exclaimed, and you could tell by the faces that all were remembering the way he prophesied about the catch. Had the tar dried at the touch of his hands maybe?

But Seoineen was dragging the currach down the shingle.

'Why wouldn't it be dry?' he cried. 'Wasn't it a fine dry night. I remember going to the door after talking to my father into the small hours, and the sky was a mass of stars, and there was a fine, sharp wind blowing that you'd be in dread it would dry up the sea itself! Stand back there, Mother,' he cried, for her face was beseeching something of him, and he didn't want to be looking at it. But without looking he knew what it was trying to say. 'Isn't it towards my ordination the money is going? Isn't that argument enough for you?'

He had the boat nearly down to the water's edge. 'No, keep back there, young Jimeen,' he said. 'I'm able to manage it on my own, but let you get the nets and put them in and then be ready to skip in before I push out, because I'll need someone to help haul in the nets.'

'Is it Jimeen?' said one of the women, and she laughed, and then all the women laughed. 'Sure, he's more precious again nor you!' they said.

But they turned to his mother all the same.

'If you're ever going to let him go out at all, this is your one chance, surely? Isn't it like as if it was into the Hands of God Himself you were putting him, woman?'

'Will you let me, Ma?' It was the biggest moment in his life. He couldn't look at her for fear of a refusal.

'Come on, didn't you hear her saying yes – what are you waiting for?' cried Seoineen, giving him a push, and the next minute he was in the currach, and Seoineen had given it a great shove and he running out into the water in his fine shoes and all. He vaulted in across the keel. 'I'm destroyed already at the very start!' he cried, laughing down at his feet and trouser legs, and that itself seemed part of the sport for him. 'I'll take them off,' he cried, kicking the shoes off him, and pulling off his socks, till he was in his bare white feet. 'Give me the oars,' he cried, but as he gripped them he laughed again, and loosed his fingers for a minute, as one after the other he rubbed his hands on a bit of sacking on the seat beside him. For, like the marks left by the trawler men on the white bollard at the pier, the two bleached oars were marked with the track of his hands, palms, and fingers, in pitch-black tar.

'The tar was wet!'

'And what of it?' cried Seoineen. 'Isn't it easy to give it another lick of a brush?'

But he wasn't looking at Jimeen and saying it, his eyes were lepping along the tops of the waves to see if they were pulling near the other currachs.

The other currachs were far out in the bay already: the sea was running strong. For all that, there was a strange, still look about the water, unbroken by any spray. Jimeen sat still, exulting in his luck. The waves did not slap against the sides of the currach like he'd have thought they would do, and they didn't even break into spray where the oars split their surface. Instead, they seemed to go lolloping under the currach and lollop up again the far side, till it might have been on great glass rollers they were slipping around.

'God! Isn't it good to be out on the water!' cried Seoineen, and he stood up in the currach, nearly toppling them over in his exuberance, drawing in deep breaths, first with his nose, and then as if he were drinking it with his mouth, and his eyes at the same time taking big draughts of the coastline that was getting farther and farther away.

'Ah, this is the life: this is the real life,' he cried again, but they had to look to the oars and look to the nets, then, for a while, and for a while they couldn't look up at sea or sky.

When Jimeen looked up at last, the shore was only a narrow line of green.

'There's a bit of a change, I think,' said Seoineen, and it was true.

The waves were no longer around and soft, like the little cnoceens in the fields back of the shore, but they had small sharp points on them now, like the rocks around the Point that would rip the bottom out of a boat with one tip, the way a tip of a knife would slit the belly of a fish.

That was a venomous comparison though, and for all their appearance, when they hit against the flank of the boat, it was only the waves themselves that broke and patterned the water with splotches of spray.

It was while he was looking down at these white splotches that Jimeen saw the fish.

'Oh look, Seoineen, look!' he cried, because never had he seen the like.

They were not swimming free, or separate, like you'd think they'd be, but a great mass of them together, till you'd think it was at the floor of the sea you were looking, only it nearer and shallower.

There must have been a million fish; a million million, Jimeen reckoned wildly, and they pressed as close as the pebbles on the shore. And they might well have been motionless and only seeming to move like on a windy day you'd think the grass on the top of the promontory was running free like the waves, with the way it rippled and ran along a little with each breeze.

'Holy God, such a sight!' cried Seoineen. 'Look at them!'

But Jimeen was puzzled.

'How will we get them into the net?' he asked, because it didn't seem that there was any place for the net to slip down between them, but that it must lie on the top of that solid mass of fish, like on a floor.

'The nets: begod, I nearly forgot what we came out here for!' cried Seoineen, and at the same time they became aware of the activity in the other boats, which had drawn near without their knowing. He yelled at Jimeen. 'Catch hold of the nets there, you lazy good-for-nothing. What did I bring you with me for if it wasn't to put you to some use!' and he himself caught at a length of the brown mesh, thrown in the bottom of the boat, and began to haul it up with one hand, and with the other to feed it out over the side.

Jimeen, too, began to pull and haul, so that for a few minutes there was only a sound of the net swishing over the wood, and every now and then a bit of a curse, under his breath, from Seoineen as one of the cork floats caught in the thole pins.

At first it shocked Jimeen to hear Seoineen curse, but he reflected that Seoineen wasn't ordained yet, and that, even if he were, it must be a hard thing for a man to go against his nature.

'Come on, get it over the side, damn you,' cried Seoineen again, as Jimeen had slowed up a bit owing to thinking about the cursing. 'It isn't one netful but thirty could be filled this day! Sure you could fill the boat in fistfuls,' he cried, suddenly leaning down over the side, delving his bare hand into the water. With a shout, he brought up his hand with two fish, held one against the other in the same grip, so that they were as rigid as if they were dead. 'They're overlaying each other a foot deep,' he cried, and then he opened his fist and freed them. Immediately they writhed apart to either side of his hand in two bright arcs and then fell, both of them, into the bottom of the boat. But next moment they writhed into the air again, and flashed over the side of the currach.

'Ah begorras, you'll get less elbow room there than here, my boys,' cried Seoineen, and he roared laughing, and he and Jimeen leant over the side, and saw that sure enough, the two mackerel were floundering for a place in the glut of fishes.

But a shout in one of the other currachs made them look up.

It was the same story all over the bay. The currachs were tossing tipsily in the water with the antics of the crew, that were standing up and shouting and feeding the nets ravenously over the sides. In some of the boats that had got away early, they were still more ravenously hauling them up, strained and swollen with the biggest catch they had ever held.

There was not time for Seoineen or Jimeen to look around either, for just then the keel of their own currach began to dip into the water.

'Look out! Pull it up − ! Catch a better grip than that, damn you. Do you want to be pulled into the sea. Pull, damn you, pull!' cried Seoineen.

Now every other word that broke from his throat was a curse, or what you'd call a curse if you heard them from another man, or in another place, but in this place, from this man, hearing them issue wild and free, Jimeen understood that they were a kind of psalm. They rang out over the sea in a kind of praise to God for all his plenitude.

'Up! Pull hard − up, now, up!' he cried, and he was pulling at his end like a madman.

Jimeen pulled too, till he thought his heart would crack, and then suddenly the big white belly of the loaded net came in sight over the water.

Jimeen gave a groan, though, when he saw it.

'Is it dead they are?' he cried, and there was anguish in his voice.

Up to this, the only live fish he had ever seen were the few fish tangled in the roomy nets, let down by the old men over the end of the pier, and *they* were always full of life, needling back and forth insanely in the spacious mesh till he used to swallow hard, and press his lips close together fearing one of them would dart down his gullet, and he'd have it ever after needling this way and that inside him! But here was no stir at all in the great white mass that had been hauled up now in the nets.

'Is it dead they are?' he cried again.

'Aahh, why would they be dead? It's suffocating they are, even below in the water, with the welter of them is in it,' cried Seoineen.

He dragged the net over the side where it emptied and spilled itself into the bottom of the boat. They came alive then, all right! Flipping and floundering, and some of them flashing back into the sea. But it was only a few on the top that got away, the rest were kept down by the very weight and mass of them that was in it. And when, after a minute, Seoineen had freed the end of the net, he flailed them right and left till most of them fell back flat. Then, suddenly, he straightened up and swiped a hand across his face to clear it of the sweat that was pouring out of him.

'Ah sure, what harm if an odd one leps for it,' he cried. 'We'll deaden them under another netful! Throw out your end,' he cried.

As Jimeen rose up to his full height to throw the net wide out, there was a sudden terrible sound in the sky over him, and the next minute a bolt of thunder went volleying overhead, and with it, in the same instant it seemed, the sky was knifed from end to end with a lightning flash.

Were they blinded by the flash? Or had it suddenly gone as black as night over the whole sea?

'Oh God's Cross!' cried Seoineen. 'What is coming? Why didn't someone give us a shout? Where are the others? Can you see them? Hoy there! Marteen! Seumas? Can you hear – ?'

For they could see nothing. And it was as if they were all alone in the whole world. Then, suddenly, they made out Marteen's currach near to them, so near that, but for Seoineen flinging himself forward and grabbing the oars, the two currachs would have knocked together. Yet no sooner had they been saved from knocking together than they suddenly seemed so far sundered again they could hardly hear each other when they called out.

'What's happening, in Christ's name?' bawled Seoineen, but he had to put up his hands to trumpet his voice, for the waves were now so steep and high that even one was enough to blot out the sight of Marteen. Angry white spume dashed in their faces.

'It's maybe the end of the world,' said Jimeen, terror-stricken.

'Shut up and let me hear Marteen!' said Seoineen, for Marteen was bawling at them again.

'Let go the nets,' Marteen was bawling. 'Let go the nets or they'll drag you out of the boat.'

Under them then they could feel the big pull of the net that was filled up again in an instant with its dead weight of suffocating fish.

'Let it go, I tell you,' bawled Marteen.

'Did you hear? He's telling us to let it go,' piped Jimeen in terror, and he tried to free his own fingers of the brown mesh that had closed tight upon them with the increasing weight. 'I can't let go,' he cried, looking to Seoineen, but he shrank back from the strange wild look in Seoineen's eyes. 'Take care would you do anything of the kind!'

'It's cutting off my fingers!' he screamed.

Seoineen glared at him.

'A pity about them!' he cried, but when he darted a look at them, and saw them swelling and reddening, he cursed. 'Here – wait till I take it from you,' he cried, and he went to free his own right hand, but first he locked the laden fingers of his left hand into the mesh above the right hand, and even then, blood spurted out in the air when he finally dragged it free of the mesh.

For a minute Seoineen shoved his bleeding fingers into his mouth and sucked them, then he reached out and caught the net below where Jimeen gripped it. As the weight slackened, the pain of the searing strings lessened, but next minute as the pull below got stronger, the pain tore into Jimeen's flesh again.

'Let go now, if you like, now I have a bit of hold of it anyway – now I'm taking the weight of it off you,' said Seoineen.

Jimeen tried to drag free.

'I can't,' he screamed in terror, 'the strings are eating into my bones!'

Seoineen altered his balance and took more weight off the net at that place.

'Now!'

'I can't! I can't!' screamed Jimeen.

From far over the waves the voice of Marteen came to them again, faint, unreal, like the voices you'd hear in a shell if you held it to your ear.

'Cut free – cut free,' it cried, 'or else you'll be destroyed altogether.'

'Have they cut free themselves? That's what I'd like to know!' cried Seoineen.

'Oh, do as he says, Seoineen. Do as he says!' screamed Jimeen.

And then, as he saw a bit of ragged net, and then another and another rush past like the briary patches of foam on the water that was now almost level with the rowlocks, he knew that they had indeed all done what Marteen said; cut free.

'For the love of God, Seoineen,' he cried.

Seoineen hesitated for another instant. Then suddenly he made up his mind and, reaching along the seat, felt without looking for the knife that was kept there for slashing dogfish.

'Here goes,' he cried, and with one true cut of the knife he freed Jimeen's hands, the two together at the same time, but, letting the knife drop into the water, he reached out wildly to catch the ends of the net before they slid into it, or shed any of their precious freight.

Not a single silver fish was lost.

'What a fool I'd be,' he gasped, 'to let go. They think because of the collar I haven't a man's strength about me any more. Then I'll show them. I'll not let go this net, not if it pull me down to hell.' And he gave another wild laugh. 'And you along with me!' he cried. 'Murder?' he asked then, as if he had picked up the word from a voice in the wind. 'Is it murder? Ah sure, I often think it's all one to God what a man's sin is, as long as it's sin at all. Isn't sin poison – any sin at all, even the smallest drop of it? Isn't it death to the soul that it touches at any time? Ah then! I'll not let go!' And even when, just then, the whole sea seemed littered with tattered threads of net, he still held tight to his hold. 'Is that the way? They've all let go! Well then, I'll show them one man will not be so easy beat! Can you hear me?' he cried, because it was hard to hear him with the crazy noise of the wind and the waves.

'Oh, cut free, Seoineen,' Jimeen implored, although he remembered the knife was gone now to the bottom of the sea, and although the terrible swollen fingers were beyond help in the mangling ropes of the net.

'Cut free is it? Faith now! I'll show them all,' cried Seoineen. 'We'll be the only boat'll bring back a catch this night, and the sea seething with fish.' He gave a laugh. 'Sure that was the only thing that was spoiling my pleasure in the plenty, thinking that when the boats got back the whole island would be fuller of fish than the sea itself, and it all of no more value than if it was washed of its own accord on to the dirty counters of the shop! Sure it wouldn't be worth a farthing a barrel! But it will be a different story now, I'm thinking. Oh, but I'll have the laugh on them with their hollow boats, and their nets cut to flitters! I'll show them a man is a man, no matter what vows he takes, or what way he's called to deny his manhood! I'll show them! Where are they, anyway? Can you – see them – at all?' he cried, but he had begun to gasp worse than the fishes in the bottom of the boat. 'Can you – see them – at all? Damn you, don't sit there like that! Stand up – there – and tell me – can – you – see – them?'

It wasn't the others Jimeen saw though, when he raised his eyes from the torn hands in the meshes. All he saw was a great wall, a great green wall of water. No currachs anywhere. It was as if the whole sea had been stood up on its edge, like a plate on a dresser. And down that wall of water there slid a multitude of dead fish.

And then, down the same terrible wall, sliding like the dead fish, came an oar; a solitary oar. And a moment afterwards, but inside the glass wall, imprisoned, like under a glass dome, he saw – oh God! – a face, looking out at him, staring out at him through a foot of clear green water. And he saw it was the face of Marteen. For a minute the eyes of the dead man stared into his eyes.

With a scream he threw himself against Seoineen, and clung to him tight as iron.

How many years ago was that? The bishop opened his eyes. They were so near the shore he could pick out the people by name that stood on the pierhead. His stomach had stopped rolling. It was mostly psychological; that feeling of nausea. But he knew it would come back in an instant if he looked leftward from the shore, leftwards and upwards, where, over the little cement pier and over the crane-bill steeple of the church, the promontory that they called the Point rose up black with its own shadow.

For it was on that promontory – four times the height of the steeple – they had found themselves, he and Seoineen, in the white dawn of the day after the Wave, lying in a litter of dead fish, with the netful of fish like an anchor sunk into the green grass.

When he came to himself in that terrible dawn, and felt the slippy bellies of the fish all about him, he thought he was still in the boat, lying in the bottom among the mackerel, but when he opened his eyes and saw a darkness as of night, over his head, he thought it was still the darkness of the storm and he closed them again in terror.

Just before he closed them, though, he thought he saw a star, and he ventured to open them again, and then he saw that the dark sky over him was a sky of skin, stretched taught over timber laths, and the star was only a glint of light – and the blue light of day at that – coming through a split in the bottom of the currach. For the currach was on top of him! Not he in the bottom of it.

Why then was he not falling down and down and down through the green waters? His hands rushed out to feel around him. But even then, the most miraculous thing he thought to grasp was a fistful of sand, the most miraculous thing he thought to have to believe was that they were cast up safe upon the shore.

Under his hands though, that groped through the fishes, he came, not on sand, but on grass, and not upon the coarse dune grass that grew back from the shore at the foot of the Point. It was soft, sweet little grass, that was like the grass he saw once when Seoineen and he had climbed up the face of the Point, and stood up there, in the sun, looking down at all below, the sea and the pier, and the shore and the fields, and the thatch of their own houses, and on a level with them, the grey spire of the chapel itself!

It was, when opening his eyes wide at last, he saw, out from him a bit, the black tip of that same chapel spire that he knew where he was.

Throwing the fish to left and right he struggled to get to his feet.

It was a miracle! And it must have been granted because Seoineen was in the boat. He remembered how he prophesied the seed would be on the tide, and in his mind he pictured their currach being lifted up in the air and flown, like a bird, to this grassy point.

But where was Seoineen?

'Oh, Seoineen, Seoineen!' he cried, when he saw him standing on the edge of the Point looking downward, like they looked, that day, on all below. 'Oh, Seoineen, was it a miracle?' he cried, and he didn't wait for an answer, but he began to shout and jump in the air.

'Quit, will you!' said Seoineen, and for a minute he thought it must be modesty on Seoineen's part, it being through him the miracle was granted, and then he thought it must be the pain in his hands that was at him, not letting him enjoy the miracle, because he had his two hands pressed under his armpits.

Then suddenly he remembered the face of Marteen he had seen under the wall of water, and his eyes flew out over the sea that was as flat and even now as the field of grass under their feet. Was Marteen's currach lost? And what of the others?

Craning over the edge of the promontory he tried to see what currachs were back in their places under the little wall dividing the sand from the dune, turned upside down and leaning a little to one side, so you could crawl under them if you were caught in a sudden shower.

There were no currachs under the wall: none at all.

There were no currachs on the sea.

Once, when he was still wearing a red petticoat like a girsha, there had been a terrible storm and half a score of currachs were lost. He remembered the night with all the women on the island down on the shore with storm lamps, swinging them and calling out over the noise of the waves. And the next day they were still there, only kneeling on the pier, praying and keening.

'Why aren't they praying and keening?' he cried then, for he knew at last the other currachs, all but theirs, were lost.

'God help them,' said Seoineen, 'at least they were spared that.'

And he pointed to where, stuck in the latticed shutters on the side of the steeple, there were bits of seaweed, and – yes – a bit of the brown mesh of a net.

'God help you,' he said then, 'how can your child's mind take in what a grown man's mind can hardly hold – but you'll have to know sometime – we're all alone – the two of us – on the whole island. All that was spared by that wall of water – '

'All that was on the sea, you mean?' he cried.

'And on the land too,' said Seoineen.

'Not my mother – ?' he whimpered.

'Yes, and my poor mother,' said Seoineen. 'My poor mother that tried to stop us from going out with the rest.'

But it was a grief too great to grasp, and yet, even in the face of it, Jimeen's mind was enslaved to the thought of their miraculous salvation.

'Was it a miracle, Seoineen?' he whispered. 'Was it a miracle we were spared?'

But Seoineen closed his eyes, and pushed his crossed arms deeper under his armpits. The grimace of pain he made was – even without words – a rebuke to Jimeen's exaltation. Then he opened his eyes again.

'It was my greed that was the cause of all,' he said, and there was such a terrible sorrow in his face that Jimeen, only then, began to cry.

'It has cost me my two living hands,' said Seoineen, and there was a terrible anguish in his voice.

'But it saved your life, Seoineen,' he cried, wanting to comfort him.
Never did he forget the face Seoineen turned to him.

'For what?' he asked. 'For what?'

And there was, in his voice, such despair that Jimeen knew it wasn't a question but an answer; so he said no more for a few minutes. Then he raised his voice again, timidly.

'You saved my life too, Seoineen.'

Seoineen turned dully and looked at him.

'For what?'

But as he uttered them, those same words took on a change, and a change came over his face, too, and when he repeated them, the change was violent.

'For what?' he demanded. 'For what?'

Just then, on the flat sea below, Jimeen saw the boats, coming across from the mainland, not currachs like they had on the island, but boats of wood made inland, in Athlone, and brought down on lorries.

'Look at the boats,' he called out, four, five, six, any amount of them; they came rowing for the island.

Less than an hour later Seoineen was on his way to the hospital on the mainland, where he was to spend long months before he saw the island again. Jimeen was taken across a few hours later, but when he went it was to be for good. He was going to an aunt, far in from the sea, of whom he had never heard tell till that day.

Nor was he to see Seoineen again, in all the years that followed. On the three occasions that he was over on the island he had not seen him. He had made enquiries, but all he could ever get out of people was that he was a bit odd.

'And why wouldn't he be?' they added.

But although he never came down to the pier to greet the bishop like the rest of the islanders, it was said he used to slip into the church after it had filled up and he'd think he was unnoticed. And afterwards, although he never once would go down to the pier to see the boat off, he never went back into his little house until it was gone clear across to the other side of the bay. From some part of the island it was certain he'd be the last to take leave of the sight.

It had been the same on each visit the bishop made, and it would be the same on this one.

When he would be leaving the island, there would be the same solicitous entreaties with him to put on his overcoat. Certainly he was always colder going back in the late day. But he'd never give in to do more than throw it over his shoulders, from which it would soon slip down on to the seat behind him.

'You'd do right to put it on like they told you,' said the secretary, buttoning up his own thick coat.

But there was no use trying to make him do a thing he was set against. He was a man who had deep reasons for the least of his actions.

IN A CAFÉ

THE CAFÉ WAS IN A BACK STREET. MARY'S ANKLES ACHED AND SHE WAS glad Maudie had not got there before her. She sat down at a table near the door.

It was a place she had only recently found, and she dropped in often, whenever she came up to Dublin. She hated to go anywhere else now. For one thing, she knew that she would be unlikely ever to have set foot in it if Richard were still alive. And this knowledge helped to give her back a semblance of the identity she lost willingly in marriage, but lost doubly, and unwillingly, in widowhood.

Not that Richard would have disliked the café. It was the kind of place they went to when they were students. Too much water had gone under the bridge since those days, though. Say what you liked, there was something faintly snobby about a farm in Meath, and together she and Richard would have been out of place here. But it was a different matter to come here alone. There could be nothing – oh, nothing – snobby about a widow. Just by being one, she fitted into this kind of café. It was an unusual little place. She looked around.

The walls were distempered red above and the lower part was boarded, with the boards painted white. It was probably the boarded walls that gave it the peculiarly functional look you get in the snuggery of a public house or in the confessional of a small and poor parish church. For furniture there were only deal tables and chairs, with black-and-white checked tablecloths that were either unironed or badly ironed. But there was a decided feeling that money was not so much in short supply as dedicated to other purposes – as witness the paintings on the walls, and a notice over the fire grate to say that there were others on view in a studio overhead, in rather the same way as pictures in an exhibition. The paintings were for the most part experimental in their technique.

The café was run by two students from the Art College. They often went out and left the place quite empty – as now – while they had a cup of coffee in another café – across the street. Regular clients sometimes helped themselves to coffee from the pot on the gas ring, behind a curtain at the back; or, if they only came in for company and found none, merely warmed themselves at the big fire always blazing in the little black grate that was the original grate when the café was a warehouse office. Today, the fire was banked up with coke. The coffee was spitting on the gas ring.

Would Maudie like the place? That it might not be exactly the right place to have arranged to meet her, above all under the present circumstances, occurred vaguely to Mary, but there was nothing that could be done about it now. When Maudie got there, if she didn't like it, they could go somewhere else. On the other hand, perhaps she might like it? Or perhaps she would be too upset to take notice of her surroundings? The paintings might interest her. They were certainly stimulating. There were two new ones today, which Mary herself had not seen before: two flower paintings, just inside the door. From where she sat she could read the signature, Johann van Stiegler. Or at least they suggested flowers. They were nameable as roses surely in spite of being a bit angular. She knew what Richard would have said about them. But she and Richard were no longer one. So what would *she* say about them? She would say – she would say –

But what was keeping Maudie? It was all very well to be glad of a few minutes' time in which to gather herself together; it was a different thing altogether to be kept a quarter of an hour.

Mary leaned back against the boarding. She was less tired than when she came in, but she was still in no way prepared for the encounter in front of her.

What had she to say to a young widow recently bereaved? Why on earth had she arranged to meet her? The incongruity of their both being widowed came forcibly upon her. Would Maudie, too, be in black with touches of white? Two widows! It was like two magpies: one for sorrow, two for joy. The absurdity of it was all at once so great she had an impulse to get up and make off out of the place. She felt herself vibrating all over with resentment at being coupled with anyone, and urgently she began to sever them, seeking out their disparities.

Maudie was only a year married! And her parents had been only too ready to take care of her child, greedily possessing themselves of it. Maudie was as free as a girl. Then – if it mattered? – she had a nice little income in her own right too, apart from all Michael had left her. So?

But what was keeping her? Was she not coming at all?

Ah! the little iron bell that was over the door – it too, since the warehouse days – tinkled to tell there was another customer coming into the café.

It wasn't Maudie though. It was a young man – youngish anyway – and Mary would say that he was an artist. Yet his hands, at which, when he sat down, he began to stare, were not like the hands of an artist. They were peculiarly plump soft-skinned hands, and there was something touching in the relaxed way in which, lightly clasped one in the other, they rested on the table. Had they a womanish look perhaps? No; that was not the word, but she couldn't for the life of her find the right word to describe them. And her mind was teased by trying to find it. Fascinated, her eyes were drawn to those hands, time and again, no matter how resolutely she tore them away. It was almost as if it was by touch, not sight, that she knew their warm fleshiness.

Even when she closed her eyes – as she did – she could still see them. And so, innocent of where she was being led, she made no real effort to free her thoughts from them, and not until it was too late did she see before her the familiar shape of her recurring nightmare. All at once it was Richard's hands she saw, so different from those others, wiry, supple, thin. There they were for an instant in her mind, limned by love and anguish, before they vanished.

It happened so often. In her mind she would see a part of him, his hand – his arm, his foot perhaps, in the finely worked leather shoes he always wore – and from it, frantically, she would try to build up the whole man. Sometimes she succeeded better than others, built him up from foot to shoulder, seeing his hands, his grey suit, his tie, knotted always in a slightly special way, his neck, even his chin that was rather sharp, a little less attractive than his other features –

But always at that point she would be defeated. Never once voluntarily since the day he died had she been able to see his face again.

And if she could not remember him, at will, what meaning had time at all? What use was it to have lived the past, if behind us it fell away so sheer?

In the hour of his death, for her it was part of the pain that she knew this would happen. She was standing beside him when, outside the hospital window, a bird called out with a sweet, clear whistle, and hearing it she knew that he was dead, because not for years had she really heard birdsong or birdcall, so loud was the noise of their love in her ears. When she looked down it was a strange face, the look of death itself, that lay on the pillow. And after that brief moment of silence that let in the birdsong for an instant, a new noise started in her head; the noise of a nameless panic that did not always roar, but never altogether died down.

And now – here in the little café – she caught at the table edge – for the conflagration had started again and her mind was a roaring furnace.

It was just then the man at the end of the table stood up and reached for the menu card on which, as a matter of fact, she was leaning – breasts and elbows – with her face in her hands. Hastily, apologetically, she pushed it towards him, and at once the roar died down in her mind. She looked at him. Could he have known? Her heart was filled with gratitude, and she saw that his eyes were soft and gentle. But she had to admit that he didn't look as if he were much aware of her. No matter! She still was grateful to him.

'Don't you want this, too?' she cried, thankful, warm, as she saw that the small slip of paper with the speciality for the day that had been clipped to the menu card with a paper pin had come off and remained under her elbow, caught on the rough sleeve of her jacket. She stood up and leant over the table with it.

'Ah! thank you!' he said, and bowed. She smiled. There was such gallantry in a bow. He was a foreigner, of course. And then, before she sat down again she saw that he had been sketching, making little pencil sketches all over a newspaper on the table, in the margins and in the spaces between the newsprint. Such intricate minutely involuted little figures – she was fascinated, but of course she could not stare.

Yet, when she sat down, she watched him covertly, and every now and then she saw that he made a particular flourish: it was his signature, she felt sure, and she tried to make it out from where she sat. A disproportionate, a ridiculous excitement rushed through her, when she realised it was Johann van Stiegler, the name on the new flower paintings that had preoccupied her when she first came into the place.

But it's impossible, she thought. The sketches were so meticulous; the paintings so –

But the little bell tinkled again.

'Ah! Maudie!'

For all her waiting, taken by surprise in the end, she got to her feet in her embarrassment, like a man.

'Maudie, my dear!' She had to stare fixedly at her in an effort to convey the sympathy, which, tongue-tied, she could express in no other way.

They shook hands, wordlessly.

'I'm deliberately refraining from expressing sympathy – you know that?' said Mary then, as they sat down at the checkered table.

'Oh, I do!' cried Maudie. And she seemed genuinely appreciative. 'It's so awful trying to think of something to say back! – Isn't it? It has to come right out of yourself, and sometimes what comes is something you can't even say out loud when you do think of it!'

It was so true. Mary looked at her in surprise. Her mind ran back over the things people had said to her, and the replies.

Them: It's a good thing it wasn't one of the children.
Her: I'd give them all for him.
Them: Time is a great healer.
Her: Thief would be more like: taking away even my memory of him.
Them: God's ways are wonderful. Some day you'll see His plan in all this.
Her: Do you mean, some day I'll be glad he's dead?

So Maudie apprehended these subtleties too? Mary looked hard at her. 'I know, I know,' she said. 'In the end you have to say what is expected of you – and you feel so cheapened by it.'

'Worse still, you cheapen the dead!' said Maudie.

Mary looked really hard at her now. Was it possible for a young girl – a simple person at that – to have wrung from one single experience so much bitter knowledge? In spite of herself, she felt she was being drawn into complicity with her. She drew back resolutely.

'Of course, you were more or less expecting it, weren't you?' she said, spitefully.

Unrepulsed, Maudie looked back at her. 'Does that matter?' she asked, and then, unexpectedly, she herself put a rift between them. 'You have the children, of course!' she said, and then, hastily, before Mary could say anything, she rushed on. 'Oh, I know I have my baby, but there seems so little link between him and his father! I just can't believe that it's me, sometimes, wheeling him round the park in his pram: it's like as if he was illegitimate. No! I mean it really. I'm not just trying to be shocking. It must be so different when there has been time for a relationship to be started between children and their father, like there was in your case.'

'Oh, I don't know that that matters,' said Mary. 'And you'll be glad to have him some day.' This time she spoke with deliberate malice, for she knew so well how those same words had lacerated her. She knew what they were meant to say: the children would be better than nothing.

But the poison of her words did not penetrate Maudie. And with another stab she knew why this was so. Maudie was so young; so beautiful. Looking at her, it seemed quite inaccurate to say that she had lost her husband: it was Michael who had lost her, fallen out, as it were, while she perforce went outward. She didn't even look like a widow. There was nothing about her to suggest that she was in any way bereft or maimed.

'You'll marry again, Maudie,' she said, impulsively. 'Don't mind my saying it,' she added quickly, hastily. 'It's not a criticism. It's because I know how you're suffering that I say it. Don't take offence.'

Maudie didn't really look offended though, she only looked on the defensive. Then she relaxed.

'Not coming from you,' she said. 'You know what it's like.' Mary saw she was trying to cover up the fact that she simply could not violently refute the suggestion. 'Not that I think I will,' she added, but weakly, 'After all, you didn't!'

It was Mary who was put upon the defensive now.

'After all, it's only two years – less, even,' she said stiffly.

'Oh, it's not altogether a matter of time,' said Maudie, seeing she had erred, but not clear how or where. 'It's the kind of person you are, I think. I admire you so much! It's what I'd want to be like myself if I had the strength. With remarriage it is largely the effect on oneself that matters I think, don't you? I don't think it really matters to – to the dead! Do you? I'm sure Michael would want me to marry again if he were able to express a wish. After all, people say it's a compliment to a man if his widow marries again, did you ever hear that?'

'I did,' said Mary, curtly. 'But I wouldn't pay much heed to it. A fat lot the dead care about compliments.'

So Maudie *was* already thinking about remarriage? Mary's irritation was succeeded by a vague feeling of envy, and then the irritation returned tenfold.

How easily it was accepted that *she* would not marry again. This girl regards me as too old, of course. And she's right – or she ought to be right! She remembered the way, even two years ago, people had said she 'had' her children. They meant, even then, that it was unlikely, unlooked for, that she'd remarry.

Other things that had been said crowded back into her mind as well. So many people had spoken of the special quality of her marriage – hers and Richard's – their remarkable suitability one for the other, and the uniqueness of the bond between them. She was avid to hear this said at the time.

But suddenly, in this little café, the light that had played over those words flickered and went out. Did they perhaps mean that if Richard had not appeared when he did, no one else would have been interested in her?

Whereas Maudie – ! If she looked so attractive now, when she must still be suffering from shock, what would she be like a year from now, when she would be 'out of mourning,' as it would be put? Why, right now, she was so fresh and – looking at her there was no other word for it – virginal. Of course she was only a year married. A year! You could hardly call it being married at all.

But Maudie knew a thing or two about men for all that. There was no denying it. And in her eyes at that moment there was a strange expression. Seeing it, Mary remembered at once that they were not alone in the café. She wondered urgently how much the man at the other end of the table had heard and could hear of what they were saying. But it was too late to stop Maudie.

'Oh, Mary,' cried Maudie, leaning forward, 'it's not what they give us – I've got over wanting things like a child – it's what we have to give them! It's something – ' and she pressed her hands suddenly to her breasts, 'something in here!'

'Maudie!'

Sharply, urgently, Mary tried to make her lower her voice, and with a quick movement of her head she did manage at last to convey some caution to her.

'In case you might say something,' she said, in a low voice.

'Oh, there was no fear,' said Maudie. 'I was aware all the time.' She didn't speak quite so low as Mary, but did lower her voice. 'I was aware of him *all the time*,' she said. 'It was *him* that put it into my mind – about what we have to give.' She pressed her hands to her breasts again. 'He looks so lonely, don't you think? He is a foreigner, isn't he? I always think it's sad for them; they don't have many friends, and even when they do, there is always a barrier, don't you agree?'

But Mary was too embarrassed to let her go on. Almost frantically she made a diversion.

'What are you going to have, Maudie?' she said, loudly. 'Coffee? Tea? And is there no one to take an order?'

Immediately she felt a fool. To whom had she spoken? She looked across at Johann van Stiegler. As if he were waiting to meet her glance, his mild and patient eyes looked into hers.

'There is no one there,' he said, nodding at the curtained gas ring, 'but one can serve oneself. Perhaps you would wish that I – '

'Oh, not at all,' cried Mary. 'Please don't trouble! We're in absolutely no hurry! Please don't trouble yourself,' she said, 'not on our account.'

But she saw at once that he was very much a foreigner, and that he was at a disadvantage, not knowing if he had not perhaps made a gaffe. 'I have perhaps intruded?' he said, miserably.

'Oh, not at all,' cried Mary, and he was so serious she had to laugh.

The laugh was another mistake though. His face took on a look of despair that could come upon a foreigner, it seemed, at the slightest provocation, as if suddenly everything was obscure to him – everything.

'Please,' she murmured, and then vaguely, 'your work,' meaning that she did not wish to interrupt his sketching.

'Ah, you know my work?' he said, brightening immediately, pleased and with a small and quite endearing vanity. 'We have met before? Yes?'

'Oh no, we haven't met,' she said, quickly, and she sat down, but of course after that it was impossible to go on acting as if he were a complete stranger. She turned to see what Maudie would make of the situation. It was then she felt the full force of her irritation with Maudie. She could have given her a slap in the face. Yes: a slap right in the face! For there she sat, remotely, her face indeed partly averted from them.

Maudie was waiting to be introduced! To be *introduced*, as if she, Mary, did not need any conventional preliminaries. As if it was all right that she, Mary, should begin an unprefaced conversation with a strange man in a café because – and of course that was what was so infuriating, that she knew Maudie's unconscious thought – it was all right for a woman of *her* age to strike up a conversation like that, but that it wouldn't have done for a young woman. Yet, on her still partly averted face, Mary could see the quickened look of interest. She had a good mind not to make any gesture to draw her into the conversation at all, but she had the young man to consider. She had to bring them together whether she liked it or not.

'Maudie, this is – ' She turned back and smiled at van Stiegler. 'This is – ' But she was confused and she had to abandon the introduction altogether. Instead, she broke into a direct question.

'Those are your flower pictures, aren't they?' she asked.

It was enough for Maudie – more than enough, you might say.

She turned to the young man, obviously greatly impressed; her lips apart, her eyes shining. My God, how attractive she was!

'Oh no, not really?' she cried. 'How marvellous of you!'

But Johann van Stiegler was looking at Mary.

'You are sure we have not met before?'

'Oh no, but you were scribbling your signature all over that newspaper,' she looked around to show it to him, but it had fallen on to the floor.

'Ah yes,' he said, and – she couldn't be certain, of course – she thought he was disappointed.

'Ah yes, you saw my signature,' he said, flatly. He looked dejected. Mary felt helpless. She turned to Maudie. It was up to her to say something now.

Just then the little warehouse bell tinkled again, and this time it was one of the proprietors who came in, casually, like a client.

'Ah, good!' said van Stiegler. 'Coffee,' he called out. Then he turned to Mary. 'Coffee for you, too?'

'Oh yes, coffee for us,' said Mary, but she couldn't help wondering who was going to pay for it, and simultaneously she couldn't help noticing the shabbiness of his jacket. Well – they'd see! Meanwhile, she determined to ignore the plate of cakes that was put down with the coffee. And she hoped Maudie would too. She pushed the plate aside as a kind of hint to her, but Maudie leaned across and took a large bun filled with cream.

'Do you mind my asking you something – about your work – ?' said Mary.

But Maudie interrupted.

'You are living in Ireland? I mean, you are not just here on a visit?'

There was intimacy and intimacy, and Mary felt nervous in case the young man might resent this question.

'I teach art in a college here,' he said, and he did seem a little surprised, but Mary could see, too, that he was not at all displeased. He seemed to settle more comfortably into the conversation.

'It is very good for a while to go to another country,' he said, 'and this country is cheap. I have a flat in the next street to here, and it is very private. If I hang myself from the ceiling, it is all right – nobody knows; nobody cares. That is a good way to live when you paint.'

Mary was prepared to ponder. 'Do you think so?'

Maudie was not prepared to ponder. 'How odd,' she said, shortly, and then she looked at her watch. 'I'll have to go,' she said inexplicably.

They had finished the coffee. Immediately Mary's thoughts returned to the problem of who was to pay for it. It was a small affair for which to call up all one's spiritual resources, but she felt enormously courageous and determined when she heard herself ask in a loud voice for her bill.

'My bill, please,' she called out, over the sound of spitting coffee on the gas stove.

Johann van Stiegler made no move to ask for his bill, and yet he was buttoning his jacket and folding his newspaper as if to leave too. Would his coffee go on her bill? Mary wondered.

It was all settled, however, in a second. The bill was for two eight-penny coffees, and one bun, and there was no charge for van Stiegler's coffee. He had some understanding with the owners, she supposed. Or perhaps he was not really going to leave then at all?

As they stood up, however, gloved and ready to depart, the young man bowed.

'Perhaps we go the same way?' They could see he was anxious to be polite.

'Oh, not at all,' they said together, as if he had offered to escort them, and Maudie even laughed openly.

Then there was, of course, another ridiculous situation. Van Stiegler sat down again. Had they been too brusque? Had they hurt his feelings?

Oh, if only he wasn't a foreigner, thought Mary, and she hesitated. Maudie already had her hand on the door.

'I hope I will see some more of your work sometime,' said Mary. It was not a question, merely a compliment.

But van Stiegler sprang to his feet again.

'Tonight after my classes I am bringing another picture to hang here,' he said. 'You would like to see it? I would be here – ' He pulled out a large, old-fashioned watch. 'At ten minutes past nine.'

'Oh, not tonight – I couldn't come back tonight,' said Mary. 'I live in the country, you see,' she said, explaining and excusing herself. 'Another time perhaps? It will be here for how long?'

She wasn't really listening to what he said. She was thinking that he had not asked if Maudie could come. Perhaps it was that, of the two of them, she looked the most likely to buy a picture, whereas Maudie, although in actual fact more likely to do so, looked less so. Or was it that he coupled them so that he thought if one came, both came? Or was it really Maudie he'd like to see again, and that he regarded her as a chaperone? Or was it – ?

There was no knowing, however, and so she said goodbye again, and the next minute the little bell had tinkled over the door and they were in the street. In the street they looked at each other.

'Well! If ever there was – ' began Maudie, but she didn't get time to finish her sentence. Behind them the little bell tinkled yet again, and their painter was out in the street with them.

'I forgot to give you the address of my flat – it is also my studio,' he said. 'I would be glad to show you my paintings at any time.' He pulled out a notebook and tore out a sheet. 'I will write it down,' he said, concisely. And he did. But when he went to hand it to them, it was Maudie who took it. 'I am nearly always there, except when I am at my classes,' he said. And bowing, he turned and went back into the café.

They dared not laugh until they had walked some distance away, until they turned into the next street, in fact.

'Well, I never!' said Maudie, and she handed the paper to Mary.

'Chatham Row,' Mary read, 'number eight.'

'Will you go to see them?' asked Maudie.

Mary felt outraged.

'What do you take me for?' she asked. 'I may be a bit unconventional, but can you see me presenting myself at his place? Would *you* go?'

'Oh, it's different for me,' said Maudie, enigmatically. 'And anyway, it was you he asked. But I see your point – it's a pity. Poor fellow! He must be very lonely. I wish there was something we could do for him – someone to whom we could introduce him.'

Mary looked at her. It had never occurred to her that he might be lonely! How was it that the obvious always escaped her?

They were in Grafton Street by this time.

'Well, I have some shopping to do. I suppose it's the same with you,' said Maudie. 'I am glad I had that talk with you. We must have another chat soon.'

'Oh yes,' said Mary, over-readily, replying to her adieux though, and not to the suggestion of their meeting again! She was anxious all at once to be rid of Maudie.

And yet, as she watched her walk away from her, making her passage quickly and expertly through the crowds in the street, Mary felt a sudden terrible aimlessness descend upon herself like a physical paralysis. She walked along, pausing to look in at the shop windows.

It was the evening hour when everyone in the streets was hurrying home, purposeful and intent. Even those who paused to look into the shop windows did so with direction and aim, darting their bright glances keenly, like birds. Their minds were all intent upon substantives; tangibles, while her mind was straying back to the student café, and the strange flower pictures on the walls; to the young man who was so vulnerable in his vanity: the legitimate vanity of his art.

It was so like Maudie to laugh at him. What did she know of an artist's mind? If Maudie had not been with her, it would have been so different. She might, for one thing, have got him to talk about his work, to explain the discrepancy between the loose style of the pictures on the wall and the exact, small sketches he'd been drawing on the margins of the paper.

She might even have taken up his invitation to go and see his paintings. Why had that seemed so unconventional – so laughable? Because of Maudie, that was why.

How ridiculous their scruples would have seemed to the young man. She could only hope he had not guessed them. She looked up at a clock. Supposing, right now, she were to slip back to the café and suggest that after all she found she would have time for a quick visit to his studio? Or would he have left the café? Better perhaps to call around to the studio? He would surely be back there now!

For a moment she stood debating the arguments for and against going back. Would it seem odd to him? Would he be surprised? But as if it were Maudie who put the questions, she frowned them down and all at once purposeful as anyone in the street, began to go back, headlong, you might say, towards Chatham Street.

At the point where two small streets crossed each other she had to pause, while a team of Guinness's dray horses turned with difficulty in the narrow cube of the intersection. And, while she waited impatiently, she caught sight of herself in the gilded mirror of a public house. For a second, the familiar sight gave her a misgiving of her mission, but as the dray horses moved out of the way, she told herself that her dowdy, lumpish, and unromantic figure vouched for her spiritual integrity. She pulled herself away from the face in the glass and hurried across the street.

Between two lock-up shops, down a short alley – roofed by the second storey of the premises overhead, till it was like a tunnel – was his door. Away at the end of the tunnel the door could clearly be seen even from the middle of the street, for it was painted bright yellow. Odd that she had never seen it in the times she had passed that way. She crossed the street.

Once across the street, she ran down the tunnel, her footsteps echoing loud in her ears. And there on the door, tied to the latchet of the letter box, was a piece of white cardboard with his name on it. Grabbing the knocker, she gave three clear hammer strokes on the door.

The little alley was a sort of cul-de-sac; except for the street behind her and the door in front of her, it had no outlet. There was not even a skylight or an aperture of any kind. As for the premises into which the door led, there was no way of telling its size or its extent, or anything at all about it, until the door was opened.

Irresponsibly, she giggled. It was like the mystifying doors in the trunks of trees that beguiled her as a child in fairy tales and fantasies. Did this door, too, like those fairy doors, lead into rooms of impossible amplitude, or would it be a cramped and poky place?

As she pondered upon what was within, seemingly so mysteriously sealed, she saw that – just as in a fairy tale – after all there was an aperture. The letter box had lost its shutter, or lid, and it gaped open, a vacant hole in the wood, reminding her of a sleeping doll whose eyeballs had been poked back in its head, and creating an expression of vacancy and emptiness.

Impulsively, going down on one knee, she peered in through the slit.

At first she could see only segments of the objects within, but by moving her head, she was able to identify things: an unfinished canvas up against the splattered white wainscot, a bicycle pump flat on the floor, the leg of a table, black iron bed legs, and, to her amusement, dangling down by the leg of the table, dripping their moisture in a pool on the floor, a pair of elongated grey wool socks. It was, of course, only possible to see the lower portion of the room, but it seemed enough to infer conclusively that this was indeed a little room in a tree, no bigger than the bulk of the outer trunk, leading nowhere, and – sufficient or no – itself its own end.

There was just one break in the wainscot, where a door ran down to the floor, but this was so narrow and made of roughly jointed boards that she took it to be the door of a press. And then, as she started moving, she saw something else, an intricate segment of fine wire spokes. It was a second before she realised it was the wheel of a bicycle.

So, a bicycle, too, lived here, in this little room in a tree trunk!

Oh, poor young man, poor painter: poor foreigner, inept at finding the good lodgings in a strange city. Her heart went out to him.

It was just then that the boarded door – it couldn't have been a press after all – opened into the room, and she found herself staring at two feet. They were large feet, shoved into unlaced shoes, and they were bare to the white ankles. For, of course, she thought wildly, focusing her thoughts, his socks are washed! But her power to think clearly only lasted an instant. She sprang to her feet.

'Who iss that?' asked a voice. 'Did someone knock?'

It was the voice of the man in the café. But where was she to find a voice with which to reply? And who was she to say what she was? Who – to this stranger – was she?

And if he opened the door, what then? All the thoughts and words that had, like a wind, blown her down this tunnel, subsided suddenly, and she stood, appalled, at where they had brought her.

'Who iss that?' came the voice within, troubled.

Staring at those white feet, thrust into the unlaced shoes, she felt that she would die on the spot if they moved an inch. She turned.

Ahead of her, bright, shining, and clear, as if it were at the end of a powerful telescope, was the street. Not caring if her feet were heard, volleying and echoing as if she ran through a mighty drainpipe, she kept running till she reached the street, kept running even then, jostling surprised shoppers, hitting her ankles off the wheel knobs of pushcars and prams. Only when she came to the junction of the streets again, did she stop, as in the pub mirror she caught sight again of her familiar face. That face steadied her. How absurd to think that anyone would sinisterly follow this middle-aged woman?

But suppose he had been in the outer room when she knocked! If he had opened the door? What would have happened then? What would she have said? A flush spread over her face. The only true words that she could have uttered were those that had sunk into her mind in the café; put there by Maudie.

'I'm lonely!' That was all she could have said. 'I'm lonely. Are you?'

A deep shame came over her with this admission and, guiltily, she began to walk quickly onward again, towards Grafton Street. If anyone had seen her, there in that dark alleyway! If anyone could have looked into her mind, her heart!

And yet, was it so unnatural? Was it so hard to understand? So unforgivable?

As she passed the open door of the Carmelite Church she paused. Could she rid herself of her feeling of shame in the dark of the confessional? To the sin-accustomed ears of the wise old fathers her story would be lightweight; a tedious tale of scrupulosity. Was there no one, no one who'd understand?

She had reached Grafton Street once more, and stepped into its crowded thoroughfare. It was only a few minutes since she left it, but in the street the evasion of light had begun. Only the bustle of people, and the activity of traffic, made it seem that it was yet day. Away at the top of the street, in Stephen's Green, to which she turned, although the tops of the trees were still clear, branch for branch, in the last of the light, mist muted the outline of the bushes. If one were to put a hand between the railings now, it would be with a slight shock that the fingers would feel the little branches, like fine bones, under the feathers of mist. And in their secret nests the smaller birds were making faint avowals in the last of the day. It was the time at which she used to meet Richard.

'Oh, Richard!' she cried, almost out loud, as she walked along by the railings to where the car was parked. 'Oh, Richard! It's you I want.'

And as she cried out, her mind presented him to her, as she so often saw him, coming towards her: tall, handsome, and with his curious air of apartness from those around him. He had his hat in his hand, down by his side, as on a summer day he might trail a hand in water from the side of a boat. She wanted to preserve that picture of him for ever in an image, and only as she struggled to hold on to it did she realise there was no urgency in the search. She had a sense of having all the time in the world to look and look and look at him. That was the very way he used to come to meet her – indolently trailing the old felt hat, glad to be done with the day; and when they got nearer to each other she used to take such joy in his unsmiling face, with its happiness integral to it in all its features. It was the first time in the two years he'd been gone from her that she'd seen his face.

Not till she had taken out the key of the car, and gone straight around to the driver's side, not stupidly, as so often, to the passenger seat – not till then did she realise what she had achieved. Yet she had no more than got back her rights. No more. It was not a subject for amazement. By what means exactly had she got them back though – in that little café? That was the wonder.

ASIGH

ONLY ONCE IN ALL THE YEARS DID HE SAY ANYTHING ABOUT IT, AND that was a few days before he died. He was lying so still she thought he was asleep, but his eyes were open and staring at the rags on her leg.

'Does it trouble you much?' he asked. That was all, but her fear of him flared up as fierce as the day he struck her. And ill though he was, helpless – dying – she wanted to tell a lie and say it didn't trouble her at all. Perhaps she felt that to exonerate him might have freed him from the guilt that smouldered behind his terrible eyes. But the saturated rags wrapped round her leg would show up the lie.

'Only a bit, Father,' she said. 'Not much.'

'It was the brass buckle did it,' he said, speaking as if it were only yesterday. It was sort of an apology. She knew that. But not for his action! No! Never for that! Only for its unfortunate outcome. 'There must have been verdigris on that buckle,' he said. 'And verdigris is poison. If your mother was alive she'd have put something on the cut to take the poison out of it.' He kept looking at her leg, and feeling awkward she moved away. She was going out of the room, when he rapped on the table by his bed. 'Why didn't you know it was poison?' he said. 'Well, you know it now!'

Then, as unexpectedly as he had opened them, he closed his eyes again, and whatever need had made him break the silence of a lifetime must at last have been satisfied because he was asleep almost at once. She went back and stood looking down at him. He was in one of the heavy, unnatural sleeps that of late came down so often upon him. Soon sleep would close in upon his consciousness altogether. He couldn't last much longer. It would be all over then, the long imprisonment of her life with him. But she took no pleasure in the thought. Her brother, Tom, was as much to be pitied, or more, and he never complained. Lately the thought of her father's death passed through her mind with greater and greater frequency. Now, to banish it, she looked out at the fields that washed up almost to the hall door.

Closed in by summer, the fields were deeper and lonelier than ever, and the laneway that led out to the road was narrowed by overhanging briars and the wild summer growth of bank and ditch. Away in a far field down by the river her brother was scything weeds. He was cutting away with an easy rhythmical movement. As she watched he stopped to put a new edge on the blade, and when he reached down for the whetstone she was startled to see how stiff and awkward he was. The man on the bed was suppler than him! A feeling of pity for Tom's dried and wasted years assailed her, but her leg had begun to throb again. It may have been that her father's words had wakened the pain. She put her hand to it. The pain was so bad it might have been the moment it happened, when he'd come upon her suddenly in the churchyard, talking with one of his own workmen, and in the sight of all the other stragglers, raised the head-collar in the air and swung it over her. Sparkling like a star in the day sky the buckle had held her eyes for an instant before it darkened down upon her.

She'd fallen with the pain. And as she fell, she saw Jake take to his heels across the slabstones. But her father didn't give him a glance.

'Get up!' he'd said to her. 'Get up!' And as if she was a beast that had fallen, he struck her again to rise her. Not that he was a man who ever ill-treated a beast. Nor for that matter had he ever before objected to her having a word with a man. Indeed, he used to give her a coarse encouragement.

'You'd better watch your step in that jacket, girl,' he'd say of an evening when she was going out for a walk, even when she was too young to know what he meant. She often thought there might have been a queer meaning in his words, but if so she didn't want to uncover it. Indeed she used to laugh and run outdoors. And as for some of the dresses he bought her in the town when he'd go to the fair, the neighbours' tongues used to clack at them.

'It's easily seen you have no mother, you poor child.' That was said to her more than once when her father had decked her out as fancily on plain ordinary days of the week as if it was a Sunday or a holy day. She couldn't play in the kind of dresses he bought her. Maybe that was how she got into the habit of standing about drawing looks from the boys in the schoolyard, and later, bolder looks from their own workmen, particularly Jake. It was behind her father's back for the most part that she got those looks – especially from Jake, but her father knew about them and he never seemed to mind. She used to think he put some construction of his own on them, that they were a measure of something in his mind.

In her own mind that was all they were too, a measure of her attraction. Obscurely she knew, even then, that nature made use of small affinities to prepare the heart for the final, the fatal, the immortal affinity of love.

One day, a week before she was seventeen, when a spanking back-to-back trap drove into the yard, she was drawn to the doorway by something more compelling than curiosity.

'The name is Mallon – Tod Mallon,' the owner of the trap said, jumping down and going to meet her father, who'd come out of the cowshed at the sound of the wheels rattling over the cobbles. She stayed where she was, standing at the yard door. But Mallon had seen her. And if she knew in that instant what she had been waiting for, there was a look in his eyes that made her feel that he, too, had come to the end of some kind of waiting. In his case, though, it had been a longer wait than hers, he being a mature man. She heard him announce to her father that he had just bought the farm next to them. It was as big a farm as their own.

'Both divisions,' he said proudly, 'and it's the best of land. But it was overstocked at the back end of the year, and I'll be short of hay. I'm told you have a field of second-crop meadow for sale on foot?'

'The hay will be for sale all right,' her father said slowly, 'but I was thinking of making it up myself.' His shrewd eyes were trying to sum up the stranger, but afterwards she knew it was for other reasons than she'd thought at the time. In his mind her father had paired them up, herself and Mallon in that first moment. Because her father, too, had been waiting – waiting for someone like Tod to come along as a husband for her.

Of course at that time all was looks. In the silent fields living close to the mute beasts, there was more meaning to be got out of looks and glances than there was for people in the towns. She used to think sometimes that for people like them – her, and her father and Tod – words only ran alongside looks like the song of the stream runs alongside the meaningful ripples. All the same there were times when words had their full potency, and never more than when men were making a deal.

'Will you give me the first refusal one way or another?' Mallon asked.

'Would you like to have a deal here and now?'

'That depends on what you're asking,' Mallon said.

'How much is the worth of it?' her father asked.

The two men had moved across the yard towards where a gate led into the meadow. Her father leant back against the gate, facing away from it, for he knew every blade of grass that was in it; but Tod Mallon leant forward and looked deep into the grass that swelled like a sea, and was as green as the sea, with not a blotch of blossom marring it, from mearing to mearing, but only darker clots of green where cow pads had coarsened the growth. And she, standing to one side of the men, could see how Mallon coveted the rich grass, and how he coveted the skill that had brought a crop like it out of their light, gravelly land. But above all, she saw how his eyes took pleasure in its rippling waves.

Then the bargaining broke out again involuntarily.

'Well, what is it worth?' her father asked.

'To me? Or to you?'

'What's the differ?' Her father seemed surprised.

'Oh, there's a big difference,' said Mr Mallon. 'And what's more, I'd say you're a man that sets a steep value on anything you have to offer.'

Her father laughed. And seeing she had come up to them, he flung his arm around her waist, like he might have done perhaps with her mother when he was early married to her.

'I can afford to ask a nice price,' he said. 'I never put anything on the market that I'm ashamed to stand behind!'

Mr Mallon looked for a minute into her father's eyes, and then he looked into hers, and again like when he first rode into the yard she felt a fated weight in the moment, and knew that it wasn't altogether about the meadow grass the men were talking, either of them. It was no longer the olden times, when marriages were arranged. Now such carry-on was laughed at and mocked, but her father and Mallon were making a match for her all the same. There and then.

And she wanted it that way! Yes. And her heart was so filled with joy that when just then, high up in the blue sky, out of sight, a lark began to trill, it seemed as if it was her heart singing out for all to hear. She looked at Tod Mallon. And he looked at her.

'Well, I'm a man that's willing to pay a good price for a thing if it's true to its worth,' he said. He turned back to her father. 'But there's no hurry, I suppose,' he said, and he nodded at the grass. 'It can be let go a while longer, wouldn't you say?'

'Oh, a good while longer,' her father said, as if glad he could be prodigal with something. 'Take your time. You'll have the first refusal anyway, I promise you that!'

They shook hands then, with a strong manly clasp of their hands that dipped them forward and downward as if they were two middle-sized men, instead of the tall men they both were. Tod Mallon straightened up first.

'Goodbye, sir,' he said to her father.

'Goodbye, miss!' he said to her. No more. The next minute he was in the trap and spanking down the road. She and her father stayed looking after him for as long as they could see the tip of his whip over the road hedge.

'Well, that's that!' her father said then. He was in great spirits. As they moved back into the middle of the yard and met Jake coming against them he was almost gloating. 'I told you that was the best bit of meadow in the countryside.'

'Did he make an offer?' Jake asked dourly.

'No,' said her father, 'but I put out a feeler and I'm well satisfied.'

But when her father went into the cowshed Jake looked at her queerly.

'What did you think of the fine Mr Mallon? He'll be looking for more than the meadow before long, I'd say!'

'I don't know what you mean.'

Jake only sneered. 'Oh, not you!' he said.

She walked away from him and went back towards the gate leading into the meadow. Leaning over the gate she remembered the covetous look in Mr Mallon's eyes. Her own eyes seemed to see the field for the first time. Was I blind before? she thought wonderingly. Then she went after her father into the cowshed.

'Well, girl?' he said gaily, when she came up to him in the semi-darkness that was slatted with light from the loosely jointed boards.

In the weeks that followed she got on better with her father than ever before. And even poor Tom didn't seem to rub him up the wrong way either, or at least not as often as he usually did.

'What has him in such good form these days?' Tom asked her with a puzzled look on his face.

'I don't know,' she lied, but later that evening she returned to the subject. 'Tom,' she said impulsively, 'why don't you take courage while he's in good humour and tell him about you and Flossie?'

Because, cautious and all as Tom was, she knew he and Flossie Sauran were meeting oftener and oftener after dark in the evenings and on Sunday afternoons. If her father knew he'd flay him. Tom got no encouragement at all in that line. She didn't know why their father made this difference between her brother and herself, unless it was that he identified something of himself in her and not in Tom. One day, when she was in town with him, they met a cattle dealer who told her he knew her when she was only a sparkle in her father's eyes. Her father was delighted.

'She has the same sparkle in her eye, I can tell you!' he said meaningfully.

There was very little sparkle in Tom's eye. All the same she couldn't see why he was so covert about his meetings with Flossie.

'He can't kill you, Tom!' she said. 'Why don't you tell him! He might think the more of you for it. Tell him!'

But Tom was terrified of him.

'Take care would he hear you!' he said, looking over his shoulder nervously, although at the time their father was out in the fields counting the cattle.

'He'll have to know sometime!' she said, but lightly, because already her mind was running ahead to the time when she herself would be married. She'd have some authority over her father then, and she'd talk to him about Tom; straight talk too. And she'd ask Flossie to her house, and let her and Tom meet openly and naturally. Tod might put in a word for them, then, too.

For Tod Mallon had come again. He'd bought the meadow. And he'd called after that again to bargain for the after-grass.

'That fellow means business,' her father said, making no disguise now about his meaning. He pulled her hair affectionately. 'After-grass indeed! No beast could want for after-grass that has the sweet pickings Mallon's can get any day down between the flaggers in his own river field. Mark my words, if he takes our after-grass, there's more in his mind than he's declared!'

As if she didn't know! The old collie in the yard knew! He had given up barking at Tod, and he a cross dog that barked at people going past the house every day of their lives.

She would of course have liked Mallon to show his hand more

plainly, and to her instead of only to her father. She was unsettled. Most of the day she hung about the yard or stood at the door to see if there might be a trap coming up the road, with the tip of a whip showing over the hedge. She was happy all the same, and it was good to look out over the fields. How sweet must be the moment when feelings roused by such beauty could be shared with another soul? She was only impatient for the moment of sharing to come. And it was slow in coming.

For one thing Tod never came to the house unless he had business with her father. She would have begun to think there was nothing at all between her and him if it weren't for Jake. Since Mallon appeared on the scene Jake had got bolder because he felt that now he would be playing safe. More than ever her flirting with him was only a whiling away of the long, tedious summer evenings.

But her father seemed to take a different view of things, and several times now when she and Jake met at the pump in the yard, or when Jake came to the kitchen door to get the pig mash, she'd seen her father glaring at him. But she no more feared her father than she feared the feints of Jake, because she felt wiser and more knowing than either of them. For all the fears the farmers had of their daughters getting mixed up with a labouring man, those fears were nothing to the fears the fellows themselves had of making trouble between them and the men that gave them their hire. Oh, she knew Jake! She knew him better than her father knew him.

If only her father had known, that day in the churchyard, that it was talking about Mallon she and Jake were!

She had come out from the service, and was going through the churchyard, down the grass path to the stile that led into their own fields, when she'd seen Jake standing under the old yew trees that vaulted the path. He was going back to the yard to rinse the milk cans, a job that was often left till after church on Sunday. And when he saw her he waited.

'I suppose you'll be going home the other way one of these days,' he said, and he nodded towards the path that led out to the road. And she knew Tod must have been somewhere in sight. She'd seen him in the church, but he'd left before her, and although that was why she had hurried out she hadn't seen him anywhere. She hadn't wanted to stare around too obviously. She was so glad to see Jake, because it gave her an excuse for lingering a bit, and while she was talking to him she was looking back casually over her shoulder. It wouldn't matter if Tod saw her as long as she was talking to someone. It might provoke him. Jake was only a workman, but he was a fine-looking man, and young blood didn't make the same distinctions as old blood.

Jake wasn't one for hanging back though. He wanted to get his work done; he was going to a football match after his dinner.

'Are you coming?' he said.

'What's the hurry?' she said, stealing another backward glance as she spoke. Tod was still in the churchyard. He was standing at the gate talking to an old woman from a cottage near him, who did a bit of baking for him and washed his shirts. He was facing her way, but she couldn't be sure if he'd seen her or not. 'What's the hurry, Jake?' she repeated absently.

But Jake gave her arm a pull, and his voice was rough. 'I know what's in your mind,' he said. 'Be careful. You're not going to make a teaser out of me!'

She turned to laugh at him, but there was a look in his eyes that made her restless. If only she could bring that look into the eyes of the other one!

That was the moment her father came over the stile.

Her first feeling when she saw him was only simple surprise. She thought he was far away in the upland pasture putting a head collar on a mare, to bring her down to the home fields. What had brought him back? What had brought him here?

The next minute he raised the head collar.

'Don't!' she screamed, when she realised why he'd swung the strap, and she saw the buckle glittering in the air. 'We were only talking, Father,' she screamed.

For one instant it seemed that he had stayed the buckle in mid-air, and she saw by his eyes that her father did, in that moment, believe her. But she knew him. Her innocence would not save her. He must have glimpsed her from the fields, and thought it was with Tod Mallon she was dallying. When he'd seen it was not Mallon, but Jake, he'd been bitterly disappointed. It was for his disappointment she would suffer.

To this day, she wasn't sure if he'd missed or not with his first lash at her. She fell on the ground all right, but she could have flung herself down cowering, cowering before the blow.

'Father, Father! Do you want to make a show of me before everyone?'

It was the wrong thing to say. He threw a glance beyond her to where the few people who were still standing around the church gate had drawn together astonished, not knowing what to do. And among them, rooted to the ground with astonishment, was Tod.

Then, before her father swung the head collar again, she covered her face and chest. He would strike her now for sure. He was in the wrong, but it was she who'd put him in the wrong, and he'd strike her for it. Mortified at what he had done, and unable to undo it, he would put himself altogether beyond the comprehension of gapers and gossipers, by hitting her again.

It was the second blow did the harm. It fell on her leg and tore open the skin. Yet at the time she hadn't felt any bitterness. If anything, it was pity for her father himself that she felt, pity for the damage that, through her, he had done to his own secret vanities and ambitions. But of course, then, no one knew, neither her father, nor herself, nor Tod, nor anyone, that the cut was going to fester and fail to heal.

In the days that followed, her father must often have felt guilty.

She'd caught him slyly looking at her at times, and about a week afterwards – it must have been the next Sunday – when she was getting ready to go out to church he shouted at her.

'Take off that stocking!' he said. 'Do you want to get dye into the cut and destroy yourself altogether!'

She took off the stocking. Her leg was throbbing and she wasn't sorry to stay at home that day. After a few weeks tied to the house though, it was a different matter. And one lovely evening – such a lovely evening – she decided to take a walk if it was only a little limp of a one.

Her father was in the yard when she opened the door.

'A person would think you'd want to hide your shame, instead of going out to show it off!'

Tears rushed into her eyes. How could he speak to her like that? Him who did it? How could he? She had a lot to learn. She didn't know then of all the years that lay ahead when it would have been a relief if he sneered at her instead of her having to endure the terrible silence that came down with respect to her infirmity. Not only her father's silence, but Tom's. Not only the silence of those in the house with her, but of the whole parish. No one ever spoke directly of it to her. Except Tod. He always asked about it, right from the start.

The first night, after it happened, he'd come straight up to the house to ask openly about it. Her father was out, and Tom and she were in the kitchen.

'It's Mallon!' Tom said when he saw him coming. 'You'd better not let him see you.' But she limped to the door.

'How are you?' Tod asked, and his eyes went at once to the rag she had tied around her leg. It was an old sheet torn up for the purpose.

'You saw what happened?'

'I only saw him strike you. I didn't see why he did it.'

'You saw all there was to see!' she flashed. 'I was only talking to Jake Hewett.'

He looked unbelievingly at her.

'A father would hardly strike his daughter for that!' he said, and his voice was harsh. But she was hardly going to bother to clear herself, such a feeling of joy went through her at that harsh note in his voice. Now I know he cares, she thought. But she had to say something.

'Don't you believe me?' she said.

'I don't know,' he said. 'I don't know!' And with that he turned and went away, without a word to Tom, who had come out and was standing beside them like a fool while all this was going on.

'I thought he wanted to see Father?' Tom said, looking stupidly after Mallon as he drove out of the yard.

'Did you!' she cried, and she laughed. 'That's all you know!'

If it weren't for the ache in her leg she would have thought what happened was lucky and that it might be the cause of bringing things to a head. She went back to the kitchen and rolled down her stocking and looked at the cut. It might be a good thing to stoup it again, because it would want to heal quickly if she was to follow up whatever advantage she had gained.

But every time she cleaned out the cut, pus formed in it again. No matter how often she stouped it, no scab stuck to it for long enough to let it dry.

At last one day about six months after it happened, when her father and Tom were at the Three Day Fair of Ballinasloe, she got Jake to drive her in to the dispensary in the town, but she didn't put much stock on what the doctor told her.

Next morning when she and her brother were alone together for a minute in the kitchen, she asked Tom a question cautiously. 'Is an ulcer a bad thing, Tom?'

Tom was sharpening the scythe up against the kitchen table, and drawing the whetstone slowly along the blade, as if it was to get music out of it.

'In a beast, is it?' he asked absently.

'Man or beast,' she said weakly.

'They say it's bad,' he said. 'Why?'

'No why!' she said dejectedly.

Tod knew all about ulcers though.

'Is that leg no better?' he asked her irritably one day when he had come on some business with her father. 'Would it be ulcerating? Did you see a doctor about it? An ulcer can get incurable if it's neglected.'

His voice was cruel, but she knew what made it cruel, and she wouldn't have had it any other way.

'You believe me now, Tod, don't you?' she said softly. 'It was only because he was a working man that my father was annoyed with me for talking to him, and – '

'I know,' he said sharply, interrupting her. 'I believe you.' But there was a look on his face that made her heart go cold. It was a look she had seen once on Tom's face when they were children. He'd lost the new watch that their father had given him for his Confirmation. He'd looked for it all day on the fringe of the meadow, and in the matted grass of the headland. Then just as they were going to go home, she heard him draw a breath like a cry, and when she ran over to where he was standing in the middle of a plank that served as a footbridge across a ditch, she thought he was daft, because there was the watch on the bottom of the ditch, yet he had looked as if he was going to cry.

'But you've found it, Tom!' she'd said.

'I wish I hadn't,' he said, and looking again she saw the watch was under a foot of water and she understood then the look on his face.

That was the look on Tod's face. He wished he didn't believe her. Now that she was useless to him.

Because, by then she knew herself that her leg was never going to heal. It didn't come against her too much. She could work about the house and the inner yard, she could churn and bake, but she'd be no use for the heavier jobs of a farmer's wife, calf-rearing or pig-feeding or the like.

A fierce resentment went through her. That was country life for you! In the town it would have been different. But in the country, the only thing men thought about was breeding a family, and getting as much work out of a woman as a beast. But she regretted her bitterness when she remembered the first day Tod had driven across the cobbles, and their eyes had met. She knew she was doing him an injustice. He, too, would have welcomed a bit of romance in his life, only he wasn't prepared to have it at the cost of everything else.

He came less and less often to the house. Sometimes he didn't call for months, and always when he called he had a strict purpose. Now, though, instead of being glad, her father found it hard to be civil to him. The only chance she got to as much as see him was in church on Sundays. She used to sit behind him, on the other side of the aisle so she could look across slantways, without being seen, but he must have felt her eyes upon him, because after a time he took to standing at the back of the church. And always when the service was over he went out quickly and drove away. He had given up the trap. He was one of the first in the countryside to have a motor car. She hated that car. It seemed to take him still further out of her life. It would keep him eligible a long time in the eyes of the giddy young girls growing up around them, in spite of his ageing appearance and his solitary ways.

Tod was ageing fast. On the rare occasions when she met him she could see that. And her heart was stabbed with sadness for them both. But he never married – and in this her heart could still exult, and standing at the window sometimes looking into the fields, she was unable to stem the little false feelings of hope that stirred in her, above all in summertime, the time she first met him. Then, when the fields were rich and flowering, the hedges flecked with blossom, and when the scent of the clover sweetened the air, she used to argue with herself.

It ought to be enough, she'd tell herself, the beauty and the peace of it all. But it wasn't. It was meant to be shared.

And as the years wore on, and as her leg got a lot less painful and gave her less trouble, sometimes when she looked around her in the church, it seemed to her that the forced rest she had got from having to mind it had left her, in the end, a younger-looking woman than the women who were girls when she was a girl, and who were now worn out with child-bearing and the brutal work on the land.

Even Tod remarked on it one day in the town.

'You're looking well,' he said, and although it was a mild enough remark, she knew it meant she must be looking well indeed.

'I'm feeling well!' she said. And she laughed recklessly. 'I was thinking only the other Sunday that I'm wearing better than a lot of my neighbours.'

It was a flash of her old boldness, a boldness that had gone utterly from her spirit much less her tongue. But Tod turned aside abruptly.

'They had their strength when they needed it,' he said. Somehow she didn't feel humiliated or hurt. It showed he still cared, and it came into her mind that if she really knew – for certain – not just by hints and insinuations, but *for certain*, that he had loved her, and that that was why he never married – and never would – she would have been satisfied. He'd be hers in a kind of way, then, at least.

It might be too small a thing to satisfy most women, but it would satisfy her – or so she thought. But would she be able to keep such knowledge a secret? she wondered. If she didn't tell someone, just one person, wouldn't the truth be little better than her dreamings and imaginings? But who could she tell? Flossie Sauren was the only one who might come near to understanding.

Poor Flossie! She and Tom had never married either, so although Flossie and herself didn't meet often there was a bond between them. Not that she had much sympathy for Flossie, for it seemed to her that whereas she and Tod had been kept apart by inmost, unknowable causes hidden in the human heart – Tom and Flossie were unmarried only because they hadn't any spirit.

One evening she tried to goad Tom into doing something about Flossie even at that late date. It was again the eve of the Three Day Fair in Ballinasloe, and for the first time in their lives their father was not going. Tom was going on his own. He was in the kitchen blacking his shoes.

'He mustn't be feeling well if he's not going, Tom,' she said. 'Will you manage by yourself?' He would be buying springers, a knacky job.

When Tom didn't answer she saw how stupid she'd been. He was glad to be going alone. He looked younger and livelier than he'd done for a long time. He was excited too, almost queerly excited.

'You'd think you were going to a wedding,' she said.

She didn't often make jokes, but the look he gave her that evening cured her for good.

'What made you say that?' He stopped in the middle of blacking the shoe in his hand.

'Tom! Don't look at me like that!' she said. 'I was only thinking how well you looked. And anyway, I don't see what harm it was! By rights it ought to be a wedding – your own!' She ran over to him. 'Oh, Tom, I'm not standing in your way, am I? You know what I mean! If you're waiting for me to be gone out of here and the way clear for you to take in a wife, then you'll never marry. Because I'll never be gone. It's not my fault! You know that, don't you, Tom? But I wouldn't be in anyone's way. You can tell Flossie I'd be good to her. I would. I promise you!'

He'd started blacking the other shoe while she was saying this, but he left down the blacking brush and taking his foot off the chair he went to the window and pointed out towards the yard where their father could be seen clattering across the cobbles with the yard lamp, seeing everything was in order.

'What life would a woman have in this house with him?' Tom asked.

It was true.

'Here, let me do those shoes for you,' she said, in amendment for her insensitivity.

'They're done enough,' he said.

They were shining like laurel leaves. She couldn't help exclaiming. 'Aren't they very light-soled shoes for wearing to the fair?'

But oh, how touchy he was! She could have bitten out her tongue for noticing them.

'I want something besides hobnail boots to wear in the evenings in the lodging-house parlour, don't I?' he said.

'That's right, Tom,' she said weakly, thinking that when his father went with him it must have been very little Tom saw of the parlour. No doubt he'd always been sent off to bed like a gossoon, to be up at the first screech of daylight.

He'd be a new man if he was his own master, she thought. And, where she would have felt guilty thinking of gain to herself if anything happened to their father, it seemed different altogether to think of the gain to Tom.

How long will it be till he gets the place, she wondered? It seemed that their life would go on, day after day, for ever, as it had always done, until it was less of a duration than a kind of immediate successiveness: a kind of eternity.

'Ah well, he'll enjoy the fair anyway,' she thought. And next morning she felt happy for him as she watched him go off in the dawn. Maybe he'd have things to tell her when he came back.

She tried to imagine the lodging-house parlour. Would there be young women there, playing the piano to amuse the farmers and the dealers? It would be hard on poor Flossie if Tom were to put his eye on some young one, but somehow she couldn't think of him making advances to any woman, but only sitting down, pleased with being away from home, and proud of his shoes, shining like laurel leaves.

The whole three days of the fair he was in her mind continually and she tried hard not to be impatient for his return. Their father, too, was looking forward to his return home. The fair seemed to have gained in importance for their father by his being unable to go to it. He never quit reading the newspaper, noting the weights of the beasts and the prices they were making.

'I ought to have gone, no matter how I felt,' he said. 'He'll buy backward springers: that's what he'll do. He has no experience.'

Tom didn't buy backward springers. He bought none.

'They were going too dear,' he said, and she thought at the time he said it lamely.

'You didn't buy any beast at all?' she echoed.

She was nearly speechless with surprise.

Their father wasn't speechless though: far from it.

'Is it pay for four days' food and lodgings and nothing to show for it?' he shouted. 'God damn it, what kind of a fool are you?' He looked as if he might strike him. Then he sat down heavily on a chair behind him.

'Are you all right, Father?' she cried. 'Tom! Tom! There's something the matter with him! Quick! Hold him.'

There was something wrong. They got him to bed and sent for the doctor. He'd had a stroke.

She forgot about Tom and Flossie for a long time after that.

In seven years from that day their father never left the bed. When she did occasionally think about Tom and Flossie she didn't like to mention the matter again. It was linked in her mind with her unfortunate joke on the eve of the fair. And when once, after many years, she did mention it, Tom cut her short.

'I've had enough of that!' he said crossly.

She felt he, too, was thinking of the night before the fair, and he didn't want to be reminded of what she'd said. But a few minutes later he spoke of that night himself.

'I killed him!' he said.

'Nonsense,' she said. 'Anyway, he's far from dead,' she added.

Their father was not far from death though. It was the very next day he asked about her leg. And the day after that he was dead.

When their father was laid out and she sat beside the bed, she found herself pondering on the changes that would come. Already the house was filling with people. One by one the neighbours had congregated. It was almost like the way, one by one, cattle are drawn over to a part of a field where something unusual has happened, where a tree has fallen, or where one of themselves has been lamed and is unable to rise.

At first the voices were subdued, but as the house filled up, and the neighbouring women saw small things to be done, and set about doing them, there was more live air about the house than there had been for years. If there ever had!

It was like a breaking of ice. And as when the ice of winter is breaking, and the growth of spring is seen to have already started underneath, she felt within her a great expectancy. But expectancy of what? She didn't know. She did wonder, though, if Tod would come to the funeral.

He didn't come. He was the only one for miles around who stayed away from both the house and the cemetery.

'A nice neighbour, that fellow!' Tom said, when all was over and he and she were alone on the day after the burial.

'He never forgave Father,' she said.

Tom stood up abruptly. He was still in his best clothes, but he was restless, and didn't seem to have much fancy for sitting talking. Above all, he didn't seem to like the turn the talk had taken.

'I think I'll change my clothes,' he said.

She knew what that meant. He was going out with the old scythe to cut weeds. He's married to that old scythe, she thought, partly bitter, partly amused. And a few minutes later, when she heard steps in the yard, she thought it was him coming back for something he'd forgotten: the whetstone or the wrench.

But it was Tod.

'You didn't come to the funeral,' she said, for the sake of saying something. She didn't ask him in, but went out to him, and they both walked across the yard towards the gate leading into the meadow. It was summertime again.

'I never forgave him,' he said, leaning over the gate and looking down into the deep grass.

They were the words she had used only a moment before to Tom.

'For what he did to me?' she asked softly.

He looked straight at her face.

'And to me,' he said.

Like a lark in the sky – like when she was young – her heart sang out for joy. But under a hedge of the field in front of them, a corncrake made himself heard with a harsh sound, not like a song at all, more like the sound of the clappers at Tenebrae.

'He came between us: he spoiled everything for us.'

It was true, she thought. At last – at last – after all these years it was said. Not in the words of youth. Not in the way she would once have wanted to hear it – but in the only way it could be said now. She looked at him with pity.

He saw the look in her eyes, and he took a step nearer to her, but she moved back. Long ago she had condemned him for not knowing that love was enough, and for thinking only of breeding a family. Now, when the days of her fertility were over, she saw things in another light. Her heart was flooded with the old familiar feeling of hope in the future, but she realised at last that it wasn't from Tod any more that she looked for hope's fulfillment. It was too late. In the intensity of this realisation her mind fastened urgently on her brother. Tom! He was younger than her. And Flossie was younger still. There was time yet surely for them to be fruitful if they married!

I must talk to Tom again, she thought. It was no longer a vague romantic notion that animated her mind. Nor was it Flossie and Tom's satisfaction either that she looked for from their union. It isn't us that matter any more, she thought, Tod or me, or Tom or Flossie. It's those who come after us.

Looking past Tod, she let her eyes fill with the beauty of the field he had once bid for, the field that was again heavy with meadow. Oh, to stand leaning over that gate with a crowd of youngsters around her – or even one small creature, gripping her hand – oh, the joy of that!

Impatiently, she put out her hand.

'Thank you for coming, Tod,' she said, but when he looked as if he was going to say something else, she gathered her arms to her breast. 'I have to see Tom about something. I was going down to him when you came.'

He had to stand aside to let her pass, and when she did, he must have seen there was nothing for him to do but to go back out to where he had left his car on the road. Once she looked back at him, and she saw he was standing by the door of the car looking after her. She, too, stood for a minute looking at him, but it was taking leave of him she was, in that last backward look. Then she hurried on downward to the river.

Tom and Flossie would have to be married at once. At once. They mustn't be let wait any longer, not even in decency to the dead.

'Tom! Tom!' she called out as she drew near him. Already she had forgotten Tod Mallon. He was unimportant to her at last. 'I couldn't stay in the house, Tom,' she cried when she reached him. 'I had to come down to you. I know you hated talking about it the last time, but it's different now, isn't it?' She hesitated, but only for a minute. 'About you and Flossie, I mean?'

He had stopped scything when she first spoke, but when he took in her words, he assumed the stiffness of a stranger. Then deliberately, and without answering her, he began again to pull the scythe heavily through the reeds.

She tried to take his silence for attentiveness.

'You'll have to wait a little while, I know that,' she said apologetically, 'but we could have everything planned.' Her excitement rushed back and overwhelmed her. She didn't notice the pronoun she had used. 'We could talk it over with Flossie, and begin to get things ready for the wedding without anybody knowing. With me in the know, she could come up here, and she and I could both be getting the house in order. We could – '

Tom stopped scything again, but he took up the whetstone and drew it across the blade. Then he looked coldly at her.

'Take it easy,' he said. 'Take it easy, will you!'

'Oh, but Tom! How can you say that? After all the years that have been wasted. Time is so precious now – for both of you.'

But her eagerness seemed to annoy him.

'Didn't you hear me telling you to take it easy!' he said. 'For God's sake! Death always brings changes, but there's no hurry. There is no hurry, I tell you,' he repeated, and this time he said it so positively and so meaningfully she felt perhaps there was more to him, that he was perhaps deeper than she had ever known.

'It wouldn't be the same as long ago,' she said less confidently, 'but surely it would be – '

'Better than nothing? Is that what you mean?' His voice was so bitter she began to get frightened.

'No,' she said, standing firm all the same, 'that's not what I mean. But wouldn't you like to have a family growing up around you, Tom? Wouldn't any man?'

When he seemed to ponder this thought for a moment, her hopes rose, but the next minute he looked her full in the face with a strange expression.

'I'll have no family,' he said shortly. 'I can tell you that now.'

'How do you know?' she cried. 'You never can tell. I – '

He put out his hand then and caught her by the arm, and his grip was so fierce she nearly fainted.

'How do I know? How does any man know? My father thought I was a gom. I put up with that, but I didn't know you took me for one too? I may have been afraid of him – afraid to face up to him openly – but that didn't say I let him own me body and soul. When I said we'd have no family I meant what I said. Don't look so stupid! You know what I mean!' She didn't, but as she struggled to understand, he sneered. 'Oh, it's not what you think now either,' he said. 'It was all respectable and as it ought to be, or as near as we could make it to what it ought to be. We're properly married and all that, but it's not the great cause for rejoicing that you seem to think it. Not in the way you mean anyway. If we were going to have a child we'd have had one long ago.'

She stared at him as if he was a stranger. She said nothing for a minute. She was only beginning to understand. If they'd had a child he'd have had to tell his father, she thought, and he was glad he hadn't had to face up to it.

They were standing near an old thorn tree, and she sank back against it weakly. She was utterly confounded by what he had told her. Looking at him, she could see he felt bad for her. He probably didn't know what injury he had done her, but she could see he wanted to make amends.

'I was going to tell you a couple of times,' he said, 'but I thought it was safer for your own sake not to be wise to it. And then as the years went by – '

She looked up quickly. 'Years? How many years?'

'Oh, I don't know,' he said indifferently. Then he made an effort. 'Before Father got ill, of course! Nine or ten years I'd say, and about six or seven since we got married. As a matter of fact I thought you had got wind of our plans the night before the wedding. It was the night I was supposed to be going to Ballinasloe to the fair.' Suddenly he put his hand up to his forehead in a mild distress. 'You remember when I came back I told him I didn't buy the springers – and he flew into a rage – it brought on that first stroke he got. I used to think for a long time that it was my fault he was stricken. Because I wasn't at the fair at all. I didn't go near Ballinasloe. Flossie met me in the town and we went up to Dublin and got married.'

It all came back to her. The thin shoes she thought he was polishing for the lodging-house parlour! She'd thought him odd that night: she remembered it well. So that was what he'd been up to! She looked at him. She never thought he would have had it in him.

Seeing the surprise on her face, her brother may have felt a momentary flash of the liveliness and spirit that had led to his one solitary escapade, but no doubt it died away, at the thought of the long unproductive years that were ushered in by that brief bravado.

'Well, that's the way things are,' he said matter-of-factly. 'You see what I mean when I say there's no hurry. There'll have to be changes, I realise that — but I don't know yet what they'll be. I doubt if Flossie will want to come to live here in the fields now, being used for so long to living near the road. It's lonely in there, you know. I might go down and live in her place if her sister went to Dublin, and there's some talk of that. It might work out. Their place is small, but we'll have no use for a big place.' He looked at her suddenly and he looked tired and helpless. 'There's you to consider, too, of course. It'd be very lonely for you here on your own. I suppose you might find some place in Dublin too and then we could sell this place. But as I said, there's no hurry. And now, will you leave me alone for God's sake and let me get on with the scything. You know it's the only bit of pleasure I get.'

There was no choice for her but to turn and make her way back to the house. Evening was coming down quickly, and the western sky glowed with so fierce a light that as the homing rooks flew across the flaming path of the burning sun, they became transparent as glass birds.

Reaching the door of the house she stood and looked back. The light of day had not yet faded, but a few stars had made their way through the heavens. Their beauty stabbed her through and through. She used to want to share that beauty, first with Tod, and then, in a last hysterical longing, she'd wanted to share it with anyone — anyone — even the unborn. But now there would be no one with whom to share it, ever. Why did she have this terrible need? We try to make nature a part of our life, she thought, and what are we but a part of it?

She looked down towards the river field. It was almost too dark to see Tom, and it must have been too dark for him to see what he was doing, but he was still swinging the scythe expertly from side to side, slicing through the reeds and the wild grasses, with a gesture so true and natural it might have been a branch swaying in the wind.

HAPPINESS

MOTHER HAD A LOT TO SAY. THIS DOES NOT MEAN SHE WAS ALWAYS talking but that we children felt the wells she drew upon were deep, deep, deep. Her theme was happiness: what it was, what it was not; where we might find it, where not; and how, if found, it must be guarded. Never must we confound it with pleasure. Nor think sorrow its exact opposite.

'Take Father Hugh.' Mother's eyes flashed as she looked at him. 'According to him, sorrow is an ingredient of happiness, a necessary ingredient, if you please.' And when he tried to protest she put up her hand. 'There may be a freakish truth in the theory for some people. But not for me. And not, I hope, for my children.' She looked severely at us three girls. We laughed. None of us had had much experience of sorrow. Bea and I were children and Linda only a year old when our father died suddenly after a short illness that had not at first seemed serious. 'I've known people to make sorrow a substitute for happiness,' Mother said.

Father Hugh protested again. 'You're not putting me in that class, I hope?'

Father Hugh, ever since our father died, had been the closest of anyone to us as a family, without being close to any one of us in particular, even to Mother. He lived in a monastery near our farm in County Meath, and he had been one of the celebrants at the Requiem High Mass our father's political importance had demanded. He met us that day for the first time, but he took to dropping in to see us, with the idea of filling the crater of loneliness left at our centre. He did not know that there was a cavity in his own life, much less that we would fill it. He and Mother were both young in those days, and perhaps it gave scandal to some that he was so often in our house, staying till late into the night and, indeed, thinking nothing of stopping all night if there was any special reason, such as one of us being sick. He had even on occasion slept there if the night was too wet for tramping home across the fields.

When we girls were young, we were so used to having Father Hugh around that we never stood on ceremony with him but in his presence dried our hair and pared our nails and never minded what garments were strewn about. As for Mother, she thought nothing of running out of the bathroom in her slip, brushing her teeth or combing her hair, if she wanted to tell him something she might otherwise forget. And she brooked no criticism of her behaviour. 'Celibacy was never meant to take all the warmth and homeliness out of their lives,' she said.

On this point, too, Bea was adamant. Bea, the middle sister, was our oracle. 'I'm so glad he has Mother,' she said, 'as well as her having him, because it must be awful the way most women treat them, priests, I mean, as if they were pariahs. Mother treats him like a human being, that's all.'

When it came to Mother's ears that there had been gossip about her making free with Father Hugh, she opened her eyes wide in astonishment. 'But he's only a priest,' she said.

Bea giggled. 'It's a good job he didn't hear that,' she said to me afterwards. 'It would undo the good she's done him. You'd think he was a eunuch.'

'Bea, do you think he's in love with her?' I said.

'If so, he doesn't know it,' Bea said firmly. 'It's her soul he's after. Maybe he wants to make sure of her in the next world.'

But thoughts of the world to come never troubled Mother. 'If anything ever happens to me, children,' she said, 'suddenly, I mean, or when you are not near me, or I cannot speak to you, I want you to promise you won't feel bad. There's no need. Just remember that I had a happy life and if I had to choose my kind of heaven I'd take it on this earth with you again, no matter how much you might at times annoy me.'

You see, according to Mother, annoyance and fatigue, and even illness and pain, could coexist with happiness. She had a habit of asking people if they were happy at times and in places that, to say the least of it, seemed to us inappropriate. 'But are you happy?' she'd probe as one lay sick and bathed in sweat, or in the throes of a jumping toothache. And once in our presence she made the inquiry of an old friend as he lay upon his deathbed. 'Why not?' she asked when we took her to task for it later. 'Isn't it more important than ever to be happy when you're dying? Take my own father, do you know what he said in his last moments? On his deathbed, he defied me to name a man who had enjoyed a better life. In spite of dreadful pain, his face radiated happiness.' Mother nodded her head comfortably. 'Happiness drives out pain, as fire burns out fire.'

Having no knowledge of our own to pit against hers, we thirstily drank in her rhetoric. Only Bea was sceptical. 'Perhaps you got it from him, like spots, or fever,' she said. 'Or something that could at least be slipped from hand to hand.'

'Do you think I'd have taken it if that were the case?' Mother cried. 'Then, when he needed it most?'

'Not there and then,' Bea said stubbornly. 'I meant as a sort of legacy.'

'Don't you think in that case,' Mother said, exasperated, 'he would have felt obliged to leave it to your grandmother?'

Certainly we knew that in spite of his lavish heart our grandfather had failed to provide our grandmother with enduring happiness. He had passed that job on to Mother. And Mother had not made too good a fist of it, even when Father was living and she had him, and later us children, to help.

As for Father Hugh, he had given our grandmother up early in the game. 'God Almighty couldn't make that woman happy,' he said one day, seeing Mother's face, drawn and pale with fatigue, preparing for the nightly run over to her own mother's house that would exhaust her utterly. There were evenings after she came home from the county library where she worked, when we saw her stand with the car keys in her hand, trying to think which would be worse, to slog over there on foot or take out the car again. And yet the distance was short. It was

Mother's day that had been too long. 'Weren't you over to see her this morning?' Father Hugh demanded.

'No matter,' said Mother. She was no doubt thinking of the forlorn face our grandmother always put on when she was leaving.

'Don't say good night, Vera,' Grandmother would plead. 'It makes me feel too lonely. And you never can tell, you might slip over again before you go to bed.'

'Do you know the time?' Bea would ask impatiently if she happened to be with Mother. Not indeed that the lateness of the hour counted for anything, because in all likelihood Mother would go back, if only to pass by under the window and see that the lights were out, or stand and listen and make sure that as far as she could tell all was well.

'I wouldn't mind if she was happy,' Mother once said to us.

'And how do you know she's not?' we asked.

'When people are happy, I can feel it. Can't you?'

We were not sure. Most people thought our grandmother was a gay creature, a small birdy being who even at a great age laughed like a girl, and more remarkably sang like one, as she went about her day. But beak and claw were of steel. She'd think nothing of sending Mother back to a shop three times if her errands were not exactly right. 'Not sugar like that, that's too fine; it's not castor sugar I want. But not as coarse as that, either. I want an in-between kind.'

Provoked one day, my youngest sister, Linda, turned and gave battle. 'You're mean!' she cried. 'You love ordering people about.'

Grandmother preened, as if Linda had paid her a compliment. 'I was always hard to please,' she said. 'As a girl, I used to be called Miss Imperious.'

And Miss Imperious she remained as long as she lived, even when she was a great age. Her orders were then given a wry twist by the fact that as she advanced in age she took to calling her daughter Mother, as we did.

There was one great phrase with which our grandmother opened every sentence: '*if only*'. 'If only,' she'd say, when we came to visit her, 'if only you'd come earlier, before I was worn out expecting you.' Or if we were early, then she'd say, if only it was later, after she'd had a rest and could enjoy us, be able for us. And if we brought her flowers, she'd sigh to think that if only we'd brought them the previous day when she'd had a visitor to appreciate them or if only the stems were longer, or that we had picked a few green leaves, and included a few buds. Because, she'd say disparagingly, the poor flowers we'd brought were already wilting. We used to feel we might just as well not have brought them. As the years went on Grandmother had a new bead to add to her rosary: if only her friends were not all dead. By their absence, they reduced to nil all real enjoyment in anything. Our own father, her son-in-law, was the one person who had ever gone close to pleasing her. But even here there had been a snag. 'If only he was my real son,' she used to say, with a sigh.

Mother's mother lived on through our childhood and into our early maturity, although she outlived the money our grandfather left her, and in our minds she was a complicated mixture of valiance and defeat. Courageous and generous within the limits of her own life, her simplest demand was yet enormous in the larger frame of Mother's life, and so we never could see her with the same clarity of vision with which we saw our grandfather, or our own father. Them we saw only through Mother's eyes.

'Take your grandfather,' she'd cry, and instantly we'd see him, his eyes turning upon us, yes, upon us, although in his day only one of us had been born: me. At another time, Mother would cry, 'Take your own father,' and instantly we'd see him, tall, handsome, young, and much more suited to marry one of us than poor bedraggled Mother. Most fascinating of all were the times Mother would say, 'Take me.' By magic then, staring down the years, we'd see blazingly clear a small girl with black hair and buttoned boots, who, though plain and pouting, burned bright, like a star. 'I was happy, you see,' Mother said. And we'd strain hard to try and understand the mystery of the light that still radiated from her. 'I used to lean along a tree that grew out over the river,' she said, 'and look down through the grey leaves at the water flowing past below, and I used to think it was not the stream that flowed but me, spread-eagled over it, who flew through the air like a bird. That I'd found the secret.' She made it seem there might be such a secret, just waiting to be found. Another time she used to dream that she'd be a great singer.

'We didn't know you sang, Mother?'

She had to laugh. 'Like a crow,' she said.

Sometimes she used to think she'd swim the Channel.

'Did you swim that well, Mother?'

'Oh, not really, just the breaststroke,' she said. 'And only then by the aid of two pig bladders blown up by my father and tied round my middle. But I used to throb, yes, throb with happiness.'

Behind Mother's back, Bea raised her eyebrows.

What was it, we used to ask ourselves, that quality that she, we felt sure, misnamed? Was it courage? Was it strength, health, or high spirits? Something you could not give or take? A conundrum, or a game of catch-as-catch-can?

'I know what it was,' cried Bea one day. 'A sham.'

Whatever it was, we knew that Mother would let no wind of violence from within or without tear it from her. Although, one evening when Father Hugh was with us, our astonished ears heard her proclaim that there might be a time when one had to slacken hold on it, let it go for a moment, to catch at it again with a surer hand. In the way, we supposed, that the high-wire walker up among the painted stars of his canvas sky must wait to fling himself through the air until the bar he catches at has started to sway perversely from him. Oh no, no! That downward drag at our innards we could not bear, the belly swelling to the shape of a pear. Let happiness go by the board. 'After all, lots of people seem to make out without it,' Bea said. It was too tricky a business. And might it not be that one had to be born with a flair for it?

'A flair would not be enough,' Mother said when we once asked her. 'Take Father Hugh. He, if anyone, had a flair for it, a natural capacity. You've only to look at him when he's off guard with you children, or helping me in the garden. But he rejects happiness. He casts it from him.'

'That is simply not true, Vera,' said Father Hugh, overhearing her. 'It's just that I don't place an inordinate value on it like you. I don't think it's enough to carry one all the way. To the end, I mean – and after.'

'Oh, don't talk about the end when we're only in the middle,' said Mother. And, indeed, at that moment her own face shone with such happiness it was hard to believe that her earth was not her heaven. Certainly it was her constant contention that of happiness she had had a lion's share. This, however, we, in private, doubted. Perhaps there were times when she had had a surplus of it, when she was young, say, with her redoubtable father, whose love blazed circles around her, making winter into summer and ice into fire. Perhaps she did have a brimming measure in her early married years. By straining hard, we could find traces left in our minds from those days of milk and honey. Our father, while he lived, had cast a magic over everything, for us as well as for her. He held his love up over us like an umbrella and kept off the troubles that afterwards came down on us, pouring cats and dogs.

But if she did have more than the common lot of happiness in those early days, what use was that when we could remember so clearly how our father's death had ravaged her? And how could we forget the distress it brought on us when, afraid to let her out of our sight, Bea and I stumbled after her everywhere, through the woods and along the bank of the river, where, in the weeks that followed, she tried vainly to find peace.

The summer after Father died, we were invited to France to stay with friends, and when she went walking on the cliffs at Fécamp our fears for her grew frenzied, so that we hung on to her arm and dragged at her skirt, hoping that like leaded weights we'd pin her down if she went too near to the edge. But at night we had to abandon our watch, being forced to follow the conventions of a family still whole, a home still intact, and go to bed at the same time as the children of the house. It was at that hour, when the coast guard was gone from his rowing boat offshore, and the sand was as cold and grey as the sea, that Mother liked to swim. And when she had washed, kissed, and left us, our hearts almost died inside us and we'd creep out of bed again to stand in our bare feet at the mansard and watch as she ran down the shingle, striking out when she reached the water where, far out, wave and sky and mist were one, and the greyness closed over her. If we took our eyes off her for an instant, it was impossible to find her again.

'Oh, make her turn back, God, please!' I prayed out loud one night.

Startled, Bea turned away from the window. 'She'll have to turn back sometime, won't she? Unless – ?'

Locking our cold hands together, we'd stare out again. 'She wouldn't,' I whispered. 'It would be a sin.'

Secure in the deterring power of sin, we let out our breath. Then Bea's breath caught again. 'What if she went out so far she used up all her strength and couldn't swim back? It wouldn't be a sin then.'

'It's the intention that counts,' I said.

A second later, we could see the arm lift heavily up and wearily cleave down, and at last Mother was in the shallows, wading back to shore.

'Don't let her see us!' cried Bea. As if our chattering teeth would not give us away when she looked in at us before she went to her own room on the other side of the corridor, where later in the night the sound of her weeping would reach us.

What was it worth, a happiness bought that dearly?

But Mother had never questioned its worth. She told us once that on a wintry day she brought her own mother a snowdrop. 'It was the first one of the year,' she said, 'a bleak bud that had come up stunted before its time, and I meant it as a sign of spring to come. But do you know what your grandmother said? "What good are snowdrops to me now?" Such a thing to say! What good are snowdrops at all if they don't hold their value for us all our lives? Isn't that the whole point of a snowdrop? And that is the whole point of happiness, too. What good would it be if it could be erased without trace? Take me and those daffodils.' Stooping, she buried her face in a bunch that lay on the table waiting to be put in vases. 'If they didn't hold their beauty absolute and inviolable, do you think I could bear the sight of them after what happened when your father was in hospital?'

It was a fair question. When Father went to hospital, Mother went with him and stayed in a small hotel across the street so she could be with him all day from early to late. 'Because it was so awful for him, being in Dublin,' she said. 'You have no idea how he hated it.'

That he was dying neither of them realised. How could they know, as it rushed through the sky, that their star was a falling star? But one evening when she'd left him asleep Mother came back home for a few hours to see how we were faring, and it broke her heart to see the daffodils were out all over the place, in the woods, under the trees, and along the sides of the avenue. There had never been so many, and she thought how awful it was that Father was missing them. 'I know you send up little bunches to him, you poor dears,' she said. 'Sweet little bunches, too, squeezed tight as posies by your little fists. But stuffed into vases they can't really make up to him for not being able to see masses of them growing.' So on the way back to the hospital she stopped her car and pulled a great bunch of them, the full of her arms. 'They took up the whole back seat,' she said, 'and I was so excited at the thought of walking into his room and dumping them on his bed, you know, just plopping them down so he could smell them, and feel them. I didn't mean them to be put in vases in his room, not all of them. It would have taken a rainwater barrel to hold them. Why, I could hardly see over them as I came up the steps; I kept tripping. But when I came into the hall, that nun – I told you about her – that nun came up to me, sprang out of nowhere it seemed, although I know now that she was waiting for me, knowing that somebody had to bring me to my senses. But the cruel way she did it. Reaching out, she grabbed the flowers, letting lots of them fall. I remember some of them getting stood on. "Where are you going with those foolish flowers, you foolish woman?" she said. "Don't you know your husband is dying? Your prayers are all you can give him now." She was right. I was foolish. But I wasn't cured. And that summer it was nothing but foolishness the way I dragged you children after me all over Europe. As if any one place was going to be different from another, any better, any less desolate. But there was great satisfaction in bringing you places your father and I had planned to bring you, although in fairness to him I must say that he would not perhaps have brought you so young. And he would not have had an ulterior motive. But above all, he would not have attempted those trips in such a dilapidated car.'

Oh, that car! It was a battered old red sports car, so depleted of accessories that when, eventually, we got a new car Mother still stuck out her hand on bends, and in wet weather jumped out to wipe the windscreen with her sleeve. And if fussed, she'd let down the window and shout at people, forgetting she now had a horn. How we ever fitted into it with all our luggage was a miracle.

'Oh. There was plenty of room, you were never lumpish, any of you,' Mother said proudly. 'But you were very healthy and very strong.' She turned to me. 'Think of how you got that car up the hill in Switzerland.'

'The Alps are not hills, Mother,' I pointed out coldly, as I had done at the time, when the car failed to make it on one of the inclines. Mother let it run back until it wedged against the rock face, and I had to get out and push till she got it going again in first gear. But when it got started it couldn't be stopped to pick me up until it reached the top, where they had to wait for me. And for a very long time.

'Ah, well,' Mother said, sighing wistfully at the thought of those trips. 'You got something out of them, I hope. All that travelling must have helped you with your geography and your history.'

We looked at each other and smiled, and then Mother herself laughed. 'Remember the time when we were in Italy, and it was Easter, and all the shops were chock-full of food? The butchers' shops had poultry and game hanging up outside the doors, fully feathered, and with their poor heads dripping blood, and in the windows they had poor little lambs and suckling pigs and young goats, all skinned and hanging by their hind feet.' She shuddered. 'Continentals are so obsessed about food. I found it revolting. I had to hurry past. But Linda, who must have been only four then, dragged at me and stared and stared. You know how children at that age have a morbid fascination for what is cruel and bloody. Her face was flushed and her eyes were wide. I hurried her back to the hotel. But next morning she crept into my room, and pressed up close to me. "Can't we go back, just once, and look again at that shop?" she whispered. "The shop where they have the little children hanging up for Easter." She meant the young goats, of course, but I'd said *kids*, I suppose. How we laughed.' But here her face was grave. 'You were really very good children in general. Otherwise I would never have put so much effort into rearing you, because I wasn't a bit maternal. You brought out the best in me. I put an unnatural effort into you, of course, because I was taking my standards from your father, forgetting that his might not have remained so inflexible if he had lived to middle age and was beset by life, like other parents.'

'Well, the job is nearly over now, Vera,' said Father Hugh. 'And you didn't do so badly.'

'That's right, Hugh,' said Mother, and she straightened up, and put her hand to her back the way she sometimes did in the garden when she got up from her knees after weeding. 'I didn't go over to the enemy anyway. We survived.' Then a flash of defiance came into her eyes. 'And we were happy. That was the main thing.'

Father Hugh frowned. 'There you go again!' he said.

Mother turned on him. 'I don't think you realise the onslaughts that were made upon our happiness. The minute Robert died, they came down on me, cohorts of relatives, friends, even strangers, all draped in black, opening their arms like bats to let me pass into their company. "Life is a vale of tears," they said. "You are privileged to find it out so young." Ugh! After I staggered on to my feet and began to take hold of life once more, they fell back defeated. And the first day I gave a laugh, poof, they were blown out like candles. They weren't living in a real world at all; they belonged to a ghostly world where life was easy: all one had to do was sit and weep. It takes effort to push back the stone from the mouth of the tomb and walk out.'

Effort. Effort. Ah, but that strange-sounding word could invoke little sympathy from those who had not learned yet what it meant. Life must have been hardest for Mother in those years when we older ones were at college, no longer children, yet still dependent on her. Indeed, we made more demands on her than ever then, having moved into new areas of activity and emotion. And came and went as freely as we did ourselves, so that the house was often like a hotel, and one where pets were not prohibited but took their places on chairs and beds, as regardlessly as the people. Anyway it was hard to have sympathy for someone who got things into such a state as Mother. All over the house there was clutter. Her study was like the returned-letter department of a post office, with stacks of paper everywhere, bills paid and unpaid, letters answered and unanswered, tax returns, pamphlets, leaflets. If by mistake we left the door open on a windy day, we came back to find papers flapping through the air like frightened birds. Efficient only in that she managed eventually to conclude every task she began, it never seemed possible to outsiders that by Mother's methods anything whatever could be accomplished. In an attempt to keep order elsewhere she made her own room the clearinghouse into which the rest of us put everything: things to be given away, things to be mended, things to be stored, things to be treasured, things to be returned; even things to be thrown out. By the end of the year, the room resembled an obsolescence dump. And no one could help her; the chaos of her life was as personal as an act of creation. One might as well try to finish another person's poem.

As the years passed, Mother rushed around more hectically. And although Bea and I had married and were not at home any more, except at holiday time and for occasional weekends, Linda was noisier than the two of us put together had been, and for every follower we had brought home she brought twenty. The house was never still. Now that we were reduced to being visitors, we watched Mother's tension mount to vertigo, knowing that, like a spinning top, she could not rest till she fell. But now at the smallest pretext Father Hugh would call in the doctor and Mother would be put on the mail boat and dispatched to London. For it was essential that she get far enough away to make phoning home every night prohibitively costly.

Unfortunately, the thought of departure often drove a spur into her and she redoubled her effort to achieve order in her affairs. She would stay up until the early hours ransacking her desk. To her, as always the shortest parting entailed a preparation as for death. And as if her end was at hand, we would all be summoned, to be given last-minute instructions, although she never got time to speak a word to us, because five minutes before departure she would still be attempting to reply to letters that were the acquisition of weeks and would have taken whole days to answer.

'Don't you know the taxi is at the door, Vera?' Father Hugh would say, running his hand through his grey hair and looking very dishevelled himself. She had him at times as distracted as herself. 'You can't do any more. You'll have to leave the rest till you come back.'

'I can't, I can't!' Mother would cry. 'I'll have to cancel my plans.'

One day, Father Hugh opened the lid of her case, which was

strapped up in the hall, and with a swipe of his arm he cleared all the papers on the top of the desk pell-mell into the suitcase. 'You can sort them on the boat,' he said, 'or the train to London.'

Thereafter, Mother's luggage always included an empty case to hold the unfinished papers on her desk. And years afterwards a steward on the Irish Mail told us she was a familiar figure, working away at letters and bills nearly all the way from Holyhead to Euston. 'She usually gave it up about Rugby or Crewe,' he said. 'She'd get talking to someone in the compartment.' He smiled. 'There was one day coming down the corridor of the train I was just in time to see her close up the window with a guilty look. I didn't say anything, but I think she'd emptied those papers of hers out the window.'

Quite likely. When we were children, even a few hours away from us gave her composure. And in two weeks or less, when she'd come home, the well of her spirit would be freshened. We'd hardly know her, her step so light, her eye so bright, and her love and patience once more freely flowing. But in no time at all the house would fill up once more with the noise and confusion of too many people and too many animals, and again we'd be fighting our corner with cats and dogs, bats, mice, bees, and even wasps. 'Don't kill it!' Mother would cry if we raised a hand to an angry wasp. 'Just catch it, dear, and put it outside. Open the window and let it fly away!' But even this treatment could at times be deemed too harsh. 'Wait a minute. Close the window!' she'd cry. 'It's too cold outside. It will die. That's why it came in, I suppose. Oh dear, what will we do?' Life would be going full blast again.

There was only one place Mother found rest. When she was at breaking point and fit to fall, she'd go out into the garden, not to sit or stroll around but to dig, to drag up weeds, to move great clumps of corms or rhizomes, or indeed quite frequently to haul huge rocks from one place to another. She was always laying down a path, building a dry wall, or making compost heaps as high as hills. However jaded she might be going out, when dark forced her in at last her step had a spring of a daisy. So if she did not succeed in defining happiness to our satisfaction, we could see that whatever it was, she possessed it to the full when she was in her garden.

I said as much one Sunday when Bea and I had dropped round for the afternoon. Father Hugh was with us again. 'It's an unthinking happiness, though,' he cavilled. We were standing at the drawing-room window, looking out to where in the fading light we could see Mother on her knees weeding in the long border that stretched from the house right down to the woods. 'I wonder how she'd take it if she were stricken down and had to give up that heavy work,' he said. Was he perhaps a little jealous of how she could stoop and bend? He himself had begun to use a stick. I was often a little jealous of her myself, because although I was married and had children of my own, I had married young and felt the weight of living as heavy as a weight of years. 'She doesn't take enough care of herself,' Father Hugh said sadly. 'Look at her out there with nothing under her knees to protect her from the damp ground.' It was almost too dim for us to see her, but even in the drawing room it was chilly. 'She should not be let stay out there after the sun goes down.'

'Just you try to get her in, then,' said Linda, who had come into the room in time to hear him. 'Don't you know by now that what would kill another person only seems to make Mother thrive?'

Father Hugh shook his head again. 'You seem to forget it's not younger she's getting.' He fidgeted and fussed, and several times went to the window to stare out apprehensively. He was really getting quite elderly.

'Come and sit down, Father Hugh,' Bea said, and to take his mind off Mother she turned on the light and blotted out the garden. Instead of seeing through the window, we saw into it as into a mirror, and there between the flower-laden tables and the lamps it was ourselves we saw moving vaguely. Like Father Hugh, we, too, were waiting for her to come in before we called an end to the day.

'Oh, this is ridiculous!' Father Hugh cried at last. 'She'll have to listen to reason.' And going over to the window he threw it open. 'Vera! Vera!' he called, sternly, so sternly that, more intimate than an endearment, his tone shocked us. 'She didn't hear me,' he said, turning back blinking at us in the lighted room. 'I'm going out to get her.' And in a minute he was gone from the room. As he ran down the garden path, we stared at each other, astonished; his step, like his voice, was the step of a lover. 'I'm coming, Vera!' he cried.

Although she never failed to answer him when he called, whatever about us, Mother had not moved. In the wholehearted way she did everything, she was bent down close to the ground. It wasn't the light only that was dimming; her eyesight also was failing too, I thought, as instinctively I followed Father Hugh.

But halfway down the path I stopped. I had seen something he had not seen. Mother's hand, that appeared to support itself in a forked branch of an old tree-peony she had planted as a bride, was not in fact gripping it but impaled upon it. And the hand that appeared to be grubbing in the clay in fact was sunk into the soft mould. 'Mother!' I screamed, and I ran forward, but when I reached her I covered my face with my hands. 'Oh, Father Hugh,' I cried. 'Is she dead?'

It was Bea who answered, hysterically. 'She is! She is!' she cried, and she began to pound Father Hugh on the back with her fists, as if his pessimistic words had made this happen.

But Mother was not dead. And at first the doctor even offered hope of her pulling through. But from the moment Father Hugh lifted her up to carry her into the house we ourselves had no hope, seeing how effortlessly he, who was not strong, could carry her. When he put her down on her bed, her head hardly creased the pillow.

Mother lived for four hours. Like the days of her life, those four hours were packed tight with concern and anxiety. Partly conscious, partly delirious, she seemed to think the counterpane was her desk, and she scrabbled her fingers upon it as if trying to sort out a muddle of bills and correspondence. No longer indifferent now, we listened, anguished, to the distracted cries that had all our lifetime been so familiar to us. 'Oh, where is it? Where is it? I had it a minute ago. Where on earth did I put it?'

'Vera, Vera, stop worrying,' Father Hugh pleaded, but she waved him away and went on sifting through the sheets as if they were sheets of paper. 'Oh, Vera,' he begged. 'Listen to me! Do you not know – '

Before he could say what he was going to say Bea pushed between them. 'You're not to tell her!' she commanded. 'Why frighten her?'

'But it ought not to frighten her,' said Father Hugh. 'This is what I was always afraid would happen, that she'd be frightened when it came to the end.'

At that moment, as if to vindicate him, Mother's hands fell idle on the coverlet, palms upward and empty. And turning her head she stared at each of us in turn, beseechingly. 'I cannot face it,' she whispered. 'I can't. I can't. I can't.'

'Oh, my God!' Bea said, and she started to cry.

'Vera. For God's sake, listen to me!' Father Hugh cried, and pressing his face to hers, as close as a kiss, he kept whispering to her, trying to cast into the dark tunnel before her the powerful light of his own faith.

But it seemed to us that Mother must already be looking into God's exigent eyes. 'I can't!' she cried again. 'I can't face it.'

Then her mind came back from the stark world of the spirit to the world where her body was still detained, but even that world was now a whirling kaleidoscope of things which only she could see. Suddenly her eyes focused, and, catching at Father Hugh, she pulled herself up a little and pointed to something we could not see. 'What will be done with them?' Her voice was anxious. 'They ought to be put in water anyway,' she said, and, leaning over the edge of the bed, she pointed to the floor. 'Don't step on them,' she said sharply. Then, more sharply still, she addressed us all. 'Have them sent to the public ward,' she said peremptorily. 'Don't let that nun take them, she'll only put them on the altar. And God doesn't want them. He made them for us, not for Himself.'

It was the familiar rhetoric that all her life had characterised her utterances. For a moment we were mystified. Then Bea gasped. 'The daffodils!' she cried. 'Don't you remember? The day Father died.' And over Bea's face came the light that had so often blazed over Mother's. Leaning across the bed, she pushed Father Hugh aside. And, putting out her hands, she held Mother's face between her palms as tenderly as if it were the face of a child. 'It's all right, Mother. You don't have to face it. It's over.' Then she who had so fiercely forbade Father Hugh to do so blurted out the truth. 'You've finished with this world, Mother,' she said, and, confident that her tidings were joyous, her voice was strong.

Mother made the last effort of her life and grasped at Bea's meaning. She let out a sigh, and, closing her eyes, she sank back, and this time her head sank so deep into the pillow it seemed that it would have been dented had it been a pillow of stone.

THE YELLOW BERET

'TWO MURDERS IN THE ONE NIGHT? IN DUBLIN? NONSENSE! MAYBE IT'S the same one they're talking about?' Mag looked at her husband in mild disbelief.

'How could it be the same?' Don said. 'Wasn't the other one down at the docks? Do you never read the papers?'

'But two murders in the one night!' Mag knew that the note of doubt in her voice would annoy him, but she couldn't help it, so, to please him, she peered across the breakfast table at the newspaper in his hand. But without her glasses the sun made one blur of everything on the table – plates, napery, and newsprint – and waywardly her mind went back to her own concerns. She'd soon have to call Donny. She glanced up at the mantelpiece to see if the entrance card for his examination was still propped in front of the clock, so he couldn't possibly forget it when he was going out. Then she looked around the room to make sure there was nothing else he was likely to forget – his fountain pen, or the key of his locker in the college.

But all the time she was vaguely aware that Don was critical of her lack of attention. She'd have to make some comment.

'I hope we're not going to have a wave of crime!' she said.

Exactly the wrong thing to say. She had only revealed the full extent of her heedlessness.

'Wave of crime!' he scoffed. 'I told you there was no connection between the two crimes. You're as bad as the newspapers.' He sounded irritated. But as he read on down the long columns devoted to the two crimes he became more amiable. 'It's a disturbing business,' he conceded. 'It will have a very upsetting effect on the public, I'm afraid!'

Well, here was something Mag could discuss with a genuine interest and liveliness.

'I don't see why! Why anyone should be upset – ordinary people like us, I mean. There's always a reason for these murders! Don't tell me they come out of a clear sky! I see no reason why anyone should be concerned at all about them – beyond feeling sorry for those involved, of course! Take that girl at the docks. I'm sure what happened to her was only the end of a long story!'

'Not necessarily,' Don said curtly. 'As a matter of fact they're looking for a Dutch sailor who only went ashore a few hours before the murder – '

'But he knew her from another time, I suppose? And – '

'Not necessarily,' said Don again.

Mag reddened. She hadn't understood that it might all have happened in that doorway: not only the murder, but . . . well . . . it all.

'Oh!' she said, repulsed. Then her voice quickened. 'Oh, Don. Let's not talk about it. Let's not even think about it. You know how I feel about that kind of thing.'

It was not so much a feeling as an attitude. She had made it a point to draw a circle, as it were, around their home, and keep out all talk of violence and crime. She had always tried to let their son feel he lived in a totally different world from the world where such things happened. Don't talk about it. Don't think about it. That was her counsel to him – and to herself as well.

It wasn't as easy to practise as to preach, though. Last evening, although she had only caught a word or two about that girl who was strangled on the docks, yet she could not get the thing out of her mind all night. Although she had never been out to the Pigeon House, where it happened, and had only seen the long sea wall from the deck of the B. & I. Boat – seen it sliding past as the ship pulled out past the Alexandra Basin into the bay – yet she kept picturing the place as if it were a place she knew well.

Through the cranes and ships' rigging one could see the wide wharf narrowing into a place with no human habitation; nothing but coal yards, and warehouses, and the power station of Pigeon House itself, its windows lit by day as well as night with a cold inimical light. Then the wharf narrowed again until it seemed only a promenade for birds, with bollards here and there splattered with glaring white droppings; and where in places steps led down into the water they seemed senseless, more than half of them underwater, wobbly-looking and pale, and when a wash of water went over the top steps it lay on them thin as ice.

It was here she pictured it happening. Not at the edge near the steps, but back from them, where, in an abortive bit of wall, an iron gate stood giving entrance or egress to nowhere. She could distinctly picture that gate, reinforced top and bottom with rusty corrugated iron – cut in jags along the top as if with giant pinking shears.

How could a gateway she had never seen be so vivid in her mind? Even now, in the sunny breakfast room, with Don across the table from her, she felt the picture forming again in her mind. But this time there was a man in the picture. A Dutch sailor. It was him: the murderer! Who else could it be? Bending downward, in the gateway, with his back to her, she saw him, as clearly as she saw the gate in which he stood. His clothes – a faded blue shirt – his hair – a carroty red – were as plain as if he were standing in front of her in the flesh. She could not see his face, but he could not stand there for ever. In a minute he would have to straighten up and turn and get back to the densely peopled streets and lose himself in the crowds, and she would be forced to look at him face-to-face. And when she saw his face – ah, this was the terror – it would, she felt certain, be a face well known to her.

What was the meaning of this vision? There had never been anything psychic about her.

Desperately she closed her eyes to blot it all out – the wharf, the gateway, the figure – but against her closed lids they formed again, more clearly. And then – as she knew he must – the man turned, or half-turned rather, because only his eyes turned towards her; his face and head remained partly averted. His head, indeed, seemed fixed in an implacable pose as if he had no power to move it, and yet in another sense it was all movement, a strange and terrible inner motion. Every cell of skin and hair and membrane seemed to vibrate. His coarse orange hair quivered, and his fibrous beard, while the enormous white whorl of the one ear visible to her seemed as if it was still evolving from its first convolution. And not only the face but the very air around him seemed to whirl and spin until it, too, was all spirals and oscillations. She went rigid with tension.

Then the white whorl of that ear brought her back to her senses. Van Gogh! The self-portrait! Relief left her so limp she slumped down in her chair. What a fool she was! She glanced at Don, glad he was not always able to read her mind. Yet – wait! Why did Van Gogh come into her mind? Could there be any reason? And what did the real murderer look like?

To think that he might at that moment be walking the streets of Dublin! Oh, heavens! She could see him again. This time he was standing on Butt Bridge, leaning over the parapet and staring down the river. Terror swept over her.

'Did you say the other murder was in Dublin, too, Don?' she asked sharply.

'Still trying to link the two? I tell you, there was no connection between them, Mag. The other poor creature – ' he nodded down at the paper ' – the other poor creature was the soul of respectability – '

'The other victim was a woman too? You didn't tell me!'

'An elderly spinster,' said Don, as if not altogether corroborating her statement. 'A schoolteacher, I think it said.' He bent and looked for verity to the paper. 'Yes, a schoolteacher living in Sandford Road. Respectable enough address! Over fifty, too!'

But Mag rushed over and grabbed the paper out of his hand.

'Over fifty? Oh, no, Don! No! Why didn't you tell me? That's terribly sad. I didn't realise. I thought it was another of those ugly businesses. Why didn't you tell me it was so sad? The poor creature!'

Don stared at her.

'What's sadder about her than the girl on the docks?' he asked.

But Mag had got her glasses and was gathering up the pages of the paper. 'Where is the front page? Was there a picture of the poor thing?'

'I don't think so,' said Don. 'There was a picture of that girl, though! She was only seventeen. A lovely-looking girl. Now that was what you might call sad! Oh, I know the sort she was, and all that, but she was so young. She had her whole life ahead of her. There's no knowing but she might somehow have been influenced for good before it was too late. And anyhow,' he said limply, 'the other poor thing – ' He shrugged his shoulders, not bothering to finish the sentence. 'She can't have had much of a life. Can't have had much to look forward to in the future! Lived alone. Kept herself to herself. An odd sort apparently. Say what you like – it wasn't the same as being seventeen!'

'Oh, stop it, Don. I can't bear it. You don't understand. To come to such an end after a lifetime of service.' Mag was poring over the paper. 'Yes! She was a teacher. To make it worse, she was a kindergarten teacher – oh, the poor thing. I can't bear to think of it. The head was battered in – with a stone, they think – and bruises on the neck and back.'

'Not a sex crime, anyway,' Don said, facetiously, Mag thought.

'Oh, Don, how can you? There's no question of anything like that! She was over fifty! Fifty-four. And several people have already come forward, voluntarily, to testify to her character. She led the most normal, the most regular life and – '

'Nothing very normal or regular about wandering the streets in the small hours!'

'Oh, you didn't read it properly.' Mag consulted the paper again. 'She was found in the small hours, but it was done before midnight. They haven't given the pathologist's report yet, but the police put the time between eleven and twelve. She wasn't found earlier because the body was dragged into someone's front garden.'

'Nice for those people!' Don said.

'Oh, Don, how can you joke about it? Do you realise that if she had been left in the street there might have been a spark of life in her when she was found? As things were it seems she wouldn't have been found at all until daylight only a couple coming home from a dance happened to step inside the garden hedge.'

'Nice for them, too!' Don said irrepressibly. 'Sorry, Mag, sorry! I feel as bad as you do about it, but you never take any interest in murders, and to hear you carrying on about these women – '

She pulled him up short.

'Don't speak of them in the same breath!' she said coldly.

But he was looking down at the paper again.

'Oh, look, there's more about it in the late-news column. They're looking for any information that may lead to the recovery of a yellow beret believed to have been worn by the victim earlier in the evening.'

Mag pressed her lips together.

'The unfortunate girl! She little thought when she was putting on that beret – '

'It wasn't the girl! It was the other woman.'

'The elderly woman? Are you sure? A yellow beret? It sounds more like what a young girl would wear, surely?'

'The old girl must have fancied herself a bit, it seems.'

'Oh, Don, I asked you not to take that tone again, please. Please! I'm certain it was simply a case of some thug attacking her in the hope that she might have money on her. He probably didn't intend anything more than to stun her, but maybe she screamed, the poor thing, and he got frightened and hit her again to keep her quiet. Maybe he didn't realise he'd killed her at all.'

'Then why did he drag her into that garden?'

'Oh, I forgot about that.'

But Don had had enough of it. He glanced at the clock. 'You forgot something else! How about calling Donny?' he said, and he went out, got his hat and coat in the hall, and where he stood put them on.

'Oh, he has plenty of time yet,' Mag said, and she followed him out into the hall. But she looked up the stairs. 'All the same, I'll go up and call him before I do anything else.' At the bottom of the stairs, however, she turned. 'Don't go till I come down,' she said, quite without reason. Or was it, she thought afterwards, that even then, at the foot of the stairs, a vague uneasiness had already taken possession of her? Had she, all morning, been unconsciously aware of a sort of absolute silence upstairs, different altogether from the merely relative silence when the boy was up there, but asleep? Certainly halfway up the stairs when she looked through the banister rail she was outrageously relieved to see that her son's bed had been slept in, although he was not in it.

'Oh, you're up?' she cried, talking to him, although she wasn't sure whether he was in his room or not. He could be behind the door, perhaps, taking down his clothes from the clothes hook? Or in the bathroom? 'Where are you?' she called, when she saw he wasn't in his room. She went to the door of the bathroom. 'Are you in there, Donny?' she asked from outside the bathroom door. 'Where are you?' she called out then sharply, still addressing herself to him. But when she leaned over the banisters to see if he could have gone downstairs – to the kitchen perhaps – without their noticing him – it was to Don she called. 'Is he down there, Don?'

'Why would he be down here?' Don had come to the foot of the stairs. She thought there was an uneasy note in his voice. Then he, too, started up the stairs.

'Why are you coming up?' she cried.

She must have begun to cry at that point, because Don shouted at her.

'Stop that noise, for God's sake, Mag! The boy probably stayed out last night. But what of it? I wish I had a pound note for every time I stayed out all night when I was his age. I'd be a rich man now if I had! He has you spoiled; that's all! There's some perfectly reasonable explanation for his staying out!'

'But he didn't stay out. He was in bed when I brought up his hot jar last night!'

Don seemed taken aback by being reminded of this.

'He's gone out somewhere then, I expect,' he said, 'that's all.'

'Where? And when? I was down early. There wasn't a stir in the house. I didn't hear a sound till I heard you!'

Together they stood stupidly, one above the other, in the middle of the stairs.

'He must have gone out during the night, then,' Don insisted.

'But why? And why didn't he tell us he was going out?' Mag demanded. 'He knows I'm a light sleeper. He knows I never mind being wakened. Many a night, before his other exams, he came into my room and sat on the end of the bed to talk for a while if he couldn't get to sleep.'

'Well, come downstairs anyway, Mag,' Don said, more gently. 'There's no use standing up here in the cold. He hasn't done this before, has he? No! You'd have told me, of course. And he didn't have a sign of drink on him last night, I suppose?'

'Has he ever had?' she flashed.

In spite of the anxiety that was creeping over him too, she saw that Don was irritated by her righteous tone.

'Look here, Mag,' he said, 'it wouldn't be the end of the world, you know, if he did take a drink! We can't expect to keep him off it for ever. Moderation is all we can demand from him at his age.'

But Mag set her face tight.

'I'll never believe it of him,' she said. 'Not Donny!'

'Well, how else are you going to account for his behaviour now?'

'Maybe he thought of something he wanted to look up before the exam,' she said desperately. 'You know Donny! If it was anything important – anything for his exam – he'd think nothing of getting up and dressing and going out to quiz some of his pals about it. Not like other fellows that would be too lazy and would chance leaving it to the morning! Donny would never chance anything.'

That was true. She saw Don had to acknowledge it.

'Yes,' he said, 'but in that case he'd have been back in an hour or so.'

'Unless he stayed talking, wherever he went!'

'He would have telephoned!'

'In the middle of the night?'

They looked at each other dully.

'You don't suppose . . . that he might have met with an accident or something?'

'Funny, I never thought of that,' his father said.

Yet, now, to both of them it seemed an obvious thought.

'Hadn't we better do something?' said Mag.

'Like ring the hospitals?' Don went over to the hall table where the phone stood. There, he hesitated.

'Which hospital ought I to ring? Street accidents are usually brought to Jervis Street Hospital, I think, but I don't suppose they are brought there from all parts of the city. I suppose all hospitals have casualty wards. I wonder where I ought to try first?' Suddenly his hesitancy left him, and confidently he put out his hand to take up the receiver. 'I know what I'll do, I'll ring the police. That's the thing to do. They must get reports from every hospital.' He turned to her. 'Did he have his name on him, I wonder? Or any form of identification?'

When she didn't answer he looked up. Her face had gone white. He put down the phone. 'Don't look like that, Mag,' he said. 'I'm sure he's all right. It was only to reassure you that I was phoning at all. We've got a bit hysterical, if you ask me. I think we should wait a while longer before doing anything. He'll breeze in here any minute, I bet. Wait till you see. And look here, Mag, let me give you a bit of advice. When he does come back . . .'

But he saw that she was in no condition for taking advice.

'Don't ring the police anyway,' she said.

It was the way she said it, dully and flatly, that made him feel suddenly that whatever had come into her mind to trouble her was out of all proportion to his own vague fears.

'You're not keeping anything from me, are you, Mag?' he asked, sharply.

'Oh, no,' she cried. 'It's just that I don't think we ought to draw attention to him in case – '

' – in case he got himself into some scrape or other? Is that it? What scrape could he get into?' he asked, stupidly.

'Oh, I don't know,' she said, 'but it seems a bad time to draw attention to him – with all this going on . . .'

It was an exceedingly vague and formless reference to what they had been discussing at breakfast, but he got her meaning at once, and his face flushed angrily.

'You can't mean that! You just don't know what you're saying!' he said. 'Your own son!'

'Oh, don't go on that way,' she cried. 'You didn't wait for me to finish. Listen to me!'

But he wasn't listening then, either. He was just staring at her.

'Oh, please! Please!' Mag said wearily. 'I only meant that he might be innocently involved, drawn into something against his will, or even accidentally, and afterwards perhaps been afraid of the consequences. That was all I meant!' Then she looked sharply at him. 'What did you think I meant?'

In sudden enmity each probed the other's eyes for a fear worse than his own.

'Might I ask one thing?' said Don at last bitterly. 'Which of these killings is the one in which you think my son is involved? Battering in the head of an old woman? Or the other one?'

'You know right well the one I mean!' Mag snapped. 'How could he be involved in the other? Nothing on earth could justify killing that poor old creature.'

Don gave a kind of laugh.

'Well! You women are unbelievable. So you consider the poor girl on the docks was fair game for any kind of treatment! Bad luck if it should end as it did – bad luck for the man, that is to say!' He turned away as if in disgust, but the next minute he swung back vindictively. 'Tell me one thing,' he said. 'Just how did you think that anyone could be innocently implicated in a business like that? Your son, for instance!'

'I don't know,' cried Mag. 'It's not fair to take me up like that. I didn't say I thought anything of the kind. I was only frightened, that's all. Any woman would be the same. Many a time when we were first married, if you were late coming home, I'd be looking at the clock every minute and imagining all kinds of things.'

'About me?'

'Oh, you don't understand! What comes into one's mind at a time like this has nothing at all to do with the other person. It doesn't mean one thinks any the less of him. It's as if all the badness of the world – all the badness in oneself – rushes into one's mind, and starts up a terrible reasonless fear. I know Donny is a good boy. And I know he wouldn't harm anyone. But he might have been passing that doorway – '

'Down at the docks, on a dark night? It was raining too, the paper said.'

'Well, how do we know what might have brought him down there? How do we know where he is any night he's out, if it comes to that? He could have been passing that way just at the wrong moment, and maybe seen something. Then, who knows what might have happened!'

'But you forget he came home last night, Mag. You saw him yourself, or so you said. You said you went up and said good night to him like you always do, and gave him his hot bottle?'

Mag said nothing for a minute.

'Don,' she said in a low voice. 'There's something I didn't tell you because it seemed silly, but last night wasn't quite like other nights. His light went out as I went up the stairs. He had put it out although he heard me coming. I didn't mind it at the time – well, not much – and I tried not to be hurt – I told myself his eyes might be giving him trouble after studying so hard all the week. So I said nothing but went into the room without putting on the light and he put out his hand and took the hot bottle from me – in the dark. It wasn't quite like always.'

'Oh, now you're splitting hairs,' Don said, impatiently. Yet Mag could see he was carefully considering what she'd told him. 'I think there's something you ought to get straight in your mind, Mag,' he said then, slowly, 'even if he were to walk right in the door this minute. You've got things wrong. It's just possible that a young fellow like our Donny might on occasion have some truck with a girl like that poor girl that was strangled without its being necessarily taken that he'd be mixed up in her murder, but he couldn't be mixed up in her murder without it necessarily being taken that he had some sort of truck with her! Get clear on that!'

Mag's mind, however, had unexpectedly cleared itself not only of that, but of all her other senseless fears as well.

'Oh, I'm sure we are being ridiculous,' she cried. 'There's bound to be some simple explanation. Look, Don! If it makes you feel better, dear, go ahead and ring the police.' But when he said nothing she put out her hand timidly and laid it on his sleeve. 'What do you really think, Don?' she said.

'I don't know what to think, now,' Don said, roughly. 'You've succeeded in getting me into a fine state.' He moved over and stood at the window. Then all of a sudden he gave a loud guffaw. 'Well, well,' he said, in an altogether new tone of voice. 'They didn't hang him yet anyway: he's coming down the road!'

'Oh, thank God. Let me look. Where is he?'

Mag ran to the window, and then, when she had seen her son with her own two eyes, she ran towards the door.

'Mag!' Don's voice was so strident she turned back, but when their eyes met they were instantly at one again and could seek counsel from each other.

'What will I say to him?' she asked quickly.

'Let him speak first,' Don said, authoritatively.

What they didn't realise, either of them, was that it would be Donny who, with his sunny smile, would speak first as always – with his smile that was always so open, and had such a peculiar sweetness in it.

'I suppose I'm in for it!' he said, lightheartedly. 'Or perhaps you didn't miss me? I thought I'd be back before you woke up.' When they didn't answer, he reddened slightly. 'I meant you to come down and find me as fresh as a lark instead of like most mornings, trying to get my eyes unstuck.' He turned to Mag. 'Were you worried, Mother? I'm sorry. I'll tell you how it happened. I hope you weren't too upset?'

Mag was flustered.

'Well, it was mostly on account of your exam, Donny – ' she said, vaguely, glancing at the pink card. 'If it was an ordinary morning...'

Donny glanced at the card too, and also at the clock. He went over and took up the card and put it in his pocket. 'I mustn't forget this. It's a good job I came home. I'd have forgotten it. I wasn't going to come home at all, but go right on to the college, only for thinking about you and how you might worry.'

'It was a bit late in the day to be worrying about us then,' said Don.

'I know,' cried Donny. 'But I ought to have been home hours ago, only I got a blister on my heel. It hurts like hell still. I ought to bathe my foot, but I don't suppose I've time. If it wasn't for thinking you'd have been in a state about me I could have washed my foot in the lavatory down at the examination hall. But then I'd have had nothing to eat, and I'm starving.' Seeing some unbuttered toast, he picked it up and rammed it into his mouth.

'Oh, that toast is cold,' cried Mag. 'Let me make some more.' But Don brought his fist down on the table.

'Toast be damned,' he said, and he turned to Mag. 'Where the hell was he? Isn't that what we want to know?' He swung back towards his son again. 'Where were you? You don't seem to realise – your mother was nearly out of her mind.'

'Oh, Don, what does it matter now!' cried Mag. 'As long as he's back, and everything is all right.'

For everything was more than all right now. The absent son had been unknowable and capable of – well – capable of anything. The real Donny, standing in their midst, was once more enclosed within the limits of their loving concept of him.

But Don could be stubborn.

'How are we so sure everything is all right?' he snapped. 'My God, Mag, but you have a short memory!' He turned to Donny. 'It's a queer thing to find a person has got up out of his bed in the middle of the night, and taken himself off somewhere – God knows where – without as much as a word of explanation. Why didn't you tell your mother where you were going? You know she's a light sleeper. And you knew you needn't have been afraid of waking me. I never hear a sound once I finally drop off. Why didn't you do that? Why didn't you come in and tell us what was going on?'

'Oh, Don, don't upset him,' Mag cried. 'Look at the clock. He can tell us at supper tonight, and – '

'But there's nothing to tell!' Donny cried. 'It'll all sound foolish now. I only meant to go out for a few minutes in the first place, but the night was so fine – '

'Are you trying to tell us you just went out for a nice little walk?' said Don. 'In the middle of the night?'

Missing the ironic note in his father's voice, Donny turned round eagerly.

'Not a walk! I had no notion of taking a walk. At that hour of the night! I only intended stepping outside to get a breath of air.' He turned back to Mag. 'I couldn't sleep after I went to bed. You know how it is before an exam! Well, after I was a while tossing about, I knew I'd never sleep. I knew the state I'd be in for the exam, so I got up and dressed. I thought that after a mouthful of fresh air I might look over my notes again for a bit. But as I said – when I stepped outside I was tempted to take a few steps down the road. It was such a night! You've no idea. I just kept walking on and on, till I found myself nearly in Goatstown! I was actually standing on Milltown Bridge before I realised how far I'd walked! And there were the hills across from me when I leant over the bridge – and somehow they seemed so near and – '

'You didn't go up the hills?' Mag couldn't conceal her astonishment.

'Well, as far as the Lamb Doyle's,' Donny said proudly. 'I'd have liked to go on further, up by Ticknock, but it was beginning to get bright – not that it was really dark at all, but day was breaking – you should have seen the sky – I'd like to have stayed up there. But I had the old exam to think about, so I had to start coming down again. Oh, it was great up there: I felt wonderful. I'd been going a bit hard at the work in the last few weeks and everything was sort of bunged up in my brain. Up there, though, I could feel my mind clearing and everything falling into place. But I don't suppose you understand?' he said, suddenly aware of their lack of comment.

'If only you'd come to my door, son,' his mother said.

'As if you'd have let me go out if I did, Mother! You know you'd have got up and come downstairs, and insisted on cups of tea, and reheating jars and remaking beds. You'd never have let me out! But that breath of air, and the exercise, was just what I needed. I felt great! The good is well taken out of it now though, by all this fuss!' He looked accusingly from one to the other of them.

Mag turned to Don.

'Now! What did I tell you! He could have explained everything at supper.'

'Let's have no more of it so,' said her husband, and he took up his briefcase. 'All I'll say is, it's a pity he didn't cut short his capers by an hour or so, and save us all this commotion.'

'I told you, I got a blister on my heel,' said Donny, indignantly. 'I would have been back hours ago only for that.'

Mag had forgotten the blister. 'Oh! Let me look at it, son,' she cried. 'The dye of your sock might get into it. You could get an infection.

We'll have to see that it's clean and put a bandage on it. Sit down, Donny, son,' she said, and as he sat down she sank down on her knees in front of him like she used to do when he was a little boy and she had to tie his shoelaces for him.

'Wait till you see the bandage that's on it now,' said Donny. 'I came down partway in my bare feet – as far as Sandyford, where the bungalows begin – but people were stirring – milkmen, bus conductors, and that class of person – going to work, and I had to put on the shoes, but I wouldn't have got far in them only I found something to pad my heel. This!' he cried, and he rolled down his sock and pulled it up – a bit of sweat-stained, blood-soaked felt. 'What's the matter?' he cried, as he saw Mag's face. Then he saw Don's. 'What's the matter with you two?' he cried.

Was it the texture of the cloth? Was it the colour? What was it that made his parents know, instantly, that the bit of felt had once been part of a woman's beret?

'Why are you staring at me?' Donny cried. He looked down at the bit of stuff. At the same time he shoved his hand down into his pocket and brought up the rest of the beret. 'I felt bad about cutting it up,' he said, 'it looked brand new, but I told myself that – as the old proverb goes – somebody's loss is somebody else's gain.'

Mag and Don were staring stupidly at him.

'I suppose it wasn't all a yarn you were spinning us, was it?' Don asked at last. But he answered his own question. 'I suppose it wasn't,' he said, dejectedly. And he walked over and took up the paper. 'There's something you'd better know, boy,' he said, quietly. 'You evidently didn't see the morning paper.' He held it out to him, pointing to one paragraph only.

Donny read quickly – a line or two.

'Is this it, do you think?' he asked then, with a dazed look at the bit of yellow felt.

'That's what we want to know,' Don said. 'Where did you get it?'

'I told you! I picked it up in the gutter, somewhere about Sandyford Road. Oh, do you think it's it?' he cried again, and letting the pieces fall he ran his hands down the sides of his trouser legs, as if wiping them. 'Why didn't you tell me when I came in first?' he said, looking so pathetically young and stupid. Mag began to laugh, odd, gulping laughs.

'Don't mind me, son,' she said, between the gulps. 'I can't help it.' She didn't see the warning look Don gave her. 'It's from relief,' she said.

Donny looked at her. He had not missed his father's look. Ignoring her, he turned to Don.

'What did she mean?'

'Nothing, boy, nothing,' said Don. 'We were a bit alarmed, you must realise that. You wouldn't understand, I suppose. Some day you may. Parenthood isn't easy – it induces all kinds of hysterical states in people at times – men as well as women!' he added, staunchly, taking Mag's arm and linking them together for a minute. 'I mean – ' he said, but suddenly irritation got the better of him. 'Anyway, you've only yourself to blame,' he snapped. 'We were beside ourselves with anxiety – almost out of our minds. We were ready to think anything.'

Donny said nothing for a moment.

'You were ready to think anything? But not anything bad?' He turned to Mag. 'Not you, Mother? You didn't think anything bad about me? Why, you know me through and through, don't you, like – like as if I were made of glass. How could you think anything bad about me?'

'Oh, of course I couldn't,' Mag cried. And she longed to deny everything – words, thoughts, feelings, everything – but all she could do was show contrition. 'I was nearly crazy, Donny,' she cried. 'You don't understand.'

'You're right there! I don't understand,' said Donny, and he slumped down on a chair. After a minute, apathetically, he began to pull his sock on over his grimy foot. 'I'd better go to my exam,' he said.

'Your exam!' Don shouted. 'Are you joking? Well, let me tell you, you can kiss goodbye to your exam. Don't you know you'll have to account for that beret being in your possession, you young fool? You don't think you can walk into the house with a thing like that – like a dog'd drag in a bone – and when you've dropped it at our feet walk off unconcerned about your business?' Suddenly Don, too, slumped down on a chair. 'Oh, weren't you the fool to get us into this mess! You and your rambles! If you were safe in your bed where you ought to have been we'd have been spared all this shame and humiliation.'

Shame? Humiliation? Mag thought all that at least was over. Don gave her a withering look.

'We'll be a nice laughing stock!' he said. 'I can just see them reading about this in the office. There'll be queer smirks.' He looked at Donny. 'And I'd say your pals in the university will have many a good snigger at you too. To say nothing of what view the university authorities may take of it. And they might be nearer the mark. It's not such a laughing matter at all. It's no joke being implicated in a thing like this. There's no end to the echoes a thing like this could have – all through your life! People have queer, twisted memories. They won't remember that you were innocent: they'll only remember that your name was mentioned in connection with a murder – no matter how innocently. I'd take my oath that from this day you're liable to be pointed out as the fellow that had something to do with the murder of a woman.' In a flash of involuntary malice he turned to Mag. 'They'll probably get things mixed up, seeing both murders were the same night, and think it was in the other one he was involved.'

Donny didn't catch the last reference. He was thinking over what Don had first said.

'God help innocence, if everyone is as good at distorting things as you!' he said, angrily.

'Well, it's no harm for you to be shown what can be done in that line,' said Don, a bit shamefaced, but still stubborn. 'I'd be prepared to swear you'll want your wits about you when you're telling the police about it. They'll need a lot of convincing before they believe in your innocence – or your foolishness, as I'd be more inclined to call it. It isn't as if you only saw the thing, or picked it up and hung it on the spike of a railing, as many a one would have done – as I'd have done, if it was me! It isn't even as if you picked it up and put it in your pocket and forgot about it, as maybe another might have done. But oh no! You had to cut it up in pieces! How will that appear in the eyes of the police? And I must say I wouldn't like to be you when it comes to telling them about the blister on your heel! As if you were a young girl with feet as tender as a flower! Those detectives have powerful feet. You couldn't blister them with a firing iron! I tell you, you'll wear out the tongue in your head before you'll satisfy those fellows' questions.' He put his head in his hands. 'Oh, how did this happen to us?'

Mag ran over to him.

'Don! I can't understand you!' she cried. 'You didn't take on this bad when we thought – '

Don glared at her. 'It wasn't me thought it, but you,' he cried. 'And if it was now, I'd know better what to think. He's only a fool – that's clear.'

But Donny stood up.

'I may be a fool, but I'm not one all the way through,' he said quietly, calmly. 'How is anyone to know – about this? It was hardly light when I picked it up. There wasn't a soul in sight. And if no one knows, why should I go out of my way to tell about it? It was up to the police to find it anyway. Isn't that what they're paid for – paid for by us and people like us? Whose fault is it if they don't do their job properly? There must have been any number of them in that vicinity last night, with flashlights and car lights and the rest of it. If the beret was so important, why didn't they make it their business to find it? Why was it left for me to find? And why should I neglect my business because they don't do their business right? Here – I'm going out to my exam!'

'Oh, but, son,' cried Mag, 'you could call at the station – or phone them – yes, that would be quicker – phone them – and tell them you found the beret, but that you have to go to your exam.'

Donny sneered.

'A lot they'd care about my exam. They'd keep me half the day questioning me, like Dad said.'

'Not if you explained, son. You could say you'd be available in the afternoon.'

'As if they'd wait till then for their information, Mother! No – I'm going to the exam.'

'Oh, son! Time might be of the greatest importance!' She ran over to him. 'Oh, Donny! You don't understand. Even if you were to miss your exam – think of what this might mean – it might lead to their finding whoever did it!'

'It could as easily lead them astray,' Don said quietly. 'I know them – they could lose more time probing Donny than would find twenty murderers in another country. It might not be as bad as it seemed at first, Mag, for him to do as he says: keep his mouth shut!' He stooped and picked up the two pieces of felt and stared at them.

Donny put out his hand.

'Give them to me,' he said. 'I've got to go.' Almost absently, he fitted the two pieces together for a minute till they made a whole. 'I'll see later what I'll do,' he said. Then he looked his father in the face. 'But I think I know already,' he said.

Hastily, Don took up his briefcase again.

'I'll be down the street with you, son,' he said. 'We have to consider this from every angle.' At the door he turned. 'Are you all right, Mag?' he asked.

Mag wasn't looking at him. She was looking at Donny.

'Don't look at me like that, Mother!' Donny said. 'Nobody's made of glass, anyway. Nobody!'

CHAMOIS GLOVES

IT WAS AN IMPORTANT DAY AT THE CONVENT OF OUR LADY OF PERPETual Succour: three postulants were about to take their First Vows.

A beautifully fine day, thank God!

The sunlight glinted on the chapel windows, on the greenhouse roof, and on the windshields of the visitors' cars as they came up the driveway.

One or two cars were already drawn up in front of the chapel, which was a separate building, to the left of the convent, and the tyres had made ridges in the loose, clean gravel. It was really too thickly spread, and it rolled about under the feet of the relatives when they stepped out of the cars. No wonder there were no weeds! And there – in case even one small weed should dare to put up its head – was Joe the gardener standing by the yew hedge, with a hoe in his hand. But note he was in his best suit, and he was wearing his hat.

On the other side of the yew hedge, but magnificently unconcerned, two – no – three young nuns were walking rapidly up and down reading their Office. And finally, at an open window in one of the classrooms on the ground floor, the five small girls who were going to be bridesmaids at the ceremony were having their wreaths and veils put straight by a lay teacher.

There were countless guardian angels moving about upon diverse errands too, of course, but being unseen their actions need hardly be related. The principal ones, anyway, were the angels who belonged to the young girls about to take their vows, and they were way up on the top storey of the Novitiate at that moment; doubly out of sight, you might say.

The cars were really beginning to arrive now. Two more were coming up, and there was the sound of another one changing gear down at the gates. (The gates were situated at a bad point in the road; it could not be safely negotiated in top gear.) Ah, here it was, gathering speed, and causing the gravel to shoot out to either side of the wheels as if from a peashooter.

In the basement of the convent an old lay sister peered upwards through a window.

Had they all arrived, she wondered? She was the kitchen sister – Sister Ursula – and she was in charge of the luncheon which would be served after the ceremony. She looked back over her shoulder at a clock. In exactly fifty minutes more, she calculated, they should be sitting down to table. But would they?

Tch! tch! she said, as from yet another car, that scattered the gravel right and left, there descended a whole family, father, mother, and three small children.

I hope there won't be more than the number, like last year, she muttered. People had no consideration, no manners, you might say. Some of them thought children didn't count. But they ought to be taught a lesson. Children should not be put at the table at all; they should be put in a classroom and given a glass of milk and a plate of biscuits. But no, oh, no; nothing would do the parents but squeeze them in to the table, upsetting everything, especially the number of knives and forks.

'Here, I have two forks,' the father would say; as if the table was laid wrong!

'Oh, but they don't understand,' said the old sister.

She was the daughter of a small farmer, and it always seemed to her that the meals at the convent were very grand, and that the people who were invited to them didn't properly apprehend the formalities. Where did they see the like before? she would ask. And if after the meal a grapefruit came back untouched to the kitchen, or a piece of cutlery was unused, she was very proud. You can't blame them, she would say to the younger lay sisters. Where did they see such things before?

On the other hand, Reverend Mother, who came from a well-to-do merchant's family in the Midlands – Reverend Mother was always nervous in case everything was not correct, and on such occasions as now she hovered about the table adjusting the folds of the serviettes, and making minute alterations in the lie of the cutlery. It was a minor, but constant, source of embarrassment to her that they had not got proper grapefruit spoons. She had not quite sufficient confidence to order them, but whenever a young nun's dower included a share of family plate, or when the convent received a bequest in the form of silverware, she eagerly rummaged through it.

'Are there no grapefruit spoons?' she would exclaim, and when there were not, it was manifestly difficult for her to conceal her disappointment, no matter how rare or how valuable were the items.

Sister Ursula knew Reverend Mother's feelings about the spoons, and so, whenever she laid the table for visitors, she always gave the bowls of the teaspoons a squeeze to narrow them.

'They should be pointed, you know,' she told the younger lay sisters. 'But who'll notice the difference!' Poor Reverend Mother! God gave her wit, some of them won't ever have seen a grapefruit at all!

Today, as she peered upwards through the ivy-framed window, she was inclined to think a lot of the cutlery would come back unused. Once professed, she was prepared to accept all the choir nuns as ladies, but some of their relatives . . . she raised her brows so that the band of starched linen across her forehead shifted its place and showed the ridge it had made in her skin.

Ah! There was a familiar car. On the dot, as usual; Father Devaney. She bustled back to the range. Everything would be on time after all; Father Devaney would see to it. Thanks be to God.

The arrival of the priest's car was indeed a signal to all concerned. The young nuns pacing behind the yew hedge closed their breviaries, and walked, not so much quickly, as purposefully, back to the building. The five little communicants were bustled out of sight. Among the guests there was activity also. Some of the menfolk who had stayed sitting behind the wheels of their cars got out and, pulling up their coats by the back of the collar, as if they were their own footmen, followed their womenfolk. The womenfolk, on the other hand, confident and chattering up to this point, now became ill at ease, and inclined not to know what was to be done. It was always the men who could be relied upon in the end.

'Well, what's keeping us?' they said, and trooped up the steps of the chapel, but they wiped their feet elaborately on the scraper provided, and stepped on the golden parquet as if it were brittle yellow glass.

Yet, in a few minutes, as if the chapel door had been a swallow hole and they had been sucked into it, everyone had disappeared. No longer blocked with people, the open door gave a glimpse of hundreds of candle flames, and let out the first notes of the organ, peremptory; premonitory.

Meanwhile, in the Novitiate which was also separate from the main building, high up near the copper cupola, viridescent with verdigris, and on top of which, gay as a weathervane, there shone a gilt cross, the three young girls who were about to be received raised their arms and down over their bodies fell the beautiful white satin gowns they were to wear for their wedding with the Holy of Holies. But although the cubicles were so high up in the roof, nevertheless the lower sashes were covered with a brass grille so that only the pigeons walking about on the cupola could see those beautiful bare arms.

On account of this brass grille, the postulants could not clearly see the cars arriving; they could only hear them as they came up the drive.

That's ours, thought Veronica, the youngest of the postulants. She knew the sound of the engine, and a minute afterwards the peculiar noise of the doors slamming. In a little while – the ceremony would be so short really, and the luncheon would not take very long – she would be with the family. A feeling of absolutely delirious happiness passed through her from top to toe. It was too bad Mabel couldn't be there, of course, but even that couldn't spoil the marvellousness of it all. Oh, joy!

But all at once she bit her lip. That was the trouble, you see, she was too happy, far too happy, all the time, yesterday, today, every single day. Since the very first day she entered the Novitiate, she hadn't had one moment of sadness or regret. Surely that wasn't right? Where was the sacrifice if there were no pain of loss, no anguish of indecision?

Take the other postulants, for instance. How many times during the past year had she been awakened in the small hours by a sound of sobbing in one of the other cubicles? It was subdued sobbing, but terrible to hear, all the same, in the darkness. She had never been able to tell whether it was Sister Assumpta or Sister Concepta, but from other indications she felt sure that in both their souls there was some struggle about which she knew nothing at all. And once, at recreation, Sister Concepta had asked her a strange question.

'Do you ever have dreams?' she asked. 'Queer ones, I mean?' And when Veronica said she hadn't, Concepta had turned away with a worried expression.

It was shortly after this that Veronica had gone to the trouble of confiding in the mistress of novices, or Private Enterprise, as she was called on account of a famous reprimand she had made to a former novice whose zeal she considered excessive. 'Do what is asked of you, Sister; no less, and no more. We don't want any private enterprise in piety!'

Private Enterprise had listened for a minute or two, and then grunted.

'So you think God ought to have put more temptations in your way, do you?' she said. 'And might I ask what makes you think you'd be able to withstand them? Let me tell you, God knows what he's doing. And if, for some purpose of His own, He occasionally wants some of us poor weak creatures as well as the other kind, well then, He has to arrange matters so that there isn't too great a strain put on us.'

She spoke so sarcastically that tears had come into Veronica's eyes, but then, just before she turned aside, the old nun smiled.

'At least, that's the only way I can account for my own perseverance!' she said.

That was Private Enterprise all over. She was always putting people into their place, but somehow at the same time she managed to make them feel glad to be there.

And so, when, out on the landing, Veronica saw the pale faces of Concepta and Assumpta, even then, at the last minute, she felt an impulse to put her case once more to the older nun.

'Look at their faces,' she wanted to say. 'Anyone can see what they feel, while I am only – only what?' Scandalised, she realised that for the most part she was looking forward to seeing her family: looking beyond the ceremony, as it were, treating it almost as if it were of no great importance at all, this, the Great Day, for which they had been preparing every single day that had preceded it since they came into the convent!

Perhaps after all she had no vocation. In a panic she looked around. Where was Private Enterprise? Ah, there she was, plodding up the stairs. Veronica started forward, but before she could open her mouth, the old nun looked past her at Concepta and frowned.

'You're not going to be sick, are you?' she asked bluntly. 'You're very green in the face!'

'Wait a minute!' she commanded them all, although just then they heard the faraway sound of the organ that had been a signal for them to start moving down the stairs. 'Better be on the safe side,' she muttered, and she disappeared into the small pantry on the landing.

When she came out, she had a big enamel basin in her hand.

'I'll bring this down to the sacristy, just in case,' she said. 'I do wish you wouldn't dramatise yourself so much, Sister!' she said irritably.

Humbly, Veronica drew back. How glad she was she hadn't said anything.

And then, just before she gave them the signal to start moving, Private Enterprise held them up again for a minute.

'It will be all over in a few minutes,' she said reassuringly. 'Don't be nervous. Remember that in God's eyes every day of the past year was as important as today. You gave yourself to Him every day. All that's happening today is that you're receiving the outward sign of your union with Him. Don't be nervous. Think of how proud your people will be of you: think of how soon you'll be seeing them.'

And so, when she was walking up the aisle of the chapel, actually kneeling at the altar rails, she found herself thinking again of them, she didn't worry. It was a pity that Mabel would not be able to come to the reception, but she could offer up her disappointment. She offered it up for Mabel herself to bring her safely through things.

And then, as if there was not to be even the smallest shadow on the day, ever such a short time afterwards, as Private Enterprise had said – in their black habits now – when they followed her into the parlour – who should she see, first of all, running over to her – but Mabel. Yes – Mabel: running forward ahead of Mother and ahead of Father.

'Why, Mabel – ' she cried. 'I thought – '

But Mabel only laughed at how puzzled she was, and, all perfume as usual, she kissed her.

'What's this?' cried Father, as he and Mother came up to her, and he pretended to draw back as he was about to kiss her. 'I didn't know nuns wore perfume.'

Several people in the parlour looked around in surprise.

'Oh, I suppose it's come off Mabel,' she cried in alarm, and then they all began to laugh. And indeed, by this time, at both ends of the parlour where each of the other novices was surrounded by her own little groups of friends, there were bursts of laughter like bursts of small artillery fire, until it seemed as if each burst ought by right to be accompanied by a little puff of smoke rising into the air.

And the talk . . . it was easily seen the ceremony had been preceded by the Long Retreat.

'Did you really keep absolute silence for twenty-one days?' cried Mother. 'I mean absolute, absolute silence?'

'We can well understand your incredulity, my dear,' said Father. 'Can't we, girls?'

He was always teasing Mother.

'Oh, indeed!' cried Mother. 'You'd wonder why some people were given tongues at all: isn't that so, girls?'

To Veronica, it was just like being at home. She had forgotten, really, how they teased each other, Father and Mother, and how they all talked so much, all together too. Ever so slightly – she couldn't help it – Veronica felt superior to them; even to Father. In the Community Room, at recreation, the conversation was always happy, but somehow there was a difference. It wasn't so – so scatterbrain! But realising this might be spiritual pride, she checked herself quickly.

And anyway, she wanted to hear about Mabel. She still didn't understand how she was able to be there.

'Don't look so puzzled, darling,' cried Mabel herself just then. 'You're an auntie for the past fortnight! I simply couldn't bear to miss being here and so I got round the old doctor and made him give me a cocktail!'

Seeing that Veronica didn't understand, Mabel reddened slightly. 'Nursing home slang, pet,' she said. 'Don't let it worry you: an injection to induce me: that's all!'

But she was still a bit red in the face. An awkward silence seemed to have come over their part of the parlour.

Not that Veronica had really taken in what was said. Only vaguely did she comprehend that the baby must be born, but a nervous feeling came into her stomach, and she didn't want to hear any more details. Just that everything was all right: that was enough. And there would have been an end to it if Euphemia had not joined them just then.

Euphemia was their aunt, and she was twenty-seven years now in the order, but she considered herself a real woman of the world for all that. Even the name which she had taken in religion, although it was used by all the family instead of her name in the world – which most of them had forgotten – and Mabel and Veronica could hardly have recalled – was used without a prefix, as easily and familiarly as if it were a Christian name: a perfect compromise. She seemed to go in for compromise, Euphemia did. On this occasion she took Mabel up sharply.

'I must say I'm surprised at you, Mabel. I didn't think you'd go in for being smart. In God's good time: that was the old-fashioned way. And the best way in the long run. Things are best left in the hands of God, my dear, or even of Nature, if you prefer it that way. It isn't wise to alter the natural order of things. I don't want to alarm you, but I hope you won't find later on. Well, we'll hope not in any case. Of course, it's an altogether different story if there are sound medical grounds for interference – but I take it that was not so in your case?'

Long ago when she and Mabel were at school, they used to boast about their aunt Euphemia, because she was so broad-minded. You'd never think she was a nun at all. You could say anything to her. And you should hear her talking! That's the kind of nun I'd like to be if I had to be one at all, Mabel used to say.

Well, Veronica didn't want to be that kind. She didn't want to be priggish, but if God ordained that certain things were to be outside her experience, she didn't care to know anything about them. And anyway, there were times, in the chapel, when she had seen Euphemia's face across from her in the transept among the choir nuns, when she was still a postulant, and it had often seemed to her that there was something unreconciled in Euphemia's face. Was it possible, she had wondered, that for some people there was a struggle to be fought out, anew, every day, even *after* the taking of vows? She looked at Euphemia with new eyes. Was she ever – ?

But just at that moment, Sister Concepta came and whispered to her. One of Concepta's visitors had been at school with Mabel and she'd like to meet her again.

'Bring her over, of course!' cried Mabel, overhearing the whisper, and staring with curiosity across the parlour.

But the friend turned out to be much older than Mabel. She was in the Senior School when Mabel was still in the Lower School. And she was married long before Mabel, as could be seen by the size of the big child – four or five years old at least – who was with her, staring up at them all from under an unkempt fringe.

The child stared most of all at Veronica.

'Is *her* hair cut too, Ma?' she demanded.

'Oh, Judy, keep quiet; you are a tiresome child,' cried the mother. 'How dare you say such things.'

'But you said in the car – '

'Never mind what I said! You know you shouldn't repeat things. You're always being told so. And stop staring. Where are your manners?'

But the child's eyes were riveted on the starched linen band across Veronica's forehead. Everyone felt embarrassed for a minute. Then Father Devaney, who had been talking to Reverend Mother, detached himself and took the child by the arm.

'Well, little girl, what's your name?' he said, and before she had time to say any more he had led her over to where a glass door looked out upon the garden.

There, on a strip of vacant grass, some pigeons were walking decorously up and down.

'Why don't you try and catch one,' he said, and he opened the door.

Judy ran out: the pigeons rose into the air with a flurry.

'Oh, look; so many of them!' cried Veronica's mother. 'It's like St Mark's!'

'Only these are not so tame!' said Euphemia. There she was again! When was *she* in Venice?

'Oh, do look at them,' cried Mother again, moving over to the glass door.

Reverend Mother, too, moved over to the door.

'Sometimes when they are walking up and down, we say they are reading their office; they look so solemn,' she said. She conceived it as part of her duties always to make a mild joke like this on such occasions.

And certainly everyone laughed. Following her lead too, everyone – except Veronica and Father – moved over to the glass door.

Father laid a hand on Veronica's arm.

'Let's stay on this side of the ship to make weight,' he said.

Veronica laughed. As a family, analogy was irresistible to them. She knew exactly what he meant. The pigeons had acted upon the company as a floating canister or a bottle will act upon the passengers of a ship, drawing them all to one side to lean over the deck rail, the insignificance of the object that focuses so much attention making explicit a boredom that they would hardly otherwise have realised.

It was getting boring: there was no doubt about it. Much as she loved her own people, Veronica kept thinking of what would happen when the visitors left, and took their place for the first time in the community.

Meanwhile, her mother, usually restless, had put her head out the French window.

'Couldn't we go out?' she cried, meaning to compliment the garden, but in reality giving the effect of criticising the parlour.

Reverend Mother's narrow cheeks reddened profusely. Was the room stuffy? Was she at fault in not having had the glass doors open? She nodded her head vigorously at a young nun, who rushed to unhook the other half of the door.

'Perhaps you'd like to see the garden,' said Reverend Mother, speaking generally to the whole company, and stepping out into the air.

As they were leaving the parlour, Father looked back over his shoulder.

'You must have a good greenhouse,' he said to Veronica, because, now that it was empty of people, the parlour seemed to be full of ferns, dotted about everywhere in ornamental pots.

Veronica looked back. Even when she was a child, visiting Euphemia, the parlour had always fascinated her, with its strong odour of beeswax, and the stiff, unrelaxing arrangement of its furniture. Once it was the only part of the convent she knew, and it hinted at deeper discipline and coldness to be found beyond it.

'It's a lovely room, isn't it?' she said impulsively.

But her mother had come within earshot once more.

'Personally I can't abide pot plants,' she said. And then impulsively she looked straight at Veronica. 'Aren't you ever lonely for home, darling?' she said bluntly.

It was so easy to see the course her thoughts had taken. She was thinking of the drawing room at home, always filled with masses of cut flowers: simply masses of them.

Veronica didn't want to hurt her, but she just wasn't one bit lonely. It even seemed to her now that cut flowers were out of place anywhere except on the altar. But naturally she wasn't going to say that.

And anyway, at last, for a moment only perhaps, she was alone with Mabel. Something or other engaged the attention of the rest.

'Well, old thing?' said Mabel. 'You look marvellous – in your habit, I mean. Of course, you looked divine in' – but Mabel just couldn't bring herself to use the words 'wedding gown' – 'in the satin gown,' she said quickly. 'But then, who wouldn't cut a dash in that!' She looked critically at her sister. 'It takes a good figure to look well in that rig-out,' she said, 'although it can't be denied that figure or no figure, you look a bit like a penguin, my dear!'

It was an old joke. When they were at school they always called the nuns penguins.

Veronica laughed.

'Do you know, Mabel – ' she began, but their mother was calling Mabel.

'Isn't it about time someone made a move to leave?' she said.

'Oh, bother!' said Mabel to Veronica. 'I wanted to have a word with you – oh, nothing in particular, just a little chat like long ago, but I dare say I'll get a chance again. Or perhaps I could pop in and see you tomorrow before my train leaves, if that's all right.'

Veronica didn't know.

'I'd have to ask permission to have a visitor,' she said.

'Good lord!' cried Mabel. 'It's plain to be seen I'd never have made a nun.'

Euphemia and Father Devaney had joined them by this time.

'God help us, Mabel, if we had to depend on the like of you to fill our convents,' said Father Devaney. He was an old friend of Mabel. 'In the name of God, what have you on your fingernails?' he asked.

'Oh, go on now, Father. Don't take the good out of that nice sermon you gave this morning. You should have heard it, Vera,' she said, 'and you too, Euphemia – in case you get too puffed up with vanity – it was all about us poor mothers. It's the poor mothers of this world who deserve their crowns in heaven, I can tell you. Do you know what time the baby woke this morning?'

'It's a bit soon for you to complain about your job, Mabel,' said her mother. She had a vague feeling that the topic of the baby's feeds was not quite seemly on this particular occasion. It might be different if he were on a bottle. 'Oh, the young women nowadays,' she said, and she raised her eyebrows – anything to prevent Mabel from saying something indiscreet – 'I don't know what they have to complain about – compared with us, I mean.' She sighed. 'When I think of what we – my generation, I mean – when I think of what *we* suffered.' Suddenly she turned to Father Devaney. 'Do you know, Father, these young people are so smart they've put an end to all that! It seems there is some young man – a doctor, of course – who has written a book, and they are all reading it – Mabel never left it out of her hands the whole nine months – and he claims – at least Mabel claims – that having a baby is a pleasure now. Did you ever – ?'

But suddenly she stopped short. She had jumped into the conversation so hastily to prevent Mabel from going too far, and now what was she saying herself? To make matters worse, she had fallen foul of Mabel.

'It's nothing to joke about, Mother,' she said stiffly. 'After the first contraction – '

But Father, *dear* Father, came up just then and put his hand firmly on Mabel's shoulder.

'Another time, Mabel dear, another time,' he said. 'You've had your thunder – this is Veronica's day.'

Veronica's day: it was so true. They all looked at her proudly.

'Are you happy about me now, Mother,' said Veronica, impulsively.

'Of course, my dear,' said her mother. 'It was only that I wanted you to be sure you knew what you were doing.' Unaccountably, there was another moment of awkwardness. 'I do feel we ought to start going – ' she said once more.

And so, very shortly, it was all over: the Great Day.

Once more the cars were crunching the gravel, and there was the sound of doors slamming.

Until the last car disappeared, the three new choir nuns stood at the door, and then turned uncertainly back into the hall. What did they do now?

A mild consternation stirred in them as they saw Private Enterprise, without a glance at them, going down the corridor leading from the chapel to the Novitiate, and passing through that little door – more familiar now than all the doors of home – through which they would pass no more. Like the doors of home, it too was closed to them now.

Veronica glanced at the big clock in the hall. It was only five o'clock.

Suddenly she realised that she was so fatigued she could hardly stand.

Then Reverend Mother approached them.

'Sister Eucharia will tell you your new duties,' she said. Then she looked in particular at Veronica. 'Why, you look exhausted, Sister,' she said. 'I think you had better go to bed tonight, as soon as you've had your tea. In fact, you'd better have your tea right now and then go straight to your cell.'

A great feeling of relief came over Veronica. It had been a terrible strain, really, the whole day.

As the other two, Concepta and Assumpta, moved away after Sister Eucharia, Veronica stood for a minute in the empty hall. Then she went down the corridor towards the refectory. Fatigue had brought a certain dejection, and her shoulders drooped slightly. And could she but have seen it, beside her, the feathered wings of her guardian angel drooped still more. It was all very well for Private Enterprise to take a practical view of things, but with the other guardian angels, bragging and boasting about the sacrifices they had to offer up for their clients, it was a bit hard for Veronica's angel to have absolutely nothing but words to offer on her behalf. Naturally, as Veronica enunciated her vows, her angel had flown off with them at once, engraved on a golden scroll, but she couldn't help feeling that the golden words had a hollow sound.

Ah, well, the Lord's ways were His own, she thought, and one had to be satisfied. She followed Veronica dutifully down the corridor. Thank goodness they were going to call an end to the Great Day. Just then, however, a voice called after them.

'Just a minute, Sister,' said a voice. It was Reverend Mother again. 'I think your sister must have left these behind. Will you be seeing her soon again, or will we post them to her?' In her hand she had a pair of chamois gloves. 'Perhaps you could keep them till you see her?' said Reverend Mother.

Veronica took the gloves and bowed to Reverend Mother.

Sister Ursula was not in the refectory, but the tables were laid, and Veronica sat down and ate some bread and butter, and took a glass of milk from the big jug on the side table. That was enough for her. She wasn't hungry anyway, only tired, deadly tired.

As she passed back along the corridor, she could hear the choir starting the Tantum Ergo. Benediction was nearly over. She went upstairs to the new cubicle in which she had changed out of her white satin dress into her habit. But as she reached the landing, she noticed a small hand-basin on one side of the wall, with two taps, which meant there was hot water as well as cold. In her hand she still held Mabel's gloves.

Tired and all as she was, it suddenly occurred to her that it would be a nice thing to wash out the gloves and give them back clean. Chamois gloves were so easily soiled. And she and Mabel always made a point of never wearing the same pair twice without being washed.

Impulsively taking off her stiff linen cuffs, and leaving them on the shelf over the hand-basin, Veronica ran the hot tap. The steam rose up in a cloud. She made a lather, pulled the gloves on her hands, and plunged them into the water.

Oh, that slimy feel of wet chamois! How well she remembered it. She might almost have been standing in the little wash-up pantry at the top of the house which she and Mabel used all their lives. It used to be a housemaid's pantry in the time of the previous occupiers, but she and Mabel had it for their own.

Very rarely did their mother go up there to it, and when she did she closed her eyes in horror at its condition.

'This place is a disgrace. It will have to be done up. I do wish at least you wouldn't get it so littered.'

Because Mabel's pots and tubes were all over the place, on the window ledges and the edges of the cracked hand-basin. Yes, there was a big crack across the bottom that got filled with plain dirt. Yes, and more than once the down-pipe got clogged with hair combings but they managed to free it with a knitting needle.

'Ugh!' cried mother, when she heard. 'And to think you do hygiene at school. Ugh!'

It was pretty disgusting really, compared with the rest of the house, that was really so beautifully kept. Mother never tolerated anything that wasn't beautiful.

Yet she and Mabel spent such a lot of time up there gossiping and exchanging confidences when they were supposed to be brushing their teeth or buffing their nails.

It was there, one afternoon, that she plucked up courage to tell Mabel her plans.

But all at once Veronica couldn't bear to recall any more. Two big tears welled into her eyes and coursed down her face.

Astonished, her guardian angel stared. As far as she knew, Veronica's mind was filled only with memories of cracked sanitary ware, steamy walls, and a litter of quite unsightly broken combs and misused tubes of toothpaste.

No matter! The tears were there: and more of them, a regular flood of tears were streaming down her face. All the little angel's fatigue was dispelled in an instant. She was as fresh as a daisy once more. The other angels had got ahead of her, of course, but better late than never, and cupping two tears in her hand, she sped for Heaven.

As for Veronica, she soon dried her eyes, and rinsing the gloves she took them into her cell to hang up and dry. In a few minutes she was asleep.

THE LONG AGO

EVERYONE WAS KIND TO HALLIE. YOU'D BE SURPRISED AT THE NUMBER of young people in the town who visited her, and went for walks with her, and did little messages on her behalf. But, although she was always nice to them and offered them tea when they called, there were only two people in the town whose company Hallie really enjoyed. One was Ella Fallon, who used to be Ella White. The other was Dolly Feeny, who used to be Dolly Frewen. For Dolly and Ella and Hallie had all been girls together, and they had a great many memories in common. Their main bond was that Dolly and Ella had been in Hallie's confidence in the days long ago when all three of them were young, and Dolly knew for a fact, what other people took to be gossip, that in happier circumstances – and if it had not been for the intervention of a certain person – Hallie, too, would have been married like them, and have a home of her own. Dolly and Ella had read every note that had passed between Hallie and Dominie Sinnot. And they knew it was Dominie who had given Hallie the brooch which she always wore; a gold brooch with the word 'Dearest' written on it in seed pearls. They both stoutly maintained that Dominie had once as good as told them, although not in so many words, that he would never marry any other girl but Hallie.

Ah well, that was all long ago, and Dominie at the time was only a law student, apprenticed to old Jasper Kane. And being young and innocent Dominie perhaps had not realised that an ageing solicitor would hardly make an offer of partnership to a penniless young apprentice unless there was more to the offer than met the eye. There was a string to it. And the string was Blossom – Jasper's only daughter.

Hallie never blamed Dominie, when he married Blossom, but she felt it no injustice to Blossom that a small spark of the truth should be kept alive and tended, particularly when poor Dominie lived so short a time.

'He would be alive today if it was you he married, Hallie!' Dolly said, one day, and Ella agreed. They were a great comfort to Hallie. She felt she could speak her heart to them at any time. And indeed, shortly after Dominie's death, when an awkward situation developed with Blossom, Ella and Dolly took a firm stand in Hallie's defence. Why shouldn't she visit Dominie Sinnot's grave if she wanted? they cried. They knew all about the dream she'd had – three nights in a row – a dream in which Dominie had come to her, and in which he seemed to be trying to convey some message that she did not at first understand, until quite suddenly one day she guessed what he wanted. He wanted her to visit his grave! And promptly that very evening she went down to the cemetery and knelt beside the mound. She not only said a few prayers for him. She shed a few tears for him as well. And after that she went down to the cemetery every evening.

Those moments kneeling by Dominie's grave were the happiest moments of Hallie's day. But even those moments were sometimes spoiled by the appearance of Blossom draped to the waist in widow's weeds, and when Blossom arrived Hallie, of course, had to get up off her knees and move away. In fact she had to pretend she was visiting her own family plot – as if, like everyone else in the town, Blossom didn't know quite well that Hallie's parents had been laid to rest in the burial grounds of the old Friary before it was closed. No one had been buried in the Friary for at least a decade.

The situation could have been difficult for Blossom too, if matters had not settled themselves unexpectedly. Because a short time after Dominie's death Blossom married again. And unlike Dominie, her second husband was a big, assertive fellow who would not let Blossom out of his sight. She was always hanging from his arm. And since the main gates of the cemetery were kept locked except on the days of funerals, and the side gates were so narrow two people could not go through linked, Blossom soon gave up visiting the grave. She ordered a headstone to be erected, and never went near the cemetery again. The grave was all Hallie's after that.

Hallie soon had the grave a regular showpiece. A yew tree she planted back of the headstone did remarkably well. A box hedge she put inside the curbstone did not do quite so well, but Hallie took it up and put down a small privet hedge. People thought this behaviour a bit odd. There were raised eyebrows. And one or two unkind remarks were carried back to Hallie. But with Dolly and Ella to take her part she rose superior to all criticism.

'Don't mind what people say, Hallie,' Dolly urged. 'As for the Kanes – their consciences can't be too clear about the way you were treated.'

Those were the kind of remarks Hallie treasured.

The year that Hallie decided to buy a plot for herself in the new cemetery right beside the plot in which Dominie lay, people felt that she was going altogether too far. But again, Ella and Dolly took her part.

'We know how you feel,' Ella said. 'If things had gone as they should, we know where your coffin would go by rights – down into the same grave with Dominie!'

'I thought over it for a long time,' Hallie assured her friends, 'and I would not have bought the plot if Blossom had stayed a widow.'

After that particular conversation, however, Dolly and Ella felt sadder for her than ever.

'She doesn't seem to realise that Blossom will have to be buried with Dominie anyway, whether she likes it or not,' Dolly said. 'A wife is buried with her first husband no matter how many times she marries.'

'I hope nobody will tell her that,' Ella said kindly. 'Let her have what small comforts she can get.'

Ella was always softer hearted towards Hallie than Dolly was, because, as far as these things can be known, it seemed that Ella was happier in her marriage than Dolly. Not that Dolly was dissatisfied; Sam Feeny was a man in a million. He was making money fast. He was buying up property hand over fist. And Dolly would have an easy life of it some day, although, for the moment, she had to fall in with his ideas about economy and thrift. The marriage was not the love match of Ella and Oliver. Dolly had married Sam for security. And so it was a terrible blow to her when Sam was brought down with pneumonia one day and – putting up hardly any fight – was dead three days from the day he took bad.

Strange to say, it was to Hallie that Dolly turned. It was Hallie who held her together and gave her strength on the day of the funeral. No one would ever have imagined that an inexperienced spinster could have acted so tactfully, but it was she who, after the coffin had been got downstairs, put her arms around Dolly and persuaded her to control herself enough to go to the cemetery.

'Think of me,' Hallie said. 'When Dominie died I had to stand at the back of the crowd, like a stranger. It's different for you. You'll be standing at the lip of the grave, knowing no one has a better right to stand there.'

Dolly recovered her composure at once.

'Poor Hallie,' she said. 'I never realised how you must have suffered that day.' Her mind was taken off her own trouble for a few minutes. 'Do you know, Hallie,' she said, 'I had forgotten until this minute, but now I distinctly remember that when Dominie's coffin was being lowered into the clay, Blossom was looking across the grave at the man she is married to today! He had only just come to town. I'm certain she was wondering who he was and already sizing him up! There were tears in her eyes, but there was curiosity in them as well.' At the thought of Blossom's infidelity to Dominie, Dolly had braced up, and seen where her own duty lay. 'Give me my hat,' she said. 'I mustn't keep the hearse waiting. Sam was always on time wherever he went. I won't delay him now.'

Hallie was proud of the way Dolly behaved at the graveside. People were more impressed by her silence than they would have been by any amount of sobbing and screaming. Her behaviour was certainly most edifying by comparison with Blossom, whose screams could have been heard a mile away when the first sod thudded down on Dominie's coffin.

Indeed, Ella was astonished at Dolly's calm – and told her so. 'I don't know how you did it, Dolly. I'd have broken down. I'd have thrown myself into the grave if it was Oliver – God forbid that the like should happen,' she added tactlessly, and she hastily made the sign of the cross. Dolly and Hallie exchanged glances. There are times when the silent heart grieves deepest, they seemed to say, each to the other.

After Sam's death it was Ella who was the odd one out, as Dolly and Hallie saw more and more of each other. Not that Dolly had much time to spare. She had two children and they took up a good part of her time. As well as that Sam's affairs were not in as good order as might have been expected – or desired – and his widow was in and out of old Jasper Kane's office every other day. There was even talk of a lawsuit. Nevertheless, it was undeniable that she had more free time than formerly, and it became an almost regular thing for Hallie and herself to go for a walk every evening after supper – just as they used to do in the long ago. No one could have known what those walks meant to Hallie. The thought of them bore her up through the long day, in a house that was empty and dark and cold, for nothing she did – no fire she lit, no light she burned – could bring back the warmth and brightness of the time when she was young. Young! Her faded face, and her faded hair, and her thin body that had dried up without giving out any of its sweetness, had been a bitter sight to her in her mirror for many a day. But somehow her ageing appearance did not trouble her as much after she took up her old companionship with Dolly. The days went quicker when there was something she could look forward to in the evenings. True, she, Dolly, and Ella had occasionally taken a walk together, even after the other two were married, but it was a different thing altogether to look forward to a walk every evening – regularly. It was, she told herself, just like long ago. And as she and Dolly strolled along the country roads in the soft twilight it sometimes seemed to Hallie that they were indeed back in that long ago. Walking idly along, sometimes softly humming a tune together in part time, it was so like when they were young! The evening skies were the same as ever, darkening away to the east, with a gleam still lingering in the branches of the western trees. There were bats striking through the dark air in fits and starts. There was the sweet sound of a little stream, that ran alongside the road, hidden by a high hedge from behind which came the same sound of cattle moving noisily in the rushy bottom. The same. The same. All around them the countryside was the same. The night sky was the same. And deep, deep down under the changed shape of their bodies, weren't they – she and Dolly – the same Hallie and Dolly of long ago?

More and more of the past was dragged back into their conversation as they walked and talked in the twilight.

'Do you remember the first day Ella put up her hair?' Hallie said one evening.

'Do I!' Dolly said. 'It was a Sunday! In the chapel at last Mass! It fell down when she was genuflecting. I thought she'd die of embarrassment.'

'So did I,' Hallie said, and she laughed heartily, seeing Ella again in her mind's eye as clearly as she saw her that day – thin as a rod, with her toppling heap of pale hair, standing all confused halfway up the centre aisle, her cheeks flaming, not knowing whether to stoop and pick up her hairpins, or get into a pew as if nothing had happened, letting her hair hang down her back as it always had. She squeezed Dolly's arm. 'Do you remember the day you first put up your own hair, Dolly?' she said.

'Will I ever forget it!' Dolly smiled as she thought of the day when she herself stood in her bedroom looking into the spotted mirror that reflected a saucy seventeen-year-old, her mouth filled with hairpins and a pile of chestnut hair caught on top of her head, while the rest of her hair rambled over her shoulder. She gave Hallie's arm a squeeze. 'I'll never forget the day *you* put up your hair, Hallie,' she said generously. 'And I know there was someone else who never forgot it either.'

'Who?' breathed Hallie, her heart fluttering. As if she needed to be told! Oh that day! Oh! Oh! Such a day. A Sunday, too, of course. She'd let her hair loose from its braids and piled it up on the top of her head, but all the way down the street to the chapel she was trembling with apprehension in case it might fall down like Ella's. And when she went into the chapel, although she did not turn her head to look in his direction, she knew that Dominie was kneeling just inside the door. And she knew he would be staring at her. If *her* hair had fallen down then what would she have done?

'Oh, what would I have done, Dolly, if my hair had come undone?' she cried. 'At least Ella knew Oliver wasn't in the chapel the day hers fell down. He was laid up with a cold. How lucky she was: just think how awful it would have been for her if he had been there!'

'Oh, I don't suppose it would have mattered very much,' Dolly said, indifferently. She was willing to talk endlessly about those days long ago, but she could not relive them. And sometimes she wished Ella were with them. But Ella seldom got out in the evening. The children had to be put to bed, and after that she was usually tired. Dolly sighed. She understood why Ella did not want to come with them, whereas Hallie never understood. Hallie was always bemoaning Ella's absence, and regretting she was not with them. She got quite censorious at times. 'Ella ought to get out in the evenings, if only for half an hour. Just for a change. Just for the fresh air.' She wouldn't listen to any excuses from Dolly. 'You have children too, Dolly!' she said.

'My girls are older than Ella's little people,' Dolly said. 'And anyway girls are able to do a lot for themselves.'

'Why doesn't she come out after she's put them to bed?'

'But that's the only time she has alone with Oliver,' Dolly blurted out at last, although she had regrets at once. Hallie unlinked her arm.

'I should think she'd have seen enough of him by now,' she said.

That annoyed Dolly. It was all she could do not to say something mean – to let Hallie see, for once and for all, that there was a big difference between a married woman and a spinster, and even a widow was not the same as a woman who had never had a man in the house at all!

But as soon as these bitter words came into Dolly's mind she suppressed them. After all, it wasn't fair to regard Hallie as an old maid. She had been the prettiest of the three of them, and she had a nicer disposition. If Dominie Sinnot had not been a worthless weakling, Hallie would have been married before either her or Ella. If it came to that, Hallie could have married someone else, even after Dominie married Blossom, if she hadn't remained so absurdly wrapped up in him. It really wasn't fair to call her an old maid.

'Don't walk so fast, Hallie,' she said. 'My shoe is hurting me.' She was trying to pretend that it was she who lagged back, and not Hallie who had gone on ahead in a huff. 'Isn't it chilly?' she added, as they drew abreast again, making this as an excuse for drawing Hallie's arm through hers again. And then, deliberately, she herself tried to feel critical of Ella. Ella should be more considerate. It was not very tactful of her to keep talking about Oliver all the time, considering poor Sam, and where *he* was now, poor soul. Ella and Oliver may have been nearer to each other in age than she and Sam, but that didn't necessarily mean their marriage was any happier. Love wasn't everything! But try as she might to turn against Ella, Dolly found herself echoing Hallie's regret that she was not with them on their evening walks. For one thing, the past to Ella – as to her – was a misty place, in which it was nice to let their minds wander, but which they knew they could never reenter, whereas Hallie had never left it.

But they had reached the crossroads at which they usually turned back. Beyond this the road ran between tall trees, lonely and dark, and on the left somewhere – they weren't quite sure where – a man had once been done to death by thieves, or so they had always been told. One night in the long ago Ella had insisted that they should go further. It was a moonlit night, full of light and shadow.

'Oh, come on. Let's go down the ghosty road,' Ella urged. 'Come on.' But they wouldn't go. She, Hallie, claimed to have a stone in her shoe, and Dolly flatly refused to go a step further, saying she was too scared.

'All right, go home!' Ella said. 'I'll go by myself!' And away she went, with her sprightly gait, down the lonely road that was lit only in the centre where the moon played down through the branches of the trees, but dark and gloomy to either side where tangles of undergrowth cast their shadows. On Ella went, firm and straight, and fearless! And there they stood, feeling foolish at the thought that they who were two years older than Ella had less spirit than she. But a few seconds after Ella had gone out of sight around the first bend of the road, they heard her calling to them and, next thing, she came flying back, her skirt held up with both hands and her silk stockings flashing. 'Run, run!' she cried as she caught up with them, but they only laughed, because they knew that she had fancied her courage so great, her imagination had had to supply terrors to equal it. And ever after, when they came to that crossroads they used to tease her about that night. 'How about going on another few yards?' they used to say, just to rattle her. Even after Ella married, Hallie tried to keep up the joke. 'If we had Ella with us we might go a bit further,' she'd say when they reached that point.

It was the kind of remark Hallie was always making – a remark that concentrated so much of the past in its essence, and Dolly didn't object as long as she didn't elaborate on it too much. But she always did. 'I wonder if Ella really saw something that night or if her imagination ran away with her?' she asked this very evening as she and Dolly stood at the crossroads and looked down the ghostly road. 'What do you think Hallie?' she said. 'We must remember to ask her next time we see her.' Unfortunately at that moment Dolly had been thinking of something quite different she herself wanted to ask Ella – a practical question about the future. She was having trouble filling in some forms that came in the post, relating to Sam's insurance policy, and she was wondering if Ella could help her with them. She didn't reply to Hallie.

'What are you thinking about, Dolly?' Hallie asked peevishly, having seen that she was preoccupied.

'I was just wondering if Oliver has his life insured,' Dolly said.

Hallie turned her head away. She wasn't interested.

However, if Hallie was not interested in what Dolly said that night, she had reason next day to recall Dolly's words. She ran down the street and knocked on her door.

'Wasn't it queer you should speak of Oliver the other night?' she said, breathless from running.

'Why? What did I say anyway?' Dolly asked.

'Oh, don't you remember?' Hallie was impatient. 'You were wondering if he had his life insured.'

'Well? What was queer about that?'

'But haven't you heard?' Hallie cried. 'He's ill.'

Dolly had an unpleasant feeling that Hallie was overstraining the coincidence.

'I don't see anything queer about that. What's the matter with him anyway? I suppose he has a cold? He's hardly likely to give anyone the benefit of his insurance!'

Hallie drew an enormous breath. 'Oh, but it's not a cold, Dolly. It's more than that. The doctor doesn't know what's the matter with him. Yes! He's had the doctor. And a nurse. And there's talk of getting a night nurse. Ella is nearly out of her mind.'

Dolly was still reluctant to believe it was serious, but she began to feel uncomfortable about having made that remark about the insurance policy. She was determined Hallie must be exaggerating Oliver's condition.

'Oh, I wouldn't mind Ella,' she said scathingly. 'Look at me. I was nearly out of my mind when Sam got ill.' She had no sooner mentioned poor Sam, however, than she saw the look on Hallie's face, and her own face fell, thinking of where Sam had finished up. 'Well,' she said crossly. 'If he is bad, we'd better go up there at once. Ella is no person for dealing with an emergency. Think of that houseful of children! Think of the turmoil! Oh! If anything should happen! Hurry! Hurry!' She grabbed her coat and together they hurried up the street to Ella's.

When they got to Ella's house Hallie and Dolly found they were not the only ones who thought it their duty to be there. It was Ella's mother who opened the door. She showed them into the parlour – a room that was rarely used and in which they had hardly ever before set foot. And on their way into the room they had to stand aside to let Ella's sister-in-law pass out with a tray. The parlour was crowded. And in the middle was Ella, sitting down like a visitor.

'Oh, Hallie! Oh, Dolly!' When she saw them, Ella's face lit up, and she tried to get to her feet but several people urged her back into her chair. She sat back again docile as a child. They saw that her poor face was as white as a sheet, and that she looked as if she did not know where she was or what she was supposed to do. It was someone else who provided them with chairs, and when the sister-in-law returned a few minutes later with fresh cups of tea, as she proffered them tea she pressed upon them also the information that Oliver's condition was grave. The crisis was expected any minute.

Hallie and Dolly felt awkward. They had come to help. To take charge of the children. To see that everything possible was being done for Oliver. And instead of that they were being treated like visitors. In other parts of the house they could hear people charging themselves with the tasks they had intended to undertake.

'Is the doctor with him?' Dolly asked, reluctant to stay in the background.

'The doctor has been here twice already,' Ella's mother said. 'He's upstairs with him now.' Then she glanced at the clock and frowned. 'He ought to be brought down for a cup of tea,' she said and she turned away importantly, pausing only to whisper something to a cousin of Ella's sitting near the door, who promptly rose and followed her out of the parlour, closing the door.

'Can't we do something?' Dolly whispered to Hallie. 'Did you say there was a nurse?'

'I believe so,' Hallie said, 'but I don't know if she's a proper nurse.'

'What do you mean by that?'

'She's a cousin of Oliver's. They say she has some kind of a nursing diploma.' She needed to say no more.

'A nursing diploma!' Dolly exclaimed contemptuously, but she had to lower her voice hastily because at that moment the so-called nurse put her head around the corner of the door, looking for someone who was not there. Then she went out again, and she, too, closed the door after her. But Dolly and Hallie had seen that although she wore a nurse's cap all right and a white coat, the coat was too short and under it showed a gaudy dress with a flowery pattern. But what they objected to most was that her long legs were covered with flashy flesh-coloured stockings, and stuck into small fashionable shoes with high heels.

'I don't think much of her,' Dolly said. 'Someone ought to send down for the district nurse.' She stood up.

But just then the young nurse appeared again. This time she tiptoed over and whispered to the women on either side of Ella, who immediately began to assist Ella to her feet. Indeed, this assistance was given with such vigour that, almost before Hallie and Dolly knew what had happened, Ella had been whisked from the room.

'The crisis!' Everyone whispered the same word at the same time, so the whisper ran around the parlour like a breeze. 'The crisis!'

Up to then most people had been talking quietly, but now, subdued, they sat silent, straining to interpret the sounds from above. But where, formerly, there had been an occasional soft footfall, and the sound of an occasional voice, there was now absolute silence.

The silence lasted a long time. And the longer it lasted, the more oppressive it became, until those who had occasion to move – to cross their legs, or open their handbags – did so with exaggerated care and self-consciousness. Once during this vigil, there was a short diversion when a child was heard outside in the passage, asking a question in a shrill voice. In the parlour several people started to their feet in dismay. But the child's voice stopped in the middle of a word, and then heavy footsteps were heard again, hurrying away. The child had obviously been snatched up and carried out of earshot. After that such stillness settled over the room, Hallie and Dolly were weighted down by it. On Dolly it lay so heavily, her indignation could do no more than smoulder. But Hallie found it easy enough to yield to silence. Wasn't she used to it? One by one her thoughts began to drift away to their usual strolling ground: the past.

First she thought about Oliver, and of how strong and hearty he was long ago. It was sad to think of him, now, flat on his back, and helpless with strange women whispering and tiptoeing around him. Even the resentment she had borne against him for being best man at Dominie's wedding began to wear away. After all, he could hardly have refused. He had nothing against Blossom either, she supposed. He would have been best man for Dominie no matter who Dominie married. Poor Oliver! Was he really going to die? Did he know he was so low? When Dominie was dying, it was said he didn't know it. Even when they had brought the priest to him he thought the priest had just dropped in for a friendly chat. And he was unconscious when he was anointed. Would it have made any difference to her, she wondered, if Dominie had known he was dying? Would he have sent her any message? Suddenly a startling thought entered her mind. Perhaps Dominie had sent her a message. Perhaps Blossom had kept it from her. But at this point she pulled herself up. It was by never putting the strain of incredulity upon it that she had kept intact through the years the thin web of her romance. She had no doubt whatever that Dominie's last thoughts had been of her, but to think that he had expressed them would have been straining things too much.

Her mind returned to Oliver. Was he conscious? she wondered. Did he know that Ella was beside him? Not for anything in the world would Hallie want to deprive Ella of anything that might solace her in her sorrow, but if it should happen that Oliver was too far gone to recognise her at the end, then it was to her, Hallie, that Ella could turn. She would understand. After all, Sam had been fully conscious right up to the end. Hadn't his last words to Dolly been something about an insurance policy? Yes, it was to her, and not to Dolly, Ella would turn.

Hallie felt very close to Ella at that moment. After all they had both felt, at the time of Dolly's marriage, that there was something a bit too practical about Dolly's choice. Dolly had picked out Sam. There had not been the instantaneous, mutual attraction between them that there had been between Ella and Oliver, and between her and Dominie. She had never forgotten something Ella said the night before her wedding.

'Oliver will never have much money, Hallie,' she said. 'I'll never have things nice, the way I planned.'

'That doesn't matter,' Hallie had confidently answered.

Ella had pressed her hand. 'I knew you'd say that, Hallie,' she said. 'You and Dominie wouldn't have cared about money either.'

That was why it had hurt so bitterly, after Dominie married Blossom, to have to stand in the chapel and smile and smile when Ella and Oliver were married. That wound had never healed. It was strange, but even now when she'd sigh and say to Dolly that it would have been like long ago if Ella was with them she knew in her heart it wasn't really true. Things wouldn't have been the same. Because Ella would never have stopped talking about Oliver all the time. And it hurt. It hurt.

But now Oliver was ill and Hallie knew she mustn't bear resentment against him. He was ill, and maybe dying.

Just then the nurse threw open the parlour door again. 'Where are the children?' she demanded to know. 'I thought they were here.' When she saw they were not in the parlour she withdrew her head, and shut the door with a slam. Those in the parlour exchanged glances.

'The children are wanted to say goodbye to him. He must be sinking fast.'

A woman who was only distantly related to Oliver threw up her hands and burst into tears.

'Hush, hush!' the woman beside her murmured, not to silence her but to direct her grief into more suitable channels. 'Poor Oliver is not the one to be pitied,' they cried. 'He's going to a better world. But think of his poor young widow. Think of her! Poor Ella!' And everyone in the room broke into the same refrain. 'Poor Ella. Poor Ella.' What in the world would she do now, with those young children and no father to look after them? 'Poor Ella.'

'Poor Ella. Where was she? She shouldn't be up there till the very end. Poor Ella. Had she any arrangements made? And the children. Where were they? They ought to be taken to a neighbour's, otherwise they'd be under everyone's feet!'

Everyone was aware of things to be done, and eager to undertake those tasks. No one could be expected to remain shut up in a small front parlour when now, all over the house, in the kitchen and in the passages, there were people running back and forth, and running up and down the stairs, and people dragging articles of furniture across the floors. For the suspense was over. Oliver was sinking fast. The death rattle had been heard in his throat. Not a minute was to be wasted if everything was to be ready when death imposed a final and absolute decorum. Dolly, certainly, could not sit in the parlour a minute longer. She got up and ran out.

Hallie found herself alone at last. She had no urge to join in the tumult. Looking around her, she began indifferently to gather up cups and saucers and pile them on a tray, but she left the tray down on a side table inside the door and sat down again herself, by the dying fire. Poor Ella. It was strange to think that all three of them – Dolly, Ella, and herself – had been left alone within so short a time. Dominie was only seven years dead – Sam less than a year. And now Oliver. She sighed. In various ways all three of them had been preyed upon by the years that once, far off on the horizon, had appeared like beautiful birds of paradise, laden with sweetness. The tears came into her eyes. She had been the first to feel Time's bitter beak and claw. She had been torn apart even before Dominie died. And, after he died, it was still a long time before the others suffered anything like what she had gone through.

But now they were all three alike again in their grief and loss as they had once been alike in their hopes and dreams. Never, never would she have admitted it before, but now she faced it, that in her heart she had always resented the happiness the other two had known, and she had missed. And that was why when she and Dolly talked about their girlhood, it had secretly made her heart ache to think of Ella, snug and warm between the four walls of her home, occupying herself by attending to the needs of her children, and satisfying the demands made on her by Oliver, her husband.

Oliver's demands upon Ella had always been very obvious. Whenever Hallie met her she was never able to stop and talk to them for more than a minute or two. 'I must get back. I have to iron Oliver's shirt!' she'd say. Or some such nonsense. Even after Mass on Sundays he'd be waiting impatiently for her outside the chapel gate, and she'd be in a hurry to join him. 'I must fly,' she'd say. 'I mustn't keep him waiting.'

But now Ella, too, would be lonely. Now she would be glad enough to go out walking with Dolly and herself of an evening. And whereas she used to put the present before the past, now she too would begin to put the past before the present. She would be willing and even eager to talk about when they were young. Those golden days. That leafy springtime.

For a moment as Hallie sat there in the stuffy parlour it seemed to her that the leafy boughs of youth and springtime were about to form a bower about her, when, abruptly she was recalled to her whereabouts by a piercing scream. Oliver was gone!

Poor Ella. It was all over.

The next minute there were voices in the passage, among which Hallie distinguished the voice of Dolly, who had clearly taken command.

'Bring her into the parlour,' Dolly was saying. 'And keep her there.' Then the door opened and Dolly and Ella's mother appeared in the doorway with Ella between them. Ella was struggling to free herself, but over her head the others spoke authoritatively to each other – entirely disregarding her. 'Keep her in here,' Dolly ordered. 'Don't let her upstairs again. It's no place for her now. Is there any brandy in the house? She should be given a sip of it, whether she likes it or not.'

Hallie stood up. She was dazed and disconcerted. And indeed Dolly herself, who thought they were showing Ella into an empty room, was just as taken aback. 'Oh, are you here?' she said, surprised.

But to Ella it seemed the most natural thing in the world to see Hallie standing there.

'Oh, Hallie!' she cried, and where until then she had hung back protesting she now rushed forward and threw out her arms. 'Oh, Hallie! He's dead. Oliver is dead. He's gone from me.'

Hallie came to life at that, and her arms flew out to enlace with Ella's. This was how they had always flung themselves upon each other in their tempests of girlish grief.

'Oh, Hallie, Hallie, what will I do?' Ella cried, as she clung to her. And where she had been deaf to the others, she seemed willing and eager to listen to Hallie. Behind Ella's back Dolly made signs to Hallie. 'See if you can calm her,' she said out loud, feeling justified perhaps in disregarding Ella since Ella had buried her face in Hallie's bosom.

Hallie realised she was the centre of attention. They were all waiting for her to speak. And after a minute, Ella, too, raised her head and looked up at her with swollen eyes.

'Oh, Hallie, Hallie! What will become of me? How will I live without him?' she cried.

All at once Hallie knew what to say. 'Oh, Ellie darling,' she cried and she pressed her close. 'Hush – hush. Time heals everything.' Then her voice grew softer and more persuasive. 'While you were all upstairs,' she said, almost crooning the words, 'I was sitting here thinking how lovely it would be when you, Dolly, and I would be together again like we used to be. Like long ago.'

But almost before she finished, Ella broke away from her, and began to scream again and to struggle to get out of the room again. Her mother had to take hold of her and try to pacify her.

'Don't mind her, Ella. She didn't mean it,' she said. 'She didn't know what she was saying.'

What was the matter? What had she said? Hallie looked around for Dolly, but Dolly was staring at her with eyes that would take the heat out of the sun.

'Have you gone out of your mind, Hallie?' Dolly said. Hallie got more confused. 'What did I say?' she cried. But Dolly pushed her to one side, and dropping down on her knees she put her arms around Ella, and whispered something into her ear. Ella stopped screaming at once.

Hallie stared at them. She hadn't heard what Dolly whispered, but her eyes fastened on the hands of her friends, that were tightly clasped. And on their hands she saw their wedding rings. She knew then what Dolly had said.

AT SALLYGAP

THE BUS CLIMBED UP THE HILLY ROADS ON ITS WAY THROUGH THE Dublin Mountains to the town of Enniskerry. On either side the hedges were so high that the passengers had nothing more interesting to look at than each other. But after a short time the road became steeper and then the fields that had been hidden were bared to view, slanting smoothly downward to the edge of the distant city.

Dublin was all exposed. The passengers could see every inch of it. They could certainly see every steeple and tower, although the dark spires and steeples rising out of the blue pools of distance looked little better than thistles rising up defiant in a pale pasture.

The sea that half-circled this indistinct city seemed as grey and motionless as the air. Suddenly, however, it was seen that the five o'clock mail boat, looking no bigger than a child's toy boat, was pushing aside the plastery waves and curving around the pier at Dunlaoghaire on its way to the shores of England.

'There she goes!' Manny Ryan said to the young man in a grey flannel suit who shared the bus seat with him. 'The fastest little boat for her size in the whole of the British Isles.'

'What time does it take her to do the crossing?' the young man asked.

'Two hours and five minutes,' said Manny, and he took out a watch and stared at it. 'It's three thirty-nine now. She's out about four minutes, I'd say. That leaves her right to the dot. She'll dock at Holyhead at exactly five forty.'

'She's dipping a bit,' said the young man. 'I suppose she's taking back a big load after the Horse Show.'

'That's right. I saw by the paper this morning she took two thousand people across yesterday evening.'

'You take a great interest in things, I see.'

'I do. That's quite right for you! I take a great interest indeed, but I have my reasons. I have my reasons.'

Manny put his elbow up against the ledge of the window and turned on his side in the tight space of the seat so that he was almost facing his companion, who, having no window ledge to lean upon, was forced to remain with his profile to Manny while they were talking.

'You wouldn't think, would you,' said Manny, 'just by looking at me, that I had my choice to sail out of Dublin on that little boat one day, and I turned it down? You wouldn't think that now, would you?'

'I don't know,' said the young man uncomfortably. 'Many a man goes over to Holyhead, for one class of thing or another.' But it was clear by his voice that he found it hard to picture Manny, with his shiny black suit and his bowler hat, in any other city than the one they had lately left. So strong was his impression that Manny was – as he'd put it – a Dubliner-coming-and-going, that he hastened to hide this impression by asking what business Manny had in Holyhead, if that wasn't an impertinence? He forgot apparently that Manny had never actually gone there, but Manny forgot that too in his haste to correct the young man on another score altogether.

'Is it Holyhead?' he asked in disgust. 'Who goes there but jobbers and journeymen?'

'London?' asked the young man, raising his eyebrows.

'Policemen and servant girls,' Manny said impatiently.

'Was it to the Continent, sir?' said the young man, and the 'sir' whistled through the wax in Manny's ears like the sweetest note of a harp, plucked by a clever finger.

'To the Continent is right,' he said. 'I was heading for Paris – "gay Paree", as they call it over there – and I often wish to God I hadn't turned my back on the idea.'

'Is it a thing you didn't go, sir?'

'Well, now, as to that question,' said Manny, 'I won't say yes and I won't say no, but I'll tell you this much: I had my chance of going. That's something, isn't it? That's more than most can say! Isn't it?'

'It is indeed. But if it's a thing that you didn't go, sir, might I make so bold as to ask the reason?'

'I'll tell you,' said Manny, 'but first of all I'll have to tell you why I was going in the first place.' Taking out a sepia-coloured photograph from an old wallet, he passed it to the young man, who looked at it, holding it close to his face because it was faded in places and in other places the glaze was cracked. But he made out quite clearly all the same a group of young men sitting stiffly on cane-backed chairs, their legs rigid in pinstripe trousers, their hair plastered down with oil, and their hands folded self-consciously over the awkward contours of trombones, fiddles, and brass cornets. In the centre of the group, turned up on its rim, was a big drum wearing a banner across its face with the words MARY STREET BAND printed on it in large block letters. 'That was us,' said Manny, 'the Mary Street Band. We used to play for all the dances in the city, and as well, we played for the half-hour interval at the Mary Street Theatre.' He leaned over. 'That was me,' he said, pointing to a young man with a fiddle on his knee, a young man who resembled him as a son might resemble a father.

'I'd recognise you all right,' said the stranger, looking up at Manny's face and down again at the photograph. Both faces had the same nervous thinness, the same pointed jaw, and the same cleft of weakness in the chin. Only the eyes were different. The eyes in the photograph were light in colour, either from bad lighting on the part of the photographer or from youthful shallowness in the sitter. The eyes of the older Manny were dark. They had a depth that might have come from sadness, but whatever it came from, it was out of keeping with the cockiness of his striped, city suiting and his bowler hat. 'There was a party of us – the few lads you see there at the back, and the one to the left of the drum – and we were planning on getting out, going across to Paris and trying the dance halls over there – palais, they call them. We'd stuck together for three years, but these few lads I'm after pointing out to you got sick of playing to the Dublin jackeens. I got sick of them, too. They were always sucking oranges, and spitting out the pips on the floor, and catcalling up at the artistes. We heard tell it was different altogether across the water. Tell me this, were you ever in Paris, young fellow? "Gay Paree", I should be saying.'

'No, I can't say that I was,' said the young man.

'Man alive!' said Manny. 'Sure, that's the place for a young fellow like you. Clear out and go. That's my advice to you. Take it or leave it: it's my advice to you, although I don't know from Adam who you are or what you are. That's what I'd say to you if you were my own son. Cut and run for it.' Manny gave a deep sigh that went down the neck of the lady in front and made her shiver and draw her collar closer. 'Paris!' he said again, and again he sighed. 'Paris, lit up all night as bright as the sun, with strings of lights pulling out of each other from one side of the street to the other, and fountains and bandstands every other yard along the way. The people go up and down linked, and singing, at all hours of the day or night, and the publicans – they have some other name on them over there, of course – keep coming to the door every minute with aprons round their middle, like women, and sweeping the pavement outside the door and finishing off maybe by swilling a bucket of wine over it to wash it down.'

'You seem to have a pretty good idea of it for a man who was never there!'

'I have a lot of postcards,' said Manny, 'and myself and the lads were never done talking about it before ever we decided on going at all. In the end we just packed up one night and said, off with us! There had been a bit of a row that night at the theatre, and somehow or other an old dead cat got flung up on the stage. Did you ever hear the like of that for ignorance? "Holy God," we said, "that's too much to take from any audience."'

'All I can say is, it's no wonder you packed your bags!' said the young man.

'Is it now?' said Manny. 'That's what I tell myself. My bag was all packed and strapped, and what was more, before very long it was up the gangplank and on the deck of that little boat you see pulling out there!'

They looked out the window of the bus, down over the falling fields of the mountainside, to the sea and the vanishing boat.

'Is that right?' said the young man.

'That's right. Me and my bag were on the deck and there was Annie below on the quay, with the tears in her eyes. That was the first time I gave a thought to her at all. Annie is my wife. At least she is now. She wasn't then. I gave one look at her standing there in the rain – it was raining at the time – with her handkerchief rolled up in her hand ready to wave as soon as the boat got going. The porters were pushing past her with their truckloads of trunks and hitting up against her. Did you ever notice how rough those fellows are? Well, with the rain and the porters and one thing and another, I got to pitying her, standing there. I got to thinking, do you know, of all the things we'd done together. Nothing bad, you know. Nothing to be ashamed of, if you understand, but still I didn't like to think of her standing there, watching me going off, maybe for good, and she thinking over the things I'd said to her at one time or another. You know yourself, I suppose, the kind of thing a man's apt to say to a girl, off and on?'

'I do,' said the young man.

'You do? Well, in that case you'll understand how I felt seeing her standing there. I felt so bad I tried to go back down the gangplank for a few last words with her before the boat pulled out, but there were people coming up against me all the time and I was having to stand aside every other step I took and crush in against the rails to let them pass. And some of them were cranky devils, telling me to get the hell out of the way, to come if I was coming, and go if I was going, and – for God Almighty's sake – to take my bloody bag out of the way. It was jabbing them in the legs without my noticing it, and as sure as I pulled it to one side it jabbed into someone on the other side. There was terrible confusion. You'd think, wouldn't you, that the officials would be able to put a stop to it? But I declare to God they were worse than the people that were travelling. There was one of them clicking tickets at the bottom of the gangway, and all he did was let a shout at me to say I was obstructing the passage. Obstructing!

'"Come on up, Manny," shouted the lads from up above on the deck.

'"Goodbye, Manny," Annie said in a little bit of a voice you'd hardly hear above the banging of cases and the screaming of the seagulls.'

'You didn't go down?'

'Down I went.'

'And the boys?'

'They were staring like as if they were transfixed. They couldn't believe their eyes. They kept calling down to me from the deck above, but the wind was going the other way and we couldn't hear one word they were saying. Then the whistles began to blow, and the sailors began spitting on their hands and pulling at the ropes to let the plank up into the boat. The train was getting ready to go back to Westland Row: it was going to pull out any minute.

'"I knew you'd come to your senses," Annie said. "Have you got your bag?" I held it up. "Your fiddle?" she said. By God, if I hadn't left the fiddle above on the deck! Would you believe that? I started shouting up at the lads, and Timmy Coyne — that's the little fellow with the moustache sitting next to me in the photo — Timmy put his hands up to his mouth like he was playing a bugle — it was the piano he played in the band, by the way — and he shouts out "Wha-a-a-at?" like that, drawing it out so's we could hear it.

'"The fiddle!" I shouted. But "fiddle" isn't a word you can stretch out, you know. No matter how slow you say it, it's said and done in a minute. "Fiddle." Try it yourself. "Fiddle." It's a funny sort of word, isn't it, when you say it over a few times like that? It sort of loses its meaning. Anyway, Timmy didn't hear me. "Ca-a-a-n'-t hea-er-ear!" says he. A couple of people round about me began to shout up too. "Fiddle. Fiddle," they shouted. The boat was pushing off from the pier.

Suddenly one real game fellow that was after putting a fine young girl on the boat, and after kissing her too in front of everyone, ups and pulls off his hat, and crooking it under his arm, like it was a fiddle, he starts pulling his right hand back and forth across it for all the world as if it was a bow and he was playing a real fiddle. Timmy takes one look at him and down he ducks and starts rooting around on the deck. The next minute he ups and rests the fiddle case on the rails.

' "Catch!" he shouts, and over comes the fiddle across the space of water that was blinding white by this time with the foam from the moving boat.

' "It's into the water!" someone shouts.

' "Not on your life!" shouts your man on the wharf, and he leaps into the air to catch it. But you know how slippy them wooden boards on the wharf are – with that green slimy stuff on them? You do? Well, to make a long story short, your man's foot slips, and down comes the fiddle on one of the iron stumps they tie the boat to, and fiddle and case, and even the little bow, were smashed to smithereens under my eyes. You should have heard the crowd laughing. I always say it's easy enough to raise a laugh when you're not doing it for money!'

'What did Annie say?'

' "It's the hand of God," she said.'

'What did you say?'

'Sure, what could I say? There was no use making the poor fellow feel bad, so I had to let on to make a joke of it. I went over and gave a kick with my foot to the bits of wood, and put them floating out on the water, along with a bucketful of potato peels and cabbage stalks that were just after being flung out of a porthole.' Manny looked down at the grey feather of smoke on the horizon that was all that now remained of the mail boat. 'Whenever I see that little boat,' he said, 'I get to thinking of the sea and the way it was that day, with the swill lapping up and down on it and the bits of the fiddle looking like bits of an old box. Walking back to the train, we could see the bits of it floating along on the water under us, through the big cracks in the boards. I never can understand why it is they leave such big spaces between those boards anyway. And just as we were going out the gate to the platform, what did I see, down through the splits, but a bit of the bow. And here's a curious thing for you! You could tell what it was the minute you looked at it, broken and all as it was. Oh, look! you'd say if you happened to be passing along the pier, going for a walk and not knowing anything about me or the boys. Look! you'd say to whoever was with you. Isn't that the bow of a fiddle?'

'Did you ever hear from the boys again?' the young man asked. Manny shook his head.

'If they wrote we never got the letter,' he said. 'I heard they broke up after a bit. When Annie and me got married we opened a shop in South King Street and went to live over the shop. You know South King Street? Our shop is down past the Gaiety. The shop took up pretty near all our time on account of us knowing nothing about business. We never got a minute to ourselves. Nor now either. Look at today! I've been out since early morning trying to find someone that would deliver eggs to the door. That's what I'm doing now, going up to Sallygap to see a man I was told about by one of the dealers in Moore Street. The dealer gets his eggs from this man twice a week, and I didn't see why he couldn't bring us in a couple of dozen at the same time. If he does, we'll put up a card on the window saying Fresh Eggs Daily. The Dublin people go mad for a fresh egg. Did you ever notice that?'

The conductor came down the aisle and leaned in to Manny.

'We're coming near to Sallygap now,' said the conductor.

'Is that right?' said Manny. 'Give a touch to the bell so, and get the driver to stop. Anywhere here will do nicely.' He turned to the young man confidentially. 'I have to look for the place, you see.'

'I hope you find it all right, sir.'

'I hope so. Well, good day to you now. Don't forget the advice I gave you.' Manny pointed with his thumb in the direction of the sea.

Then he got off the bus and for the first time in years found himself on a country road alone.

The farmhouse Manny was looking for was easy enough to find. And the farmer obligingly promised to send him down the eggs twice a week, and three times if the orders got bigger. He wanted to know if Manny ever tried selling chickens or geese? Manny said his wife took care of the orders. The farmer asked if he would mention the matter to his wife. Manny agreed to do so. They said goodbye and Manny went back to the road.

By that time Manny wanted a drink. He wasn't a drinking man, but he wanted a glass of beer just to take the thirst off him. He remembered that they had passed a public house a while before he got off the bus. He started walking back towards it.

As he walked along he thought of the boys again. It was the boat had put him in mind of them. And the young fellow that had been sitting beside him was just about the age he was himself in those days. A nice young fellow! Manny idly wondered who he was, and he wondered, just as idly, at what time he himself would get a bus going back to Dublin.

But it was nice, mind you, walking along the road. He didn't care if the bus was a bit slow in coming. It was not as if it was raining or cold. It was a nice evening. He'd often heard tell of young lads from Dublin coming up here on their bicycles of a fine evening, and leaving the bicycles inside a fence while they went walking in the heather. Just walking, mind you; just walking. He used to think it was a bit daft. Now that he was up here himself he could see how a quiet sort of chap might like that class of thing. Manny looked at the hedges that were tangled with wild vetches, and he looked at an old apple tree crocheted over with grey lichen. He looked at the gleaming grass in the wet ditch, and at the flowers and flowering reeds that grew there. They all have names, he supposed. Could you beat that!

Walking along, he soon came to a cottage with dirty brown thatch from which streaks of rain had run down the walls, leaving yellow stripes on the lime. As he got near, a woman came to the door with a black pot and swilled out a slop of green water into the road, leaving a stench of cabbage in the air when she went in. It was a queer time to be cooking her cabbage, Manny thought, and then he chuckled. 'For God's sake,' he said out loud, 'will you look at the old duck?'

A duck had flapped over from the other side of the road to see if the cabbage water made a pool big enough to swim in. 'Will you just look at him?' Manny said to himself, the road being empty. He was giving himself very superfluous advice though, because he was staring at the duck as hard as he could. But as he stood there a geranium pot was taken down from inside one of the small windows of the cottage, and a face came close to the glass. They don't like you stopping and staring, I suppose, he thought, and he moved along.

His thoughts for some time were on the smallness and darkness of the cottage. He wondered how people put up with living in a little poke like that, and his own room behind the shop in South King Street seemed better to him than it had for a long time. After all, he and Annie had a range. They had gaslight. And they had the use of the lavatory on the upper landing. He was pleased to think of the many advantages he had over those people who had been peeping out at him. He used to think sometimes that South King Street was a dungeon in which he was imprisoned for life, while other men went here and went there, and did this and did that, and some of them even went off to Paris. But at that moment he felt it was a fine thing after all to have a place of your own to keep things in, a place where you could lie down if you were sick or worn out. And it was within a stone's throw of the Pillar.

He didn't get out enough – that was the trouble. If he got out and about more he'd have the right attitude to the house, and maybe to the shop, too. No wonder he was sick of it, never leaving it except like this, to do a message. He should take an odd day off. Man! What was he talking about? He ought to take a week. He ought to run over to Paris and look up the boys. Then, as if aghast at the magnitude of his revolt, he gave himself an alternative. He should go over to Liverpool, anyway, for one of the weekend race meetings. With a bit of luck he might make his expenses, and that would shut Annie's mouth.

The public house came into view just then, and very opportunely, because Manny walked in with the confidence of one who is contemplating a sojourn in distant lands.

He ordered his drink. There were two or three locals leaning against the counter, and a large man, obviously a commercial traveller, stood cleaning his spectacles and asking questions about the locality. The locals were looking sheepishly at their empty glasses that were draped with scum. The traveller gave orders for the glasses to be filled up again. He looked down the counter at Manny as if he would like to include him in the order, but there was a repelling air of independence about Manny, due perhaps to his bowler hat, which sat self-consciously upon the bar counter.

Manny listened to the talk at the other end of the bar. Once or twice the locals mistook the traveller's meaning, but Manny felt a warmth in his heart towards them. Their dull-wittedness gave him a feeling of security. He felt a great dislike for the talkative traveller. He hoped that they would not be on the same bus going back to the city.

Just then the sound of a motor stole into the stillness outside. The bus was coming. Manny drank up, and put out his hand for his hat. Out of the corner of his eye he saw the traveller buttoning his overcoat. He heard his jocose farewells to the locals, who were already leaning back with greater ease against the counter.

Manny went towards the door. The traveller also went towards the door. In the doorway they met.

'I see you are taking this bus too?' said the traveller.

Manny had, of course, intended going back on that bus. He had no idea when there would be another one. But he took a great dislike to the idea of journeying back with the large, talkative man.

'I'm waiting for the next bus,' he said impulsively.

'Sorry!' said the traveller. 'I should have been glad of your company. Good evening.'

'Good evening,' said Manny, and he stood back from the dust of the bus as it started up again.

When the dust had blown into the hedges, Manny stepped into the middle of the road and doggedly faced the way the bus had gone. He would probably be walking for a long time before another bus caught up with him, but he did not care. A rare recklessness possessed him, and when shortly after night came down this feeling of recklessness strengthened. He walked along, looking from side to side, and in his heart the night's potent beauty was beginning to have effect. But he felt confused. The dark hills and the pale sky and the city pricking out its shape upon the sea with starry lights filled him with strangely mingled feelings of sadness and joy. And when the sky flowered into a thousand stars of forget-me-not blue he was strangled by the need to know what had come over him, and having no other way to stem the tide of desolating joy within him, he started to run the way he used to run on the roads as a young lad. And as he ran he laughed out loud to think that he, Manny Ryan, was running along a country road in the dark, not knowing but he'd run into a hedge or a ditch.

Yesterday, if anyone had come to him and suggested that he'd do such a thing, he would have split his sides laughing. And tomorrow, if he were to try and persuade Annie to take a walk out in the country, she'd look at him as if he was daft. The Dublin people couldn't tell you the difference between a bush and a tree. Manny stood to recover his breath. And he thought of his wife with her yellow elbows coming through the black unravelled sleeve of her cardigan, as she leaned across the counter in the dismal shop, giving off old shaffoge with any shawley who came the way and had an hour, or maybe two hours, to spare. He thought of the bars filled with his cronies talking about the state of the country for all they were fit, men that never saw more of it than you'd see from the top of a tram. He thought of the skitting young fellows and girls outside Whitefriar Street after late Mass on a Sunday, and he thought of the old men standing at the pub ends of the streets, ringing themselves around with spits. He thought of the old women leaning against the jambs of their doorways, with empty crockery milk jugs hanging out of their hands, forgotten in the squalor of their gossip. He thought of the children sitting among the trodden and rancid cabbage butts on the edge of the pavements, repeating the gossip they had heard when they crouched, unheeded, under some public-house counter. He thought of the young and the old, the men and the women, and the pale, frightened children, who were shuffling along the kneelers in churches all over the city, waiting their turn to snuffle out their sins in the dark wooden confessionals. And it seemed as if the cool green light of day scarcely ever reached those people, and the only breezes that blew into their lives came from under their draughty doors thickened with the warm odour of boiling potatoes. The loathing he'd felt for the city, years before, when he first came to Dublin, stole over him again as it had done on that night long ago in the little theatre in Mary Street. Dublin jackeens! he thought.

'Dublin jackeens!' he said then out loud, the gibe coming forth from a dim corner in his mind where the memory of a buttercup field and a cobbled yard pricked with grass gave him the right to feel different from them. Once more he longed to get away from Dublin. But this time there was a difference. He wanted to get away from Dublin – yes – but not from Ireland. He didn't want to go away from Ireland, he thought with anguish. Not away from her yellow fields. Not away from her emerald ditches. He wanted only to get away from the stuffy Dublin streets and the people that walked them. Even to get away occasionally for an hour like this would satisfy him.

Wasn't it well, after all, he hadn't gone to Paris? Things always turned out for the best in the end. If he had gone away he might never have come up here to Sallygap, and then he would never have found out that peace was not a matter of one city or another, but a matter of hedges and fields and waddling ducks and a handful of stars. Cities were all alike. Paris was no better or no worse than Dublin when you looked into the matter closely. Paris was a wicked place too, by all accounts, even if people did have a good time there at night, with the lights and the bandstands. Who ever heard of the boys from the Mary Street Band since they went? Where were they? God alone knew! They were playing, maybe, in some cellar done up with striped tablecloths and posters on the walls, like he'd seen in the pictures, with smoke cutting their guts, and women with big thighs and dresses torn open to the waist sitting on their knees and cracking the strings of their sinews with the weight.

A sweat broke out on Manny, and he had to stand still on the road to let the wind cool his burning face. He was damn glad he had stayed at home. What was the need in anybody going across seas when all a man had to do, if he got sick of himself, was to take a bus and come up to a place like this? As long as a fellow could come up to a place like this, what was the need of going further?

I'll come up here again, he thought. Upon my soul I will. 'I'll come back again,' he said out loud this time. 'I'll come back again all right.' He turned and took a last look at the hills before he went round a bend in the road, where the houses and shops of Rathfarnham would hide them from view.

With the first shops and the first beginnings of the city and its dazzling tramlines, its noises, and its shoving crowds, Manny felt a tiredness he had not felt in all the miles of rough road he had walked. His feet burned, and his back was weighed down with a knapsack of weariness. So at Terenure he took a tram and sat on the edge of the only seat that was vacant, his light weight joggling with every motion, and the elbow and hipbone of a fat woman on the inside of the seat nudging him with the insistence of inadvertency. Smells of gas and oil sickened him. Broken lights strained his eyes. But most of all a dread of returning home came over him as he remembered that Annie had told him to hurry back. The sharp notes of her voice echoed sudden and loud in his ears, and it seemed impossible that he had forgotten what she said. He felt like a little boy who had blotted his copy, a little boy who had lost the change, a little boy creeping home under fear of the whip.

The fear of Annie's tongue hung over Manny all the time the tram rattled through the suburbs and when he got out to walk down King Street. When he reached home and saw the closed shutters of the shop, his hand was so stiff and cold that when he put it into the letter box he could hardly find the string by which the latch of the door could be pulled back from outside. His hand clattered the letter box for a time before he found it. Then he pulled the string and the door opened. He went in and felt for the knob of the kitchen door, not seeing that the door was wide open because the room was dark and the fire only a powdering of hot grey ash. Then a red spark fell into the ashpit and he realised the door was open after all and that Annie was sitting by the range. Next minute his eyes became used to the dark, and, the customary position of things supplementing his eye where it failed, enabled him to reach the fire and sit down opposite her. He said nothing but sat watching her and wondering when she would speak.

Annie did not speak. The truth was that she had been so excited by his unusual absence that she was unfit for any emotion at his eventual return.

Marriage had been an act of unselfishness on Manny's part. He married Annie because he thought that was what would make her happy, and he was content to give up his own freedom for that object. She, however, had not thought of marriage as anything but a means of breaking the monotony. And she had soon found it a greater monotony than the one she had fled from, and, unlike the other, it was no anteroom of hope leading to something better. Manny accepted her so complacently from the first day that she was bored in a week with his unchanging kindness. At first she exhibited an artificial irritation at trifles in the hope of stirring up a little excitement, but Manny was kinder and more gentle on those occasions than he was before, and gradually her irritability and petulance became more daring until these sins could scarcely be classed as venial. Finally, what had been slyly deliberate became involuntary, and the sour expression on her face hardened into a mask. She sought in the throbbing pulse and rippling flux of anger the excitement she had unconsciously hoped to find in her marriage bed. But her angers, too, were sterile, breeding no response in Manny. He was the same always. It seemed, however, that she could never believe this, and she tried from time to time to break the strength of his weakness, and she fought against his kindness as if it were her enemy, as, in an obscure way, it was. What Annie really wanted was the flaming face, the racing pulse, the temper that raised red weals on the skin, the heat of bodies crushed together in rage. And this need of her nature had never been satisfied except vicariously, leaning over the shop counter listening to the whispered stories of other women; stories of obscene blows given in drunken lusts, stories of cunning and cupidity and flashes of anger and hate that rent the darkness of the tenement hallways in the vicinity, when she and Manny had been in bed for hours.

'Ah, woman dear,' these other women would say to her, 'sure you know nothing at all about life.' And then, as if she was to be pitied, they'd roll up their sleeves indulgently and show her scalds and scabs. 'Take a look at that!' they'd say.

And sometimes, standing at the hall door in the dark at night after the shop was shut, she might hear a scream in a room across the street, or round the corner, followed maybe by children's voices sounding as if they were frightened out of their wits. Or perhaps a neighbour might come down the street loudly sobbing, linked on either side by her children, sobbing louder and telling her in high childish voices not to mind; not to mind. Not to mind what? Annie wondered. Which of the inciting words and gestures she had heard the neighbours tell about had provoked this woman? She used to draw back a bit into the doorway while they were passing, her thin shoulder blades pressed against the wall so they wouldn't see her spying on them and she might then catch a glimpse of Manny sitting in the kitchen with his stocking feet upon the cooling range, while he read the paper. Her eyes would flicker with hatred and resentment, and she would have an impulse to be revenged on him by going in and poking the range, to send clouds of ashes over him till he'd have to get up and go to bed.

This evening, when he did not come back on time, she set her mind to planning some taunt for him when he'd come into the shop. If there were customers there, so much the better. One time she wouldn't have risked a row before the customers, but she'd found it helped trade more than it hindered it, particularly when Manny never answered back or made trouble. But as the evening wore out and there was still no sign of him, she began to think better of him. She began to think that maybe in his weak way he was defying her at last. Maybe he was getting his temper up with drink? He wasn't a drinking man, but there was always a first time for everything.

A wild elation welled up inside her, waiting for a torrential release in shouting and screaming. Perhaps she had battered in his patience at last? At last he was going to try to get even with her. Well! She was ready. She went into the kitchen, leaving the door into the shop half-open while she knotted her hair as tight as she could, the pricking pain on her neck giving her a foretaste of the fight she would have, and her eyes glittered. She let the customers go without giving them their usual bit of chitchat. She put the shutters up before the time. Where was he? It was getting very late now for a timid man like Manny. And he had had no dinner. She lifted the saucer that was covering his plate on the range. She ought to let him get a bite of food into him before she started the row. But where was he?

She was on her way out to the door to look up the street when she saw the silhouette of the poorhouse hearse passing the door. Supposing he was gone for good? The little skunk! It would be just like him to go over the river wall, like a rat in the dark, and never be heard of again. She would be cheated in this like everything else. Then the blackness lifted a little in her heart and she began to consider other possibilities. Maybe he'd skipped off to better himself somewhere and given her a miss? Again anger throbbed in her breast, but it eased when she remembered that he wouldn't have any money. Thanks be to the Almighty – and to her own good sense – she hadn't given him any money for the eggs. She wondered if he'd got them. Had he gone for them at all?

One after another, then, pictures of horror came into her mind. She saw a sodden corpse, white and hideously swollen, being carried in across the shop, dripping water from muddy clothes upon the thirsty floorboards. She saw herself at the wake, moaning and rocking from side to side, with everyone pitying her.

He wasn't a bad sort really, always wanting to take her to the Gaiety when the opera was on. He wasn't to blame for being so weak. His hands always went dead when he was cold. His face got a terrible blue colour in frosty weather. She thought about the peculiar habit he had of sleeping with his feet outside the bedclothes. And she began to feel uneasy about the past as well as about the future. She walked up and down the dark room, letting herself be mauled now by remorse.

Once in a while she went into the street and looked up and down. She did that in an effort to anticipate the terror that she felt was coming nearer every minute, rounding each corner more rapidly than the one before. But the evening winds were cooling the air and breathing their clear sweet peace even into the city streets. The lights were lighted, but their rays were not yet drawn out from them because the day had still some brightness of its own. They kept their gold carefully coiled up inside their glass globes, against the hour when their light would be needed, and it seemed as if they had no other function than to decorate the streets. The trams, too, were lit up, and they sailed like gilded galleons down the evanescent evening blue. The noises of trucks and drays sounded singly in the stillness as if to announce that they were going off as fast as they could, and that soon the city would be given over to cars and taxis travelling to gaudy cinemas and to theatres pearled with light.

The evening was so fair and so serene, so green and gilt, it threatened to rob her of all her dreads and to soothe her fears. It was better to sit by the whitening fire and imagine that the city outside was dark and vicious as she had often felt it to be, crossing it late on winter nights; a place of evil shadows, with police standing silently in the alleyways, and its shops shut down and barricaded with boards like coffin lids, and all the private houses fortified with battered ashcans lined up along the path, and, dreariest of all, the dark Green with its padlocked gates and its tree-high railings, through which you heard the agonies of a thousand cats wailing in the shrubberies.

She did not know which of her black forebodings she felt to be the more likely, but the ones that brought terror without robbing her entirely of the object of her terror were the ones that most appealed to her. And so she more or less expected a living Manny to be brought home to her, but one in whom some latent mutinous instinct had at last set up a twanging of chords that would echo throughout the rest of their lives and put reality into their relationship. She waited for his coming with more eagerness than when he was coming to court her.

But the instant she heard his footfall she knew he was the same old Manny. He was all right. And he was sober. Her fears faded out in widening ripples, leaving stillness and stagnation in her heart once more. When he put his head inside the door she knew by his apologetic cough that whatever it was had kept him out late it was no high-riding revolt, just a pale and weedy shoot from the anaemia of his character. It was certainly not a bursting into leaf of unsuspected manliness.

She sat by the fire without moving.

At last Manny was driven to break the silence himself.

'Did you keep my dinner, Annie?' he asked timidly, going over to the range, stooping his head as he went to avoid a slap of the wet sheets and towels that hung across the kitchen on a piece of string. He opened the door of the oven and bending down looked in. There was nothing there, and he shut the door quietly and stole a look at Annie. She was sitting scratching her head with a hairpin she had pulled out of the tight knot of hair on her neck. When she had finished scratching she stood up.

'Get out of my way,' she ordered tonelessly, and, taking down a damp cloth off the line over his head, she took a hot plate from the top of the stove and went over to a pile of rubbish in the corner of the room. Pulling out a piece of brown paper she put it under the plate before she set it on the table. 'Light the gas,' she ordered.

The nauseous smell of gas roamed around the room in streamers that soon ran together into one thick odour, and the glare of the gas-light took away the only dignity the room had – its darkness. Manny sat down to the meal set before him on the brown paper. It was a plate of meat flanked on two sides by tallow-yellow potatoes and a mound of soggy cabbage that still held the shape of the fork with which it had been patted. Meat, potato, and cabbage were all stuck fast to the plate. And around the rim of the plate, the gravy was crusted into a brown paper doily.

'It looks good,' Manny said appeasingly, 'and it smells good.'

'It smelled better four hours ago,' Annie said, cleaning a knife with her fingers and putting it down beside the plate.

Manny wondered if this reference to keeping the dinner hot was intended as an opening for him to say where he had been, and what had kept him, but when he looked at her he decided on saying nothing.

He ate his dinner in silence, and tried as best he could to keep the food in his mouth from making noises, but the sounds of chewing seemed so loud in his own ears that after a few mouthfuls he began to swallow down the coarse lumps of beef unchewed. Soon the silence became so terrible he could eat no more. He pushed aside his plate and sat staring at the ring of grease it had left on the absorbent brown paper. He was reminded waywardly of the brown paper he had used the night before his wedding to get a grease stain off the sleeve of his best suit. In those days he used to read in bed and he'd get his clothes covered with candle grease, because he used to hump them under the candlestick to raise it higher beside the bed. That was a long time ago, but the past had been coming into his mind all day. He used to hear his mother say that you relived all your life in your mind before you died, but he hated those ignorant old superstitions. They'd drive you mad. Yet this silence in the kitchen was enough to make a man mad too.

He turned around in the chair and deliberately drew down the lash of her rage. 'I went up to Sallygap to get the eggs, but I missed the bus and walked home.'

'From Sallygap?'

He had expected a tirade. He looked at her. She was picking her teeth with a bit of brown paper she'd leaned over and torn off the paper under the plate.

'Gets in your teeth, doesn't it?' he said, in a fainthearted hope that there was not going to be any row.

'Are you finished?' she asked.

He looked at his plate. 'Finished,' he said. 'All except my tea. I'll wet the tea myself if you like.'

'The tea is in the pot,' she said, and as he poured the spluttering water into the cold teapot she got up and went over to the dresser and took down a cup and saucer. She put them on the table.

The cup had not been washed since it had last been used. There was a sediment of moist sugar in the bottom of it, and the outside was streaked with yellow tea stains.

'This cup is a bit dirty,' he said, moving over to the sink.

'It's your own dirt, then,' she said to him. 'It was you who had it last.'

He stood irresolute, and then he said he'd like a clean cup.

'There's a quarter pound of sugar in the bottom of that cup,' Annie said, and then she snapped a question at him suddenly, with some apparent relevancy in her own mind. 'What did you do with the return ticket?'

He rooted in his pockets and took out the half-ticket. She snapped it up and looked at it closely, and then she stuck it down in a jug that was hanging by its handle on the nail of the dresser.

'Is he going to send the eggs?'

'Every Monday and Friday.'

'Give me that cup.' She went over to the sink, where she ran the cold tap on it. She clattered it back on the saucer, wet. Cold drops splashed on his hot hands from her wet hands. She stood looking down at him. 'It's a queer thing when a man disgusts to himself,' she said.

Her eyes were greener than ever. They used to remind him of the sea at Howth, where they used to go walking when they were courting. They were the same colour still, but now they reminded him suddenly of the green water under the wharf at Dunlaoghaire. And as the sticky sea that day had been flecked with splinters of his broken fiddle, Annie's eyes above him now were flecked with malevolence.

Ever since their first quarrel, he'd been afraid of her sharp tongue. But it had been the fear of a timid soul. Now, looking up into her eyes, his immature and childish fear fell from him, and instead of it there came into his heart a terrible adult fear; a fear that came from his instincts, from his blood. He thought of all the talk he had heard at different times in public houses, talk of morgues and murders, and he remembered what he had said to himself up at Sallygap about the people of Dublin: that they were ignorant, with clogged pools in their blood that clotted easily to unjust hate. They hugged their hate. He thought of Paris, with its flashing lights and its flashing hates, its quick flashing knives; but the dangers in Paris seemed vivid and vital compared with the dead anger in the sullen eyes that were watching him. Desperately he thought of the hills, but the thought of them gave him no refuge. The happy hills were fading from his mind already. He would never seek a sanctuary among them again.

For there was no sanctuary from hatred such as he saw in Annie's eyes, unless it came from behind some night, from a raised hatchet brought down with a crack on his skull, or from a queer taste in the mouth followed by a twisting in the guts. She had him imprisoned forever in her hatred. His little fiddle had crashed on the pier the day he gave up all his dreams for her, and it had floated in splintered sticks on the dirty water. He thought of it for a moment, and then he thought of nothing at all for a while, but just sat watching her as she went about the room.

Then he remembered that she had said something to him when she clattered down the wet cup on the saucer in front of him a little while before. He tried to think what it was she had said. He couldn't remember.

But he did remember, distinctly, thinking at the time, that whatever it was, it was true.

SARAH

SARAH HAD A BIT OF A BAD NAME. THAT WAS THE WORST HER NEIGHbours would say of her, although there was a certain fortuity about her choice of fathers for the three strapping sons she'd borne – all three outside wedlock.

Sarah was a great worker, strong and tireless, and a lot of women in the village got her in to scrub for them. Nobody was ever known to be unkind to her. And not one of her children was born in the County Home. It was the most upright matron in the village who slapped life into every one of them.

'She's unfortunate, that's all,' this matron used to say. 'How could she know any better – living with two rough brothers? And don't forget she had no father herself!'

If Sarah had been one to lie in bed on a Sunday and miss Mass, her neighbours might have felt differently about her, there being greater understanding in their hearts for sins against God than for sins against his Holy Church. But Sarah found it easy to keep the Commandments of the Church. She never missed Mass. She observed abstinence on all days abstinence was required. She frequently did the Stations of the Cross as well. And on Lady Day when an annual pilgrimage took place to a holy well in the neighbouring village Sarah was an example to all – with her shoes off walking over the sharp flinty stones, doing penance like a nun. If on that occasion some outsider showed disapproval of her, Sarah's neighbours were quicker than Sarah herself to take offence. All the same, charity was tempered with prudence, and women with grown sons, and women not long married, took care not to hire her.

So when Oliver Kedrigan's wife, a newcomer to the locality, spoke of getting Sarah in to keep house for her while she was going up to Dublin for a few days, two of the older women in the district felt it their duty to step across to Kedrigan's and offer a word of advice.

'I know she has a bit of a bad name,' Kathleen conceded, 'but she's a great worker. I hear it's said she can bake bread that's nearly as good as my own.'

'That may be!' said one of the women, 'but if I was you, I'd think twice before I'd leave her to mind your house while you're away!'

'Who else is there I can get?' Kathleen said stubbornly.

'Why do you want anyone? You'll only be gone for three days, isn't that all?'

'Three days is a long time to leave a house in the care of a man.'

'I'd rather let the roof fall in on him than draw Sarah Murray about my place!' said the woman. 'She has a queer way of looking at a man. I wouldn't like to have her give my man one of those looks.' Kathleen got their meaning at last.

'I can trust Oliver,' she said coldly.

'It's not right to trust any man too far,' the women said, shaking their heads.

'Oliver isn't that sort,' Kathleen said, and her pale papery face smiled back contempt for the other women.

Stung by that smile, the women stood up and prepared to take their leave.

'I suppose you know your own business,' said the first one who had raised the subject, 'but I wouldn't trust the greatest saint ever walked with Sarah Murray.'

'I'd trust Oliver with any woman in the world,' Kathleen said.

'Well, he's your man, not ours,' said the two women, speaking together as they went out the door. Kathleen looked after them resentfully. She may not have been too happy herself about hiring Sarah but as she closed the door on the women she made up her mind for once and for all to do so, goaded on by pride in her legitimate power over her man. She'd let everyone see she could trust him.

As the two women went down the road they talked for a while about the Kedrigans but gradually they began to talk about other things, until they came to the lane leading up to the cottage where Sarah Murray lived with her brothers and the houseful of children. Looking up at the cottage their thoughts went back to the Kedrigans again and they came to a stand. 'What ever took possession of Oliver Kedrigan to marry that bleached-out bloodless thing?' one of them said.

'I don't know,' said the other one. 'But I wonder why she's going up to Dublin?'

'Why do you think!' said the first woman, contemptuous of her companion's ignorance. 'Not that she looks to me like a woman would ever have a child, no matter how many doctors she might go to – in Dublin or elsewhere.'

Sarah went over to Mrs Kedrigan's the morning Mrs Kedrigan was going away and she made her a nice cup of tea. Then she carried the suitcase down to the road and helped Kathleen on to the bus because it was a busy time for Oliver. He had forty lambing ewes and there was a predatory vixen in a nearby wood that was causing him alarm. He had had to go out at the break of day to put up a new fence.

But the bus was barely out of sight when Oliver's cart rattled back into the yard. He'd forgotten to take the wire-cutters with him. He drew up outside the kitchen door and called to Sarah to hand him out the clippers, so he wouldn't have to get down off the cart. But when he looked down at her, he gave a laugh. 'Did you rub sheep raddle into your cheeks?' he asked, and he laughed again – a loud, happy laugh that could give no offence. And Sarah took none. But her cheeks went redder, and she angrily swiped a bare arm across her face as if to stem the flux of the healthy blood in her face. Oliver laughed for the third time. 'Stand back or you'll frighten the horse and he'll bolt,' he said, as he jerked the reins and the cart rattled off out of the yard again.

Sarah stared after him, keeping her eyes on him until the cart was like a toy cart in the distance, with a toy horse under it, and Oliver himself a toy farmer made out of painted wood.

When Kathleen came home the following Friday her house was cleaner than it had ever been. The boards were scrubbed white as rope, the windows glinted, and there was bread cooling on the sill. Kathleen paid Sarah and Sarah went home. Her brothers were glad to have her back to clean the house and make the beds and bake. She gave them her money. The children were glad to see her too because while she was away their uncles made them work all day footing turf and running after sheep like collie dogs.

Sarah worked hard as she had always done, for a few months. Then one night as she was handing around potato cakes to her brothers and the children who were sitting around the kitchen table with their knives and forks at the ready in their hands, the elder brother, Pat, gave a sharp look at her. He poked Joseph, the younger brother, in the ribs with the handle of his knife. 'For God's sake,' he said, 'will you look at her!'

Sarah ignored Pat's remark, except for a toss of her head. She sat down and ate her own supper greedily, swilling it down with several cups of boiling tea. When she'd finished she got up and went out into the wagon-blue night. Her brothers stared after her. 'Holy God,' Pat said, 'something will have to be done about her this time.'

'Ah, what's the use of talking like that?' Joseph said, twitching his shoulders uneasily. 'If the country is full of blackguards, what can we do about it?'

Pat put down his knife and fork and thumped the table with his closed fist.

'I thought the talking-to she got from the priest the last time would knock sense into her. The priest said a home was the only place for the like of her. I told him we'd have no part in putting her away – God Almighty, what would we do without her? There must be a woman in the house! – but we can't stand for much more of this.'

Joseph was still pondering over the plight they'd be in without her. 'Her brats need her too,' he said, 'leastways until they can be sent out to service themselves.' He looked up. 'That won't be long now though; they're shaping into fine strong boys.'

But Pat stood up. 'All the same something will have to be done.

When the priest hears about this he'll be at me again. And this time I'll have to give him a better answer than the other times.'

Joseph shrugged his shoulders. 'Ah, tell him you can get no rights of her. And isn't it the truth?' He gave an easygoing chuckle. 'Tell him to tackle the job himself!'

Pat gave a sort of a laugh too but it was less easy. 'Do you remember what he said the last time? He said if she didn't tell the name of the father, he'd make the newborn infant open its mouth and name him.'

'How well he didn't do it! Talk is easy!' Joseph said.

'He didn't do it,' said Pat, 'because Sarah took care not to let him catch sight of the child till the whole thing was put to the back of his mind by something else – the Confirmation, or the rewiring of the chapel.'

'Well, can't she do the same with this one?' Joseph said. He stood up. 'There's one good thing about the whole business, and that is that Mrs Kedrigan didn't notice anything wrong with her, or she'd never have given her an hour's work!'

Pat twitched with annoyance. 'How could Mrs Kedrigan notice anything? Isn't it six months at least since she was working in Kedrigan's?'

'It is, I suppose,' Joseph said.

The two brothers moved about the kitchen for a few minutes in silence. The day with its solidarity of work and eating was over and they were about to go their separate ways when Joseph spoke.

'Pat?'

'What?'

'Oh, nothing,' said Joseph. 'Nothing at all.'

'Ah, quit your hinting! What are you trying to say? Speak out, man.'

'I was only wondering,' said Joseph. 'Have you any idea at all who could be the father of this one?'

'Holy God,' Pat cried in fury. 'Why would you think I'd know the father of this one any more than the others? But if you think I'm going to stay here all evening gossiping like a woman, you're making a big mistake. I'm going out. I'm going over to the quarry field to see that heifer is all right that was sick this morning.'

'Ah, the heifer'll be all right,' Joseph said. But feeling his older brother's eyes were on him, he shrugged his shoulders. 'You can give me a shout if she's in a bad way and you want me.' Then when he'd let Pat get as far as the door he spoke again. 'I won't say anything to her, I suppose, when she comes in?' he asked.

Pat swung around. 'And what would you say, I'd like to know? Won't it be all beyond saying anyway in a few weeks when everyone in the countryside will see for themselves what's going on?'

'That's right,' said Joseph.

Sarah went out every night, as she had always done, when dusk began to crouch over the fields. And her brothers kept silent tongues in their heads about the child she was carrying. She worked even better than before and she sang at her work. She carried the child deep in her body and she boldly faced an abashed congregation at Mass on Sundays, walking down the centre aisle and taking her usual place under the fourth station of the cross.

Meantime Mrs Kedrigan, too, was expecting her long-delayed child, but she didn't go to Mass: the priest came to her. She was looking bad. By day she crept from chair to chair around the kitchen, and only went out at night for a bit of a walk up and down their own lane.

She was self-conscious about her condition and her nerves were frayed. Oliver used to have to sit up half the night with her and hold her moist hands in his until she fell asleep, but all the same she woke often and was frightened and peevish and, in bursts of hysteria, she called him a cruel brute. One evening she was taking a drop of tea by the fire. Oliver had gone down to the post office to see if there was a letter from the maternity hospital in Dublin, where she had engaged a bed for the following month. When he came back Oliver had a letter in his hand. Before he gave it to her, he told her what was in it. It was an anonymous letter and it named him as the father of the child Sarah Murray was going to bring into the world in a few weeks. He told Kathleen it was an unjust accusation.

'For God's sake, say something, Katty,' he said. 'You don't believe the bloody letter, do you?' Kathleen didn't answer. 'You don't believe it, sure you don't.' He went over to the window and laid his burning face against the cold pane of glass. 'What will I do, Katty?'

'You'll do nothing,' Kathleen said, speaking for the first time. 'Nothing. Aren't you innocent? Take no notice of that letter.'

She stooped and with a wide and grotesque swoop she plucked up the letter. Then she got to her feet and put the letter under a plate on the dresser and began to get the tea ready with slow, tedious journeyings back and forth across the silent kitchen. Oliver stood looking out at the fields until the tea was ready and once or twice he looked at his wife with curiosity. At last he turned away from the window and went over to the dresser. 'I'll tear up the letter,' he said.

'You'll do nothing of the kind,' Kathleen said, and with a lurch she reached the dresser before him. 'Here's where that letter belongs.'

There was a sound of crackling and a paper ball went into the heart of the flames. Oliver watched it burn, and although he thought it odd that he didn't see the writing on it, he still believed that it was Sarah's letter that coiled into a black spiral in the grate.

The next evening Sarah was sitting by the fire as Kathleen Kedrigan had been sitting by hers. She, too, was drinking a cup of tea, and she didn't look up when her brothers came into the kitchen. No one spoke, but after a minute or two Sarah went to get up to prepare the supper. Her brother Pat pushed her down again on the chair. The cup shattered against the range and the tea slopped over the floor.

'Is this letter yours? Did you write it?' he shouted at her, holding out a letter addressed to Oliver Kedrigan – a letter that had gone through the post, and been delivered and opened. 'Do you hear me talking to you? Did you write this letter?'

'What business is it of yours?' Sarah said sullenly, and again she tried to get to her feet.

'Sit down, I tell you,' Pat shouted, and he pressed her back. 'Answer my question. Did you write this letter?'

Sarah stared dully at the letter in her brother's hand. The firelight flickered in her yellow eyes. 'Give it to me,' she snarled, and she snatched it from him. 'What business is it of yours, you thief?'

'Did you hear that, Pat? She called you a thief!' the younger brother shouted.

'Shut up, you,' Pat said. He turned back to his sister. 'Answer me. Is it true what it says in this letter?'

'How do I know what it says! And what if it is true? It's no business of yours.'

'I'll show you whose business it is!' Pat said. For a minute he stood as if not knowing what to do. Then he ran into the room off the kitchen where Sarah slept with the three children. He came out with an armful of clothes, a red dress, a coat, and a few bits of underwear. Sarah watched him. There was no one holding her down now but she didn't attempt to rise. Again her brother stood for a moment in the middle of the floor irresolute. Then he heard the outer door rattle in a gust of wind, and he ran towards it and dragging it open he threw out the armful of clothing, and ran back into the room. This time he came out with a jumper and a red cap, an alarm clock, and a few other odds and ends. He threw them out the door, too.

'Do you know it's raining, Pat?' the younger brother asked cautiously.

'What do I care if it's raining?' Pat said. He went into the other room a third time. He was a while in there rummaging and when he came out he had a picture frame, a prayer book, a pair of high-heeled shoes, a box of powder, and a little green velvet box stuck all over with pearly shells.

Sarah sprang to her feet. 'My green box. Oh! Give me my box!' She tried to snatch it from him.

But Joseph suddenly put out a foot and tripped her.

When Sarah got to her feet Pat was standing at the door throwing her things out one by one, but he kept the green box till last and when he threw it out he fired it with all his strength as far as it would go as if trying to reach the dunghill at the other end of the yard. At first Sarah made as if to run out to get the things back. Then she stopped and started to pull on her coat, but her brother caught her by the hair, at the same time pulling the coat off her. Then, by the hair he dragged her across the kitchen and pushed her out into the rain, where she slipped and fell again on the wet slab stone of the doorway. Quickly then he shut out the sight from his eyes by banging the door closed.

'That ought to teach her,' he said. 'Carrying on with a married man! No one is going to say I put up with that kind of thing. I didn't mind the other times when it was probably old Molloy or his like that would have been prepared to pay for his mistakes if the need arose, but I wasn't going to stand for a thing like this.'

'You're sure it was Kedrigan?'

'Ah! Didn't you see the letter yourself! Wasn't it Sarah's writing? And didn't Mrs Kedrigan herself give it to me this morning?'

'Sarah denied it, Pat,' Joseph said. His spurt of courage had given out and his hands were shaking as he went to the window and pulled back a corner of the bleached and neatly sewn square of a flour bag that served as a curtain.

'She did! And so did he, I suppose? Well, she can deny it somewhere else now.'

'Where do you suppose she'll go?'

'She can go where she bloody well likes. And shut your mouth, you. Keep away from that window! Can't you sit down? Sit down, I tell you.'

All this took place at nine o'clock on a Tuesday night. The next morning at seven o'clock, Oliver Kedrigan went to a fair in a neighbouring town where he bought a new ram. He had had his breakfast in the town and he wanted to get on with his work, but he went to the door of the kitchen to see his wife was all right and called in to her from the yard. 'Katty! Hand me the tin of raddle. It's on top of the dresser.'

Kathleen Kedrigan came to the door and she had the tin of raddle in her hand.

'You won't be troubled with any more letters,' she said.

Oliver laughed self-consciously. 'That's a good thing, anyhow,' he said. 'Hurry, give me the raddle.'

His wife held the tin in her hand, but she didn't move. She leaned against the jamb of the door. 'I see you didn't hear the news?'

'What news?'

'Sarah Murray got what was coming to her last night. Her brothers turned her out of the house, and threw out all her things after her.'

Oliver's face darkened.

'That was a cruel class of thing for brothers to do. Where did she go?'

'She went where she and her likes belong; into a ditch on the side of the road!'

Oliver said nothing. His wife watched him closely and she clenched her hands.

'You can spare your sympathy. She won't need it.'

Oliver looked up.

'Where did she go?'

'Nowhere,' Kathleen said slowly.

Oliver tried to think clearly. It had been a bad night, wet and windy. 'She wasn't out all night in the rain?' he asked, a fierce light coming into his eyes.

'She was,' Kathleen said, and she stared at him. 'At least that's where they found her in the morning, dead as a rat. And the child dead beside her!'

Her pale eyes held his, and he stared uncomprehendingly into them. Then he looked down at her hand that held the tin of red sheep raddle. 'Give me the raddle!' he said, but before she had time to hand it to him he yelled at her again. 'Give me the raddle. Give it to me. What are you waiting for? Give me the God-damn stuff.'

THE HAYMAKING

CHRISTOPHER GLEBE WORE YELLOW LEATHER BOOTS AND NECKTIES with fancy patterns, and, moreover, his boots were never muddy. But you can't measure a man's acreage by the amount of mud on his feet, and when Christopher Glebe went to count his cattle he had to walk the best part of three hundred acres, and the farmers around about considered he was a cut above themselves. Some of the smaller farmers took off their hats in his presence. Nevertheless, in spite of the respect in which he was held it never occurred to any of the farmers that he would look beyond their own daughters when he took it into his head to pick a wife, and indeed every time he passed them on the road they took occasion to step into their kitchens and tell their own daughters that it would be a lucky girl that would get him.

'Three hundred acres of pasture and arable! And look at all the extra grass you'd have to fatten a few more bullocks if you dug up all the useless shrubs and bushes about the house, and the big trees in the middle of the fields.'

'The trees are no harm,' the young women would cry, not liking even this mild criticism of such a fine gentleman as Christopher Glebe. 'In the summer the cattle can lie down in the shade!'

'Lie down in the shade! They'd be better employed filling their bellies. If I had my way I'd cut down every tree in the county. They're only a nuisance. They're a source of encouragement to birds, that's what they are! If we had no trees we'd have no birds, and if we had no birds we'd sleep easier when the crops are in the ground.'

And with this remark the farmer would go out into the yard again, with a long face, having forgotten the hopeful thought that had prompted him to leave it a moment before.

But Christopher Glebe gave rise to many such hopeful thoughts because he was never backward about staring at the young women of the locality, looking them over with a bold eye and losing no opportunity of taking in their points on such occasions as they were exposed to view, as, for instance, on Sundays when they rode past him on the road, perched up on their fathers' sidecars and back-to-back traps, with their legs dangling down and their skirts blowing up in the wind. And there never was a gathering of young people in a farmer's house at which Christopher Glebe would not turn up at some hour of the night, and although he did not dance with any girl he stood in the open doorway and watched them all.

'It's a pity he doesn't dance with the girls,' said more than one mother regretfully.

'Leave him alone,' said their menfolk. 'He knows it's always best to pick a filly in the ring.'

As for the young girls themselves, they endeavoured to show great unconcern at his scrutiny, but after a jig or a reel they were always careful to make for the other end of the room in case they might look heated or show a few beads of perspiration at the side wings of the nostrils. They were not as unconcerned as they tried to look.

'I wonder what Christopher Glebe is saying,' said one young woman with slim hips and narrow bones who had just done a jig by herself in the centre of the floor and who was conscious at the moment of making a great stir among the young men against the wall.

But no one heard Christopher Glebe's remark except a morose young farmer who stood in the doorway with him and whose feet were not idle from unwillingness to move, but from inability to master the intricacies of the dance steps and figures.

'Look at that girl,' said Glebe. 'Look at her hips! You'd hardly call her a woman at all.' He stared reflectively at the young woman. 'How could a man expect a woman like that to bear children?'

The young farmer agreed with a mutter.

'There's not much pleasure in watching her dance either,' he said morosely.

Christopher turned around and looked at the young man, at his idle posture and his gloomy face, and he burst out laughing.

'That's true for you,' he said, and he laughed more.

He knew that the best part of the evening for most of the farmers' sons was watching the young women in the centre of the floor, watching their hips sway and their rich breasts lolloping in time to the jerky tunes of the melodeon.

And as for himself, he also knew that a man could pick a wife better by standing at the door, where he could judge a girl's parts impersonally, whereas in the heat on the floor there was no knowing what damage could be done to the reason, by the feel of a young girl close to you, or a pair of eyes glancing up at you and shyly glancing away again. Yes, you could make a good pick from among the girls, just by standing at the door and watching them out of the corner of your eye. But Christopher Glebe wasn't ready to get married for a few more years yet; or so he thought before the doctor ordered him to take a course of waters at the National Spa to see if the waters would reduce a painful rash he had developed on the back of his neck.

The spa was situated on the coast, a few miles outside Dublin, and it combined the usual seaside attractions with its course of medicinal treatments. The place had a reputation also for the remarkable number of romances that had originated there. But Christopher knew nothing of this, and he was almost as surprised as his neighbours when he came to his senses and realised he was going to marry Fanny, a girl he only knew a few months, and who was above all things else – a schoolteacher!

It all happened so quickly.

Christopher wasn't used to seaside hotels or seaside manners. He felt clumsy and out of place. The only time he felt at ease was when he caught sight of a familiar red face and realised that it was his own face reflected in a mirror. The first day seemed endless, but when evening came at last and he went into the hotel to go to bed, he saw a crowd round the piano in the dining room and there was a young woman in a black skirt and a white blouse, sitting on the piano stool, vamping tunes, with her foot on the loud pedal, and sprinkling a great many treble notes in between every bar. This was Fanny. Christopher came downstairs again and took up his place at the door, but in this case the piano was just inside the door and he was so fascinated at the way Fanny scattered her fingers up and down the keys, and smiled from one side to another with the precision of a pendulum swinging from right to left, he paid no attention to hips or bust but became quite well informed upon such irrelevancies as the shape of her ear, and the size of the small pointed shoes of patent leather that went up and down incessantly on the pedals of the piano.

Fanny and her sister Sadie were the life and soul of the hotel. And the funny part about it was that they nearly went to another place. You see, they went somewhere every year, for a week or a fortnight at least, and having travelled around to various seaside resorts in the last twelve or fifteen years they were getting a bit sick of them all, and they decided this year that they would try some place near home; the spa, for instance. They might enjoy themselves just as well as anywhere else; and as well as that there would be a considerable saving of train fare.

The fact that Christopher had only just arrived at the hotel, and that the sisters were leaving in two days, gave him no time to gather his scattered thoughts. They remained scattered for the whole two days, and when the sisters left for the train he took them to the station in a taxicab and saw them off from the platform and made Sadie give him her sister Fanny's address.

As for Fanny, the last thing that entered her head was the thought that she would marry a farmer. She saw him the first night he came over to the piano and she saw the rash on his neck, and when Sadie joked her about him she didn't like it. But next day she laughed. And on the second day she and Sadie began to pretend, in a joke, that she was going to consider him seriously. And indeed, it was all a joke when they went away two days later, although he came to the train to see them off and although Fanny herself leaned out of the carriage window and made him stand still till she took a snap of him with her small folding camera.

When they were back at work, Sadie at the hospital and she herself at the school, she expected the whole thing to blow over, but Christopher kept writing, and one day during the winter he said he was coming to town to see her.

The day that the letter arrived it was addressed to the school and it lay on her desk, but two classes passed over before she had time to slit the envelope, and even then she could only get a chance to read a line or two at a time as she went back and forth between the blackboard and her desk. The day was cold and dark and they had to have the lights lighted in the classroom, a thing that always irritated her because it put such a gloss on the board that the children couldn't see what she wrote on it and made this an excuse for calling out to her and becoming restless and noisy.

'Miss! We can't see the board.'

She moved it to another angle.

At once there was a chorus from another side of the classroom.

'Oh, Miss! Now we can't see it.'

And so on. The more she moved the board, the more children there were who couldn't see it, until at last she began to get excited and suspect that they could all see it perfectly well but were anxious to kill time and give her trouble.

'I won't move it another inch,' she said crossly.

'Oh, Miss!' They gave a collective wail that made her look up nervously at the partition of frosted glass that divided her class from the class next door. Every sound went through the partition and was heard distinctly in the other room.

'Those who cannot see will please come up the aisle and stand where they can see,' said Fanny desperately.

That was the last straw because they crowded up around the desk and there was absolutely no opportunity then of reading her letter. She pushed it between the pages of a book and sat staring out of the foggy window while the class copied down the work from the board. In the silence every sound could be heard, the scratching of the pens, the snuffle of a fat pale girl at the back, and the constant sighs of the boarders as their pencils rubbed against their broken chilblains.

When Fanny was tired looking out the smeared window she turned and looked around the classroom in which she sat year after year but with such little attention that she could hardly have told the colour of the walls. This time, however, some relation between her unconscious thoughts and the subject of the lingual charts on the wall made her look at them more closely, and as she stared at them she felt a sudden elation. The charts represented the four seasons and depicted the seasonal changes that take place on a farm. The pictures were arranged to include as many objects as possible so that by marking them out with a pointer the teacher might enlarge the vocabulary of the class. There were men and women, children and dogs, horses, ploughs, harrows, and drays. There were forks, rakes, tip carts and barrows, cocks of hay and milking pails. There were fat cattle, mules and sheep, pigs, sows and a litter of bonhams. There were clutches of chickens and baskets of eggs. And there were a hundred and one other things that teacher much less pupil might be forgiven for not recognising by name. But it was the sun that took Fanny's eye. In each of the charts the sun was represented in the upper left corner and it was the colour of ripe wheat, and it shone down in thick rays for all the world like a bundle of wheat sheaves held upside down.

Fanny's head filled with visions of green trees and golden crops.

And suddenly she picked up the letter from Christopher and read it from end to end, holding it up in front of her boldly, and not caring whether the children stared or not. She was heartily tired of them, anyway.

Four months later, Fanny and Christopher were married. It was early in June. As Sadie said, it was a nice time to begin life on a farm; haymaking time.

They were married at seven o'clock in the morning. Sadie acted as bridesmaid and the sexton stood up for Christopher. It was all over in a few minutes, and they had breakfast in a hotel near the church. When they left Sadie an hour or so later and took the train for home, they sat opposite each other on the carpeted seats of the railway carriage, and tried to feel that they knew each other as well as could be. Christopher told her a few funny stories and she laughed in the spaces between one story and another, so that the laughing alone occupied a good part of the journey. But before the journey was over they were looking across at each other and the same thought was in each mind. She looked at his stout body as he sat with his knees apart, and at his flushed face, and she wondered at the suddenness with which she had given in to him. He looked at her thin pointed face and her thin body, and her narrow pointed shoes, and he wondered for the first time what kind of a housekeeper she was, and whether she knew anything at all about a farm.

Three weeks after she had returned from her wedding trip, Fanny woke up at five o'clock one morning. It was so bright she couldn't believe it was so early, but Christopher was lumped up in the bed without any sign of waking. Fanny got up in her bare feet and went to the window.

Outside the early summer sun was already up over the rim of the sky, illuminating the countryside with the rich slanting rays that, like the evening rays, deepen the colour of the earth and enrich the glow of the grasses. In front of the house, but on the other side of the river, there was a field of meadow and upon the tops of the grasses the sun rays shone with a rich intensity, till the ryegrass and timothy and the top stalks of the tremble grasses glowed like red copper.

Fanny looked out in rapture, and even while she looked at it, like shot silk showing its latent gleams, the tops of the copper grasses swayed in the wind and revealed not only the pale green grasses below the surface, but also the innumerable shades of yellow and purple and white of the buttercups, clovers, and daisies. Then all was still again and the meadow was calm and coppery once more. And today it was going to be cut! Today was the beginning of the haymaking. Fanny looked back at the bulk of Christopher under the bedclothes. She wondered that he was not too excited to sleep. She herself felt reluctant to go back to bed, but still, it was only five o'clock. She sighed and got back between the sheets.

It was nine o'clock before Fanny opened her eyes again, and it was the sound of a mowing machine that woke her. They were already cutting the meadow across the river. And the air was fragrant with the smell of the hay. Christopher was long gone out. But when Fanny ran downstairs ten minutes later he was coming in again across the yard. They met in the passage.

'How is the haymaking?' said Fanny.

Christopher gave her a curt look and made no answer as he pushed past her into the room where breakfast was set.

'Did you look out the window?' he said then, as she came into the room after him.

'I did!' said Fanny.

'Then you saw the sky,' said Christopher, sitting into his chair.

'The sky?' said Fanny.

'The sky is so low you could reach it with a stick,' said Christopher, and then Fanny realised that the morning was not as clear and radiant as it had been when she wakened earlier. It was heavy and warm, and in the warmth the sound of the mower was sullen, like the buzzing of bees.

The servant brought in the teapot, but before Fanny could pour out the tea, Christopher leaned over and took up the pot and poured out his own cup impatiently.

'Those damn fools never use their brains,' he said, leaving down his cup with such a clatter that the tea splashed out on the cloth. He pushed back his chair. 'I told them to cut the river meadow today, but I thought they'd have more sense than to cut it with a sky like this hanging over us.'

'But I don't think it will rain at all – ' said Fanny, pouring out her own cup of tea.

'Don't talk about something you know nothing about!' said Christopher. 'Look at that sky. It's only a matter of minutes till it's pouring bucketfuls.' He stood up and went to the open window and put out his hand to see if the first drops were falling already.

'This darkness is for heat, not for rain. I'm certain of it,' said Fanny.

'For heat! Is that so? Since when might I ask did you become an expert on the weather? It's not going to rain! Is that so? Then kindly tell me why the swallows are flying as low as the windowsills and why are the cattle lying down in the fields, all facing the same way! Those are signs of rain that I never saw fail!'

'I won't argue with you,' said Fanny, 'but if you are so sure that it's going to rain, why don't you send word for them to stop the mowing.' She stood up and went over to the window herself. 'As far as I can see they have only circled the field once. They have only cut a single strip.' She looked up at the sky. 'Although I still maintain that it won't rain, if you are sure it will why not send word for the men to stop? That would be simple as far as I can see.'

'Simple! Simple! God give me patience!' Christopher walked up and down the room two or three times rapidly without speaking and then he burst out into Fanny's face. 'It is simple, is it? That's all you know about it. Am I to pay men for wasting half a day doing something that it will take another half a day to get undone. It took those men two hours to get the machine oiled and set up, the blades sharpened and the horses tackled, and then think of the time it took them to get the machine over to the field!'

'It shouldn't have taken long to get to the field,' murmured Fanny, irresistibly, as she looked across at the field, where one of the men had stopped work to blow his nose in a red handkerchief, which he stuffed carelessly into his back pocket, leaving a small corner sticking out when he took up his work again.

Christopher's temper was rising.

'Do you think they took the mower across the river?' he sneered. 'Do you think they took a ten-ton machine across the footbridge? Don't you know they had to go around to the bridge at the other end of the village – three miles, if not more, and then at that they had to travel at walking pace to avoid jolting.' He looked balefully at Fanny. 'Perhaps you'd have whipped up the horses to a gallop? You know so much! Perhaps you'd have driven the mower down the lane like a chariot, jolting over stones as big as rocks and going into ruts as deep as drains! Is that what you'd do? Is it? Is it?'

As he asked the last question, Christopher stuck his face up so close to Fanny's that she moved backwards and the corner of the sideboard jabbed her in the middle of the back. It was the pain of the knock that brought the tears to her eyes, but Christopher had not noticed the accident.

'That's right! Cry like a child!' he shouted. 'You talk like a fool and then when you are corrected you cry like a child. Did you expect me to let you continue your fool's talk and have people laugh at me and say I married a woman that didn't know a rake from a fork? When you don't know what you're talking about keep your mouth shut, that's my advice, and don't give me cause to recall what someone said to me when he heard I was getting married. "The flies will have somewhere to go now," said he, "a schoolteacher's mouth is always open."'

At this the tears that had come to Fanny's eyes from the jab she had got in the back rolled over and down her cheeks.

'God give me patience!' cried Christopher. 'Wet weather outside the house and wet weather inside. Let me get out of here.'

There was a sound of footsteps outside the door.

'Please lower your voice,' she said. 'The servants will hear you.'

'What the hell do I care if the servants hear me!' he said in a loud voice, stamping his feet. 'This is something new. I must lower my voice so that my own servants won't hear what I have to say. This is a new idea? Where did this idea come from?'

He threw open the door and thrust out into the dark passageway where he nearly ran down the strong-limbed servant girl, who was trying to balance a tray in one hand and find the knob of the door with the other.

'Get out of the way!' he said, and then he stopped. 'What have you got there?' he asked, pulling the girl by the sleeve.

'A pot of fresh tea, sir!'

'Fresh tea! And who is that for, might I ask? What was wrong with the tea in the teapot? It was good enough for me.' He went back into the room and lifted the teapot, shaking it and feeling the sides of it with his hands. 'It's nearly full, and it's as hot as can be expected. What is the meaning of making fresh tea?'

The girl said nothing. Fanny stood up.

'I ordered fresh tea,' she said. 'The tea you drink is too strong for me. Strong tea is all right for a man, but a woman can't stand it. There is too much tannin in it.'

Glebe shrugged his shoulders. 'Have it your own way,' he said. 'I suppose it's no longer any concern of mine how the house is run. I supply the money, that is all. I hand out the money, and it is paid around to the fat shopkeepers in the town for tea and coffee that is thrown down the sink the minute my back is turned.' He straightened himself up then, and sighed. 'I won't complain,' he said. 'As long as the money lasts I'll continue to supply it. But how long will it last? That's the thing for you to think about! Money can go quicker than it can come.' He pointed out the window to the meadow across the river. 'There's a twenty-acre field of hay cut too soon and a storm threatening that will beat it into the ground so badly that we may as well try to sow gold as try to save it. There's forty pounds worth of hay in that field. That's forty pounds gone in one night. I don't suppose you ever think of things like that! Oh no, you never think of that, with your pots of fresh tea every minute. I don't grudge them to you, but all I can say is that I hope the money will always be there! As long as I can provide it I'm willing to do so, but I can't answer for the weather. A famine could wipe out a whole country in twenty-four hours. Did you not teach that to your school?' He was about to recall details of the Great Famine when he stopped up suddenly, and adopted a listening attitude. 'Is that rain I hear dripping on the skylight?'

He went out to look, and as he went down the passage with a heavy step and into the kitchen his voice could be heard, giving orders about the food that was to be brought out into the field for the mowers.

'Buttermilk? What else did you think? Do you think I was going to send them pails of champagne? All they're going to get is enough to wet their throats, and a few cuts of bread to keep them going till they get back home. I don't want any waste. Remember that.'

Fanny took the teapot from the girl's hands. It was useless to try to hide the fact that she had been crying. She hid nothing, but ignoring the fact that her face was blotched, she began to give the girl her instructions for the day.

When the instructions were given and written down, Fanny glanced out the window.

'The rain hasn't fallen yet,' she said.

'It won't rain today, ma'am. That darkness is a sign of heat.'

'That's what I thought,' said Fanny, 'but the master says it's for rain.'

'That's only because the hay is cut. My father is the same. He is as nervous as a cat from the time the first swarth is brought down to the time the last rope is tied on the top of the last cock, and the last dray loaded and gone rattling into the haggard. Men are all the same. If the sun was splitting the cobbles, they'd say that it was only a pet day, and that you'd see torrents of rain before the night.' The girl laughed. 'It's the very opposite at seeding time. At seeding time they're looking for rain and even when the drops are falling on the ground, they're looking up at the sky and telling you that you won't see rain before a week; that it's only a few drops; that the shower will pass off, that the clouds are too high for rain, that the wind is too strong for rain. And even when it comes down with a rush, flattening the grass and nearly breaking the glass in the windows, they'll still tell you that it is only a shower, and that it will pass off in a minute and that it will do about as much good as if a bird spit out, passing over the land. They say it will soak into the ground and the ground will be as hard and as dry again in a few minutes as if it never rained this twenty years.'

Fanny began to smile, and as the girl rattled on, she began to smile more and more. 'I have a lot to learn,' she said, and she smiled weakly.

When the girl went out Fanny went over to the window and looked out. It was still heavy and dull, but the scents of the clover and the honeysuckle came to the nostrils quicker. The girl's words had cheered her too, and in spite of the cross words of Christopher she was glad she was married to a man in the country and not sitting still in the stuffy school, with the windows closed, and a smell of perspiration stealing around the room as the girls concentrated on their work, with their pens screeching on the paper, and the voice of the junior mistress coming through the frosted glass partition, saying over and over again:

'Who dropped that pencil box? I will not continue this lesson till I find out. Who dropped that pencil box? Answer me please, someone. Who dropped that pencil box?'

But when Christopher came in to his dinner, somehow or other it all started over again.

'It didn't rain after all!' said Fanny, cheerily, to show him she had forgotten the bad temper of the morning.

'It will rain during the night,' said Glebe morosely, prodding at his meat with the handle of his fork to see if it was tough.

'I know what is the matter with you farmers,' said Fanny gaily. 'You are superstitious. That is it! You are afraid to admit that it may be fine in case the Household Gods would be jealous of your crops and send down a torrent!'

Christopher looked up from his plate. 'Was that the kind of rubbish you taught in the school?' he said.

Fanny bit her lip, but she remembered her resolutions. She took a piece of bread and broke it up on her plate and began again with determination to be pleasant.

'As a matter of fact,' she said, 'I have often thought that girls are not taught the right subjects in school at all. They should be taught more about the land; about the importance of the crops and the stock. They should be made to realise that the land is the backbone of society.'

Glebe looked up again.

'It isn't every girl that marries a farmer. You forget that,' he said. 'It's no use fitting a girl to marry one kind of man when everybody knows she'll marry the one she thinks can give her the easiest time!'

Fanny felt that there was a personal allusion in the last remark, but she was determined to ignore it.

'Even so!' she said. 'It wouldn't do any harm for everyone to understand a little more about the land, and appreciate the difficulties under which the farmer labours.'

'Nonsense!' said her husband. 'The trouble with this country is that there are too many people already poking their noses into what doesn't concern them. The country is filled with government officials that go to a few classes in the technical schools and then come down in their striped suits to tell us we should cut our thistles on such a day and have our sheep sheared on such and such a day, and inoculate our cattle at such and such times. They come down to see if we've done this and if we've done that, and if we put a shovel into their hands it would raise fifty blisters inside six minutes! There are too many people already meddling in what doesn't concern them. Let them leave the farmer alone. Let them stop sending their inspectors and their overseers and let them keep their pamphlets and gazettes to themselves. The men on the land knew how to treat foot rot before ever printing was discovered; and before pens were discovered too. And let me tell you this, the first man was a farmer, not a schoolmaster!'

Suddenly Fanny put up her handkerchief to her eyes. 'Why are you always throwing it in my face that I was a schoolteacher?' she cried. 'You knew that when you married me! You said you were glad I wasn't a big soft farmer's daughter.'

Glebe looked up with his mouth full. 'There are worse faults than having a big bottom,' he said.

Fanny's thin cheeks reddened. 'I refuse to be hurt by your coarseness,' she said. 'I know that this is only a passing mood, that you are upset about the hay, and that you will be different tomorrow.'

'If you know that, why don't you leave me alone?'

'But all I want to know is if there is any way in which I could help. Is there no book in the house that I could study? I might be of some assistance to you if I understood more about agriculture.'

Christopher took a potato and peeled it, throwing the skins back in the dish.

'What did I ever learn out of a book?' he asked. 'Don't talk nonsense! Could you calve a cow by reading a book?'

Fanny was silent for a few minutes.

'I see that you won't listen to me,' she said. 'You won't give me time to explain myself. I didn't expect to learn anything about the practical side of farming, but I thought that I might get some theoretical knowledge that would help you. I might study the qualities of soil, and the nature of different fertilisers.'

But Glebe was not listening. He was holding his head sideways. Then he turned his head altogether to one side, and appeared to be listening intently to something else.

'Is that rain I hear on the skylight?' he said.

'No,' said Fanny, looking out the window in front of them. 'No, it is a lovely day.' Her voice was cheerful as the voices of the birds at dawn.

'A lovely day! Is that so? Do you realise that this heavy weather is as bad for the hay as the worst shower that ever came? This is the kind of weather that causes hay to get heated and rotted. The weather is about the worst weather I could have chosen. And the worst of it is that news of that sort travels like wind. It will be all over the country before a week, and when I try to buy a bit of hay to make up for my own going to loss on me, they'll be asking every fancy price that ever was asked, thinking I'll be in a bad need of it.'

'You're looking too far ahead,' said Fanny. 'Things are not as bad as all that, yet. It's not spoiled yet. I'm sure it may be all right.'

'That's what you hope, isn't it?' said Glebe, and he pushed back his chair even more noisily than at breakfast. 'You hope it will be all right, so there won't be any shortage of money. As long as the money turns up every week that's all you care about. You never give a thought to where it comes from. If I was to be struck down one of these days, where would you be then? Answer me that?'

'I asked if I could help!' said Fanny.

'Help! A lot of help you'd be with those skinny arms,' said Christopher. 'You couldn't lift a fork. You should see some of the women. The wife of one of the men came up with his dinner pail today and she stuck her fork into the end of a sward and you never saw the shine of the prongs again until she rolled the entire sward from one end of the field to the other!'

For a moment his face relaxed, and he almost smiled at the memory of the stout woman with her fat arms. But he looked stern again.

'Of course you wouldn't think it worth your while to walk as far as the field,' he said, and before Fanny had time to explain that she wanted to go with him, he went out and banged the door.

Fanny, too, went out of the room and up the stairs, and all the way she kept muttering to herself. 'Unbearable! Unbearable!' she muttered, as she used to do at the school when some of the children were particularly upsetting. 'It's unbearable,' she said again when she got as far as her room, and her tears that trickled into her mouth had an unpleasant salty taste and the taste of them reminded her of other times when she had been unhappy and the old unhappiness combined with the new unhappiness made her rush to the window and bang down the sash, and throw herself on her bed and cry and cry and clutch at the horrible knobby white counterpane that had been in the house when she came to it.

But next day was a brilliantly sunny day. The sun danced on the ceiling and the birds were flying so bold and reckless that several times they hit against the windowpanes with a thud. When Fanny woke up she smelled the fragrance of the hay and the first thing she saw when she looked out the window was the grey stretch of the field where the hay lay whitening. She got up quickly and put on a cotton dress.

'I'm going to help to put up the hay!' she said, running downstairs. 'See! I have put on a cotton dress!'

'What are you talking about?' said Christopher, who had the window open, and was leaning out and looking up at the sky. 'Cloudy! I might have known it!' he said.

Fanny sat down to the table. 'Hurry!' she said. 'I'm longing to start!'

'Start what?'

'Didn't you hear me? I said I was going to give you a hand with putting up the hay.' She laughed. 'I'll show you that I haven't such skinny arms.' And she was going to roll up her sleeves when he looked at her with a sneer.

'Are you a fool?' he said. 'Do you think we put up hay with the dew still on it?' And then he pushed aside his plate and stood up. 'I might as well put it up wet, though, for all the good it will be now. I cut it at the wrong time.' Then he looked out the window with a morose expression. He looked at Fanny. 'Why didn't I cut my hay in the spell of fine weather we had the week before last when all the hay around here was cut. I suppose people are laughing at me now!'

But at this point Fanny could stand no more. She burst out crying and ran upstairs. The week that Christopher regretted not having spent at the hay was the week of their wedding trip, and although Christopher did not notice the unfortunate inference that would be taken from his words, he knew that something was wrong and the only thing he could think of doing to console Fanny was give her the train fare and let her go up to town to spend a few days with Sadie. So Fanny took off her cotton dress and went up to town and spent two days with Sadie. Sadie was all questions.

'How do you like the country?' she cried. 'Did you milk the cows? I wish I was you! Did they start the hay yet? I wish I was there for the haymaking!'

Fanny was not disposed to talk much about the hay. 'Christopher was unfortunate with his hay,' she said. 'He cut it the day before yesterday just as a break came in the weather.'

'But there's no break in the weather!' said Sadie. 'There isn't a cloud in the sky! Look at that sun!'

'That sun is too bright to be lasting,' said Fanny.

'Don't be silly,' said Sadie. 'We're going to have glorious weather.' Then she clapped her hands together. 'I think I'll take Saturday off and go back with you for the weekend!'

'Oh!' said Fanny in great concern. 'Wouldn't you rather wait till Christopher has the hay all up and the harvest over? It would be much nicer then. Christopher would be free to take us around.'

'I'd hate that,' said Sadie. 'What I want is to see you just as you are, in the middle of your daily life. I think it's awfully exciting to be married to a farmer. Did you find any mushrooms? I love mushrooms.'

All the way home in the train Fanny leaned back against the cushions and tried to persuade herself that it was all right to bring Sadie back with her. She was nervous and irritable all the way. But Sadie leaned out the carriage window and inhaled deep breaths from the hayfields that were down on either side of the railway track.

'Smell the hay!' she cried. 'Oh, smell the hay!' And this command she uttered every other second until it might almost be supposed that she was a child who had learned a new phrase and could not think of anything else in her joy at repeating it on all possible occasions.

'Sit down,' said Fanny at last. 'If you had to work against time to get hay up before rain you might not think it so romantic.'

'I would! I would!' cried Sadie, turning around for a moment. 'Perhaps it's just as well I came if he's short-handed and working against time. I can lend a hand.' And she hung out the window of the train again as they passed alongside another field of hay. 'Oh, smell the hay,' she cried. 'I'm glad I decided to come.'

But every minute that brought them nearer to the station at which they were to alight made Fanny more nervous of the reception they would get.

When they arrived at the station, however, Christopher was waiting for them in the dog cart.

'I knew you'd bring Sadie!' he said, and he appeared to be pleased instead of annoyed. 'I brought the trap,' he said. 'I thought that you'd be tired. Did you buy up everything in the shops? I suppose the shopkeepers are going out of business tomorrow?'

'Why?' said Sadie, springing up on the dog cart before he had time to assist her.

'Because they will be able to retire with all the money they took from the two of you yesterday.'

Sadie laughed. 'They are more likely to be closing down and going bankrupt because of the hard bargains we drove with them!'

She tilted her head pertly and Christopher threw back his own head and raised the whip in the air and laughed so loud that Fanny thought for a minute that he was drunk. She even sniffed discreetly in the region of his left ear, as they jogged along the road, but everywhere the scent of the hay was so strong and it filled the air so that she could smell nothing else.

'Did you finish the hay? Did you get it all up?' said Fanny then, drawn irresistibly to the dangerous topic, unable to restrain herself, and anxious, perhaps, to see if his return to good humour was genuine or fake.

But Christopher turned towards her amiably. 'I won't answer you,' said he. 'Instead we will drive around by the hayfield and you will see for yourself!'

'Oh, lovely!' said Sadie, and she took off her hat.

Christopher cracked the whip and the pony set off down the road and Fanny began to take heart. There was no mistaking the gay rings of the horse hooves, nor the triumphant gesture of Christopher as he spanked the reins against the brass rail of the gig.

'Smell! Smell!' cried Sadie, and she drew in deep breaths, for to either side of the road were fields of hay, some just cut, some already made up into cocks.

Christopher rode past them indifferently, till they crossed the river bridge and drew up at the wooden gate of a great lolling field from which the house could be seen on the other side of the river, as the field had been seen from the house on the day that Fanny had made her unfortunate comments on the weather.

There were no men in the field now, but from one end of it to another were rows of haycocks, as tight and precise as if they had been rolled in the gate like barrels and set where they stood. And between them already the after-grass was beginning to gleam with its matchless emerald brilliance.

'What do you think of that for hay?' cried Christopher to his sister-in-law. 'Ho there!' he cried, beckoning at two farmers who were sitting on the parapet of the bridge they had crossed. 'What do you think of that for a field of hay?'

The men got down from the parapet and began to come up to the gate, their coarse boots making great noise on the dry road that was as hard as frost after the long spell of fine weather.

'How many ton do you expect in that lot?' said one of them.

'I should imagine it's the quality of the hay that matters, not the quantity,' said Fanny, before Christopher could speak, because she was anxious to show that she had forgotten the disagreement at the beginning of the week.

'Say that again!' said Christopher delighted. 'There you are, men! See how my wife is shaping out into a farmer!'

There seemed to be some hidden joke in his words because the three men laughed, and Christopher laughed so much and hit his thigh so repeatedly with the handle of the whip that the pony got uneasy and rattled her tackle and shook her head, and Sadie, who felt in good humour, laughed as well without knowing why they were laughing. But Fanny was serious about the quality of the hay.

'Can we get down and go into the field?' she said. 'I'd like to feel it in my hand.'

Christopher looked at her proudly. 'There's no better way to test hay than by feeling it with your hand,' he said.

The ladies descended and went into the field. Christopher followed them proudly, and the two farmers moved in the same direction with something of the rich indolence of their own heavy cattle moving instinctively after some irresponsible filly or even a brightly coloured butterfly with more initiative than themselves.

Fanny took up a small fistful of the hay.

'You cannot judge with that much,' said Christopher, and he dragged out a thick wad of the hay, releasing deeper and deeper scents on the air, and showing the faint dead green of the inner blades striping the greyed and yellowed outer blades. Dead daisies and dry thistle tops, blackened clovers and faded vetches and clumps of limp buttercups showed up faintly in the hay like the flowers in pot pourri. 'What do you think of that?' said Christopher.

Fanny considered it carefully, turning it over and over and smelling it, and rubbing it between her fingers like a piece of silk releasing the soft seed that floated down through the air as gently as mist.

'I think it's very good quality,' she said.

'What did I tell you!' said Christopher delightedly, slapping his whip against his thigh again, and the farmers jerked their heads as much as to say that there was no need for words. 'I tell you it takes a schoolteacher, every time,' said Christopher, and he laughed very loudly because he saw by his wife's face that she could not tell whether he was being pleasant or unpleasant. 'I tell you, men, when you're looking for wives you couldn't do better than follow my example.' Then he looked at Sadie, who was standing a distance away from them, looking over the river with her chin stuck up as she smelled the air. He nudged the man nearest to him and spoke very loud for Sadie to hear. 'What about my sister-in-law? Don't you think she'd make a good wife for a farmer? There's one thing certain, she seems to like the smell of a farm!'

They all laughed again, and this time Fanny laughed, and as they climbed into the trap again there was a great deal of laughing and the horse pawed at the tarred road with his foot as if he wanted to make noise too, and the light-leaved ash trees shook together gaily.

'How I envy you!' said Sadie, turning from Christopher to Fanny and from Fanny to Christopher. 'Isn't Nature wonderful?'

'Tonight I will give you some of my own cider to taste,' said Christopher suddenly. 'I think I have every right to celebrate tonight. I think I can say that I have the finest hay in the county, seventy cocks, seasoned to perfection, lightly packed, tightly tied, and the whole job from mowing to topping all done inside four days. I got the best of the weather too,' he said, looking up at the sky, and then he shook his head. 'I pity the people who haven't cut their meadows yet.' He drove up the hill. At the top he stopped. 'There's a field of hay now,' he said, pointing to a field where the hay had just recently been cut and where the green colour still showed in the strands of the swards. 'I wouldn't like to be that man,' said Christopher, and he looked up at the sky with a frown, but then, flicking his head, with the generosity of indifference, he sighed. 'Ah well, who knows. The weather might keep up. But I doubt it.'

Nearing the home farm the pony galloped along faster than ever, but her master pulled her up with a swirl of dust outside a small field, at the side of the road where there were twenty-four cocks of hay ranged neatly in rows from one end of the field to the other, and so like Christopher's cocks of hay that someone might have rolled out a few of his and rolled them into this field and set them down in the bright after-grass. But Christopher saw a great difference between them and his own.

'That is poor-quality hay,' he said. 'That man cut the wrong field. I told him that he shouldn't put that field under meadow, but he had the other field ploughed up at the time I spoke, so there was nothing to be done about it. You can see, can't you, that it's of a poor quality?'

'It looks grey, I think?' said Fanny tentatively.

'It's as grey as the sky was the day he cut it,' said Christopher, and he laughed again and spanked the pony with the ends of the reins. But a few fields further on, he pulled her up again. 'There's a bad lot of hay,' he said, as he pointed with his whip to one side. 'That's not so bad,' he said, pointing to a field on the other side of the road. 'That's about the next best to mine, I should say. But I'd take a bet with any man living that I have the finest crop of hay that was put up in these parts this year!'

He turned in the gate as he said this and a few minutes later the pony drew up of her own free will at the stable gate.

'Will you ladies walk the rest of the way?' said Christopher, and then he called after them. 'Take up a bottle of cider and dust the cobwebs off it, and have it ready for me when I come up after putting the pony in her stall.'

'To think that this is made from your own apples!' said Sadie, with her eyes glittering, as she drank her third glass of the yellow wine.

'Have another glass!' urged Christopher.

'She's giddy as it is!' said Fanny, and she put her hand over her own glass as Christopher tried to fill it again.

'Take your hand away,' he said, and when she did not take it away he began to pour the cider, drop by drop over her hand until she had to give in and pull it away.

'Oh! Oh! Oh!' said Fanny, wiping her hand in her skirt and laughing.

'I'm getting tipsy,' said Sadie, looking at her empty glass with an absurd smile.

'You're not as bad as the schoolteacher,' said Christopher, pointing his finger at Fanny. 'What would your pupils say if they saw you now?' he said, reaching over and pulling a strand of her hair loose from its combs. 'Look at yourself in the mirror,' he shouted.

And, when Fanny saw herself in the mirror, with her eyes glittering and her cheeks flushed and her hair loosened out of its combs, she caught up a glass.

'One last toast,' she said. 'To life in the country! To life in the country!'

But next morning Fanny had a headache, and when she was awakened by Sadie, who ran into her room in her bare feet and let the blind cord slap against the glass, she sat up in bed and put her hand to her forehead. Christopher had gone out.

'What are you looking at?' she asked.

'What is that field of green and silver in the distance,' said Sadie, leaning back to give her a view out of the window, and pointing away to the distance to where a field of young wheat lay still wet from the dews of night, and sparkling in the early sunlight. There was no wind, but the weight of the raindrops gently waved the wheat from side to side causing the light to sparkle and glitter in the crevices of the green ears till the field was like a lake of light shot with green shafts from beneath.

'Did you ever see anything so exquisite?' said Sadie, but Fanny put her hand to her head again.

'The reaping will begin next month,' she said. 'This early morning frost ripens the harvest very quickly.'

'I hate to think of it being cut!' said Sadie. 'Do come and look at it. Did you ever see anything so exquisite?'

Fanny came across to the window in her bare feet, and pushed back her moist hair, and leaned out the window.

'It's nice, all right,' she said grudgingly, but the boards were cold under her feet and her head throbbed from the start she got when Sadie let the blind slap, and somehow Sadie irritated her, with her eager face and her exclamations. 'I hope the weather keeps up,' she said. 'It doesn't look very promising.' The wheat shimmered again at that moment. 'It looks nice now, all right,' she said. 'But I wonder how it will look in a month's time? It could be a sorry sight before then! It could get lodged inside of an hour.' She leaned out further over the sill, and looked up at the sky before she drew her head in again. 'I hope the weather will keep up,' she said. 'It doesn't look too good this morning. The sky is so low you could reach it with a stick!'

THE CUCKOO SPIT

DRENCHED WITH LIGHT UNDER THE MIDSUMMER MOON, THE FIELDS were as large as the fields of the sky. Hedges and ditches dissolved in mist, and down by the river the thornbushes floated loose like several branches. Tall trees in the middle of the fields streamed on the air, rooted by long, dragging shadows.

Vera stood at the French door, and then the night was so bright she ventured a little way down the garden path. It was a strange night. All that was real and erect had become unreal. The unreal alone had shape. And when close beside her in the long grass a beast stirred, it was only by its shadow she could see where it lay. Unnerved, she turned back to the house. The house, too, had an insubstantial air, its white gable merging in the white of the sky. But on the bright ground its shadow fell black as iron.

It was when she reached the edge of this shadow that the young man stepped out and startled her.

'I thought you saw me,' he said defensively. 'The night is so bright. I saw you. I was watching you as I was coming across the fields.' Then his voice changed. 'Are you all right?' he asked anxiously.

'Oh, yes,' she said. His concern had already made nonsense of her fright. And in the strong light pouring down she could see him as plain as day, a young man with a kind face, his thin cheekbones splattered with large, flaky freckles. Their eyes met, and they smiled at each other, surprised and happy. 'I ought to know you, I am sure,' she said, since it was late and he wore no coat.

'I don't think so,' he said. 'I'm only down here sometimes in summer. I come to stay with an uncle of mine who lives across the river.'

'Oh, I know him. Tim Hynes? At least, I know him by name. I never actually met him. My husband used to talk a lot about him.'

'I know.' The young man nodded. 'Tim was very upset by his death. So, of course, was everyone,' he added hastily.

'Your uncle more than most, though. I was told he took it very badly. There was something, wasn't there, about his losing interest in the election – not voting at all?'

'That's right. He more or less gave up politics after that.'

'I remember I got a wonderful letter from him at the time.'

'Tim?' He raised his eyebrows.

Remembering the old man's spelling, Vera herself laughed. 'I never forgot it. Something he said in it. He said it might have been difficult, even for a man like Richard, to save his soul in Dáil Éireann.'

'That's like a thing he'd say, all right, but I think it could have been to comfort you. Tim had no doubt whatever about the stature of the man we'd lost in your husband.'

The plural pronoun caught her attention. 'Are you interested in politics, too?' she asked, but she was hardly heeding his reply, she was so surprised at the sudden lessening of her interest in him. All the same, I ought to ask him into the house, she thought, if only for his uncle's sake. Or was it too late?

'Oh, it's far too late,' he said. 'I didn't intend to call. I was out for a walk, and I'd crossed over the bridge in the village and was going along the bank of the river below here when I saw that the windows were all lighted. To tell you the truth, I came up closer just out of curiosity. I was always fascinated by this house. Then I saw the French door open. Somehow or other, I got a strange feeling that the house was empty. So I came up and I was about to knock when I realised the odd situation I had got myself into, and I didn't know what to do. I was just standing there when I saw you coming back. Do you do that often, go out and leave the door open?'

She turned and looked over her shoulder to where the open door let out a stream of golden light that cut its own shape on the shape of the shadow. 'I wasn't far away,' she said vaguely.

'That's true,' he said. 'And it was a lovely night for a walk.'

It annoyed her that, having been worried at the start, he was so easily satisfied about her safety. 'I shouldn't have left the door open all the same,' she said, 'but I only meant to walk a little way, just up and down the garden path.'

'I know!' he said. 'The usual thing! You were tempted to go further.'

Again she was irritated by his readiness to put his own interpretation on the situation. 'As a matter of fact, there was nothing usual about it,' she said. 'This is the first time since my husband died that I've set foot outside the house after dark alone, except in the car, of course.'

'I don't understand,' he said quietly. 'What could there possibly be to fear in the heart of the country?'

'That was what Richard used to say. But I wasn't brought up in the country, and that makes a difference. Even when he was alive, I was nervous out of doors after dark.' She laughed. 'I'll tell you something that happened one night. We kept a few hens. They were supposed to be my affair. The henhouse was over there.' She pointed to a small triangular field near the house, a small field bounded on three sides by a wood. 'I was always forgetting to shut them up at night, and we often had to go out late and do it, but once it was the middle of the night when I woke up and thought of them, and I had to wake Richard, and we had to put on our coats and go out to them.'

'Couldn't he have gone alone?'

'Of course not. They were my hens. It wouldn't have been fair to let him go alone.'

He shook his head. 'He must have been a very patient man.'

'But it was a night just like this,' she cried.

Immediately, with her words the night seemed to press closer, lapping them round, not just with its mist and moonlight but with its summer smells of new-mown hay and sweet white clover. 'We didn't go back to the house at all,' she said, remembering that other night with quick and vivid pain. 'We stayed out for ages.' But suddenly she had an uneasy feeling that she was giving something away about that night, or about herself, or Richard.

There was a little silence.

'Is he long dead?'

'Four years this summer,' she said, and turned her face away, although she felt his sympathy would not be so easily stemmed.

'You must miss him very much,' he said. 'I was thinking that as I was walking in the fields, and looking at the house. I was wondering how you were able to go on living here without him.' But he must have felt tactless, or impertinent, because he looked away from her, out over the fields. 'It's very beautiful here, of course,' he added quickly.

'Tonight, yes,' she granted. 'This is a night in a thousand,' but she gave a cold glance over the moonlit stretches of which he spoke with such unconcern. Did he not know that there were other nights, when those fields could wear a different aspect?

But he missed the glance she'd given over the lonely fields and turned back to her. 'I suppose the more beautiful it is, the more lonely it must be for you.'

She looked into his face. 'I got over the worst of it long ago,' she said harshly. 'Do you know what I was thinking? I was thinking that there is, after all, a kind of peace at last when you face up to life's defeats. It's not a question of getting stronger, as people think, or being better able to bear things; it's that you get weaker and stop trying. I think I couldn't bear anything now, even happiness.' She paused. That was true, she thought, and yet she felt she had expressed herself inadequately. 'It's just that I've got old, I suppose,' she said more simply.

'Don't be silly,' he said, but lightly, carelessly.

She sighed. 'All the same,' she said, 'there is a strange peace about knowing that the best in life is gone forever.'

'You mean love?'

She nodded. 'And youth,' she said, but she thought she saw doubt in his eyes. 'Aren't they the one thing?'

She was startled by the haggard look that came over his face. 'I don't know,' he said. 'I hope not. God knows I've never had much of either.'

'What do you mean? What age are you, anyway?' But before he could answer she realised that she didn't even know his name. 'You didn't tell me your name,' she said.

'Fergus,' he said, giving no surname.

He must be Tim's brother's child, she thought, and again at the thought of her old neighbour across the river she felt she ought to insist on his coming inside, no matter the hour.

'Oh, no, no,' he said, actually beginning to move away. 'I'm afraid to think how late it must be now.'

'Well, perhaps you'll come again,' she said formally, but she knew that in this invitation, generosity was not on her side. It was nice to see that he thought otherwise.

'That's very kind of you, Mrs Traske,' he said warmly. 'I'd like very much to come.' His pleasure was so genuine it added to hers, yet a ridiculous ache had gone through her when he used her surname, although anything else would have been unthinkable from a strange young man, a man years younger than her. Even if they got to know each other well, and he were to call again, and again, she could not imagine that he would call her Vera, ever. It was a name she had never liked. And lately she'd liked it less. At this moment, it seemed utterly unsuitable to her: a name for a young girl. It even seemed to have a strangely venal quality. But he was saying something, and she had to listen.

'I was only saying that I don't suppose you approve of calling people by their first names on a first meeting,' he said.

Taken aback by the way their thoughts had run so close together, she hesitated. 'Well, it doesn't give much chance for measuring one's progress with people, does it?'

'I never thought of that,' he said, and he looked at her, delightedly. 'I must remember that.' Again he seemed about to go, but again he stopped. 'I correct examination papers at this time of year. I may get word any day from my landlady in Dublin to say that they have arrived. I'll have to go back at once then. Would it matter, would you mind, if I came fairly soon? Very soon perhaps?'

'Whenever you like. I'm always here,' she said, and then they said good night, and he walked away.

As she went into the house, she wondered if he would come again. She hoped he would; it was a pleasant encounter. And she kept on thinking about it as she went around the house, fastening the windows and locking the door. Even when she went upstairs, she stood for a while at the open window, looking out and going over scraps of their conversation. Some of the things she had said now seemed affected. Had she lost the knack of small talk? In particular, she thought of what she had said about happiness, and not being able now to bear it. That was so absurd, but surely he understood that she meant a certain kind of happiness, possible only to the young. Indeed, it might well be that it was when one let go all hope of ever knowing it again that the heart was emptied and ready for simpler relationships, those without tie, without pain. But when she put out the light and turned back the white counterpane, breaking the skin of light on it, she felt vaguely depressed. Would there not always be something purposeless in such attachments?

Did she expect him to come again? Certainly not the very next evening. And so early. Only a short time before, she was in the garden, weeding and staking plants, working away, without noticing the day had ended. It was by the light of a big yellow moon that she was trying to see what she was doing. It was so low a moon, so close to the ground, and it shed so gold a light that, like the sun, it gilded everything. Unlike the moon of late night, it did not take all colour from the earth but left a flush of purple in the big roses and peonies, and a glow of yellow in their glossy stamens. Yet it was night. The birds were silent; a stillness had settled over the farm. Nervously, she gathered together the rake, the hoe, and the spade, but she didn't wait to put them in the toolshed. She hurried towards the house. In the doorway she delayed for a moment. There was a peculiar quality abroad. Was it expectancy? It's in the night, though, and not in me, she thought, but just then, like a high wind falling, the expectancy died down as a step sounded on the gravel.

'You didn't think I'd come so soon, did you?' Fergus said, smiling. 'It's even more marvellous than last night, though, and I thought of you not liking to go out at night alone. But you were going out?'

'No. Going in,' she said.

'Good. I'm glad I came. Get something to put over your shoulders. Hurry!'

In spite of her surprise, she didn't hesitate. 'I'll only be a minute,' she said. 'Won't you come in while you're waiting?'

He shook his head. 'Houses weren't built for nights like this.' When she came out, he was standing clear of the shadows of the house, in the full light. 'I was telling my uncle about you,' he said when she joined him. 'He wasn't in bed when I got back last night. He sends you his regards. In fact, he sent you several messages, so many I'm sure I've forgotten the half of them.' He smiled at her. 'No matter, you can take them as given; they were all compliments and good wishes. And now,' he said, surveying the view and taking her arm casually, 'which way will we go? Down by the river? Or is the grass too high?'

'We can follow the cowpaths.'

'Oh, but the cattle go in single file, and we want to talk,' he said, and he linked her more closely. It made her uncomfortable, but she knew that when they crossed over the wooden fence around the house and went into the field in front of it, they would have to unlink. He realised it, too, after a few steps. 'It's like wading through water, isn't it?' he said, amazed as the high grass weighted down their feet. 'Does it never get eaten down? The place seemed heavily stocked to me as I came along here.'

'It would take all the cattle in Ireland to graze it down at this time of year,' she said carelessly.

He returned to her with an earnestness that was touching.

'You had courage to keep it when you are so nervous here,' he said. 'Any other woman would have sold it and gone back to the city.'

'That never once entered my mind,' she said, remembering how from the first she was aware of the security she drew from this piece of ground. But she saw of his face that he thought she had kept it for the sake of the past.

'I must tell you something,' he said. 'I nearly wrote you a letter last night after I went away from here. Would you have thought it very odd? The only reason I did not was because I'd have had to come back with it, and I thought that a footstep during the night might frighten you.'

'It would have frightened the wits out of me,' she said quickly. She did not ask what he would have said in the letter.

'I knew it would,' he said. 'I'm glad I did not do it. Anyway, I think that you know without my saying it how much meeting you meant to me.'

'It was nice for me to meet you, too,' she said politely.

'There is nothing rarer in the world than happiness,' he said then.

'Happiness? Whose happiness are you talking about?' she asked sharply.

'Yours,' he said deliberately. 'I know what you're thinking, but there is a kind of happiness that is indestructible; it lives on no matter what comes after. At least, that was how it seemed to me listening to you talking last evening.'

'But we were only talking for such a little while,' she protested.

'No matter,' he said. 'Anyway, last night was not the first time I'd seen you. I used to study down by the river long ago, on our side, and I used to see you and your husband walking together in the fields. You used to go with him to count the cattle, didn't you?'

'Yes. I always went with him,' she said absently, because her mind was going back over the previous evening.

'How I used to envy your companionship,' he said. They had reached the riverbank and they had to walk slowly, because the ground was dented and uneven from where the cattle in wet weather had cut up the sod, which now was hard as rock. 'Not that I have much experience,' he went on, 'but of the marriages I've seen at close quarters, not many were like yours. They weren't failures, either; I suppose they were happy enough in a way.' He hesitated. 'Only it wouldn't be my way,' he said flatly.

'And what would be your way?' she asked laughingly.

'Well, that's just it,' he said. 'That's what I wanted to try to tell you in the letter. You see, I didn't have any clear idea of what I would want from marriage. I only knew what I wouldn't want, until last night, listening to you.'

'I don't understand?' she cried nervously, but she did remember that at one moment the night before she had felt uneasy. Had he formed some impression of his own at that moment? If so, she would probably be powerless now to alter it. Distantly, she turned away and looked down into the river. 'Supposing the impression I gave you was wrong,' she said. 'Supposing I falsified it.' When he said nothing, she turned and looked at him and she saw he was bewildered. Filled with remorse, she put out her hand to him. 'It wasn't false,' she said quickly, 'but that was one of the things I used to dread after his death, that the past would become altered in my mind, and that he would be made into something that he wasn't.'

'Not by you, though?'

'No. By others, but it might have come to the same thing in the end. You cannot imagine how awful it was in those first months, having to listen to people talking about him, going on and on about him, mostly his family, of course, but my own people were nearly as bad, and friends and neighbours. Everybody. And all the time they were getting him more and more out of focus for me. He was – but you've heard your uncle talk about him, so you'll know what I'm going to say – he was nearly perfect, guileless. He knew only candour, the kind of person who'd make you doubt the doctrine of original sin. But to listen to his family you'd think he was a man of marble. They diminished him. Instead of adding to him, they diminished him. Can you understand that? I used to think, immediately, that that was the way they would speak of him whatever he'd been; the dead are always whitewashed. And he didn't need it. In the end, instead of listening to them, I used to sit trying to think of something about him that I didn't like.'

'Did you?'

'Well, we used to quarrel when we were first married, but in all fairness to him it was usually my fault, although it always ended with his taking the blame. Not to be noble or anything like that, but just to stop us from arguing, which he hated; to get us back to being happy again. He used to say it didn't matter what happened, I'd always blame him anyway, so it might as well be first as last. Well, one evening a few weeks after his death, I was visiting his people and listening to the same old rigmarole about him, and I got into a kind of a panic. Soon I wouldn't be properly able to remember him at all; I thought I'd lose hold of what he was really like. I was so unhappy. And when I went out to the car and left it was a miserable evening outside. It was raining, for one thing, and the canvas roof of the car was leaking. I wouldn't have minded that, only just at the loneliest and darkest part of the road I got a puncture. Well! I got out and I stood there in the rain and it seemed the last straw. But suddenly, instead of pitying myself, I felt the most violent rage sweep over me. Towards him, Richard. If only I could have confronted him at that moment, there'd be no doubt of what I'd have said. "Why did you die, anyway?" I'd have shouted. "Why didn't you take better care of yourself and not leave me in this mess?" And then –'

'Don't tell me. I know what happened next,' Fergus said. 'You had him back again, just as he always was, unchanged, amused at you.'

'Yes. And I began to laugh, there in the rain.'

There was silence for a few minutes. 'Tell me,' he said then. 'What did you do about the puncture?'

'Oh, that!' She shrugged her shoulders. 'I forget. What with one thing or another, in those days I was nearly always in that sort of situation. Such things were the commonplaces of my existence. I suppose another car came along, or I called at some cottage, or perhaps I walked to the nearest village. I can't remember.'

'Things must have been hard for you in the beginning,' he said gently. 'But you managed very well.'

'Oh, I don't know,' she said deprecatingly. 'Some things were hard in the beginning, but other things only got hard long afterwards. I'll tell you a strange thing, though, if you're interested. I don't think I fairly realised until recently, but in my heart I did blame Richard all along, not for dying, but for being what he was, for leaving a void that no one less than him could fill.'

They walked along a few more paces. 'Is that why you didn't marry again?' he said. 'It seems such a pity.'

'For me?'

'Well for you, too, of course, but I wasn't thinking of you. I was thinking of how much you have to give.' But as he spoke he seemed to lose confidence in what he was saying. 'I suppose giving isn't enough, though,' he finished uncertainly.

Sadly, she shook her head. 'And yet it was a poor kind of faithfulness really, wasn't it?'

'It's the only kind there is, I think,' he said. 'Do you know something?' he added impetuously. 'When I was walking home last night, I was thinking about your husband, and I envied him.'

'A dead man?'

'It's not as absurd as it may seem. I feel certain that I'll never have one quarter of the happiness he had.'

'But you're so young!' she cried. 'How can you tell what's ahead?'

He looked away. 'It isn't a question of age. You know that. It's temperament perhaps or maybe it's merely chance.' He looked back at her. 'It's not that I haven't a normal capacity for love, either. The truth is that I have to be crazily involved or not at all. And I've never seen that kind of thing last for long. That was why, knowing what companions you were, it meant so much to me, last night, to see that you'd never lost that other quality either. Do you realise when I knew?' He faltered before the cold look she gave him, but then he rushed on. 'It was when you told me about the time you stayed out all night.'

'Except I didn't say that,' she said crossly. 'Not exactly anyway,' she added, but she knew how rightly he had interpreted her vague words about that night.

'Forgive me,' he said gently. 'It was from your face and from the love of your voice I knew what you meant. And I was certain then of how you spent that night. You see, I never really thought that kind of love could last so long. Illicit love perhaps but not married love.'

Uncomfortable, she walked a little faster so that she outdistanced him by a few steps.

'I was right, wasn't I?' he called softly.

'Yes,' she said at last. What was the use, now, of denying those dead hours? She sighed and waited for him. 'I suppose you'd like to be married,' she said, surprising herself by her words.

He answered more lightheartedly than she expected. 'To the right person,' he said. 'You'd have been just right for me!'

It was because he said it so lightly and because she was oppressed by what had gone before that she, too, spoke lightheartedly. 'Oh, don't relegate me to the past like that!' she said. 'Why not say I'm a premonition of someone to come.'

His face clouded. 'I wouldn't say there'd be two of you in one lifetime,' he said, and there was a note in his voice that was new and harsh, and, frightened by it, she was about to suggest that they turn back, when, wheeling around, he himself suggested it. 'We'd better go back,' he said. 'Anyway, the moon has gone behind a cloud.'

'Has it?' Her eyes had been upon a small field of old meadow, along the headland of which they were passing. It was so neglected that the big white daisies in it met head-to-head and gave it an unbroken sheen of white that in the dark was like the lustre of the moon. 'Just look at those daisies!' she cried, pointing to them. 'The place is getting so neglected. I'll have to plough up that piece of ground and lay it down to new grass. There is so much that is neglected.'

'Nonsense, I never noticed any neglect,' he said so aggressively that, in order not to be annoyed, she had to tell herself that he was speaking, after all, in her defence.

'You haven't seen the place by day,' she said quietly.

'I see it every day,' he said. 'There isn't a bit of it I can't see from the other bank of the river. I saw you outside this morning, didn't I?'

'Did you?' It confused her to think of being seen without knowing it, by anyone. She was glad that they were nearly back. They had been walking faster on the return than when they set out, and already they had reached the wooden paling in front of the house. 'You'll come inside this time, I hope, and have some coffee?'

'We'd better see what time it is first,' he said. 'Tim was horrified at how late I stayed last night.' Raising his arm, he was trying to see his watch, as if, she thought irrelevantly, as if with that upraised arm he was trying to ward off a blow.

'Wait! There's a light in the porch,' she said. 'It can be switched on from outside.' But the switch was almost impossible to find among the tangled and overgrown creepers. 'There's neglect for you,' she said as she plunged her arm deep into the leaves. 'The roses are almost smothered,' she said sadly. Yet when she found the switch and the light went on, the big white roses lolloped outward towards them. On long, neglected stems, blown and beautiful, they hung face down. Impulsively, he reached out and took one between the palms of his hands, tenderly, as if it were the body of a small bird. 'Would you like one?' she asked, and she tried to break a stem, but it was difficult because the sappy fibres frayed before they severed.

He took it from her, pleased. And then he gave an exclamation. 'Oh, look at what's on it. A cuckoo spit.'

'How disgusting. Throw it away,' she said. I'll get you another one.' But he put his hand protectively about it. 'Why did you say that?' he asked. 'I was only amazed that a cuckoo should come so close to the house.' Then he saw his mistake from her face before he went any further.

'I forgot,' he said, embarrassed. 'They never do come close, isn't that so?'

'Never!' She smiled. 'They're never seen at all. At least I've never met anyone who saw one.'

'That's right. I should have known,' he said.

She saw at once that he was humiliated by his mistake, and she wanted desperately to make him feel better. 'When I was a child,' she said quickly, 'I didn't know a cuckoo was a bird at all, but a sound, like an echo.'

He didn't smile. He was looking down at the rose. On the stem, in the cleft between it and the axil of a leaf, there was a white blob, as if of spittle. 'What is it, anyway?' he asked. 'I've often seen it before.'

'Give it to me,' she said quietly, stretching out her hand. With the tip of her finger, she flicked the blob of white scuff on to the back of her other hand. 'Look,' she said, as the frothy secretion began to thin away, beads of moisture winking out, one by one, until, slowly and weakly on its unformed legs, a pale sickly yellow aphis crawled out across her skin. 'That's what it is,' she said, but at the feel of it on her flesh she shuddered, and shook it violently from her.

'You shouldn't have touched it.' Throwing down the rose, he pulled out a handkerchief and took her hand, and began carefully to wipe it all over. 'It always seemed so beautiful,' he said regretfully, 'a sign of summer.'

'Ah, well, it is a sign of summer,' she said, but her mind was not really on what she was saying, because although he'd wiped away all trace of the spit, he still held her hand carelessly in his. Unused for so long to the feel of another's flesh, she felt her cheeks flush. She was affected almost as strongly by his touch as by the feel of the plant louse. Shuddering again, she drew her hand away.

'You're cold?' he said.

Cold? Was it possible you could be so near to another person and so unaware of what went on within them? 'You must be cold, too,' she said. 'Come in and we'll have a hot drink.'

'We stayed out too long,' he said, bending down and picking up his rose. 'Next time we must manage better.'

There was evidently no question of his not calling again.

'I hope you enjoyed the walk,' he said easily, and then, as he was about to turn away, he looked directly at her. 'Good night, Vera.' He strode off down the drive.

She looked after him. Why had she enjoyed it so intensely? That was the question.

When she went inside, she attended absently to what had to be done before going upstairs for the night. Then, upstairs at last, she again went to the window and looked out. The moon, free of clouds, once more cast its lustre over everything. And, standing there, looking out, she remembered the times as a girl, before she was married, when she stood at an open window on a night like this, her heart torn by a longing to share the feelings that welled up in her. Yet later, when she had Richard there was not a single night that she had gone to the window for as much as a glance at what was outside. Always, no matter what the weather, day or the night, there was him blocking out all else. This view before her now, she had only really seen it after his death. Then, oh, then its insistent beauty began to torment her. But not with the same emotion. And she thought of something Fergus had said. He was wrong. A time came when giving was enough. She stared over the moonlit fields and the high cobbled sky. And she knew what she wanted. She wanted to reach out and gather all that beauty up and shove it into his arms. To give it away and be done with it, she thought. And afterwards not ever to have to look out at it again.

Next morning, she wakened late. Downstairs there was a loud knocking on the door. It was a grey day with a mist over the river and in the fields cattle looked dark, as if they swam in the waters of a fabulous sea. The knocking came again, more urgently, and she sprang out of bed and went to the window. Below, standing back from the door, she saw him just under her window, looking up. 'Oh, just a minute. I'll come right down,' she called down, pulling back instinctively.

'Don't come down!' he called up. 'I can't wait. I haven't a minute.'

'You have to go back?' This time in spite of the cold glare of day, she leaned out.

'The exam papers came,' he said. 'When I went back to Tim's place last night, there was a message saying they'd arrived. I have to get back. To get them finished in time, I'll have to start on them at once.' He turned his head as if to listen. 'Is that the bus?' he cried, dismayed. 'I shouldn't have come. I'll miss it. But I wanted to tell you I was going, in case you'd be looking out for me tonight.'

That he had any notion of coming that night, the third night in a row, took her by surprise. That he could have thought she might have been expecting him left her speechless.

'I'll have to go!' he cried, but he put his hand to his ear. 'It's not the bus,' he said, and he relaxed. 'I didn't think the papers would come for a few days more. The exam was only last week. But the sooner they come, the sooner I'll get paid.'

Depressed already by the day and by its cold light upon her unprepared face, and, of course, by his going, this glimpse of his unknown life was too much to endure. There was something so altogether offhand about this, their last conversation, that when in the distance she did hear the bus, she was not sorry. 'Listen!' she said. 'Here it is. The bus *is* coming this time.'

'It can't be.' He listened intently. It was. At once all his offhandedness left him. 'What I really wanted is if you ever come up to Dublin.' The sound of the bus was louder and nearer. 'If you ever do come, and if you could spare the time, I needn't tell you I'd love to meet you. Perhaps you'd let me give you a cup of tea somewhere.' But as he was looking nervously over his shoulder, the bus was getting nearer.

As for her, there was no time to dissimulate her pleasure. 'I often go!' she cried. 'And I'd be pleased to meet you.' But just then she thought of a way in which she could trim the truth a little. 'I was only thinking last night, after you'd gone, that I ought perhaps to give you the names of a few people in Dublin, friends of my husband's on whom you might call. People with some political influence, I mean, if you are serious about a political career.'

'I am,' he cried. 'Write out a list and bring it up to me. That's great.' Satisfied that she was coming, he hardly saw the necessity of fixing a day, and was turning away when he realised the need. 'When?' he cried.

'And where?' she cried, leaning out across the sill.

'How about Tuesday next? Or is that too soon?'

There was no time to think. 'Tuesday,' she agreed. 'But where? How about meeting in Stephen's Green? We can decide afterwards where to go.'

It was settled.

Or was it?

'What will happen if it isn't a fine day?' he cried.

'Oh, it will be fine,' she cried recklessly. 'You'll see.'

It rained, after all, on Tuesday. At first, she wasn't going to go to Dublin at all, but she was too unsettled to stay at home. She'd go up for a few hours anyway, she decided. And then, shortly before four o'clock, unexpectedly the rain cleared. As she parked her car on the side of the Green, she could see through the railings that the park was almost deserted. Uncertainly, she went in through a side gate. She felt better when she saw the paths were already drying out and from the wet branches overhead small birds, plump and round, were everywhere dropping to the ground like apples. On the grass starlings and sparrows ran about like children, as if for once the earth was sweeter than the sky. Would he come? Would he think it too wet? Dispirited, she walked along the vacant paths till she came to the shallow lake in the centre. And there, by the lakeside, standing under a tree, she saw him.

It was, she thought, the suddenness of seeing him that made her heart leap; only that. The next moment, a line from an old mortuary card came involuntarily to her mind. The card had been given to her by an old nun at the time of Richard's death, and her own pallid belief in a life beyond the grave had been quenched entirely by its facile promise: *Oh, the joy to see you come.* But now the words rushed back to her, ready and apt. I shouldn't be here, she thought with terror. It was too late, though. He had seen her.

'You came?' he cried. 'Didn't you know I would?'

'It was raining.'

'It stopped, though.' They began to walk along the side of the shallow cemented lake.

'You must have known I'd come when you yourself came,' she said.

'I only hoped. Can we ever be sure of anything?'

'Of some things, surely,' she said, to gain time and to think what she should do. There must be no more of these meetings. That was certain. But surely she could at least enjoy this afternoon? What harm could there be in it, except for her? And then only if she gave way to barren longings that might set the past at naught. She took a sidelong look at him. He seemed so happy. What did it matter what she felt, as long as no one knew. As long as he didn't know! And he was concerned with the trivia of their conversation.

'I suppose you mean friendship?' he said. 'But can there be friendship between a man and a woman?'

It was such a young question, it endeared him still more to her. She and Richard used to talk like that long ago. 'I don't know,' she said. 'But

I remember reading somewhere that there are only two valid relationships, blood and passion.'

He was staring down at the cinder path under their feet as they paced along. 'It's an interesting thought, isn't it?' he said. Then he looked up at her. 'What about us, though?'

Disconcerted, she gave a shrug. 'Oh, we don't come into any category at all,' she said, 'except, wait a minute, I have something for you. I'd forgotten. It justifies our association.' Opening her handbag, she took out the piece of paper on which she had written a list of names. 'Here are the people on whom I thought you should call.'

'Oh, thanks,' he said, but he took it from her absently, and without looking at it he shoved it carelessly into the outer pocket of his jacket.

'Hadn't you better put it in your wallet? I went to a lot of trouble looking up some of these addresses. And, by the way, I put a mark beside the names of a few people to whom I thought I ought to introduce you personally.'

'You mean go with me?' He put his hand in his pocket and pulled out the paper again, smoothing it and looking at it this time with interest. 'That's a difference,' he said enthusiastically, but to her dismay the next minute he rolled it into a ball and tossed it into a wire basket for wastepaper that was fastened to a tree. 'That means you'll have to come up to town again. For the whole day next time, so we don't need the list.' He smiled happily. 'Let's go up this way,' he said, pointing to a narrow path that ran over a humped bridge, low and covered with ivy. The bridge was little more than a decoration, for under it the water was utterly still. They stopped and were looking over the parapet.

'The water isn't flowing at all,' she said. It was dusty and stippled with pollen from an overhanging lime tree.

He didn't look. 'What did you mean by saying we don't come into any category?' he asked. 'Is that an obscure reference to my age?'

'No. To mine,' she said, and when he laughed she thought she had distracted him.

She hadn't. 'I knew that was what you meant,' he said. With a stony expression he looked down into the water. 'Vera,' he said quietly, 'listen to me. Never once since the first night I met you have I ever felt you were a day older than me.'

'That's nothing,' she said sadly. 'I never felt you were a day younger than me. But facts are facts.' She straightened up and spoke flatly. 'I always seem to be more attracted to people younger than me than to my own contemporaries, at least since Richard died. I was beginning to think that my heart was like a clock that had stopped at the age he was when he died, and that it was him I was looking for, over and over again, wherever I went, whenever I was in a strange place or when I met new people.'

'And wasn't it?'

'I don't think so. I think it was myself I was trying to find, the person I was before I married him. When he died, I knew I had to get back to being that person again, just as he, when he was dying, had to get back to being the kind of person he was before he met me. Standing beside him in those last few minutes, I felt he was trying to drag himself free of me. Can you understand that? Does it make any sense to you?'

'I think so,' he said gravely. 'And it would explain what I said, that from the first you seemed so young to me. It was because you were making a new beginning. I felt it at once, although I knew you must be older than me, in years, I mean.'

Vera shook her head. 'Not years. Decades,' she said.

'Oh, Vera!' he cried, exasperated. 'Don't exaggerate.'

But she wasn't going to concede anything. 'It might as well be centuries,' she said bitterly.

He turned and faced her. 'No,' he said gravely. 'Two people reaching out improbably towards each other; not impossibly.' Impulsively, he took her hand. 'Vera, what are we going to do?'

The first thing to do, she knew, was snatch back her hand, but someone was passing, and she could not let them be seen struggling. Instead, she looked down at her hand in his. This is the closest we'll ever be to each other, she thought. Then, when the person had passed, she pulled her hand free.

'This is crazy!' she cried. 'What are we saying? I thought it was bad enough that I – ' Realising what she was about to admit, she turned away abruptly. 'It's just crazy, that's all. I shouldn't have come,' she said childishly. 'I knew the minute I saw you. I was going to turn and run back to the car, only you looked up and saw me and it was too late.'

'Yes, it was too late,' he said. 'It was too late the first night of all.'

'Oh, no!' she cried. 'Not from the beginning?' It was essential she be able to blame herself, to claim complicity in letting it go on, for the course it took, for the walks, the late hours, the intimacy of their conversation. Otherwise, there would be an inevitability implied that she could not face.

There would be helplessness as well as hopelessness. The tears rushed into her eyes.

'Vera, don't be upset,' he said. 'This may be unlooked for, but you must know it's not unprecedented?'

'I know nothing.' She dried her eyes. 'I've heard things, of course. I've read things. Elderly housemaids jumping out of closets at little boys.'

'Vera. Shut up. Do you hear me! Shut up.' He raised his hand and she thought he was going to hit her. 'The question is what are we going to do?'

'We must put an end to things, that's all!'

'An end? At the beginning? You can't mean that?'

'What else can we do?'

'I don't know, not at this moment,' he said, 'but surely to God whatever we've found in each other, something we both know is rare, surely that's not to be thrown away, not before we've got anything out of it,' he said, almost pettishly.

'What is there to be got out of it, only pain and heartache?'

'For which of us?' There was a pathetic eagerness in his voice.

She shook her head. 'Does that matter?'

'I suppose not,' he agreed miserably, and yet instead of resignation he had a stubborn look, and he caught at her hand again. 'Isn't pain the price of most things?' he cried. 'You're so ready to give up, Vera. I meant what I said a while ago. There *are* precedents for this. We aren't the first people in the world to be in this particular plight. I've heard of this kind of thing, and read about it. It always seemed very beautiful.'

She interrupted him. 'No, it is unnatural!'

'Oh, Vera,' he said wearily. 'Why are you so bitter? I was only trying to say that it was something altogether outside my experience.'

'And mine.'

'All right,' he said, 'but isn't everything outside our experience until it comes into it? There was a friend of my own, a close friend, too, in my first year in college, and he was in love with a woman years older than him, fourteen years, I think. They did their best to break away from each other, but in the end they got married.'

She pulled away from him roughly. 'Married?' she repeated hysterically. 'Anyway,' she said callously, 'what is fourteen years?'

He was arrested by that. 'What age are you anyway, Vera?'

'What age are you?' she demanded, but she didn't really want to know. 'Don't tell me,' she cried, taking her hand away. She knew it was worse than she'd thought. 'It doesn't matter,' she said hopelessly. 'Let's leave things as they are, and not show them up to be altogether farcical.'

He said nothing, but she saw him wince. He reached out idly and picked an ivy leaf from the parapet and dropped it into the pond below, where it lay flat on the stagnant water.

It seemed a chance for her to say what had to be said. 'We must stop seeing each other. At least by design,' she added, having caught sight of his face.

'I see,' he said. He stood up. 'And you dismissed friendship, as far as I remember, didn't you?' he said.

She shrugged. 'This isn't friendship.' She glanced at the sky. 'It's going to rain again,' she said dully.

As she spoke, a drop of rain fell singly and heavily on to the sleeve of her blouse, and as the stroke of the hammer brings the spark to iron, the heavy drop brought her flesh to the linen. She looked down, and then she saw that he was staring too. Without a word said, the air began to throb, and it was with love, with love and nothing less. Her eyes filled with tears. 'It may be rare, love, I mean,' she said, turning aside, unable to look at him any more, 'but where there is love, everything is so easy. Friendship is so exacting. Perhaps that's why they can never exist together at the same time. And why they never, never, can be substituted for each other. Let me tell you something,' she said quickly and urgently, although as she said them the words seemed to echo in her mind and she remembered the disastrous effect of the other incident she'd told him on the first night of all. But she went on. 'One evening last summer, and I was staying with friends in Howth. After dinner, we went out on the cliff, and I asked something I'd always wanted to know. I asked why the lights across the bay were always twinkling. But I was told they weren't twinkling; they were steady. It was the level of the air in between that was uneven. Do you see?' she said sadly. 'It's the same with us.'

'I see,' he said for the second time, and he threw down another leaf on to the water. Then he straightened up. For a moment, she thought everything was ended. 'Where is your car?' he asked. But nothing was ended. 'We can't settle this here,' he said. 'I'm coming down to the farm with you. We'll have to have a long talk.' He paused. 'Unless you could stay the night in town?'

'Oh, I couldn't possibly do that,' she cried.

'Well then, I'll come down,' he said.

'And stay with Tim?' She was distractedly looking in her pockets for the keys of the car. They were going out of the park gates into the street. But when she looked at him, she saw that he was staring strangely at her.

'Where else?' he asked.

'Oh, I know there is nowhere else,' she said, but she felt the ground was slipping from under her as if she were the one who was young and inexperienced, even endangered. But it was only that she was out of practice in a game where every word, every gesture counted for ten. 'I only meant that your uncle might think it odd for you to go down unexpectedly.'

'I never go any other way,' he said. 'Are you sure that's what you meant?'

'And if it wasn't?' she asked, startled at the chancy note in her voice. 'What would be the gain?'

'If we got rid of the tension that has built up between us, we might salvage something,' he said, but there was a trace of despondency in his voice again.

'There might be nothing to salvage,' she said. 'And supposing the bonds only tightened?'

'Would you care?' he asked.

'Not then. But I care now, while I'm still able to care.'

'Tell me one thing. For whose sake would you care, your own or mine?'

She looked away from him, over the street into which they had entered. 'Not for either of our sakes, I think,' she said. She nodded at the people in the street hurrying by in all directions. 'For them, perhaps.'

'Don't be nonsensical,' he said, and as they reached the car he caught the handle of the door. 'I'll come down. And you must let me stay the night, Vera. Just to talk.' He looked at his watch. 'It's a bit bright to go down yet, though, isn't it? We ought to wait till it's darker, in case it would get about that I was down.'

'And stayed with me?'

He nodded.

For a minute, she let herself dwell on the thought of having him in the house with her, under the same roof, however separate in all else. 'I'd have to drive you up again very early before it was light, wouldn't I?'

'You could go to bed for a while,' he said. 'I'd call you.'

She knew then that they fully understood each other. They got into the car.

'There's just one thing I have to do before I can go,' he said. 'I have to call at Hume Street to collect another lot of exam papers. Can we stop there? I won't keep you a minute.'

She started the car.

'You didn't really think that you could walk out of my life like that?' he said as they drove along. 'I feel certain that no matter what happens you'll never altogether leave it.'

She said nothing, and in a few minutes they had reached Hume Street. Before he got out of the car, he looked at her. 'There's something I want to say now, before we go any further,' he said. 'No matter what happens, I want you to promise me that if you ever want me for anything, you'll tell me. Will you promise that?'

'Why do you want me to promise now?' she asked, as she leaned across him and opened the door. 'Never mind. I promise,' she said quickly. Then, knowing he must have guessed what she had in mind to do, she waited till he went up the steps and drove away.

It was nearly a year later. She had not seen him in the time between, nor did she expect to, when late one afternoon there was the sound of a car at the door. 'Well?' she said weakly when she opened it and saw him standing there.

Like the first time of all, they looked at each other, and this time, too, the look was one of surprise, but not a happy surprise.

'How are you?' he asked. There was a keen edge to his voice. 'I didn't need to ask,' he added quickly.

'And you?' she asked. He looked well.

'I wasn't going to call at all,' he said then. 'But I changed my mind.' He paused.

It saddened her to see him ill at ease, standing so stiffly. Why did he come, she wondered. 'You were anxious about me? Is that it?' she asked laughingly, thinking that by making light of it she would dispel the shadow of what had been between them. But she saw at once she had only brought it back. In a moment, the old atmosphere of intimacy was recreated, and yet it was not the same, or anything like the same.

'It was because of the old man I called,' he said dully. 'He thought it odd that I hadn't come over to see you. I've been down here for two weeks.'

'Ah, well,' she said, 'he didn't understand.'

He looked at her intently. 'I'm not so sure about that,' he said. 'I didn't tell you something he said last year, one of the nights I went back late. He gave me a queer look. "If you were better favoured," he said, "you'd be putting ideas into my silly old head."'

'I'm not so sure.' They were still standing in the doorway. 'May I stay awhile?' he asked.

Almost imperceptibly, she hesitated, but he noticed it. 'You were not going out, were you?' he asked.

'I was going out,' she said reluctantly.

'Must you?'

'I'm afraid I must.'

He seemed really surprised. 'Will you be long? Could I come back later? As a matter of fact, I have to go to Dublin for an hour or two. I only intended calling for a minute.' He looked at his watch. 'I could be back in two and a half hours. Where were you going, anyway?'

'Today is Richard's anniversary,' she said, still more reluctantly. 'I was going to the cemetery. Normally I never go near it, only I got word to say the headstone has slipped, and that it must be seen to at once, in case it falls altogether. It would break, or do damage to other graves. I have to go and see what is to be done, and make arrangements about it.'

'Oh, I see,' he said. 'But it can't be all that urgent, surely? Isn't this a bad day to go in any case? Or do you usually go on his anniversary?'

'I told you I never go. Never, never. This is purely a coincidence.'

'Well, then. You certainly shouldn't go today. Besides, it's getting late. Put it off to another day.'

'I think I ought to go this afternoon,' she said. 'I don't mind, really.' Suddenly an idea struck her. 'It would make it a lot easier if there was someone with me. I don't suppose . . .' She paused, and for a minute she thought he had not seen any connection between him and her unfinished sentence.

But he had. 'Of course I'll go. There should be someone with you. You certainly should not go alone. Don't think of it. Leave it till tomorrow or the next day, and I'll go with you gladly. Better still, I'll go without you and see what's to be done. It's not a job for a woman anyway. Where is he buried, by the way?'

'Kildare.'

'So far?'

'It's not so far from here, only a few minutes.'

'I'd probably be going from Dublin, but no matter. Put it out of your head now, and I'll take care of it.'

'You couldn't come this afternoon?'

'With you?'

'With me, of course. I know it must sound superstitious, but I have to think of getting word about it today of all days, and not going, not wanting to go.'

'Rubbish!' he said easily. 'Anyway, it's my affair now.'

'You couldn't possibly come now?' she persisted. 'Why do you have to go back to Dublin? Is it urgent?'

'Oh, it's not exactly urgent, but I'd like to go. I've arranged to give a driving lesson to someone. It need only take half an hour, but I promised to do it. A half an hour would be plenty; that's why I said I'd come back if you agreed to it, but of course the light would be gone by then, for the other job, I mean.'

She was listening very attentively. 'Is it a girl?' she asked quietly.

'You know it's not a girl.'

'Why not? I only asked because if it was a girl I'd know you couldn't possibly break your word.'

He stared. 'You wouldn't mind?'

'It would be natural,' she said.

'Was that your remedy? Another man?'

She didn't bother to reply to that. 'Well, if it's not a girl, who is it?' she asked flatly.

'It's just a fellow who works in the Department of Education. It's through him I get the exam papers to correct.'

'Couldn't you get in touch with him?'

'He's not on the phone.'

She pondered this. 'You could send him a telegram.'

'He wouldn't get it in time.'

'He'd get it afterwards, and he'd understand, surely?'

'I don't know if he would. And anyway, I couldn't leave him up there in the park, hanging around waiting for me, thinking every minute I was coming and afraid to go away.'

She gave a short laugh.

'I suppose you think that if it was last summer I'd have gone with you no matter what!' he said.

'Oh, no!' she cried. 'Last summer I wouldn't have let you come. I wouldn't have needed you. It would have been enough to know you'd have come if you could.' Her coat was lying across the hall table. She took it up. 'I must go,' she said simply.

'So you were right,' he said, blocking her way. 'We salvaged nothing.'

She put on her coat. Then she looked into his face. 'Don't blame me for being right,' she said. 'I sometimes think love has nothing to do with people at all.' Her voice was tired. 'It's like the weather. But isn't it strange that a love that was so unrealised should have – '

' – given such joy?' he asked quietly.

'Yes, yes,' she said. Then she closed the door behind them. 'And such pain.'

'Oh, Vera, Vera,' he said.

'Goodbye,' she said.

Goodbye.

VINTAGE CLASSICS

Vintage Classics is home to some of the greatest writers and thinkers from around the world and across the ages. Bringing you not just the books you already know and love, but new additions to your library, these are works to capture imaginations, inspire new perspectives and excite curiosity.

Renowned for our iconic red spines and bold, collectable design, Vintage Classics is an adventurous, ever-evolving list. We breathe new life into classic books for modern readers, publishing to reflect the world today, because we believe that our times can best be understood in conversation with the past.